D0344496

The Chin Kiss King

The Chin Kiss King

Ana Veciana-Suarez

Farrar, Straus & Giroux • New York

Farrar, Straus and Giroux
19 Union Square West, New York 10003

Published simultaneously in Canada by HarperCollins*CanadaLtd*
Printed in the United States of America
First edition, 1997

Designed by Abby Kagan

Library of Congress Cataloging-in-Publication Data
Veciana-Suarez, Ana.
    The chin kiss king / Ana Veciana-Suarez.
        p.   cm.
    ISBN 0–374–12130–3 (cloth : alk. paper)
    1. Cuban American Families—Florida—Miami—Fiction.   2. Cuban
American women—Florida—Miami—Fiction.   3. Cuban Americans—
Florida—Miami—Fiction.   I. Title.
PS3572.E27C48   1997
813'.54—dc21   96–53313

To Victor
and all the other sequin-winged angels

*Happen what may, we must risk everything,
place ourselves into the hands of God and
go willingly wherever we are carried away.*
—Teresa of Avila

The Chin Kiss King

1

On the morning before the night Cuca's great-grandson came into this hard world, a mist thickened with the scent of honeysuckle seeped beneath her carved-oak front door, invaded the living room, saturated the kitchen, and impregnated her bedroom with a melancholy so deep and so impenetrable she awoke with a start.

"*Llegó*," she said aloud, though there was no one else in the tiny, low-ceiling bedroom—no one, that is, of this life.

(She did not believe in ghosts, not really; but she accepted the hovering presence of the spirits of her lost loved ones as a blessing. They followed her everywhere, even to the bathroom, for guidance and protection, for reminders of duty, and they spoke to her in her sleep, or in church during the homily, or at the bus stop on Seventh Street, their soft, clarion voices sounding sometimes like young pupils vying for a teacher's attention.)

"*Llegó*," she repeated, this time much louder, conviction smoothing the early-morning hoarseness from her throat.

He's here.

She sat up in bed, straightened the Print of Paradise comforter she had bought at Kmart in the last white sale, and sniffed the heavy air for clues. They were there, the hints, the evidence, the telltale traces of what was to come; she felt them prick her skin, taunting, teasing, like the cool fingertips of a warm man. And yet . . . yet, honeysuckle . . . honeysuckle. What did that mean? Honeysuckle . . . honeysuckle. Melancholy. No, please no. Maybe peace? Great joy? Deep sadness? Revolution? Who knows? She sighed, an inhalation so total in its resignation that she could see the hole it sucked from the mist suspended in front of her, a perfect circle, complete and without end, beautiful.

Ay, she was losing her faculties. No doubt about it. Like smooth skin, like shiny hair and clear eyes, like desire itself, her abilities were following the call of age much too obediently. Time pardoned nobody. But she would not dwell on it, no. She had never taken well to melancholy; it did not suit her, never had, not even in the tuberculosis-infested era of her youth, when melancholy among demure young ladies was all the rage. It made her skin sallow, which was worse than age spots; it made her breasts sag and her belly bloat and her hair kink. Yes, melancholy did.

"Go!" she ordered the mist, but it went nowhere. In fact, it became so sweet that she gasped for air and so dense she could not see the green and purple and pink and indigo of her bedspread.

"Go!" she shouted. "Go! Go! Go!"

It refused to recede. It settled over her in a candied, cloying blanket.

Very well, she thought, and lay back in bed. Give in, give in. Become what it is, what you are not. Accept that which is unacceptable, what is inexplicable, what no one can find. She pulled the covers over her head and closed her eyes. She glimpsed the blinking essences that were the faithful spirits of her lost loved ones in the vast darkness of infinity, so many of them, so many. (She realized suddenly that she knew more dead people than living.) A smile escaped her lips in recognition: her father, a man with a straight back and a crooked heart. Her mother, a queen without throne or vassals. Her youngest sister, drowned in Varadero Beach, tight curls still wet. Her brothers, both the hairy one and the bald, as sternly serious in the afterlife as ever. Her maternal grandmother, Cleofe, faint, growing fainter, too long dead. And the blinking star of her bullnecked husband, hotter and closer than all the others. She gig-gled: the bastard. He called to her in the silent voice she always answered; it was replete with longing and recriminations. How long had she survived him? How long had they been separated by the diaphanous sheet of death and six feet of soil? Too long, he said, too long. Come.

She was tempted, she was. She missed him, the bad and the good, the long days and the short nights, the feel of his callused hands and the muscles on his chest and the bristle of his beard and the thrusts of his lust and the song in his voice and the rhythm of his step and the smell of sweat on his skin. They had battled like fighting cocks, as elegantly and as fiercely, and made love with the same intensity, heaving, biting, clawing, screaming, singing. A man was for that, after all, for those base, earthy, wanton feelings, that sensation of control and disorder. Ay, to have a man, her man, and his instrument in her bed, under this Print of Paradise comforter, naked and hard. How many times she had tried to explain that to her granddaughter, who lived without a man, on the other side of the duplex, in a place that was as antiseptic as hers was teeming with unclassified organisms? Many times, too many. And for im-parting this wisdom, what did she get in return? She shut her eyes tight, tighter, closing dry skin into her sockets like a drawstring purse. She knew, without being told, that this flesh of her flesh, blood of her blood, one generation removed, thought her ignorant, backward, foolishly romantic. Her granddaughter had never put it in so many words, of course. She was polite to a fault and correct beyond expectations, but there was no need to imprison intuition in the frame of words, no need whatsoever. And now, with the baby to be born today, *this very day*, a being the flesh of her flesh, blood of her blood, two generations removed, where was the father, the man and his instrument? Where, where? The girl had driven him away.

Come, Cuca, her husband called.

What is it? she asked, grateful to forget about her rejected min-istrations.

Do you see it? he asked. *The star near me.*

Where? I don't see it.

Look with your heart, mi cielo, my sky.

And she did, and she saw it, a star smaller than a hummingbird's pupil but as brilliant, as steady, as needed as a lone votive candle in a dark cave.

Llegó, her husband announced.

Sí.

Then she fell asleep suddenly, with the air still redolent of honeysuckle, and dreamed of the mosquito netting her mother-in-law had made for her eldest son's crib fifty-nine years ago. It was a good dream, so pleasant that she did not remember the baby had died at three weeks from a malady no country doctor could diagnose.

It occurred to her, when she awoke again with the mist gone and the midmorning light dappling her bed, that she had erred in reading the heady sweetness around her. It was not melancholy she felt, but a comfortable joy, one without peaks or valleys, steady, constant—the type she rarely experienced. This realization boosted her energy, and she threw back the Print of Paradise comforter and shuffled to the bathroom humming a song she could not name. She splashed her face with tepid water—no soap, of course, never—and brushed her teeth cautiously with baking soda and a white washcloth. Toothbrush bristles hurt her gums. (She still had all her teeth, a miracle she attributed to her weekly consumption of the marrow from chicken bones.)

At seventy-seven, Cuca still took a great interest in her appearance, and she was methodical in the way she cared for her body and her clothing. In anything else, she despised routine. Today, from her closet, she chose a blue-and-purple-print housedress with three-quarter cuffed sleeves because it was February and, even in Miami, one could feel a slight chill in arthritic bones. She looked closely at the dress: was the print of flowers or was it paisley? She blinked, squinted, sighed. Yes, her daughter was right; she needed to wear her glasses everywhere. But paisley or flower, who cared? She liked the colors, and the style, and the way it felt, soft cotton on old skin. She stood across from the mirror on her white wicker dresser—wasn't white wicker absolutely gorgeous and youthful?—and stared at her image. Not bad. Disheveled, old, but not altogether bad. The colors heightened the doughy whiteness of her skin and paid homage to her luxuriant hair. She had not ever been a beautiful woman, but in her youth she possessed an attractive feminine roundness, like a Botticelli model, and a compassionate face that belied a stubborn will. She had always worn her hair long, waist-length, first when it was the blue-black color of a raven, and now when it was like an undergarment washed too many times, a mother-of-pearl tone with filaments of steel gray. Her hair was her treasure, and though it was much work, washing it weekly in a tin basin outside, then sitting for hours in indirect sun to let it dry, she fiercely opposed her granddaughter's insistence that she cut it. Of course it was not practical at her age. Of course it pained her back to bend over the basin to rinse it. Of course she looked like a wild woman when she loosened the single braid every evening. But her hair was a mantilla, a work of art and effort, a promise kept. When her third baby had died, a boy born too soon and too weak, and after she had cried so many tears that her face and the tips of her fingers and toes had begun to crinkle prune-like, she vowed to La Virgen de la Caridad del Cobre that she would keep her hair long forever and ever, or at least until she died, if she was able to see a child, just one child, grow into adulthood. The Virgin kept her end of the bargain; she would, too.

Thoughts of the Virgin reminded her of the impending arrival, and she knew she must hurry, there was little time to waste, if she was going to prepare for her great-grandchild. With long, hard strokes she untangled her hair and then braided it, dabbed Agustín Reyes's Royal Violet cologne water behind each ear and between her breasts (just in case; you never know), powdered her face lightly, and applied her new Cape Coral to her lips. Then, she began the comforting ritual of slipping on her forty-six gold bracelets, twenty-three onto each arm, one for each year her marriage had endured. This took more time than it should because she liked to put the bracelets on one by one, remembering the occasion on which she had received each gift, but also because her agility was not what it used to be. Once finished, she jangled them, the noise filling the room in a merry way, like Christmas bells. (Try it, she often told her friends, the few who were still left. Sour moods and bad thoughts and migraine headaches surely will dissipate.) Then she shod her delicate size-six feet in white Reeboks, a concession to her granddaughter.

Ready. What to do first? She wasn't good at planning; her schedule was whatever pleased her, always had been, which used to infuriate her husband, particularly when she didn't starch his white shirts in time for Sunday Mass or didn't have dinner ready at seven. But his screams, his veins bulging in his thick neck, the crimson of his face—they had done little to change her. She was a mother herself, ostensibly responsible for her family, and still running to the market, over the rough cobblestones or dirt roads of her beautiful, beautiful Cuban town, dust collecting after her like a veil of hope, praying she would catch the old woman in the chicken stall before she closed shop for the day.

"Ay, mamita," she screamed between her labored breaths and the jabs of pain in her side. "Rápido, rápido, un pollito."

Then she would pay an exorbitant price for the old woman to swing the puny chicken into lifelessness, then pluck it, before she ran back home to cook it. Dinner was always late.

She had a microwave now. It was her daughter's, but Adela did not allow her to cook. She used the microwave to warm the cantina they purchased five days a week from the son of a man who had lived down the street from her in the beautiful, beautiful pueblo. The son of this former neighbor had grown rich in Miami because no one wanted to cook anymore and no one ran breathless down cobblestone streets to plead with old women for the last of their chickens as the sun slipped like an egg yolk into the black skillet that is earth. Just as well. She had better things to do. She had herbs to plant, medicines to mix, potions to label, leaves to simmer, ideas to test. She was busy without the burden of survival, and she was becoming very good at it.

She shuffled into the living room, expecting to see Adela engrossed in the newspaper's religious reporting of the previous day's lottery numbers, but she realized that she had awakened too late this morning and surely her daughter was in the market playing the Cash 3 for the day. Ay. She had the house to herself. Good. She had lived on this side of the duplex for twenty-nine years, first with her husband and daughter, then with her husband alone (when her daughter married), then with her daughter and granddaughter, then alone, and now only with her daughter. Was that right? She wasn't sure. The chronology of events often befuddled her, so the past tricked her into the present and the future hurled her back into the years of youth. It was confusing, the comings and goings of this family. In any event, she had lived here long enough to be confused: when she remembered her houses in Cuba, the one of her childhood and the one of her marriage, the layout she recalled was that of the duplex. She had never been good at spatial relationships.

About a year ago, when Adela had moved back in with her from the other side of the duplex, she had allowed her granddaughter to donate her old furniture, everything except her bedroom set and four black velvet paintings, to a charity for old people. A big yellow truck had come to pick everything up—the Formica coffee table, the matching Oriental lamps, the plaid sofa with the bad springs, the five-piece dinette set—and she had watched solemnly as two stocky, hairy men in sleeveless T-shirts carted off her belongings. She noticed the name of the organization painted in large red letters on the side ("The Useful Aged"), and she laughed at the irony because she knew she could no longer cry. She should have been overwhelmed with an unbearable sadness, for each piece of furniture served as marker and guidepost of her life in exile, but that morning, as a precaution, she had put a little rum in her breakfast *tilo* and two extra spoonfuls of brown sugar. It had done her good. Besides, Adela had gotten some nice modern furniture as replacement, a teal Boltaflex sofa and a flower-print upholstered chair, a glass-and-wrought-iron center table with a matching end piece, and a dinette set made of real wood. The furniture was nearly identical to the set her granddaughter had on her side of the duplex, except that Maribel's sofa was leather, the real thing. No one had made any suggestions about changing anything in the kitchen, and her collection of herbs and spices and ointments and liniments and potions and other mysterious brews remained untouched in their labeled boxes and jars. God had kept an eye out for her.

It was not difficult to live with Adela, although she was a little sloppy, and when Cuca spied (without meaning to) the mess in her daughter's room—stacks of newspapers in one corner, clothes that needed to be washed, hemmed, given away, or thrown out, unopened bills, torn-out magazine recipes, crumpled paper, and piles of books (*Interpreting Your Dreams, Numbers and Visions, Unlock the Power of the Mind, Playing on Hope and a Dollar, One Hundred and*

Three Ways to Riches)—she understood why her daughter's daughter had turned out to be such an uptight know-it-all. Clutter demanded order; complications prescribed simplicity. Life was an ordeal of balancing opposing forces, or a travesty, some would say, and neither daughter nor granddaughter apparently had learned that.

Cuca had always liked the duplex, from the very first time her husband had brought her to see it on a spectacular spring morning in 1963. It was neither large nor small, just the perfect size for a family of three, and provided a source of rental income, for the first few months at least. (Her daughter married less than a year later in a hurried ceremony, almost four months pregnant though as flat but not as pure as a Communion wafer, and at the urging of her mother moved next door with the no-good-for-nothing husband.) The duplex was centrally located, too: just around the corner from the pharmacy and the bodega, a couple of blocks from the Flagler Dog Track and the bus stop, and a ten-minute walk from a strip shopping center that, over the years, had been home to a cafeteria, a botanica, a pawnshop that fronted for a cocaine kingpin, an auto-parts shop, the office of a physician who had turned out to be a quack, a temporary Avon pickup site, and a housing and urban development agency. She knew by name all the neighbors on her block, and the Nicaraguan couple who recently had moved behind her, too, though most of the old-timers had fled to the suburbs after the Mariel boatlift. Those who remained behind, as she and Adela did, would never move, not to Westchester or Kendall or Miami Lakes, because this was where their Chevy Chevettes and Toyota Corollas and Ford Escorts belonged. Besides, she could walk almost anywhere, but especially to the pharmacy to buy the ingredients that kept the surface of her life polished just so.

Which reminded her: the impending arrival of the baby. She had not forgotten that, and though the honeysuckle scent had evaporated with the fierceness of the morning sun, the indecipherable sensation brought on by the sweet mist had not. Did she have everything? Didn't she need to buy something? She opened the faux-oak kitchen cabinet and squinted at the bounty in her homemade apothecary: chamomile for blisters, echinacea for migraines, willow bark for headaches, ginger root for motion sickness, ginkgo to stimulate circulation, powder valerian for insomnia, castor oil for warts, charcoal tablets for gas, Adolph's meat tenderizer for fire-ant bites, a can of WD-40 for her arthritis, an airline-sample bottle of cheap whiskey for cold sores, Preparation H for puffy eyes, an entire shelf of Progresso chicken soup cans for colds and flus (used in place of the real thing only in emergencies), a small jar of water and salt for a stuffy nose, oatmeal for weeping rashes, and so many other goodies she did not bother reading her scribbled labels. Oh, it was good to be old and useful and smart.

She did notice the little bottle of anise was nearly empty, and because anise was a miracle cure for colic, an ailment every baby in the family had suffered from, she would need to buy more of it soon. And she had run out of garlic, too. Couldn't forget that, no; she was convinced it kept her cholesterol down. Now, what else? Oh, yes, she also needed red-raspberry leaf for the tea she would give her granddaughter after labor to strengthen her uterus and relieve the post-birth cramps and, let's see, let's see, some *anón* (mosquito bites), Maalox (diaper rash), and dry mustard (insomnia). Otherwise, she was prepared for apocalypse.

The phone rang as she searched through the kitchen drawers for a pencil and a piece of paper to jot down a shopping list, and she was loathe to answer it lest she forget her items. (Her memory was not what it used to be; actually, it never had been, but now she had a believable excuse.) She found a green, eraserless stub the size of her thumb but no paper, none anywhere, not even paper towels or napkins. Then she remembered the almanac Adela kept on the wall near the back door. Beautiful almanac, too, with color photographs of Cuba—the Morro fort, balconies in Old Havana, a sugar plantation in Matanzas, a narrow street in a country town, lovers on the Malecón—and she decided to borrow a day from it. The phone continued to ring, but she hardly heard it now, so anxious was she to get a piece of paper before she forgot her mental list of anise, *anón*, dry mustard, Maalox, red-raspberry leaf. She repeated the list (aniseanondrymustardMaaloxredraspberryleaf) six times before she reached the almanac and discovered that Adela had already ripped off the previous-day page and she was staring at today's date: February 29. Leap Day, it said in red print under the numerals. Hmmm. With a firm tug, the day ended up in her small hand. She moistened the tip of the pencil with her tongue and began the laborious writing of her list. She was at Maalox when she realized the phone had not stopped ringing.

RINGRINGRINGRINGRINGRINGRINGRINGRING! How persistent! Slowed by the damnable arthritis, she hobbled over to the annoying sound.

"Abuela, my water broke." The words were curt, but the under-tone in her granddaughter's voice was one of desperation.

Cuca laughed and jangled her bracelets. How wonderful: Maribel's water had broken. She managed a few slow mambo steps across the kitchen linoleum.

"I will call your mother to pick you up."

"No, no. Caleb will drive me home. Where is Mami?"

"Where else?"

Maribel made an exasperated guttural sound that carried its message of disgust over the miles of telephone wire.

"Call her." Click.

Without hurry, Cuca wrote the last two items on February 29—Maalox and red-raspberry leaf—and added camphor to her list before dialing La Ferrolana. Adela shrieked with excitement into the phone.

"Oh! Oh! Oh! A Leap Day baby! I must make sure to play the two and the nine."

"And the twenty-nine for the Lotto Saturday."

"Of course. You know, Mamá, I have this feeling that our baby will be very lucky. He will be born with a loaf of bread under his arm."

"I think you are right, *hija*. I had a very strange feeling this morning, too, and maybe that is what it was. Good fortune on the way."

Why then, she thought and chided herself for the thought, why then did she feel the weight of a thousand sorrows on her soul?

2

The fortuitousness of her grandchild's birth date was not lost on Adela. She was a woman who constantly searched for such lucky accidents, and after so much looking she certainly recognized one when she saw it. Of course this had smacked her right in the face. Chica, a Leap Day baby.

"*Oye*, Fefa," she told the wife of the owner of the bodega after she hung up with Cuca, "my daughter's water broke."

"*¡Dios mío!*" gasped Fefa, and leaned over the counter to hug her friend. "A Leap Day baby. She will be forever young, this child. Some luck to have birthdays only every four years, eh?"

"It is a boy."

"You know already? They told you from those sono pictures they take now?"

"No, no, I just know." Adela's voice was soft as down feathers but secure in its certainty.

"A male among so many women," said Fefa pensively, shaking her head. She was gullible, easily led by the prevailing thought of the day. "You will have to be careful. Look at all those fruitcakes."

Adela shrugged. She noticed the black roots in her friend's dyed-blond hair and giggled softly with something just short of malicious satisfaction. So many of her old hairdressing clients looked like hell since she had been forced to quit work after the nasty fall. (But easy disability checks weren't so bad, and if they meant other people's bad dye jobs, ah, well, what could she do about it?) She pressed a finely manicured finger to her lips.

"I am not a woman with prejudices," Adela replied, and she spoke truth. Her daughter complained too often of her lack of judgment, discernment, boundaries.

"It is not a matter of prejudices," Fefa insisted. "It is a matter of what is normal, of what God intended for us."

"And you know what God intended for you? For me?" she asked, raising both arms toward the sky she could not see. Then, just as dramatically, she clasped her hands over her heart, a penitent pilgrim, a faithful follower. Adela spoke with her hands, hands that were quick and loud and demanding and forgiving, sometimes anxious, usually extravagant, and always, always hopeful. They were her instruments of song, bands of blinding light, twin swords of honesty and justice. In any given conversation, they ruffled like the turquoise plumes of a strutting peacock, then dazzled like an uncut diamond meeting daylight for the first time. With these hands, she had cut, combed, teased, curled, straightened, and tinted the hair of thousands of women—and fed her daughter. With these hands, she had filed and polished the nails of other hands, softened cuticles, smoothed calluses, trimmed hangnails, massaged gnarled fingers— and supported her mother. Hands, wonderful hands, gifts from God.

"I will love him no matter what, Fefa," she continued. "Even if he looks like cooked cauliflower. Even if he walks like a clown."

"I do not doubt you," her friend said. "You know what they say. If a mother's love is blind, a grandmother's is . . ."

"Depthless, widthless, lengthless. Immeasurable!" Adela shouted, and laughed her distinct laugh, the sound of a knife blade against fine crystal, sharp but resonant.

The few customers in the bodega stopped what they were doing and turned, mesmerized, to locate the source of the fantastic sound, her laugh was so notable, and they discovered they could not continue with their shopping until they had figured out what this mysterious, mystifying racket meant. It was open to interpretation. An old blue-haired woman pinching the avocados in the produce aisle thought, for a fleeting but uplifting moment, that she was once again listening to the ring of chimes in her old stone church in Ciego de Avila. Thank Jesus, thank the Virgin. Three whiskerless teenagers skipping school and plotting, in the back corner of the store, how to buy two six-packs of Corona beer without the proper identification also paused. The boys were sure it was Mrs. Harris, their guidance counselor, strong with authority, high on power: they had been found out. And the middle-aged man who was buying guava paste and cheese for his young lover, a sixteen-year-old girl who wanted a new Ford Mustang for her birthday and God knows how he would manage that, cupped his hands to his ears to preserve the ringing in his brain. He was willing to swear on a stack of Bibles, on the very grave of his saintly mother, that he had heard the laughter of the late María del Carmen, a gorgeous, voluptuous mulata from Oriente who had taught him the intricacies of lovemaking at thirteen. He adjusted his fly and willed his thumping heart to slow.

Needless to say, Adela was used to such attention and did not mind it one bit. She never went to great lengths to seek it, though, not like other women her age who wore spandex—for God's sake, spandex!—or shopped in the Juniors Department at Burdines. At fifty, she was blessed with a youthful look and outlook—petite, naturally black hair cut pixie-style, animated at all hours of the day (and, if need be, at night). She was Tinker Bell near retirement, aging in fits and spurts and not always with good sense. She cultivated the ingenue image, the wide-eyed, broad-smiling look of the innocent. Yet she was, if anything, cunning in a healthy survivalist's sense and also fiercely, passionately loyal to those she loved.

"Yes, immeasurable and irrational," Adela added. She tried to imagine how anyone could ever quantify or qualify the love she felt for this unborn being. Already it overwhelmed her. She had embroidered bibs and sheets and pajamas, added lace to curtains, Mickey Mouse decals to walls. She had even considered taking back a few of her most esteemed clients for manicures and pedicures to supplement her daughter's salary and her own disability check. She would not have entertained this thought for anyone else, not even Maribel. But a grandchild, another link in the endless, endless chain . . .

"You know, Fefa, I thought I would not be a good grandmother. It would make me feel old, no? But it has not been like that at all. On the contrary."

"New life stimulates the old," Fefa agreed, probably the wisest words she had ever spoken.

"A child changes your life, burdens you with responsibilities."

"You are telling me." Fefa was mother to eight.

"But a grandchild . . . I do not know how to explain." Her hands fluttered, grasping for meaning, seeking help. "A grandchild is like, well, like affirmation."

"Joy without responsibility." Fefa knowingly pointed her long chin at the three teenagers as they left the store empty-handed.

"This will change Maribel. If anything can, this will."

"Do not hope too much."

"It is not a hope. It is a necessity. What life can a girl like that expect? What man will want to have her? So inflexible, so programmed."

"There are worse things."

"Yes, you are right. She could have been a whore. She could have disowned her family. She could have taken a job in New York. No, she has done nothing like that. But do not blame me for wanting what I want for my daughter."

"And Eduardo?"

Adela shrugged. She liked her fugitive son-in-law and was grateful for his futile attempts to improve her life, her daughter's. All the same, he had left Maribel pregnant, *desamparada*, and most of the money he had made in his apparently-not-so-secret midnight runs had vanished or been confiscated by the government the day before Thanksgiving, the day they last saw him. She had thought he possessed more sense, certainly he had abundant charm. She had been wrong.

"You are a good woman, Adela," said Fefa, as she rung up the *membrillo* and goat cheese for the middle-aged man. "I hope you live long enough to see your grandson a man."

"I plan to."

As Fefa gathered the shopper's goods into a plastic bag, Adela scratched out the numbers on her lottery tickets in the corner of the checkout counter. She sighed. Not one was a winner. She was disappointed—but only briefly. She already had bet five Lotto tickets for that night's drawing, and with the surprising news of the impending birth and the three dollars left in her change purse she planned to invest in two more Lottos plus a Fantasy Five.

"Fefa, I have a complaint," she singsonged. "I have not won a penny, not even a free ticket in the past three weeks. I am going to boycott your place here. Take my lucky money to the Amoco down the block."

"What do you expect? To win every week?"

"I am greedy."

Adela laughed again. The old, blue-haired woman, now past the plump avocados, crossed herself with the ñame root she held in her right hand when she heard the tittering a second time. Oh, such sound! Thank Jesus, thank the Virgin.

"Well, I expect you to share your good fortune with me someday. At least take Carlos and me to dinner in Coral Gables, no?"

Actually, Adela thought, I have shared with you more than you know. And I wouldn't mind taking Carlos to dinner again—or to bed. Her heart stuttered at the image but, castigating herself for the indecency she had vowed to eliminate completely from her thoughts, she offered an apology.

"If I win tonight's Lotto, I will take you to the fanciest dinner you will ever eat. Now, be a doll and get me two more Lottos and one Fantasy Five."

It was the twenty-ninth day of the second month of the year of Our Lord nineteen hundred and ninety-two, and Adela repeated those numbers in her head, smiling quietly at the echo of their sound. Lovely. She bet the two, the nine, and the twenty-nine on each ticket. She added the one and the nineteen, and for Lotto threw in the six, a nice, unassuming, round number, to balance the lot. Also, Saturday, today, was the sixth day of the week.

She tucked the tickets into her bra, under her left breast, and, nodding goodbye, approached the exit. A loud call from the back of the store stopped her in her tracks. (Dainty tracks, if she said so herself, for she always wore heels when she left the house, even with slacks or Bermuda shorts, because they accentuated her firm and veinless calves.)

"No ham this week?" Carlos cried from the *carnicería*.

"No."

"Well, don't be a stranger and come say hello."

"Hello!" she called out, and scurried out the door. That should keep him guessing.

Traffic on Northwest Seventh Street grew heavy heading west to the weekend flea market at the dog track, but she did not mind. The raucous neighborhood exuded a vibrancy that made her feel young and buoyant. It was a balmy day, cloudless, with birdsong serving as harmonious counterpoint to the harried cars' screeches and the tic-tac of her heels against pavement. She felt no sense of urgency, no need to rush home to tend to her daughter. It would be a long time before her grandson would be born, a long day that would unfold its surprises as coyly as a letter from Publishers Clearing House.

Pain. She thought suddenly of pain. Childbirth involved excruciating pain. As did child-rearing, but at least in labor—how aptly named, eh?—it was controlled, finite, expected, and rewarded. She was not sure about the slow torture of child-rearing. For one, she did not remember the birth of Maribel. She remembered her water breaking while she was standing in line at the Grand Union one Friday afternoon. She remembered the flood, its magnitude explained only in biblical terms, and she remembered her initial embarrassment as the cashiers and store manager, the shoppers, gasped as wave after wave of yellowish fluid poured from between her legs. Then she remembered giggling. She could not, would not, stop giggling. She couldn't explain the hilarity of the situation then; she could not explain it almost thirty years later either. She could only giggle giggle giggle, as she was doing now, crossing Seventh Street, her thin shoulders shaking and her head thrown back, her eyes rolling and her butt swaying sensuously to a rhythm only she heard.

In any event, she could not remember timing contractions or counting her breathing or pushing. At the hospital, doctors must have put her to sleep, because the next thing she recalled was her mother's face close to hers as she awoke in a white hospital bed, and her mother's voice saying: "It's a girl, and she looks Chinese."

Which Maribel had.

Raising Maribel was altogether a different tale. She was a difficult baby, colicky and finicky, easily startled by her mother's laughter and her grandmother's song. She did, indeed, look Chinese, with broad, high cheekbones and slanted eyes, perfect mahogany skin and hair as black and as straight as a thief's intentions. Chinita, her father cooed, Chinita. His words were the only sound that stilled her cry. (Why? Adela thought now. Why why why why?) He said the baby reminded him of his grandmother, a diminutive woman who claimed that her own father, a man married to another woman, was the first Chinese doctor in Cuba. Ha! His family never amounted to a barrel of mangoes. He was a prime example of ruinous genes, that lazy, alcoholic, cheating excuse for a man, and Chinita was not enough to keep him nearby or straight. He disappeared from Adela's map shortly after Maribel turned five. He was dead, she was sure, and good riddance.

Maribel grew into an observant toddler, then a quiet child with a maniacal sense of order. She kept to herself in school and around the neighborhood. Family and friends complained she was a snob. Argh! how this infuriated Adela. Maribel simply enjoyed her own company and eschewed that which she could not control. She was not a problem, not the way other children are. Never did Adela shout at her daughter to pick up her room. Never did Maribel refuse to do her chores or take a bath or trim her hair. Adela's concerns for her daughter were of a different sort. She realized that unequivocally the summer afternoon her parents brought home the first coloring book.

The scene is frozen in Adela's mind, a sepia-toned snapshot that defined their lives: The kitchen of her duplex, long before the remodeling. Maribel in an immaculate pink gingham frock. Adela on the phone to Pepe, the *bolita* guy across the street from Grapeland Park. Enter Abuela Cuca and Abuelo Tony, laden with packages from G. C. Murphy's.

Maribel (politely): "Good afternoon, Abuela, Abuelo."

Cuca (characteristically effusive): "Look what we brought, *mi cielo*. Look."

Cuca hands the little girl a coloring book and a box of eight Crayola crayons—a bounty in those hard refugee times.

Maribel: "Thank you."

(She climbs onto a dining-room chair, brings out a crayon—Adela has forgotten which color—and begins filling in the blanks. She colors within the lines instinctively, as if she knows too soon, too young, the boundaries that will encase and harness her thoughts.)

Cuca: "How smart. She already knows how to color."

Adela's heart did not rejoice at her daughter's precociousness, not at all. It flip-flopped and stayed face-down. It occurred to her, with dreadful clarity, that her daughter would never know the heady joy of coloring outside the lines, of being carried along by impulse and curiosity. This pained her beyond any physical ache; it sat, a soreness, a twinge, just below her heart.

At the corner of Thirty-seventh Avenue, a police officer in a tight blue shirt and shiny black shoes held up an orange-gloved hand to halt traffic. She walked primly across the intersection and thanked the young man. Cute, and nice biceps! She smiled: such beauty and youth in this world. Farther down the block, Chucho the Sno-Kone man raised a pink ice in salutation. They exchanged pleasantries, serious advice.

"In my pueblo," Chucho told her, "every baby wore an *azabache*. The poor, the rich, the black, the white, Catholic, Protestant, Jew. No one dared to risk temptation."

Adela did not have the heart to be frank. She had bought an *azabache* pin from Ciro, the traveling jeweler, and presented it to her daughter last month. It was beautiful, 14-karat gold with a sizable, smooth black stone to ward off the evil eye.

"Mami, for God's sake," Maribel said, snickering, "do not tell me you still believe in that. It is so . . . so . . . so barbarian. So ignorant."

Adela's feelings were hurt but only briefly; she had grown accustomed to such words. Shrugging off her daughter's own ignorance, she tucked the *azabache* pin in the stack of receiving blankets and promptly forgot the rejection. Now Chucho's words reminded her of a concern she could not explain with words, only with sharp, fretful movements of her hands. Her daughter defied . . . defied what? Adela could not articulate, without sounding superstitious (which she was not), what her daughter snubbed in her arrogant disregard. Maribel walked under ladders, opened umbrellas inside houses, refused to cross herself at the beginning of long car trips. So did others. That did not worry Adela. It was something else, an element she could not touch. What, what?

Maribel had passed from childhood into womanhood without any discernible changes, except, of course, a physical blossoming that was expected. Her mind, her expectations of life, her method of approaching and deliberating and finalizing details did not change. She was, as always, reluctant to deviate and quick to doubt, a stranger to risk and adventure. Methodical, meticulous, she provided a stability and routine that were simultaneously comforting and oppressing. It was as if she had never been young, and maybe that was not so bad, not so bad at all. Could be worse, as Fefa said. Yes, all mothers should have that complaint.

By the time Adela turned the corner to the duplex, Cuca had left for the pharmacy and Maribel had not yet arrived. Adela sighed in relief. It was nice, if only for a few minutes, to enjoy the quiet of her home before the onslaught of orders from her daughter. She knew not to worry about packing Maribel's toiletries or the baby's layette, or about calling the obstetrician or the hospital. Maribel had done everything herself in plenty of time. Her daughter kept a list beside her bed of last-minute details, and had begun checking each off—preregister at hospital, notify Eduardo's parents, order cloth diapers, pack overnight bag—in the past month. She should be thankful for her daughter's organizational skills, a necessary attribute in this country of time clocks and schedules, but life had taught Adela that even the most careful plans fell victim to fate.

She immediately spotted the spectacular color of the impatiens bordering the house, riotous pink and red and fuchsia. She smiled at the first white bloom of the neighbor's mango tree and at the scent of freshly mowed lawn. She chirped at twin blue jays perched on the chain-link fence, at the dazed ladybug that flew splat onto her arm without warning, at the wind that carried the gift of rain. Generous, generous land.

Taped to the door was a note from her mother: "Daughter," the old woman had written with exaggerated loops and swirls, "I am at

the pharmacy. Drink the *tilo* on the stove. Will be back by eleven."
The signature curled into an indecipherable flourish.

Inside, the house smelled of cinnamon and clover. The mingled
homey scent sparked her hunger, so she poured the *tilo* into a flowered mug, cut herself a hardening sliver of Cuban bread from yesterday's loaf, and sat at the kitchen table to breathe the ingredients
of heaven and earth. From the living-room wall, the iridescent green
eyes of the black velvet Sacred Heart of Jesus followed her every
move: this gave her strength and comfort. She looked forward to
the time when her grandson, in bib and overalls, would sit across
from her, pleading for the soft and chewy inside of the bread. Right
then, in her momentary aloneness, she wanted more than anything
to hold him tight to her breast, to hum a lullaby of long ago (*Duérmete, mi niño, duérmete, mi amor* . . .), to breathe his baby smell of
talcum and slobber, to kiss the soft underside of his fat chin. She
hugged herself in the delight of her sensual imagination. Oh, the
places they would go together! The fun they would have! The people
they would meet! He would bring her luck: she knew that better
than she knew the beating of her own heart.

Charmed with her musings, she danced from the kitchen to the
chaos in her room. With the baby coming so suddenly, her intention
of clearing and sorting and throwing out was thankfully where it
belonged: on the back burner. Still, she wanted to find a safe and
favored place to store her lottery tickets. From her night table, she
began picking up old newspapers, unopened letters, a stack of word
puzzle sheets she had intended to complete over Christmas, several
Vanidades magazines, two Butterick maternity patterns she had forgotten she had, and a spool of green velvet ribbon. (Hmmm—what
had she been keeping the ribbon for?) Finally, buried under all this
junk, she found her twelve-inch Virgen de la Caridad smiling dole-
fully at the mess. She kissed the black plaster hair, rubbed the tiny
dark hands folded in prayer, and slipped the tickets under the pedestal of blue sea and black toes. (A wonder what some artists could
do with plaster of Paris.)

She then heard a car slow down into the driveway, the slam of
a door, then another. Two voices: Maribel's and the man from work.
Footfalls. A key turned in the lock.

"Mami!" called Maribel, and the sound was like wind forced through a funnel.

Chica! Adela suddenly thought as the voice gusted through the room. She knew what worried her about her daughter, and it was this: Maribel did not believe in the power of dreams.

3

Bupbupbupbup went the baby's heart.

"You hear your baby?" the nurse asks Maribel. Bupbupbup.

"Fine fine fine," Maribel answers.

She had forgotten to finish something? What, what? At work? In the house? How could she have forgotten!

The teacher lied. The labor coach from the hospital classes, the overweight woman with the hyena's laugh who had taught her to breathe, to hold air, to focus, to meditate, had lied. Lies lies lies.

There was pain. Exquisite, tormenting pain, breaking her back, spreading to her lungs, her ass, her legs, splintering her knees, hammering her belly, squeezing her intestines.

Pain. Peaking. A mountain so tall. No snow. So high, so steep. She had always wanted to see snow. Where does it snow? Cold snow. Canada.

Pain. Torture. Agony.

"Breathe, *mi cielo*."

Phew phew phew. Focus. Phew phew phew phew. The fat woman had lied.

Not a mountain, the pain, no. A wave. An ocean wave, yes, rising, rising, cresting. Ay, *Dios. Carajo. Puta. Maricón.*

Subsiding, going, going. Away to sea, past the horizon. Stay away.

"*¿Hielito, mi cielo?*" Her mother offers her ice chips on a plastic spoon. She is wrapped in a green hospital gown, a matching cap. Ice, manna.

"Mami. Caca."

"Same sensation, *hija.* Soon you will be ready to push. Soon it will be over."

"How long?"

"Not much."

What was time? How did one measure it? Watch, anyone? Clock? She has been at this a very long time. A day, a year, a century. Her lifetime. Night has fallen outside her window. She sees the dark gray of winter settling over the marble sill. She is confused. Her water broke . . . yesterday. No, today. This morning. Saturday. What day was today?

She forgot to lock her desk. That's what she has forgotten.

Had she turned off the computer monitor? Ay, *Dios.* Coming, it was coming, slowly, increasing, steady, marching, ripping, searing, splitting, burning. Pain. The wave rises splendidly, look at it, look at it, breaking her back, exploding her belly, her pipi, her eyes, her brain. *Carajo. Puta. Maricón.* Pain. Phewphewphew-O-phewphew-phew.

Sweat stings her eyes. The wave rolls out. Her mother washes her face with a white washcloth. Phew. Phew. Bup bup bup bup, her baby's heart. The monitor.

Oh, Eve, why did you sin?

The nurse taps her legs apart, shows her a gloved hand.

"Relax, honey. I'm going to see how you're coming along."

One finger, two fingers, three, a hand. Humiliation. Bupbupbup-bupbupb, her baby's heart fast.

The nurse smiles. "You're coming right along, honey. In no time."

The doctor. Bald. Bespectacled. Respectable. Warm. She wishes he would hug her. Her father. No, no, father dead . . . alive . . . somewhere else.

"How we doing?" He has a Cuban accent. He is from Havana. Studied in Ohio. Her father's age.

She gasps an answer. She does not know what she says.

"Tiene mucho dolor, doctor." Her mother.

"You want something for the pain?" the doctor asks. He is holding her hand now. Warm hands, with short hard black hair on the knuckles. Man's hands.

Bupbupbupbubbup, her baby's heart.

"Abuela . . ."

A tidal wave. She feels it coming. A block of water, one hundred feet tall. Phew phew phew. Focus. *Tilo, Abuela.* Tea of white willow bark. A bomb in her belly. Back breaking. Phew phew phew phew phew phew.

"Yes, breathe, honey." The nurse.

"Hold my hand, *mi cielo.*" Her mother.

Bupbupbupbup, her baby.

It's killing her, the pain. The water . . . drowning. Wave, high high. *Maricón. Puta.* AY AY AY. The doctor stares at the graph paper spilling from the monitor. The nurse listens to his whisper. He rests a hand on her sweaty forehead, like her father once did. The nurse fiddles with the IV.

"Good, good, good," the good doctor says.

No, not good. She has a knife in her side, a nail in her belly button. Her back . . . her back. Breathe. Focus. Seismic wave.

She's drowning. Too much.

"Soon, my girl. Soon you can push." A man's voice.

A male voice, baritone, resonant, vibrating . . .

. . . "Soon," her father said.

"How soon, Papi?"

"When I get a job."

"What kind of job?"

"Any job that pays."

"Will you buy me a doll, Papi, with money from your job?"

He did not answer. He was tall, very tall, oh so tall. The brown belt around his waist seemed as high as the sky. He had a black mustache, black hair on his knuckles. He had green eyes, slanted like hers. (Like the devil, her grandmother said. Why?)

She was four, no, maybe five, in a pink gingham dress and white pinafore. She wore black Mary Janes inherited from an older play-mate two houses down, with white bobby socks cuffed with lace, straight black hair cut in a bob. A little doll.

Muñeca, her father said. *Chinita. Mi muñequita china.* And when she climbs onto her mother's bed to look in the dresser mirror she knows why. She is a Chinese doll. Her father's China doll.

The calliope music from the ice-cream truck filled the block. She jumped up from the tiled doorstep and clapped in delight.

"Papi papi papi papi!"

He fumbled in his pocket for change, then followed her to the truck. She chose a red Popsicle, her favorite. They returned to the stoop, knees pressed against chests. She was very careful with the Popsicle, licking it from the bottom up, quickly, darting tongue slurping droplets. She did not want to get her dress dirty. She was the cleanest little girl she knew. She hated dirt, dust, spots, stains, clutter.

"*Una viejita*, too old for her age," observed her grandmother, who was an old lady herself, ancient. Forty, she thinks, or fifty.

"I have to go, Chinita," he said.

She gulped the last ruby Popsicle piece. Her head hurt from the cold. So did her heart. It felt compressed, refrigerated.

"Are you coming tomorrow?"

"Saturday. Next Saturday." He kissed her forehead, and she re-mained ever vigilant to keep her sticky hands away from his stiff brown pants. She watched him walk down the block, to the next, past where Marianito, the boy with no upper lip, lived. Oh, how handsome he was, her papi! She watched him until he turned left and disappeared into tall Australian pines. Sighing, she knocked on the door.

Her grandmother leaned against the doorway, bracelets jangling, looked left, looked right, let out a long hrrrrmph. She pushed past her grandmother, past that sweet scent of violet cologne, and dropped her Popsicle sticks in the kitchen trash can. In the bath-room she washed her hands—twice, for good measure—and wished it were next Saturday, whatever that meant. She hadn't learned the days of the week yet, but Saturday was a fine-sounding name for a day, any day.

Bupbupbupbupbup, her baby's heart.

"Breathe!" commands the nurse.

Oh, what pain. A saw across her intestines. A lash against her back. The wave . . . the wave. Smashing crashing blasting slicing slashing cracking tearing splitting. Breaking breaking. *Puta. Carajo. Maricón. Carajo Carajo Carajo.* Something has punctured her insides. She is hollow.

"Caca."

"No, not quite."

The nurse puts her feet in stirrups, clasps her hands around two bars on each side of the bed. The doctor slips his man-hands into gloves.

"Almost there, *querida.*"

Almost . . . but what has she forgotten? Is her underwear clean? The floor mopped in the kitchen? Dustballs swept from under her bed?

Oh, it's coming, up her legs, up her ass, in her belly exploding. Her mother will make a mess of . . .

"Push!"

The front porch stoop again. The herbal smell of freshly mowed lawn. Poincianas in bloom.

"What would you like to play?"

"The kiss game, Papi, the kiss game."

"You are not bored with that?"

"Never!"

"*Mi Chinita.*"

"Let's start with the fingers first."

"Fine. Press your fingers to mine. How sweet."

"The fingers are kissing, Papi. Watch them kiss."

"Smooch, smooch."

"Now both hands."

"That was a short kiss. What next?"

"Our knuckles."

"That is new, eh? We have never tried knuckle kissing."

"The wrists now, Papi. Okay, the elbows."

"This is awkward. I did not know elbows could kiss."

"Outside elbows can."

"What next?"

"Knees."

"Oh, those are hard kisses. Knees give hard, knobby kisses."

"Shoulder kisses now."

"How about ankle kisses, Chinita? Did you forget your ankles? They must be hard kisses just like the knee kisses."

"I know how to say ankle in English, Papi."

"You do? You are a smart girl."

"I learned in school. Can we give toe kisses?"

"What about the shoes?"

"I do not want to take off my shoes, no. Let them just meet through the shoes."

"A demure kiss, that."

"Papi, we have forgotten the hair kiss."

"I did not forget. My hair is ready. Lean forward."

"Ear kiss, but do not rub too hard, okay?"

"You have tiny ears, Chinita."

"Eyelash kisses."

"Those are very hard to give. My eyelashes are not long enough."

"I do not care, Papi. Try anyway."

"Okay. How about nose kisses, like the Eskimos?"

"Do the Eskimos really give only nose kisses?"

"I do not know. Ask your mother. She knows everything."

"Cheek kisses, Papi."

"First, the right cheek, then the left cheek. Do not forget both, because we only did one of the ears, and one of the eyelashes."

"Goody, goody. Now for the end. Tatatum: the chin kiss."

"Jut your chin out, Chinita."

"Your beard, Papi, your beard. It tickles."

• • •

"PUSH!"

"The head."

"*M'ija*, it has black hair, like yours."

Again again. Bomb. EXPLOSION. Heave heave.

"Push. Good good good."

She is breaking, splitting in half. Where is her left leg? She can't anymore. An ice chip. It's coming again. Again.

"PUSH!"

UNNNUNNNUNNNUNN. Oh, how long. *Dios mío.* Bitch. bupbupbupbup, baby's heart. Too fast. It stops.

"Check the monitor."

"Okay, sweetheart." The nurse has grabbed her face. "I don't want you pushing just yet. Okay? No pushing."

But she has to. She has to push.

"Look at my face. DO NOT PUSH!"

The pain. She wants to go caca. To push. PPPPPPUSH! She cannot see the doctor, only the green cap. He has disappeared between her legs. She's broken. Forgotten.

"MAMI!!!"

Saturday. *Sábado.* She dressed in green shorts and a matching pullover top with scalloped neck and sleeves to wait for her papi. White canvas pull-on sneakers from G. C. Murphy's, no socks. Her mother brushed her hair back in a ponytail after breakfast, but wisps escaped the rubber-band imprisonment to frame her face. She has waited a long time, since morning. In the same place, in the same way: knees pressed against chest, on the tiled stoop of the duplex doorway. Now the sun has pushed west, where her gaze has been fixed for some time. Sweat has collected on her upper lip, glistening beads, but she has refused to seek refuge inside, beside her grandmother's big fan. She has not left her post. Never. Though she hates sweat, sticky, smelly sweat, she has not left, no. She has remained seated here, stoop-warming, in hopes of spotting his tall-tall figure emerging from the cluster of Australian pines blocks away.

Her grandmother brought her a *papa rellena*, a stuffed potato, when the sun was directly overhead, before it began slipping that-away. She devoured it, then sucked on the green olive in the middle.

"Come inside, *niña*," her grandmother urged. Her grandmother's long braid wound around her gray head to form a crown.

"No, Abuela, I want to make sure he finds me."

Her grandmother started to say something but stopped. Finally, her grandmother offered: "Something must have happened."

The ice-cream truck turned the corner, its calliope music muted. Her grandmother bought her a red Popsicle, and she licked it long and lovingly, allowing the liquid ruby to drip on the porch's tiled floor. Then she flung the sticks into the ixora bushes.

She waited some more. She has waited a long time.

She never saw him again. Several months later, maybe years, an eternity (she still cannot figure out time), her mother told her that her papi died in a car accident. She was sad. She cried herself to sleep every night but never in the day, when others could see her. She eventually forgot how her heart felt that Saturday she sat with him on her stoop, so cold, so compressed, but she remembered their kiss game, the knuckle kiss, the ankle kiss, the chin kiss.

"Okay." The doctor. "Push, *querida*. Push. One more time. The shoulders."

HMMMMMMMMMMMPH.

"Push, *cielo*."

"PUSH."

So hard. Breaking. Tearing. Stuck. Oh, like constipation. But no, no, no, there it goes, wheffff. There, there, out, out out. What a relief. Oh oh oh oh.

The baby emerges blue, covered in a white film, black hair plastered against pointy head. Slimy.

"A boy!" her mother screams.

The doctor holds him up. He is tiny, smaller than she ever imagined, and scrawny. He stares at her, wide-eyed and quiet, wet and blue and as still as a dead fish. The doctor hands him to the nurse. A phalanx of green in padded shoes and hospital gowns invades her room. One, two, three, four gowns. They take the baby like a football.

"My baby!" she cries out.

No one answers. She cannot see her baby. They have formed a line against her vision in a corner of the room. Her heart has stopped, she is sure. The quartet of green has stolen him. Abduction. Kidnapping.

"My baby!"

"*Ya ya ya, querida.* One more push. Come on, come on." The doctor presses on her deflated belly.

"My baby!"

"Let her see! Let her see!" her mother screams. She scythes the air with her hands.

The wave of green parts into distinctive arms, shoulders, and heads. She watches, in awe and in fear, her son's torturous path into life. He is on a board, under a blue light, head down, feet up. His neck is slightly extended. One woman is drying him. Another is suctioning his nose with a blue bulb. They are whispering . . . what? She cannot hear.

Oh, he is so tiny, so very very very little. The size of a man's hand. Too small. But his head, so big and misshapen, so much black wet hair. And the ears, too low, too close to his jaw. What . . . what . . . A large nose. What bony arms, what skeletal legs! A rat. They have switched her son with a rat.

"Doctor . . ." She loses her voice. Something pricks and stings her pipi. Tears spill from her eyes.

A man moves the woman with the bulb aside. He slaps the baby's feet, then flicks his right heel, his left.

"Stop! Stop!" she yells. "Don't hurt him!"

"*¡Ay, Dios mío! ¿Qué hacen? Ese pobre angelito de Dios.*"

"Doctor," she pleads, trying to pull herself up on her elbows, "what are they doing to him?"

"Relax, *querida.* Relax. Let me finish you up here."

The man keeps slapping the little feet.

"Stop it! Stop it!"

And then, softly, so softly she thinks she is dreaming, a mew breaks from her son's throat, a cry as pitiful as her pain, as weak as her heart.

"There he goes," says the doctor.

"What is it, doctor?" Her mother. "What is it?"

They ignore her, the medical team in green. They call out numbers. They clean him, dry him. Sixteen and a half inches. Three pounds seven ounces. More numbers. Then, wrapped tight in a blue-and-pink-striped receiving blanket, head ensconced in a white knit cap, eyes scrunched shut, brow furrowed, gasping, mewing, the boy, the rat-boy, is delivered into her arms.

"Congratulations!" The woman smiles.

The baby is placed on her chest and, sobbing, hiccuping, blinded, she cradles him in her arms, under her strengthening heart.

He looks so strange.

"A possible chromosome abnormality, possibly a trisomy . . ."

Maribel tries hard to listen, but she doesn't understand the part about the tricycle. Her father gave her a red-and-black tricycle with a loud horn a long time ago. Her grandfather taught her to steer it.

". . . we will know for sure after the blood work is done in . . ."

The neonatologist, Maribel notices, is a young man, not much older than she. He resembles Caleb, though their coloring is much different, and the doctor's features are aligned. Still, there is something in the face—a malleable sensitivity, an openness to pain—that reminds her of her boss.

". . . the medical literature shows . . ."

Why does his voice sound so strange?

Her mother begins to cry. She is so dramatic, her mother. Sobbing, imagine! At least her grandmother is not here jangling her bracelets. What a spectacle!

"Several complications occur . . ."

She wants to hold her baby, her rat-boy, her son, but several hours ago the nurses whisked him away to the nursery. In a few minutes, when the neonatologist and his friends have left the room, she will ask her mother to help her walk down the hall to her rat-boy.

". . . Severe mental retardation, heart defects and organs . . ."

"I don't care," she interrupts. "I want to see my baby."

4

Adela examined the events of the morning in much the same way she once inspected her clients' nails for chips, marks, indentations, weaknesses of character, idiosyncrasies. After a few seconds, a longer than normal introspective period for her, Adela concluded that she had slept all morning and forgotten to wake. This seemed the only plausible explanation for what had happened—or for what she thought had happened. The visit from the doctors earlier, when the sun was barely a lozenge over the hospital's east parking lot, had the makings of a dream, a bad dream, and she would do well to pretend it never happened. That was the trick to interpreting dreams. You had to learn to distinguish which really counted. This one didn't, obviously. She laughed to dispel her doubt, but the sound forced out her throat and through her mouth was something she had never heard. It rumbled like the deep-throated neighing of a horse, a wounded mare.

Across the mauve-and-violet-wallpapered room, in the freshly made hospital bed, Maribel stirred at the strange sound but did not wake. The bliss of exhaustion. Her daughter looked radiantly dark in the bleached whiteness of the sheets (Adela was convinced the hospital's laundry room used Clorox. Shame! At the salon she had treated the damage it wreaked on skin) and her breathing came soft and peaceful, not at all like the desperate raggedness she had emitted during labor. Adela knew that Maribel was having her own dream, a pleasant one apparently, for she showed no sign of distress. Her lips drooped, her hands were curled like a baby's, and her black hair was splayed around her head in a halo.

Adela wanted to borrow the halo. She was a woman governed by her instinct, and rarely had it failed her. (A notable exception, of course, was choosing Maribel's father, but she wasn't going to allow him to intrude in this nightmare. No, absolutely not. He could star in his own, with a different billing.) Right now her gut instinct was telling her—screaming shrilly, actually—that she needed a halo, the protection of her guardian angel, the intercession of her Virgencita.

Adela knew, just as she had known that the baby was a boy, just as she had sensed that he would be born *con el pan debajo del brazo*, a loaf of bread under his arm, she knew she would soon awaken in her own bed beside her loyal Virgencita and the stash of Lotto tickets, surrounded by stacks of books, unopened bills, torn magazine recipes, maternity patterns, and a lone spool of green velvet ribbon. Yes, yes, she would be jolted awake by the melodic clang of her mother's forty-six gold bracelets. And she would realize the morning's conversation had been mistaken dialogue, temporarily displaced from someone's else life. And she would laugh, and the laugh would sound like church bells, not a horse giving birth.

Chica, for starters consider the impostors who masqueraded as doctors in this horrible apparition. She listed them on the fingers of her left hand: The one who had done the most talking, the neo-something or other, had appeared in blue jeans. Imagine that! Blue jeans. Sure, he had the obligatory white robe and a stethoscope draped like a snake around his neck—but blue jeans! Really, this happened only in dreams or in movies. All the doctors she knew wore Italian suits and dry-clean-only shirts. They reeked of imported cologne; their hands were smooth and effeminate. The blue-jean man had large, strong hands with thick fingers. She had noticed them, oh definitely. He had hands that made a woman wonder. A medical doctor? Really! Like she was born yesterday.

And the other one, the geneticist who so painstakingly tried to explain some mysterious blood work, some karyotyping, being conducted in the laboratory downstairs. So much mumbo jumbo. *Pues*, he was too young to shave. She had noticed that too smooth jaw, too, before being blinded by those tears. (Funny, she had never cried in any of her dreams before.) He was even younger than Dr. Neo-something-or-other, perhaps in his mid-twenties—and that was if one piled on the years generously. A geneticist yes, in the same dimension she had been John Kennedy's mistress.

Then, of course, the pediatrician Maribel had selected several months earlier, she recognized him and it gave authenticity to the nightmare. He was tall and stoop-shouldered, his weathered face like the planes of a rumpled paper bag. His furrowed brow creased companion lines above his nose, two parallel roadways to distracted thoughts. He had patted Maribel's hand while the others talked, his eyes staring out the window at the misty beginnings of a morning. Had he spoken? Adela wasn't sure. She could not always remember her dreams clearly.

¡Qué pesadilla! The netherworld of her subconscious had created these characters to torment her for some past peccadillo. It did that, you know. *El cura* at St. Michael's, Father Peace, said those twinges were remorse, guilt tweaking a conscience. She had felt it before, and therefore she could recognize it. But why the torment now? What had she done, how had she *sinned?* The answer flashed into her thoughts, and she smiled. Okay, okay, there had been those minor indiscretions with Carlos. She stretched her legs in front of her, luxuriating in the thought. He had such a strong, firm body, hard-hard, unusual for a man his age—and those biceps, that muscled chest! Chica, it must have been from the heavy work at the *carnicería*, all that hauling around of sides of beef and wielding those sharp knives. He was patient, too, that's what she had liked most about him, had admired him for even before their relationship had moved to a level she had not yet defined. He was comfortable with himself, with her, and it had been a sweet pleasure—like sneaking a thick slice of flan while on a diet. Despite this, she had refrained

lately. She had realized that the stakes, even for a woman who enjoyed risk, were too high, that she had little time for a relationship without a future, that, when you came right down to it, she could not face Fefa with ease if she had gone to bed with her husband the week before.

So, okay, okay, the priest was right. Guilt, real or imagined, tormented, but could it do so through such vivid dreams? Could it create characters, pooof-like-that, to people a nightmare? She did not know what to make of it. It did not seem fair that a moment of ecstasy (four, actually) would result in a lifetime of perdition, and perdition it was if something were to happen to her first grandchild.

Adela stood up quickly from her chair to dispel the thought. Such gloomy reflections gave her the chills. Her right leg was asleep, and she had to shake it and lean on it to feel the tiny ants of her blood circulating. Tottering on her high-heeled sandals as she tried for firmer footing, Adela approached the window. It was midmorning, perhaps later. She never wore a watch, but she could tell the approximate time of day by the slant of the sun in the cloudless sky outside. She watched people parking their cars, opening and closing their doors, bringing down flowers, baskets, balloons. She concentrated on an elderly couple in a blue car. The man was thin and wore plaid pants, a brown jacket. He appeared bald, but she could not tell from this distance; maybe he had wisps of white hair. He took his time fumbling with his car keys, then locking the door, and hobbling around to the other side, where he fumbled some more before opening the door. He bent over into the car, and she lost sight of him, except for the plaid bottom of his pants legs and dark shoes. His pants moved forward then backward several times before the top of him finally emerged, straightened and pulled at something. With him appeared an immense blue-haired woman. He closed the door behind her with his right hand and held her elbow with his left. That done, they walked past the row of cars, down to the sidewalk and out of sight, neither of them very limber but hand in hand just the same, the old man and the fat woman.

This gave Adela pause. She did not have anyone to publicly hold hands with, had not had for a very long time. She should have remarried and once, maybe twice, had considered it with other men, long before Carlos, but she wasn't quite sure what had happened.

Those other men had never asked, and the relationships had cooled. Well, maybe not cooled, as in silence and cold shoulders, but grown tepid like bathtub water left out too long. One of the men might have suited her if nothing better had come along, but she had waited for something better, and it had not come along. She wondered now, looking down at a hospital parking lot, watching strangers walking, talking, hugging, car doors opening and closing, and fighting off a hovering sense of doom and delinquency, if she had not missed out on something more precious than her freedom. There was something to laud in longtime companionship, in the ease of such intimacy, about a friendship that had weathered years and familiarity and sex. Maybe she should have settled; maybe she shouldn't have been so picky; maybe she shouldn't have been so sure.

And maybe then she would not have been alone in this room, trying to make sense of what was increasingly insensible nonsense. Maybe she would have had somebody to discuss the impossibility of these three doctors. Somebody who would have lifted her. Somebody who would have chided her. Somebody who would have cared as much as she did. She had, she realized with a shudder, very little: a mother who would have dropped dead long ago if not for her herbal remedies, a daughter who was embarrassed by her and . . .

And a grandson. Oh, what would Maribel name him? Not an American name, she hoped, not a name her tongue would trip over. Nothing with W, nothing that started with a J or Ch. Such difficult pronunciations. Adela preferred something masculine, something that evoked both certainty and curiosity. Antonio, for instance, like his great-grandfather. Or Leonardo, so classy. Even Pablo, though that brought memories of one of her lovers. Eduardo would do, after the baby's father. Adela preferred, though, hoped fervently actually, that Maribel not name the boy after her dear departed father. Miguel. Oh, she couldn't bear the reminder of her husband.

She sighed and turned away from the window. She had been up most of the night before the dream, and now she felt the exhaustion in her bones, the heaviness of her thoughts. There was no use in second-guessing or in lamentations. She had learned young that the past was unchangeable; all you had were memories but to those you could put a spin, add a twist, omit, edit, trim.

She eased herself into the mauve hospital chair and slipped off her sandals. She wiggled her toes, arched her feet. If she had a chance later today or tomorrow, before the baby came home, she would soak her feet in her mother's Epsom salts and give herself a pedicure. That always lifted her spirits. Besides, she wouldn't have time after everybody came home, what with caring for a newborn and, of course, Maribel.

Maribel. Bewildered, confused Maribel. How little her daughter knew of the world! For all her community-college education, her reading, her hoity-toity manners and plans, she was a mere babe. What an eye-opener an infant would be! Her schedules would go out the window and her impeccable house would gather dust balls. Nipples and bottles and burp rags and diapers and pacifiers and bibs and all that modern paraphernalia that now seemed indispensable for the raising of a baby would clutter the living room, overflow into the bedroom, invade the kitchen. How would Maribel, Ms. Everything in Its Place, accept this sudden takeover? Adela wondered. If she was smart, and her daughter was, Maribel would realize that, quite simply, she had to—how did *los americanos* put it?—go with the flow. *Se tendrá que dejar llevar por la corriente.* Sometimes that was not so bad, for we could only *pretend* to have control. In the end, no matter the amount of programming, scheming, and ordering, fate had its way. Destiny determined. A helpless baby would teach Maribel about the randomness of life, and that would not be a bad lesson to learn. Not at all.

Certainly a baby would make Maribel relax, not take herself so seriously. This, in turn, would help to improve their mother-daughter relationship. The thought perked Adela up, and she straightened, smiled, and forced herself to pursue the thought. Not that their relationship was terrible. She knew of daughters estranged from their mothers, who did not speak to them, who cared little, if anything, when the old women took sick. Their relationship was not like that, but it tended to be strained and, honestly, not very close. It pained her that Maribel never came to her for advice. She could understand such a situation when Maribel was a teenager, but those years were long gone and her daughter still maintained a haughty distance, as if Adela were an eccentric relative one had to put up with. That hurt.

They seemed to disagree about everything, large or small, significant or trivial. Two Christmases ago, for instance, they had had a falling-out over a present Maribel had bought Eduardo. It had been a stupid discussion, yes, just short of an argument, but the discussion—Maribel never raised her voice, Adela had taught her well—underscored their differences in a symbolic way.

Maribel had bought Eduardo socks for Christmas. Adela had, very patiently and very carefully, tried to give her daughter a morsel of advice.

"*Hija*," she had said, measuring her words for her audience, "let me explain to you a little about men."

"What, Mami?" That tone of voice. That narrowing of eyes.

"Socks are not an appropriate gift for your lover at Christmas."

"Who says?"

"It does not matter who says. It simply is not . . ."

"He needs some."

"It is not what he needs that you should get him."

"So I should get him cologne?"

"Well, that would be an improvement, but I meant something more romantic."

"Ay, Mami," Maribel said, snickering.

"Silk boxers are . . . how would you say . . ."

"Overpriced underwear."

"No, they are not, but if you prefer not to give underwear, fine. How about matching velour robes?"

"In Miami? We would die of heat stroke."

"I suppose you have never heard of air-conditioning. But that is beside the point. How about a gift certificate for a massage? Or a night in one of those motels by the airport with heart-shaped tubs?"

Maribel stood up. She had been gift wrapping at the kitchen table, a task that was tedious and time-consuming for someone so fastidious.

"Mami, *really*." She did not need to say anything more.

That "really" had blasted Adela's heart. To be dismissed in such a way by your own daughter!

There was a knock and the face of a middle-aged woman peered around the hospital door.

"Adela?" she asked.

"Yes." Adela quickly put on her sandals and patted her hair into place. "Come in."

The woman was dressed in hospital whites, with a badge. Finally, thought Adela, a nurse to clear up this terrible misunderstanding. Maybe the doctors had come into the wrong room. A mistake, a correction.

"I'm Clara, Fefa's cousin."

Clara? Clara?

"Fefa told me you were here. I work up on the fourth floor, in oncology, but I'm on my break and Fefa asked me to look in on you."

Adela struggled to get up while running through the files of her memory. There was something familiar about the woman—the long nose, the round face, the black hair, a familial resemblance, yes, to Fefa.

"Don't get up. You must be exhausted, and I'll just be a minute." Clara pointed to the sleeping Maribel with her chin. "How is she?"

"Very tired, as you can imagine."

"First ones are always so difficult, so painful."

"I only had one, so I don't know about the others."

"Of course. And how is she taking the news?"

"What do you mean?" Adela stood now, quickly, firmly.

"I read in the chart . . ." Clara became flustered. She wrung her hands. "They have told you, no? The neonatologist has come . . ."

Clara continued talking, but Adela could not hear. The voice drifted away, an annoying drone, like a dentist's drill. For the first time Adela noticed that there was something wrong with the room. It wasn't quite straight. The linoleum floor tilted, as did the walls, the mirror, the door. The blankets on Maribel's bed slouched forward, as if pulled by gravity, and the black wastebasket with the plastic bag—it seemed almost to be on its side! And her chair, the one she had been sitting on, was at an angle. The small bleached-oak chifforobe leaned. A framed poster of a ballerina dipped slightly toward the left.

How come she had not noticed before?

"Surely they told Maribel already," Clara was saying, and she too swayed. "I did not mean to intrude." Sway, dip.

Adela walked toward Clara. One step, two, three. She realized she was moving on an incline, uphill.

"I am so sorry, Adela. If there is anything I can do, I am upstairs until 7 p.m. tonight."

"Clara . . ." she said, and realized no words had been spoken. Her hands fluttered.

"I work twelve-hour shifts on weekends."

It was difficult to climb, Adela realized, especially on high heels. Her calf muscles cramped. Her heart beat irregularly, as if missing a note to its inner music. She herself felt off-key, displaced.

"Well, I have to be back, but you know that . . . Ooops. See what we have here. The newspaper cart."

A tiny white-haired woman in pink pushed the cart through the door, bumping Clara as the nurse walked backward out of the room. Clara took a paper and placed it on the corner of Maribel's bed.

"Really, I am so sorry."

Clara's words echoed long after she had left the room, long after Adela had stopped trying to walk uphill. She was short of breath. So much exertion, this. And she felt an increasing pressure on her chest, a terrible, terrible oppression. A giant stepping on her. A million bricks weighing down on her. Two metal plates squeezing her in. Her heart was about to burst. The pain stabbed then spread, stabbed then spread. It burned. It throbbed. It stung. She had never known anything like this: so suffocating, so overwhelming, so intense. The absolute clarity of her realization was omnipotent.

She opened her mouth to scream, but the sound she heard was her grandson's small, high-pitched voice, a forlorn but melodious note. She had heard his voice before he ever spoke, smelled his warm breath before he ever breathed, felt the softness of his belly, his legs, his face, before his skin cells had ever formed. She had known the taste of his kiss, wet and slightly sour from breast milk, before he learned to pucker, before he learned to suck. So how could she miss something she had never had?

Adela glanced at the newspaper on the bed. She could not decipher the headlines; the paper lay miles away, a lifetime ago. She did not think to look up the winning Lotto numbers on Page 2A of *The Miami Herald*, and she did not remember to call her mother. She worried instead about how she would roll down the incline on her high heels, to the beckoning chair and a level plane. She did not care about getting hurt; she simply wanted to arrive there. Reality already had forged a terrible pact with her dreams.

She asked little of this world, Cuca did. Never a woman to cling to possessions, never a wife to demand of her husband or a daughter to expect from her parents, Cuca had faced life with the open-hearted, wide-eyed, palms-up acceptance of a child who has known no evil and therefore cannot recognize it. In her case, she had known evil, just as she had known overwhelming generosity and weakness and ambivalence and terrible pain, but she had managed to pick her way through the emotional rose garden of her life: a gardener selecting the finest blooms with the fewest thorns. (I'll take this but not that. I want the bunch over there and over there. This? Definitely not.) At times, out of sheer frustration and a heart that rebelled against pain, she had opened her mouth and laughed. Laughed hard and well, better even than her precocious daughter. She had flicked back her braid, so long and so full and so black, and belted out the sound of mockery and triumph at that which attacked her. Invariably it worked: muscles relaxed, tears dried, energy returned. Laughter and the jangle of her bracelets, ay. What antidotes to depression. Cynics might say life had betrayed her. She could have, should have, had this. Life owed her: she deserved. But it was not her line of thinking. Never. No, no, no. It occasionally crossed her mind, of course. Self-pity tempted her with the lure of self-righteousness, but she was too proud, too strong, too full of herself, to confuse courage with defiance, defeat with acceptance. She had simply been given a different script to live. The producer of her play had changed the lines on her—and the plot, too. But what could she do, eh? Laugh and jangle her bracelets. And love. Do not forget that. Ever ever ever. Love was the aspirin for heartache. You had to love without thought, *entregándose completamente*, no holding back, no doubting.

As she loved her great-grandchild, this flesh of her flesh, blood of her blood, two generations removed (and probably a boy, no less. A boy! A boy!). If only Adela would call. Ring, phone, ring. Bring me the news. *Cuéntame lo que ha pasado.*

Cuca struggled up from the sofa and shuffled over to the kitchen phone. She checked for a dial tone: it was working. Hrrrmph! What could be taking Maribel so long to spit out that child, *Dios mío?* They had been gone all afternoon and all night and even for a *primeriza* that was a long time. Although, come to think of it, her cousin Hilda had been in labor three days with her first one fifty years ago. Three days! She had been lucky in that way, Cuca had. She labored, she grunted, she cursed, she sweated, she panted, she bit her lips raw—then she pushed, pushed hard and long and with the might of a woman who saw herself in the context of centuries of women doing the same. Out the baby came, a swoosh of blood and sinew and mucus and cord. Within hours, and sometimes not in the most sanitary of conditions, she had herself a new crying, hungry life. But then they had not lasted for more than a few days or weeks: maybe they had been frightened by this world and fled into the next, still blotchy-skinned and peak-headed from birth. She would have chosen a labor of three days—or a week or a month or a year, for that matter!—if it had meant she could have kept her babies. She had not been given that choice. Limitations had come early and hard to her.

She checked for the dial tone a second time. Still working. She slammed the receiver down and sighed. Patience, woman, patience. She opened the kitchen cupboard for a little pick-me-up tea, and the odor, oh that telltale scent of honeysuckle, sweet and cloying and unforgettable, wafted out, enveloping the tiny kitchen, grabbing her by the throat. Light-headed, she sniffed. Light-headed, she collapsed on a chair.

¿Qué es?

¿Qué significa?

¿Por qué?

She put her head down on the dining table and closed her eyes tight, her hard-earned wrinkles scrunching and folding over each other. Concentrate, she told herself. Join it, don't fight it. Go along, go along. What is it? What do you have for me? Think of the honeysuckle shrub. Focus only on that, not on Hilda or her son or the phone that doesn't ring and Adela's carelessness and Maribel's struggle. Concentrate.

Cuca had never seen honeysuckle in Miami, never spotted its profusion of trumpet-shaped flowers or the berries that formed after the petals dropped off. So then where was the heady, cloying scent coming from?

You blind?

Tony, my dearest!

Use your imagination—and your grandmother. She will help.

Mamá Cleofe! Oh, Mamá Cleofe, you too. So long . . .

Concentrate, Cuca, on the issue at hand. Where can that honeysuckle come from?

Granddaughter, concentrate.

Cuca slammed her head against the table to dislodge any stuck thoughts. She did it twice. Nothing. But the third time, with a red bump forming furiously on her forehead, the idea shook itself free.

Honeysuckle is very fragrant, isn't it, Mamá Cleofe?

Yes, go on, granddaughter.

And . . . I don't know anymore, Mamá Cleofe.

Cuca, mi cielo. Think of the berries.

Oh, yes, Tony. The berries. The birds eat them.

And they carry the seeds away, Cuca. They carry them far, to places you would not think honeysuckle could survive. Sometimes by mistake.

And, Tony, and? What are you getting at?

Honeysuckle—better known by the family name of Caprifoliaceae— is easy to grow. It is quite hardy and propagates easily.

Oh, Rizos, my sweet brother! It is you, the scientist. Rizos, help me please. What is this?

Concentrate!

Concentrate!

Concentrate!

The three of you are teaming up against me, eh? My husband, my brother, and my grandmother—what a trio.

Concentrate, Cuca.

Bueno, Mamá Cleofe, Tony, and Rizos. So the honeysuckle is hardy and propagates easily.

It even grows well in rock gardens, wife.

Thank you, Tony. I also know it can be trained to twine over porches and fences and trellises.

Yes, sister.

And I know the flowers are sweet because hummingbirds love its nectar.

Yes, my granddaughter.

Hardy. Propagates easily. Trainable. Sweet. So that is what we have, no?

The one you are smelling, sister, is the species L. fragrantissima.

You are an angel, Rizos.

Yes, I am.

Hardy. Trainable. Sweet.

Hardy Trainable Sweet: her great-grandson. Oh oh oh! Why had she worried? Why had she been so suspicious of the scent yesterday, worrying that it meant melancholy, bracing herself for a thousand sorrows. It was a good sign, this honeysuckle. She sniffed, taking the sweetness into her lungs, pushing it through her blood into each of her organs, but especially into her heart, which needed sweetness and gentleness and all things beautiful.

Thank you, Tony. Thank you, Mamá Cleofe, Rizos.

But they were gone.

Cuca shimmied out of the chair and to the refrigerator. She packed ice in a kitchen towel and pressed it against her forehead. Ay. Hardy. Trainable. Sweet. And all night she had been unable to close her eyes, fearful that sorrow had found her again. Silly!

Cuidado, mujer.

Eh, Tony! I thought you had left. What do you mean?

Tread carefully, my wife.

What do you mean?

Tread carefully. Not everything is what it seems.

What? Tony? Tony! Come back.

Still, the damn phone didn't ring. She sat down again and stared at the kitchen almanac—the photograph of the Morro fort especially—thinking about what her husband had said. She always tread carefully. She never took anything at face value, either. So what had that been all about?

Oh, she needed a little help from her friends. A little tea to go with the honeysuckle. A touch of chamomile tea. She prepared it automatically. Sipped, then gargled. Checked the phone for a dial tone again. Moved to the sofa. Waited.

She spent a lot of time waiting, sometimes for something she did not want but usually for something she suspected was to arrive shortly (as now, with her grandchild, her grand*son*!). More and more as she aged she waited for what she did not understand except to accept. After her husband had died, she too had waited for death. Waited, waited, waited. But death betrayed her, not once but twice. It teased her, smiled at her with its black teeth and foul breath, but left her empty, hollow, passed over. The first time death taunted her she got so sick she passed out and landed in a hospital, the very first (and only) time she had been a patient, victim of food poisoning. (Such sterility in these places. So many contraptions. So many people poking at her. Touching the inside of her wrist. Listening to her heart. Taking her blood pressure, her temperature.) Her heart beat furiously against its stalker, refused to resign itself. Then several years later, she fell on the front-door stoop, a step she had taken a trillion times, up-down, down-up, so many steps over the course of thirty years. Who would have thought, eh? But unlike most old women, she did not break a hip, only her right wrist, which had slammed against the floor as she tried to break her fall. Immobilized equally by her cast as by her mortifying anger, she could not putter around the kitchen for two months and was forced to depend on Adela—think of it: depend on undependable Adela!—to concoct the bilberry cream to strengthen the capillaries that had suffered considerable bruising from her misstep.

Honeysuckle. Sweet. Trainable. Hardy. It still filled the room. And no matter what her spirits had said, no matter what they had hinted and led her through, she could not help but feel a weight in her bones. Right now she was staring at the open kitchen cupboard, thinking, "I must close it and imprison that odor. Prevent it from invading the house," but she remained immobilized on the sofa, paralyzed by the eyes of the black velvet Sacred Heart and her inexplicable confusion, as anxiously silent as a woman left mute by a lover's unexpected leave-taking.

She jangled her bracelets. Ay. She laughed hard and true. The scent, it hardly dissipated.

• • •

When she woke, Maribel asked her mother to accompany her to the nursery. She so wanted to see the baby, couldn't understand why he had not been allowed to room with her, cocooned in the warmth of a pink-and-blue-striped blanket, asleep in one of those cute rolling bassinets. She could not wait to hold him, to feel the pull of him at her nipple, the weight of his heart against hers. Oooh! to squeeze him tight, shower him with kisses.

It was not a long walk, though her new terry-cloth slippers, bought for the occasion to match her peach-colored robe, fit snug around the toes. She noticed her mother had lost some of her characteristic oomph and shuffled as if walking through water, but Maribel did not think much of it. Adela probably was exhausted and who, anyway, would think of wearing stiletto-heeled sandals to the hospital? Sometimes her mother . . .

"Maribel," Adela began hoarsely. She pressed a red-nailed finger to her lips, a pretentious gesture that got on Maribel's nerves because those who didn't know Adela misinterpreted it as a pause for thought and reflection.

"If you have a cold, Mami," Maribel replied curtly, "you can't get near the baby."

"No, no cold." Adela's frantic hands dismissed the suggestion. She tried again: "I don't know if you understand exactly what . . ."

Then there they were outside the nursery, peeking through the window at the newborns and the brightly colored clown-and-balloon wallpaper, and Adela was not sure what she wanted to say or how she would explain it.

There were five babies in the nursery, three with pink cards taped to the side of their bassinets, two with blue. All wrapped in the same way, like chorizos, in the standard-issue striped hospital blanket. One squalled furiously, her face red, her mouth wide open. Maribel could see right down the baby's throat when she screamed. The rest slept peacefully, unaware of their crying neighbor.

Maribel concentrated on the blue cards: Jeremy Jones, Adam Fishman. Fishman was bald, Jones was black. Neither was hers. Where could the rat-boy have gone?

"Mami, I don't see the baby." She tried to keep the tone of alarm out of her voice because Adela tended to overreact, but

Maribel heard her own surprised desperation clearly. "Ay, *hija* . . ."

Then Maribel realized she had not named him and perhaps the nurses took all the unnamed babies, those poor unidentified, untethered souls, to another room. Relieved, she knocked on the window to get the attention of the two nurses in the corner. When they turned, she signaled her search by pretending to cradle a baby in her arms. One nurse smiled and slid quickly, as if on wheels, to unlock the door.

"Mrs. Garcia," the nurse greeted her. "Do you want to see your baby?"

"He's here?"

"Of course. But I'm sorry"—looking at Adela—"only the mother can come in for now."

Maribel translated; Adela nodded listlessly. She understood English perfectly, though she always spoke Spanish to her daughter and Maribel, in her infinite meddling, felt a need to interpret. Just as well. Still staring through the nursery window, she spotted her grandson, a speck of a child in the corner incubator, bathed in bright light and crisscrossed with plastic tubing.

The nurse—"Hi, I'm Joanne!"—asked Maribel to wash her hands in a corner sink.

"We have to take certain precautions," she said, and Maribel thought the nurse spoke much too loud. Surely, her voice—throaty, resonant—would awaken the sleeping babies if the furious crying and the constant alarms and coded messages over the loudspeakers hadn't already. Didn't she know how to whisper?

Joanne led Maribel to a blinding light in the far end of the room.

"He's darling, isn't he?" Joanne asked.

Maribel stared. Her baby was nothing like she remembered him. He was not wrapped in a blanket like the others. Instead, he wore a diaper and a white T-shirt. Around him everywhere there were tubes: machines talking, beeping, invading.

"Have y'all thought of a name yet?" Joanne had a Southern accent, Mississippi woods.

Maribel did not hear. She looked from one machine to another, entranced.

"I don't . . ."

"Oh, that's okay, honey. You don't have to come up with a name right away, just as long as we get it on the birth certificate before you leave the hospital."

Maribel wasn't referring to the name. What she had meant to say was that this baby did not look anything like the one she had delivered in last night's sweaty, heaving agony. This was not her rat-boy. This was a bird. He was so tiny, so itsy-bitsy-teeny, as fragile and new as dawn. He had spindly limbs, slight like a sparrow's bones, and hands the size of a quarter. His red, wrinkled face reminded her of the photograph of a baby condor she had once seen in a *National Geographic* magazine: beak nose that covered a dot of a lipless mouth on one end and curved into a bony, broad forehead on the other; ears so round and so low on his face as to appear like small wings; and a thatch of black hair like a cock's comb. His abdomen was certainly too heavy for his arms and legs, too, a bird's breast. And those diminutive feet, claw-feet! Bird-boy, bird-boy.

She had never seen anything so beautiful.

"What's that for?" Maribel asked, pointing.

"The IV? For medicine."

"Medicine? Why does he need medicine?" Maribel's heart fluttered.

"Apnea."

"What?"

"Apnea. For when you stop breathing temporarily."

Maribel felt light-headed.

"We are watching him very carefully, honey," Joanne assured her.

"Can I hold him?"

"I'm sorry, Mrs. Garcia. You can touch him, though."

"I can't hold him? Why?"

"Talk to your doctor, okay? For now, why don't you just touch him and rub him. He'll like that."

Maribel touched the baby's right knee gingerly. It was warm and bony, yielding. And so very soft. Then she touched his left knee. It felt the same, like just-baked clay. She touched one foot, then the other, counted toes on both sides. Ten, all ten. She stroked his scrawny legs, his thighs, up, down, up down round.

"*Mi cielito, mi chinito, mi tesorito, mi caramelito . . .*" she whispered, using all the endearments she had stored in her heart for so long.

She caressed his long, narrow face, the prominent bridge on his nose, the low-set ears and closed, protruding eyes, the almost lipless mouth, the sparse lashes and brows, the hard forehead.

"*. . . precioso mío, corazón de melón, sol de mi mañana . . .*"

Maribel slipped her finger into his minuscule fist. He held on to it tightly, with surprising strength.

"*Mi hombrecito. Mi machito. Mi querubín.*"

The baby opened his beak-mouth slightly. He seemed to pucker his lips in the air, sucking, sucking, a bird stretching for nourishment beyond its protected nest. Joanne reached around Maribel and put the baby's free hand in his mouth. He sucked loudly.

"That's good," she said. "I reckon he'll suck real good."

That's a good sign, Maribel thought. Isn't it? She had read about rooting somewhere, maybe in a baby book or a magazine. A good sign, this suck-sucking. Apnea be damned!

"Who does he look like?" Adela asked as they shuffled back to the room. It had taken an incredible amount of energy, more than she thought she had, for Adela to watch her daughter leaning over the bassinet, mouthing words, reaching delicately to touch, to love.

"The baby?"

"Yes, the baby."

"He looked like a bird to me."

"Hmmm."

"Mami, did I ever tell you I thought I saw Papi once during a focus group Caleb organized?"

"Impossible."

"I know, I know. But listen, this man looked just like Papi would have looked now."

"What do you mean?" Adela imagined—hoped—that, had he lived, time would have woven grooves and valleys in Miguel's face. Time would have worn him down.

"The features. The way he walked. Do you remember how he walked, with his toes pointing out, kind of like a penguin? I could recognize that walk anywhere."

"Well, it wasn't your father. Okay! And how would you remember?" Adela was adamant. Here was her daughter, a child who washed the dishes every night in the same way—glasses and cups first, cutlery next, plates last (soup bowls and saucers followed by dinner platters)—telling her she had seen her long-ago disappeared, safely-dead, what-have-you dad. No wonder Adela was feeling just this side of normal.

"Yes, but he even had the same mannerisms—you know, shrugging his shoulders after asking a question, curling the tips of his mustache."

"Your father is dead. What would make you think of something like that at this time?"

Maribel shrugged, but Adela knew the answer to her question: a newborn always made you invoke the past. Unavoidable, for only the future made us recognize how inexorably tied we are to the past. Perhaps, Adela hoped, motherhood would mean a forging of new bonds between her and Maribel, a forgiveness on both sides of past transgressions. So who was she to discourage a revelation? If Maribel wanted to believe that good-for-nothing was someone special, maybe Adela should keep her mouth shut. Let her daughter cling to whatever fantasy she wanted. Now more than ever this grownup child of hers would need a salve, and memory had such redemptive powers.

"They say all of us have doubles," Adela said, more gently now.

"This man looked just like Papi," Maribel continued. She nodded her head. It seemed she was trying to convince herself. "It was just a real strange coincidence."

They were standing in the hallway outside Maribel's room, watching an orderly hand out lunch trays several doors down. Adela felt faint, as if she were dieting, but at least the floor had evened out and the paintings no longer appeared to dip. Still, she was suspicious. An uncomfortable sensation in the shape of a doughnut both filled and emptied her. She could not make sense of it, and she could not forget the tubes and machines surrounding her grandson.

"Did you talk to him, Maribel? Maybe he was a relative."

"I couldn't. I was behind the mirror." What Maribel did not tell her mother was that she had discounted the possibility of any relation as the session proceeded. The man was shorter than she remembered her father, and much too fat. His paunch hung over his belt. He was bald and her father had possessed thick, wavy, very black hair. In the questionnaire, he had identified himself as an unemployed bookkeeper, last job seven years ago. Her father, she knew, loved to work. Besides, she was not an ignoramus or a believer in the occult. Dead was dead, and dead relatives did not return as spirits to guide—or torment—you, as her grandmother so often hinted.

Down the hall, a blond woman in a blue bathrobe rolled her baby's bassinet past the orderly, toward Maribel and Adela. Maribel watched as mother and child—a baby girl, for the taped identifying card was pink—passed them, then turned into the nursery. She was not able to catch a glimpse of the infant's face, only a fleeting vision of blond wisps and small fists, but the mother had left behind a scent of purpose and importance, like a newly opened package of school pencils. Maribel sighed.

After lunch, she would ask Joanne if she could bring the baby into her room. She wanted to roll him down the hall in the bassinet, coo and woo him with silly words, even try out different names. Maybe she could hold him.

Instead, after lunch, Maribel fell asleep.

5

Eduardo was handsome in a frivolous sort of way, like a flourish or a curlicue on the swirl of a rococo column. He had a gap-toothed, crooked smile, which Maribel had found endearing from the beginning, and the body of a lumberjack, stolid, wide, dependable. Maribel fell for him like a scaffold that's lost its pulley. They had met on a Saturday morning, when he arrived at her doorstep dressed in a white uniform, matching cap and black Reebok sneakers. She was cleaning the duplex and had answered the knock with a can of Lemon Pledge in one hand and a rag (one of her old panties) in the other.

"The p-p-pest man," he stuttered.

She was speechless.

"The p-p-pest man," he repeated, and smiled sideways.

"Do you have the right address?" she managed to whisper in Spanish. Her heart was beating so! She wondered what it would feel like to run one's tongue between the gap in the exterminator's front teeth.

He looked at a pink paper and nodded. Maribel leaned over the wall that divided the two front doors and knocked on her grand-mother's. As it turned out, yes, her mother had requested the exterminator.

"For those *cucarachitas*, especially in the kitchen," Adela said, wringing her hands to underscore the repulsive nature of the insects. "I am sure they come because of all those herbs and ointments my mother keeps in the kitchen."

Maribel forgot all about her cleaning and stood in her grand-mother's doorway while Eduardo sprayed the nooks and crannies of the duplex. She then insisted he do the same to her side, though Adela said it was not needed. Maribel wrote him a check for twenty-five dollars and watched him ride away in a white Toyota truck with red lettering: A-1 Pest Control.

For several minutes Maribel did not know what she was supposed to do. She was very methodical in her cleaning, always doing the bathroom first, then her bedroom, the hallway, the living room, and leaving the kitchen-dining room for last. She never bothered with her mother's room: so much trash and clutter, papers, magazines, ticket stubs, thread, ribbon, and paperback books. Junk, plain junk. She couldn't stand it. So she closed the door of her mother's room and worked her magic elsewhere. She dusted from the top down, left to right, with short, firm strokes. Quite effective. But after Eduardo's visit she wasn't sure if she was between the bedroom and the hallway or still in the bathroom. Had she dusted her shelves? Her dresser?

"Nice," observed Adela after Eduardo left. She had noticed her daughter's interest in the brown curls and the bedroom eyes and was tickled beyond fancy. That was about three years ago, and Maribel was twenty-five, nearly twenty-six, and had never had a serious suitor. She showed little interest in the opposite sex, though her striking looks made men stare.

"What?"

"The exterminator, a nice young man."

"Oh, Mami! That's all you think about."

Maribel stomped back into her house, Adela at her heels. "Well, maybe you should, too. Do you want to be an old maid?"

Maribel did not answer. She was busy staring at her reflection in the foyer mirror. She was dressed in a man's faded blue T-shirt with a frayed collar. It was so enormous her denim shorts were not visible. She wore no makeup, not even the trace of blush, and her hair was disheveled. She spotted a pink bump in the middle of her chin, a wannabe pimple. Had he noticed?

"Do not worry," her mother said, patting her on the shoulder. "You look stunning. Youth always looks stunning."

Maribel shook off her mother's hand. "I wish you would stop saying things like that." Secretly, though, she hoped Adela was right.

The next day Eduardo called. They went out for ice cream, to the Carvel on Thirty-seventh Avenue. He stuttered; she listened. He admired her eyes; she wanted to trace the outline of his biceps. She was somewhat disappointed that he had not worn his white uniform.

But he wore his uniform in her dream, the incredibly erotic dream she had after a heavy hospital lunch of dry meat loaf, soggy green beans, and canned peaches. And Maribel, knowing within her dream that it was a dream, was surprised. Eduardo had stopped wearing the uniform to work when he joined a couple of high-school friends in the export-import business a year or so ago. Of course sometimes, at her request, he wore it to bed.

"W-w-whatever gets your m-m-motor running," he told her in the dream, and it sounded exactly the way he said it when they were home together.

How sweet!

Except for the conspicuous absence of his black sneakers and white cap, the uniform in the dream was the same one he'd worn when they first met, even to the last detail of the rolled-up sleeves.

"Eddy," she called him.

He bent down to brush his lips against hers and slowly unbuttoned her shirt, her shorts. He slipped off her panties and nuzzled her private place. Then, working his way up with his tongue, he reached her breasts and unsnapped her bra.

"They're f-f-free," he whispered. He licked one nipple, then the other.

They lay down. His breath smelled like licorice on her face. He was so big, so strong. She wanted to scream. Drifting in and out, in and out, in and out, the rhythm as steady as a river's flow, she noticed the shadows the full midnight moon cast on the window-pane: a branch, a leaf, a bird.

She realized those were the images she had seen the night her son was conceived, and she settled into her dream, her delightful dream, with a sigh.

When Cuca worried, she ate. That afternoon she had a guava pastry, a tart apple, leftover black beans cold from the refrigerator, and bread and butter. She considered a banana, but it was still green, too hard. She then made herself some Cuban coffee, which she had vowed to give up, and jangled her bracelets because she wanted to hear the music of clinking gold. But the coffee only got her nerves worked up, which made her remember the delicious, haunting smell of honeysuckle this morning and the previous day, which made her realize that, of course, she had every reason to worry, which made her hungry all over again. Ay. She decided to brew more chamomile tea.

A blue feather floated down to the counter when she opened the kitchen cupboard. It was tiny, the size of her thumbnail, and the blue of ocean on a clear day. The wing feather of a very small bird, she decided, perhaps a hummingbird. She examined the rest of the shelves but found no other feathers. Hmmm! She opened several kitchen drawers before finding a Ziploc bag to store her discovery. Where had the feather come from? How had it landed in her kitchen? What use could she have for it? Why was it blue? So many questions she had! But she wasn't up to such analysis. She simply wanted to soothe her nerves. Stretching, on her tiptoes, she placed the bag with the feather on the left-hand corner of the middle shelf, propped against the blue bottle of Maalox. That way it wouldn't get lost if she ever needed it.

Hmmm. No scent of honeysuckle assaulted her. The only odor was a spicy one, of stored herbs and pent-up intentions. Hmmm. She'd have to think about that later.

She added extra sugar to the tea, though she also had vowed to cut back on that, and sat down to savor the hot liquid on this balmy day. Cuca had never fooled herself into thinking she was smart, not like her younger sister, who could do her times tables, *como si nada,* by the time she started grammar school. She wasn't as smart as her brother Rizos, either, the one with the curly hair who had been murdered by government thugs during one of Cuba's so-called free elections in the late twenties. She was shrewd, though, and she was patient enough to ponder and turn and twist and observe a problem until a solution eased itself out. In this case, though, she wasn't sure what the problem was; she could neither define nor give it a name. Perhaps it was not a problem at all.

Adela had been so unusually cryptic over the phone earlier. So tongue-tied. Her voice rang brittle, like a dry chicken bone rattling in a can.

"A boy," Adela had said as soon as Cuca picked up the receiver.

"Finally," Cuca replied. "Finally. What does he look like?"

"Like a baby."

"I mean, how much does he weigh? How long is he? Does he have a lot of hair? You know, Maribel had such heartburn."

Adela had already hung up, leaving Cuca speaking to the air. Maybe Adela was overwhelmed with the experience of being a grandmother, but Cuca doubted it. There was something more, something unspoken, a mystery that Adela had yet to accept or understand. So of course how could she tell her mother about it?

The tea was not sweet enough. Cuca added another heaping teaspoon of brown sugar. Soon they would need more from Pancho at the mill. She inhaled the pungent aroma and sipped. ¡Ay, qué rico! A great-grandson! How proud her husband would have been. Though he had adored Adela, spoiled her past reason and relatives' complaints, Cuca knew he had secretly longed for a boy, someone to carry on the family name. She had tried. Dios mío, she had tried. She had made love until her insides felt like a scoured pot. She had tried to carry every single one of her pregnancies to full term, not bending too much, not lifting, not looking sideways at people she hated (just in case). And when they had been born, how she had cared for those babies! Her mother-in-law, a wise woman from the mountains who signed her name with an X and counted on her fingers, once observed: "M'ija, you are afflicted with a chronic case of hope." The old woman spoke truth. The world, Cuca thought, was made miserable and ornery by its lack. And in the end, after all, she had been proven right. She finally was able to keep one, one of eight pregnancies. A singular but powerful one, Adela.

The doorbell rang. With reluctance, she shuffled to the door. *El carnicero*, Adela's friend, in guayabera and blue jeans.

"*Vieja*," he said, with a familiarity she found offensive, "I wanted to leave something for the family."

He showed her a basket of fruit; lots of bananas, she saw, and some apples, pears, grapes, cantaloupe. A fruit or two she didn't recognize. Then he walked past her, past the teal sofa and glass-and-wrought-iron table, to the kitchen, where he deposited the basket on the counter. Cuca caught a whiff of aftershave.

"I included some Granny Smith apples for . . ."

"Adela," Cuca interrupted. "Yes, I know." She said the last three words in a way she hoped he would not misconstrue. She knew about them, Adela and Carlos, though the two were discreet, oh so discreet, pretending not to look at each other and silliness such as that. But she hadn't arrived at old age by being fooled for long, and neither could ever fool her. You know the saying: *Más sabe el diablo por viejo que por diablo.* The devil knows more because he's old than because he's the devil.

"How is the new mother?"

"I am not sure. I haven't heard from Adela since early this morning. I do not want to call and wake them. A new mother must get her rest."

"Of course." The texture of his voice was like a wool sweater, warm and scratchy.

Carlos stood in the middle of the kitchen, shifting his weight from one leg to another, obviously uncomfortable. Cuca knew she should ask him to sit down, invite him to a drink of tea or *café*, but she didn't want company. She wanted to be alone. She wanted time to figure out what had not yet been said.

"Any more news on the baby?" Carlos asked.

"No, nothing."

She walked toward the door, trying to hint at his departure by her movements, but he stood as still as a dead chicken in the kitchen. Maybe that's what Adela liked about him, that maddening slowness, that lack of perception of another's intent. Of course, perhaps it was simply a physical attraction, for, if anything, Carlos was a very physical and very attractive man. Broad-shouldered, narrow-hipped, with forearms like Popeye's, he inspired a surrender to base thoughts. And he had green eyes, too, the color and opaqueness of a Coca-Cola bottle, overpowering eyes against dark skin. (Like Miguel's, the good-for-nothing. What was it with Adela and green eyes?) It was easy to forget that he was graying at the temples and that his forehead appeared to be broadening. Women tended to overlook details like that, anyway.

"I was sorry to hear about the baby. If there's anything—"

"What do you mean?"

Carlos appeared panic-stricken. He opened his mouth and uttered nonsense syllables.

"What do you mean?" Cuca asked again, this time louder.

"Have you spoken to Adela?" He walked backward, toward the kitchen door.

"Early morning, I told you. Now, what's wrong with the baby?"

Carlos's back was pressed against the kitchen wall. He looked around, a trapped animal in search of escape.

"It is not my place, *vieja*."

"Well, you're here, aren't you? And how is it that you should know what I don't?" She pointed her finger at him; the bracelets jingled.

"Fefa's cousin is a nurse at the hospital."

"So?"

"The doctors are concerned about the baby."

"¿*Preocupados*? In what way?"

Carlos nodded, but did not answer. He stared at the calendar. "March 1, my dead mother's birthday," he realized, frowning.

"Have you been to the cemetery?" Cuca asked.

"I plan to," he replied emphatically, but Cuca knew he had just thought of this. "I will place some red carnations on her grave."

"Well, son, you better do as you say. Don't promise a dead woman something you're not going to deliver. Or any other woman, for that matter."

Carlos smiled sheepishly. "Listen," he said, walking quickly past her, "I have to go."

He was already out on the porch by the time Cuca had finished crossing the living room. So he was quick when he had to be, an important trait in a man.

"Phone Adela, okay?" he called from the car. "She should be better informed than I am."

Then Cuca couldn't resist: "Say hello to *your* Fefa for me, eh."

But she realized his car motor had probably drowned out her voice. *¡Qué pena!* For all his initial slowness and big-boned awkwardness, in the end Carlos was able to flee her house as quickly as a man trying to win a footrace against death.

Back inside, she found her chamomile tea had grown cold, so she poured it down the drain. Just as well. She wasn't hungry anymore, and her head felt clearer, her nerves steadier. Answers, that's what she wanted. Answers to questions she had not yet voiced. Answers that were not as circuitous as what she was getting, and certainly not answers delivered by unlikely messengers: by *el carnicero*, no less. She dialed the hospital. *El americano* answered.

When Caleb Constant walked into the hospital room, Adela was so pleased to see her daughter's boss that she jumped from her chair and ran to give him a hug—no mean feat, this, for running on those sandals' heels was like stomping on five-inch nails. Caleb was surprised by the sudden display of emotion, and pleased as well. He inspired anything but spontaneity in other people, so he didn't mind that the pink polo shirt, which he had picked up from the dry cleaner's yesterday after dropping Maribel at her home, now bore the imprint of her mother's mouth.

"Oh, I am so sorry," Adela said, covering her face with her hands in embarrassment. "I have dirtied your shirt."

She did not try to rub it clean, though. She knew how fastidious he was. He always looked as if he had just been starched and pressed, and he preferred suits, even when he worked Saturdays, and thin ties knotted hard against his neck. Occasionally, such as today, he dropped his guard, choosing casual elegance. Last time Adela checked, people at Sunday Mass didn't dress as formally.

When Maribel told her three years ago that Caleb's wife had left him after twenty-four years of marriage, she wondered how the woman had put up with such fussiness for so long, and with no children to bind them either. But as she learned more about him, as she spoke to him over the phone, saw how he treated her daughter, heard stories of his attention to detail, Adela knew that Caleb was a generous man, kindhearted, well-intentioned, if a little stiff. He was not pleasant-looking, though one eventually grew accustomed to his face, which seemed to be in perpetual misalignment. That was the only way Adela could explain the asymmetry of his features. His thick, uneven eyebrows winged over pale blue eyes, one of which remained at half-mast at all times, and he had a straight nose, thin lips, and cheeks pocked like a raisin. Yet, when he smiled, the sudden flash of white, perfect teeth and childish dimples erased whatever momentary obsession one had with his brows or half-closed eye or acne-scarred skin.

"It's quite all right, señora." Caleb patted Adela on the shoulder. "This will wash off. I see our new mother is exhausted already."

"Oh, Caleb." Adela pronounced his name in such a way that it made Caleb stop in midstride as he walked to Maribel's bed.

"The baby," Adela blurted. "It's the baby."

"What?"

"There is something wrong with the baby. He has something in his chromosomes."

"Down's syndrome?" he whispered.

"No, not Mongoloid. But something like that."

"Oh, my God!" Caleb gasped, then blushed. Adela realized the man was sorry he had let his emotions get the best of him. Caleb, Maribel had once told her mother, did not like surprises that could not be controlled. And Adela had replied then: *Tal para cual.* Two peas in a pod.

"The doctors—"

"How do they know?"

"His facial features and a few other things. They told us this morning, but they are running some special blood tests."

"Maribel knows?"

Adela nodded.

"What's the prognosis for the baby?"

Adela had to think about the question. She was sure the doctors had referred to the future, the possibility of death, trouble, worry, agony, but she could not recall if they had said something specific. Three days of life? Two months? Six years? What *had* they said? And how could she have forgotten?

"I think," she said slowly, "that he is severely retarded."

The words hung in the air between them. Adela could see them floating like dust motes, polluting the room. She reached out for them—with her hands, her magical wands, her weapons, her source and her force—and touched nothing.

"His health?"

Adela shrugged. She pressed her finger to her mouth. Caleb hobbled to the recliner and let himself slide into it. He crossed his legs, then uncrossed them. He rubbed his chin, looked out the window, shook his head. Then, as if realizing he had an audience, he straightened himself in the chair.

"I should be comforting you, señora. How selfish of me."

Adela waved her hands in dismissal.

"I must apologize," he insisted. "How thoughtless of me."

"Please, Caleb, no need. I am just getting used to the idea. I have spent most of the morning convincing myself that I was dreaming."

"A nightmare!"

"It seems like that, no?"

"How has Maribel reacted? Oh, I don't know if I even dare to listen to the answer."

"Maribel?" Adela stared at her sleeping daughter.

"Oh, where are my manners?" Caleb stood quickly. "Please sit down."

"I have been sitting all morning. But Maribel."

"Yes, how is Maribel?"

"I don't know how to explain this because she is either taking it very well or she didn't understand anything the doctors told her."

"She's in shock, señora."

"Maybe."

"Denial. That is how our bodies deal with emotional pain."

"I know about that. I was in denial until just a while ago."

"Now?"

"Now I feel like my world has caved in around me."

"Oh, señora." Caleb stood and walked to Adela, took her hand to comfort her. "We must get all the information before we can make a judgment. Despair is often a result of misinformation or lack of information."

"In my case, no. Despair is a result of foresight."

Maribel awoke with a groan. She did not want to leave her dream. She clung to the fading image of Eduardo in his white uniform with rolled-up sleeves. When she spotted instead tufted eyebrows, a half-opened blue eye and dazzling smile, she blinked and stretched. Caleb. Caleb Constant. How reassuring! She liked him, not in the same way she longed for Eduardo, but she was quite fond of him just the same. He could explain most of life in a summary paragraph or an executive outline for every client, and she considered that admirable—to reduce what consumers wanted, how they wanted it, where and why, to a dizzying plethora of tidy charts. She imagined you could do the same with the intangibles of life if you cared to, if you were smart enough to draw up a formula that transformed the complex into the simple, the inexplicable into the obvious. She had once. She was proud of the equation, though too timid to show anyone: Love = intensity + attachment squared by time − distraction.

"Hey!" she greeted him groggily. "Have you seen my baby?"

"I just walked in."

"He looks like a little bird."

Adela realized Caleb wasn't sure what to say. Would Maribel tell him about the doctors?

"How are *you*?" he asked finally.

"Beat."

Caleb laughed.

"Want to go see him?"

Caleb nodded enthusiastically, though he was nervous about what he should expect. He helped Maribel climb out of bed and shuffle to the nursery, where they stared from behind the window. The baby remained in the plastic bassinet face-up, bathed in the radiant light of the lamp, sleeping peacefully.

"Lots of tubes," Maribel commented matter-of-factly.

"Yes, why?"

"The doctors said he has a little problem of some sort. Something with his blood, I think. Maybe because he's so little. And he has apnea."

"What about his blood?"

Maribel shrugged. "Something to do with his chromosomes. I'm not too clear about all of it."

"Shouldn't you check it out, Maribel? That sounds important to me."

She ignored the comment. "Want to go in and hold the baby?"

"No, no," Caleb said, laughing and backing away.

"Chicken."

"He sure is tiny. How much does he weigh?"

"Three pounds and change."

"I don't think I've ever seen anything so small. Even when my sister had twins."

"Oh, he'll grow. Give him time."

When they returned to the room, Adela greeted them at the door with an enormous cellophane-wrapped basket of plush toys, rattles, foam balls, and a large blue balloon.

"It's from Caleb," Adela announced.

Maribel smiled at him.

"Read the card," he told her.

She recited aloud:

> *A bundle of flannel and lace,*
> *Today you have brought a smile*
> *to your sweet mother's face.*
>
> *Tomorrow when you trade diapers for skates,*
> *bottles for balls, pacifiers for pencils,*
> *remember to always hurry home and not to be late.*
>
> *Remember the smile on your sweet mother's face.*

"That is so sweet," Adela said, clapping her hands in delight.

"I wrote it for the baby." Caleb beamed.

"Thank you, Caleb. I'm going to place it on the first page of the baby's book."

"I didn't know his name, so I couldn't write a more personal one."

"You have a real talent," Adela said.

"He does, doesn't he, Mami? He's very shy about it, though."

"You shouldn't be, Caleb. If you have a talent or a special skill, proclaim it to the four winds. I did. I realized what wonders my hands could do for others' hands, for others' hair, and I proclaimed it." Adela stomped her foot for emphasis.

"Well, señora, eventually I hope to launch my own verse-writing company. I'm looking for a contract with one of the greeting-card manufacturers. In the meantime, I still have to eat and pay the mortgage."

"Aaah! Sadly, we must still meet the demands of the body, no matter our ambitions." But Adela was glad to know that his conscientiousness didn't have the hard edge Maribel's did.

As Adela and Caleb bid Maribel farewell, Cuca's call came through. Caleb answered in his serviceable Spanish.

"What is going on?" Cuca demanded when Adela came on. "Why haven't you told me about the baby?"

"We'll talk when we get home," Adela replied.

"Tell me now, Adela." If there was anything Cuca disliked, more so even than people without any imagination or the desire for one, it was being kept in the dark.

"Wait until I get home."

"Then it must not be so bad." Cuca's voice was so hopeful it pained Adela to tell her anything.

"No, Mamá," she said softly, all the excitement over the basket and Caleb's verse gone. "It is worse."

Caleb walked Adela to her 1984 blue Ford Escort with the plastic carnation on the antenna.

"What do you think?" Adela asked.

Caleb sighed.

"You can be honest with me," she insisted.

"I think she is in denial."

"Yes, I believe so, too. She'll come out of it eventually, though. Then what?"

Caleb shuddered. His eyes widened at the question, gleamed. The tears confirmed Adela's suspicions—not only about her daughter's reaction once the fog lifted, as it surely would, but also about this man's feelings for a woman who was beyond his reach. Both realizations made her want to weep with despair.

At home, in the shower, after eating a Granny Smith apple and after explaining to Cuca as best and as simply as she could, Adela finally did weep: a deluge of despondency.

Cuca, in the meantime, undid the rubber band at the bottom of her braid and shook her hair loose. She put a half-dozen fresh sprigs of mint into a teacup, filled it with boiling water, and set a saucer on top. She waited five minutes—thinking of nothing, ignoring her husband's call, her heart's thunder, focusing only on the weight of her hair on her scalp—then added a pinch of bicarbonate of soda to the hot water. She stirred; she sipped. Mint, her grandmother used to tell her, helped relieve inner aches of unknown origins. But experience had taught her that no medicine could truly lighten the load or the darkness. No medicine of this world ever would.

6

There is an art to washing hair, a technique that requires concentration at the outset but then comes naturally with time and patience and conscientiousness. As with anything in life, practice makes not perfect—no, never, because perfection does not exist and shouldn't; life would be too boring, too flat, too empty—but practice does achieve a certain superiority, ensure a condition of quality. With the washing of hair this is true; this is true, too, with washing dirty collars or stained underwear, or frying a tasty *sofrito*, or making love to a man, or sewing a pleated skirt so the pleats remain flat even with any movement of the leg. Practice. Technique. Perseverance to do the former and desire to master the latter.

Her mother's mother taught Cuca how to wash her hair when she was five years old. No shampoos then. No showers either, but they made do.

"It will not rain today," Mamá Cleofe would tell her at dawn, as she gathered the eggs, fed the pigs, shooed the chickens, milked the cow, lit the coals, swept the porch, kneaded the dough, boiled the water, churned the butter.

"How can you tell?" little Cuca would ask.

Mamá Cleofe answered by pointing a callused finger to the brightening sky, sniffing the air like a dog and sticking out her tongue to taste the air.

"I just know."

No one doubted Mamá Cleofe. In the pueblo she was known as the only one who could predict the angry winds and fierce rains that toppled trees and snatched animals and flooded fields and scared children for years afterward. She could foresee the splitting of the earth, the falling of the sky, the swelling of the rivers beyond their banks. Once she spotted a streak of blood in the sky and three days later the government was toppled by an upstart colonel in South America. She just *knew*.

Ay, but Cuca was getting away from the memory which was . . . which was . . . come on, come on . . . which was which was . . . *Dios mío*, she should not have had all those *tilos*, but her nerves—her nerves! (That mint tea in the early evening was delicious, but it had done little for her insomnia or anxiety.) Where had her thoughts been leading to? Ah, yes. Mamá Cleofe had taught her how to wash her hair, and she always did it on a sunny day, when the breeze blew strong and warm. Wait for late morning, Mamá Cleofe ordered, after the chores are done and the men gone about their business (not always to work, mind you, but too often to loafing or to other women). Use clean soap, from a batch just made. Haul the tin basin outside to the well. Soak your hair with well water. (Lots of iron. Plenty of other minerals.) Then suds. Soap firmly, in circular motion, round and round and round in small circles that overlap, massaging the scalp with your fingertips, especially over the forehead, around the ears, just above the neck. Massage. Massage again. Work in the soap. Massage. Massage until the muscles in your arm twitch. Rinse well, making sure to free your hair of soapy deposits. Use a lot of water.

"We can always dig another well," Mamá Cleofe liked to say. (Which was true. Neighbors for miles around sought her water-divining skills.)

Do this twice, always massaging firmly, never missing the hairline or the ear area, working in the soap gently. Then rinse, rinse, rinse.

"*Agua, agua, agua. Mucha agua,*" chanted Mamá Cleofe, as the ugly mole on her chin danced to the rhythm of her words. Getting the soap out was the key to healthy, shiny hair, hair that curled in ringlets, swept back from the forehead, cascaded down the neckline.

Later, when Cuca grew older and before Mamá Cleofe died unexpectedly, gored by a bull she had raised since he was a calf, Cuca the coquettish child also learned to soak her hair in beer, work in egg yolk, rinse with baking soda, rub in homemade mayonnaise, squirt with lemon juice. Her hair was always beautiful and smooth, like the black satin cape of a nineteenth-century caballero. She owed that to Mamá Cleofe, who had taught her well, and not just about washing hair but about many other things, too: how to thread a needle in dim light, how to calm a cow that refuses to be milked, how to feed a sparrow fallen from its nest, how to avoid a man who arrives home drunk, when to press a point and when to drop an argument, the shortest way to the outhouse in the middle of the night, why elders should be treated with deference, who in town should be reviled or who should be respected, and, perhaps more important, about the miracle of herbs and other details and dosages of back-yard medicine.

Cuca longed to develop a similar relationship with her granddaughter. (She had tried, at various times and with varying degrees of success, with Adela, but there were lessons her daughter learned better and more quickly than others, unfortunately.) Cuca wanted to be teacher and guide, scout, heroine and escort, mistress and equal. And Maribel had so much potential! Now, especially now, more than ever now. Cuca had listened to Adela's explanation carefully and felt herself illuminated with the intense heat of purpose: It is time, my granddaughter. The baby, healthy or ill, is a gift, our gift. Let's share it.

Cuca had tried before, felt it her duty to impart the wisdom that is independent of knowledge. (After all, Maribel had been through so many years of school. As many as Rizos. A lifetime of education but with little sense and insight to accompany it.) Years ago, while she was in the hospital purging her blood and organs of unknown poisons, Cuca had jotted down a list of the lessons she wanted to pass to the next of the next generation. In her underwear drawer, beside her panties and bras, next to an old girdle and a long slip she rarely wore, tucked beneath the lace and potpourri sachet, Cuca kept the yellow legal-pad paper, folded in thirds horizontally, then again in thirds vertically, one end over the other to form a narrow rectangle. Occasionally she read it, usually at the beginning of a new year when, inspired by holiday festivities, she vowed to renew acquaintance with forgotten goals and old dreams. Tonight she reread it because anxiety had chomped the lining in her stomach and because the silence of the house, with Adela asleep and Maribel gone, had shattered her conception of what solitary peace had once meant to her. (To be alone and without demands was not at all what others swore it to be.)

Anyway, to the point. The list. She unfolded the paper, smoothed the creases with her hand, situated her bifocals on the bridge of her nose, and read the familiar handwriting with its exaggerated loops and swirls·

1   To love.
2   To care for one's own.
3   To accept, to fight, to surrender.
4   To build a home (not to be mistaken for keeping house).
5   To allow one's children to take flight.
6   To laugh. To dance. To cook a coconut flan.
7   To never forget.
8   To never say never.

Quite complete, eh? And, she thought, wonderful, ingenious ideas to live by. (Or did she actually mean *survive* by?) How she had managed not to bombard her granddaughter with her wisdom, her insight, her cleverness was a true test of self-control, but then again she had known that time would favor her and that patience was truly a virtue when dealing with children and the children of children. She jangled her bracelets in delight.

She shuffled to the kitchen in the darkness, clutching the list to her breast, then flattening it against the table. She flipped on the light switch. Miracle: the invention of electricity never ceased to amaze her. She opened the refrigerator and began to rummage through its contents. (Her appetite was getting the best of her.) She settled for a cold piece of fried chicken—ay, such tasty, greasy delight!—then washed her hands carefully and dried them on the kitchen towel. She sniffed the towel suspiciously. Oh, that Adela! Her housekeeping left something to be desired. Anyway, anyway, anyway. She wanted to delve further into her eight lessons to live by. Each needed an explanation, a footnote of justification, and though no audience was immediately available to appreciate it, no adoring fans clamoring for attention, eventually there would be and she would be prepared by having practiced. The endless night beckoned with its dark susurrations.

1. *Love without reserve*, blindly, because and in spite of, defying logic, pushing boundaries, forging new conventions, molding, creating, fighting. Already this is how she loved her great-grandson. Didn't know what he looked like. Didn't understand all that talky-talk of monochromes or chromosomes or crossovers. But so what; didn't matter. This was flesh of her flesh, blood of her blood; this was surprise and answer, gift and trial. She loved him just because he was.

Maribel must love the same way, and Cuca did not doubt she would. But Cuca also knew that Maribel would fight and that her brain would rebel—useless uprising, for in the end the surrender would be complete. Maribel was lucky, as she had been, despite losing all those babies. Oh, and yes, there would be pain, an ache so absolute that at times, for long periods, it would seem there was nothing else but this total agony. Not true, not true. The pain was simply the thorn on the rose of love. One could not exist without the other.

Cuca stared at the naked chicken leg on the plate. No use wasting it, so she slammed the bone against the edge of the table, splitting it evenly in half. She sucked the insides: a taste one had to acquire. (By the way, Mamá Cleofe had taught her about chicken-bone marrow, too.)

2. *To care for one's own* required more than love and certainly more than the basics of feeding and clothing and sheltering. All animals did that. (Of course there were those that ate their young, not unlike the heartless humans who cared for nothing but their own skin and sometimes not even that.) Caring was patience, duty, and perseverance; it was sometimes inconvenient and not always

pleasant, simultaneously altruistic and selfish and resentful. But it was a debt owed which demanded payment.

Cuca worried about this especially because she had lived longer, much longer than she had ever expected. And all around her she saw what she had never seen before, what frightened her: the old and the sick carted off to special places. No one had any time to wipe their slobber or change their bedsheets anymore. Too much to do, too much money to make, too much television to watch and clothes to buy and cars to flaunt. And sometimes the old were not even sick. Sometimes the sick were not even old but defective, found lacking in some way. Off they went, removed from the clear view of the horizon, from the tug of needing.

Remember Cousin Hilda, the poor woman who had labored for three days with her first son, then almost bled to death with her daughter, nearly gone crazy from work with the twins that followed a year later? She deserved a throne in one of her children's castles, no? She deserved repayment, to reap what she had sown. But the children had put her in a special building with floor after floor of older people. She watched movies in the morning and played bingo in the evenings. Her children took turns visiting, she reported in her Christmas card, and the heat was always turned up so she wasn't cold in the merciless Chicago winters. But her grandchildren? Her grandchildren! What grandchildren? They didn't take care of her. They never came to visit.

Oh, Cuca, she told herself with one final suck of the bone, best not to dwell on that. Move on, move on.

3. *To accept, to fight, to surrender.* Cuca laughed uproariously. This was a real doozy. On the surface, this series of lessons seemed contradictory. How could one accept and fight at the same time? What was the difference between acceptance and surrender? Good questions, excellent inquiries, and even at her age she was struggling to distinguish the finer points of this balance. This was the type of wisdom that demanded a lifetime of practice, not only because of its difficulty but also because one had to learn which was needed under a particular situation.

"A good batter," she remembered her husband telling her during one of their rare visits to Havana's impressive stadium, "must know as soon as the pitcher releases the ball, sometimes just by the pitcher's form, what to expect: a curve, a knuckleball, a slider, a fastball, a change-up."

"How can he do that?" she had wondered.

"Experience. Careful observation. Intuition. Luck."

The same was true for many of life's situations. When do you accept what until yesterday would have been unacceptable? She could only answer with an example: When she and Tony had first married, her mother-in-law would visit them every day, inspecting drawers in their armoire, the enamel of their tub, the food simmering in their pots. Oh, how she had resented it! She had broached the subject with her husband, who could not understand—or refused to understand—her annoyance. She had complained to her mother then, who had shrugged off her daughter's irritation with words Cuca later realized were good advice: "*Olvídate de eso, hija.* Forget it. The old lady will soon get bored." And the old lady did, when a younger daughter married, and she began the same field inspection in the other home. Later, having forgotten her mother-in-law's initial meddling, or maybe simply having forgiven it, Cuca cobbled a respectful friendship with the old woman.

Fighting required some of the same delicate differentiation. And the method of battle, the weapon, the duration, and the conditions for peace, also—how would you say?—also had to be handled deftly. Very deftly. Another example: About eight or nine years after they had married, a period in which Cuca had known both exquisite love and heart-wrenching pain (see lesson #1), Tony began to skip out at nights only to return at dawn, smelling of cheap perfume and the undeniable muskiness of down-there. The first month, she denied anything was wrong. The second month, she cried, accused, threatened, left home twice, turned away from him in bed. The third month, she formulated a plan. The fourth, she implemented it. At the start of the fifth month, he was too tired to go anywhere at night and she was pregnant. Ay, delicious revenge!

And surrender? When and where? How? Well, she was still learning. This required such a release of will, such total faith, that a lifetime of lessons sometimes was not enough. So far, she had been a bit spotty in this area—oh, how difficult it was to yield!—but she had managed to acquire dignity in the process. That was essential in surrender: dignity.

Cuca savored the chicken-bone marrow and wondered how it was possible that one could hold ideas in one's head that, at first glance, seem to be in opposition. Ideas that were equally demanding, of equal necessity, but headed in different directions. Ay, the mind, the human mind. *¡Dios mío!*

4. *To build a home*, yes, was not to be mistaken for keeping house. Let us be very clear about that. A maid can keep house, dusting counters, sweeping under furniture, scrubbing bathrooms. Maribel kept house well, a direct and opposing reaction to her mother's carelessness, of course. But building a home was something much broader; it encompassed mood, thought, creativity, and love. (Again, see lesson #1.) You knew a home by your senses: you tasted it, you smelled it, you heard and felt and saw it. Sensual, purely sensual. A home welcomed, a house accepted. A home nurtured; a house simply sheltered.

And no matter what those braless women with men's haircuts shouted. No matter what those silly magazine articles claimed were the rights of women. So many *tonterías!* Such a lack of reality! In a good home, one that welcomed, nurtured, and demanded, a woman's place was in bed, tucked under her husband.

5. *To allow a child to take flight* when one has invested so many years and so many nights requires surrender and acceptance. (See lesson #2.) Children do not belong to their parents, only to themselves. Parents are temporary guides in their lives, touchstones and kilometer markers.

And *Dios mío*, how Adela had hammered this lesson home! She and Tony had watched over their one and only with the fear of two parents who had seen too much. They had been overprotective, overcautious, over-everything. And observe the result of their overness. Phew!

Long after Adela's risk-taking, damn-all attitude had become too pronounced to ignore, she toyed around with her parents' dreams and misplaced ambitions. She wanted to run away with the circus, learn typing and shorthand, become a pediatrician, then an engineer, be a full-time housewife, volunteer as a stuntwoman, learn another language, join a holy order. (Adela as a nun—what a laugh that was!) She had finally enrolled in cosmetology school downtown: a relief for her parents, who had suffered severe emotional whiplash for two years.

Chuckling with memories, Cuca stood to pour herself a glass of orange juice. She had vowed to give it up (the acid), but she needed a little tonight. Something sweet to wash down the chicken-bone marrow.

Thinking of sweet and washing down, lesson #6. *To laugh. To dance. To cook a coconut flan.* Self-explanatory, no? Just the same, far from simple. Many times in life, it will not be easy to laugh; tears will seem more appropriate or more convenient. But if you do not fight that overwhelming feeling (lesson #3), your lips will forget how to move and your vocal cords will lose the ability to make this song of the soul. So laugh often. Laugh when you're alone or surrounded by people. Laugh softly or loudly; try different sounds. Experiment.

Some people are masters of their laughter. Adela, for one. She can laugh and ring bells. She can laugh at anything and because of anything. She learned this lesson well.

Adela also learned to dance. She even dances to the Alleluia at Sunday Mass. In fact, Cuca has noticed Adela's feet thumping when the priest intones: "Behold the Lamb of God . . ."

Dance without music but always with rhythm, even if no one else can follow. Dance close, pressing against your partner as though two are one. Dance alone, in the silence of an empty room. Dance with your eyes closed.

And the coconut flan? (Ay, she was hungry. She could go for some flan just about now. Flan that melts its sweetness into the tongue, enveloping the teeth and throat. *¡Dulce!*) Anyway, the coconut flan. The trick to the coconut flan—or any flan, for that matter—was, is, the *caramelo.* Simmer over low heat. Don't hurry. Good food (and love) takes time.

7. *To never forget.* Why had she included that, she a woman who was often sidetracked by her thoughts, who was swept away by compelling tangents to others' stories? Well, she wasn't sure why she had scribbled it, except maybe so others like her wouldn't forget the six lessons preceding this one.

No, there was more to it. Think. Think.

Ah, here. Here it is: Do not forget who you are. Do not lose yourself. Love yourself (see lesson #1). Care for yourself (lesson #2). Accept yourself (lesson #3). If you are unlucky, or maybe if you are lucky, that's all you will need.

She was nearing the end now of her lesson sheet—and of her life. She was sleepy (finally) and bone-weary (to be expected), but spiritually renewed. Inside, under the wrinkles and white hair, beneath the folds of skin, collapsing arteries, and flaccid muscles, she felt like a freshly minted coin. So on she went to lesson #8, the number of her pregnancies, four before Adela, three afterward.

8. *Never say never.* Never ever. Spit up and it will splatter your face. Deny and the denial will haunt you. You never know what you're going to do under which circumstances. You'll surprise yourself. Allow it.

Enough said.

She stood to wash the dirty glass and plate in the sink. Had she forgotten anything? Anything at all? Oh yes!

Never dry your hair in direct sunlight.

7

Maribel was in bed but wide awake when the neonatologist arrived at dawn. Unable to sleep despite her exhaustion, she had visited the baby several times during the night and each time he had appeared smaller, frailer, paler. She had stroked and rubbed, whispered, sung, giggled, cooed—and not once had he opened his eyes. But she did not desist, blinded as she was by the heat lamp's light and by the immense love she felt for her tiny bird-boy. Even in the very darkest part of night, endearments cascaded from her mouth while doubt nibbled at her elation: *Mi rey—mi cielo—mi tesoro* . . . Why so many tubes? *Chinito–Caramelito–Corazoncito* . . . Why couldn't she carry him? *Precioso mío* . . . Why the lamp? *Corazón de melón—Sol de mi mañana* . . . Why wouldn't they let her take him to her room? *Querubín* . . . Why such attention from the nurses?

She returned to her mauve-and-violet room after each visit to the nursery, frantic to tidy up and straighten out. She made her bed, wiped the sink and counters, rearranged her toiletries. She opened the blinds and closed them, turned the TV on and off, flushed the toilet several times to check if it worked properly, and inspected her face for any visible signs of change. She found what she was looking for: blotchy skin, bags under her eyes, lines on her forehead, a pinched mouth. Brimming with questions, she was anxious, therefore, to see the young doctor.

"Mrs. Garcia, I'm Dr. Rothstein. You remember me? I have news about your baby."

"Yes?" She sat up in bed. His voice sounded encouraging, didn't it? And somehow his blue eyes and thick black brows—as perfect as Caleb's were not—reminded her of her friend.

"We are monitoring him, Mrs. Garcia, and of course we are waiting for the blood work from the lab, but I must be quite frank with you."

"Please." She was standing now, trying to find the peach-colored slippers under the bed. News, any kind, every kind, should be received with your feet on the ground.

He pulled a chair close to her bed and motioned for her to sit down again. He adjusted his rimless glasses, took her hand in both of his large ones. They were like warm, heavy blankets. She liked him. She liked him already.

"One of the nurses discovered last night that your baby doesn't swallow his saliva."

She stiffened and bit her bottom lip. He rubbed her hands. "I know this is very difficult to hear, Mrs. Garcia, and, believe me, it is not pleasant to have to deliver the news either."

She managed a smile. She liked him, yes she did. Her baby would like him, too. Her baby who was the size of his warm, heavy hand.

"We ran some tests," he continued, looking straight into her eyes, "and we've found that his esophagus isn't connected to his stomach."

She tried to imagine what he was talking about but couldn't. She had never been very good at science, and her knowledge of human anatomy was sketchy. He seemed to read her confusion.

"Look," he said, and took a small notepad and pen from the right pocket of his white lab coat. He began to draw. "This long tube here reaches down to here somewhere, and over here"—he drew an oval—"is the stomach. They should be connected, but in your baby's case, there is a gap right here." He scribbled hard to fill the hole.

"So what can you do?"

"A surgeon operates to connect the two. Probably in his case, we will have to stretch the esophagus just a bit . . ."

She gasped. She felt something inside her stretching into exquisite pain.

"His is a very small gap." He held her hand tightly again.

"When?"

"In a few days. We need to run some other tests. We need to make sure he's stronger."

"Oh, my God!"

"We will need to move him to Miami Children's Hospital, too."

She nodded. Her stomach felt queasy, too big and too empty to ever be filled up.

"In addition to the medication for his apnea, we've started him on a special nutritional supplement which I think will do him good."

"Will he be able to breast-feed?" she asked. Maribel treasured, as the ultimate symbol of motherhood, the age-old image of women suckling infants. Would it be denied her?

"No, probably not," he replied softly.

One lone tear rolled down her left cheek. Dr. Rothstein handed her a tissue. She knew this couldn't be easy for him, either. How long could one be a bearer of bad news before it swallowed one's hopes, faith, ambition?

"How successful is the operation usually?"

He offered her a small smile. "It depends on various factors, but in his case I think it can be quite successful."

"Why, doctor?"

Dr. Rothstein did not answer right away. His brow furrowed. She repeated the question. It was a simple one to voice because it consisted of only one word. In her growing queasiness, that's all she could handle: Why?

"There's a scientific explanation usually for why these things happen, but that's not usually what my patients want. I think they seek a justification, an answer to why me and why not someone else, and I just don't have that."

"Oh no, doctor, not that. What I meant was why isn't his esophagus connected to his stomach?"

Dr. Rothstein sighed in relief. "Well, that's one I *can* answer. Remember our conversation after the baby was born?"

Maribel drew her hand away from the doctor's.

"We talked about the possibility of a chromosomal problem, an extra chromosome most likely."

Maribel pressed her freed hand over her mouth: she wanted to vomit. Bile erupted inside her like an acidic volcano, burning her heart.

"A trisomy, which we believe is the case here, is a serious condition, Mrs. Garcia. Many times it is life-threatening."

Maribel shivered; it was cold in the room. The air-conditioning was down too low. She wished she had worn socks to warm her feet. Goose bumps pricked her arms, her legs, her buttocks. Even her neck and face felt unusually cold, as if she had just opened the freezer door.

"Mrs. Garcia?"

The cold made her feel more alert. She sensed parts of her body she had never given a second thought to. Her left toenail chafed under the tight terry cloth of her new slipper. The pores on the edge of her face, those that ran down her hairline, past her ears, down her chin, pores she never bothered to inspect in the mirror, opened up like flowers blooming at dawn. They exhaled, a chorus of susurrations. Her right hamstring stretched without her command. One shoulder twitched, followed by the other. Her ears heard a high, shrill whistle.

"Only the karyotyping will tell us for sure, of course, but your son has some clear characteristics that point to our concerns. The incomplete esophagus is one of them."

For an interminable moment, everything became still in the room, as if someone had shouted a divine order from an old childhood game: Freeze! Dr. Rothstein spoke but his mouth did not move. The air-conditioning hummed but the curtains, in the path of the ceiling vent, hung limply. She was sure her heart had stopped, too, but if it had, why could she turn her attention to the window, where darkness had suddenly congealed?

"Dr. Burton, the geneticist, will probably be by later. And maybe two other specialists as well."

The alarm in her face must have shown clearly, for Dr. Rothstein captured her escaped hand again, held it tight between his two. The curtain fluttered. A blue jay perched outside, tapped her window, then flew away. Darkness continued to dissolve. Cold air rushed into her lungs, filled them with pain. Her chin itched. She felt herself awakening from a torpor, rising from a long sleep of comfort and complacency.

"One is a cardiologist and the other is a nephrologist."

"Nephro . . ."

"For kidneys and renal . . ."

"Will he die?" she asked. The words echoed loudly in the room. The violet of the walls flushed red. She hadn't known her voice could carry so.

"Possibly," Dr. Rothstein replied.

"Soon?"

He shrugged. "We know some things, but there are many more we don't."

"What are the chances of him surviving?" She wanted numbers, statistics, percentages, something solid, something to hold on to.

He shrugged again.

"You don't know!" Accusing.

"I'm sorry. I don't know. I can't give you a perfect answer."

"Only one answer is perfect," she retorted defiantly.

"We'll know more with other test results, and Dr. Burton may provide more information."

She was being dropped into a lightless, bottomless pit with cold walls and slimy bugs and putrid smells and water that dripped, dripped, dripped. Its pull was relentless; she had no energy to fight it. An omnipotent vacuum, its forceful sucking reached the marrow of her bones.

She began to tremble; her teeth chattered; her bones rattled. It seemed, even to the doctor, that the entire room shook—the plastic water pitcher in its foam covering, the hairbrush against the wooden counter, the mirror against the wall.

"W-w-what's wr-wr-wrong?" she whispered, her words shaking along with her.

Dr. Rothstein knew, not in a scientific way, for there was no proof in the medical world that a heart convulsed with grief made such a dreadful noise, but he had delivered enough bad news to recognize the sound of a heart being torn to shreds.

"It's the quaking of the soul, my dear," he replied, and she believed he believed that.

"My baby, is he in pain?"

Dr. Rothstein hesitated. She realized he was choosing carefully between truth and a merciful lie, and when he replied, she would not know the difference.

"We're not sure, Mrs. Garcia."

"He will die, you say."

"His condition may be serious enough . . ."

"He will die, you say," Maribel repeated, hoping that if she said it enough times it would ease the unbearable pressure in her chest.

"But he might not," Dr. Rothstein quickly added.

For the first time during the course of their conversation, she inspected the doctor's face. She noticed a tiny brown mole on the side, near his left ear. She noticed he had dark flecks in his blue eyes and a long nose that reminded her of a Greek coin.

"He might not?" she echoed.

He nodded. She clung to those words with the fierceness of epoxy glue: He might not. He might not. He might not. Dr. Rothstein squeezed her hand one last time and parted silently, leaving Maribel to find her way through the dungeon of her thoughts alone. It was so dark, so cold. Where had the morning gone?

The pain began in her legs, an electric current that shocked, pressed deep into her bones, then spread outward. It traveled to her arms, her butt, her abdomen, her neck. Finally, her face: her eyes, her nose, her mouth, her chin, her forehead, her cheeks, her skin. Until every square inch of her body throbbed. Her organs stung. Her blood coursed inflamed.

And she was so cold.

She stood without feeling her legs. She walked to the nursery, without feeling the floor. She opened the door without touching the doorknob. She spoke to the nurse without moving her mouth. She had never felt so disconsolate, not ever, not when her mother told her about her father's death, not when her grandfather died, not when Eduardo went into hiding. Never ever.

The nurse led her to the blinding light. Though she could not carry the baby, Maribel felt all of him: his knobby knees, his minuscule toes, his bony shoulders, his tiny fists. She reached over the clear plastic bassinet. She stroked, she explored, she rubbed, gingerly, afraid of the force of her emotions. He was so soft. She opened one side of the disposable diaper and peeked. He had huge balls, like twin plums. She turned his little bird-face, with his beak nose and low ears and wide forehead, to her and began to tell him about the world he had been born into, the family and the duplex and the neighborhood and the flowers and the herbs and ointments awaiting him. She told him all this while rocking on her feet, rocking and pretending she was holding him tight to her bare breast.

She rocked and talked, rocked and talked, rocked and talked. She rocked to the beat of her heart joined with his, she rocked to the echo of the waves of the beaches of her childhood and the rhythm of the salsa music her grandmother played in the mornings and to the vibration of her mother's Ford Escort when it stopped at a red light and to the pulse of Eduardo's manliness when they made love and to the beat of the vein on the baby's forehead and to the cadence of the numbers that ran down the charts Caleb drew and to the quiver of her enjoyment and the whipping of her own fear. She rocked and talked until she broke a sweat and until the baby opened his eyes and stared into her face, momentarily spellbound.

"Nurse," she called, "I have his name."

Maribel waited for the nurse to find a paper, a pen.

"His name is Victor. Victor Eduardo."

She liked the name: Victor Eduardo. Victor Eduardo. Victor Eduardo. Victor for Victory. Eduardo for his father. His lost father who had not seen him, who might never see him.

"Victor Eduardo," she repeated aloud. Musical, enchanting.

When the nurse finished taking down all the information, Maribel returned to her room. Again she said the name aloud, and it filled the room and her heart with a lyrical sound. She combed her hair and tied it back with the curling blue ribbon from Caleb's basket.

"Victor Eduardo."

Oh, what a beautiful sound, but the mauling of her heart when she said it! The pain! She felt simultaneously enlarged and diminished, paralyzed one second, enraged the next. She looked up, at the mirror above the sink, and saw a stranger with black hair and slanted eyes and a mouth contorted in anguish. Who is that? What is she doing? Where is she?

When she tried to say her son's name again, cry it out for the world to take note, to suffer along with her that torture of uncertainty, she discovered she had no voice. And she cried with the mute, depthless fury of the betrayed. She cried herself dry. She cried until she heard her grandmother say, "You have a right to anger, child." And her grandmother was at home, and she was alone.

It has always been like this, nothing more, nothing less, Cuca told the mirror as she unraveled her braid. Life gives you *mierda*, and you make fertilizer. Life gives you dust, and you pack it into a mud roof. Life gives you potholes, and you plant a vegetable garden. It was an endless chain, a pernicious cycle, never ending in its torture and sacrifice. *¿Por qué?* Why did we even bother? Just the same to be good as to be bad—you still ended six feet under. Whether you smiled or you screamed, worked hard or loafed about, prayed or cursed, what difference did it make? Where did it get you? More pain, a relentless onrush of heartache. *Como si nada.*

Cuca finished the last knot at the bottom of her braid and spread her hair, her mother-of-pearl mantilla, around her shoulders. She began to brush her hair with the Fuller brush she had bought twenty-eight years ago, when you were not afraid to open your door to a man with a briefcase. Now a man at your door . . . well, why get into that? She brushed hard, so hard her scalp hurt. She brushed close to her skin so it tingled. One stroke, two, three, four . . .

She wondered where the honeysuckle scent had gone. Tomorrow she would go to the hospital. If Adela refused to drive her, she would call a taxi. She didn't need to speak English for that. Or she would call Maribel's friend, Mr. Constant, who was a good boss and was so friendly and so genuine. If Mr. Constant was unavailable, she would stoop to *el carnicero*. That, for sure, would get Adela's goat. Ha!

. . . fourteen, fifteen, sixteen . . .

She would see for herself. She would ask Maribel questions, hard questions, specific questions, questions that would soothe her doubts—or, yes, maybe create more of them. Still, she would see for herself. She would hold the baby, look at his toes, check out his face, count his fingers. And she would inspect his dick. If there was nothing wrong with that, well then . . .

. . . twenty-seven, twenty-eight, twenty-nine, thirty . . .

Life was an exercise in acceptance. Simple as that. Acceptance of the expected and the unexpected, the welcome and the unwelcome, the bitter, the sweet, the tart, the tasteless (lesson #3). You planned, you figured, you calculated, and it went to the winds. As her mother often said, from the regal perch she commanded in the living room after her eldest son's death, a soft pallet she never left: *El hombre propone, Dios dispone.* Man proposes, God disposes.

Rizos had died when she was eleven years old. (Or had she been twelve? Thirteen? She couldn't remember exactly now, but it was three days before she began to menstruate.) Anyway, age did not matter in this story.

Was she up to thirty-six or forty-six? She had lost count of her strokes. *Coño.*

Back to Rizos. Everyone called him that because of his curly hair. She thought him unbearably handsome, but if you asked her now to detail his features, the color of his hair and eyes, she would beg you not to persist. Time had erased the distinctiveness of his face, left only a broad-brushed impression. Rizos was smart and popular. Everybody liked him; everybody trusted him. He could convince anyone he had their best interests at heart. And he was twenty-three. Ah, to be twenty-three and popular and handsome and articulate! What hope!

During one of the Machado elections, Rizos was hired by a friend of one of his professors from the University of Havana to guard the ballot box in the meeting hall of the pueblo. His father did not want him to take the job. Too dangerous. Their father was a self-righteous man with many weaknesses, to which he succumbed almost daily and for which he flagellated himself publicly.

No one ever knew what happened, though assumptions sprouted like mushrooms after a heavy rain. There were no witnesses, no overheard sounds, no suspicions. The story that emerged of Rizos's murder was pieced together with rumors taken from the air and the lips of others by Cuca's middle brother, who had straight, stiff hair like a broom before he grew bald overnight, and who presented the tale to the family in enraged hyperbole. *¿Quién sabe?* The pueblo was rife with rumors; its very existence depended on *chisme*, so everyone knew everything, but no one ever learned the truth.

Rizos had been shot by one man, maybe two. Political goons. It was said there had been a scuffle when one of the men had tried to steal the ballot box and replace it with another. Threats had been tossed. Rizos had stood his ground, then fallen to it, with a fatal shot to the heart that formed a round, bloody spot on his white suit.

Cuca's mother was overcome with grief. She cried so loud that they could hear the *jutías*, the tree rats, returning her calls in the distance. Her father and brother vowed revenge. Her little sister fled to the neighbor's house and refused to return home. (Cuca had finally coaxed her back with a fantastically red mamey, sliced and quartered and bedded on ice.)

After the Mass, the funeral, and the burial, only Cuca knew what she must do. In the midst of her agony, for Rizos had been her favorite brother and had promised she would be his firstborn's godmother, yes, even while cornered by the pain, she waited for him by the door. She waited until she succumbed to sleep, crumpled in a hardback chair, drool drying on her chin.

Rizos arrived at midnight in his signature white suit, red rose pinned to his lapel. He was luminous with anger.

"What are you doing out of bed, Sister?"

"Waiting for you."

"You fool."

Cuca began to cry. Rizos had never spoken to her so harshly.

"Why do you cry?"

"For you."

"For me?" He drifted closer, and she realized she could see through his coat, through his vest and tie and shirt, to the doorknob behind him. "Do not weep for me. Weep for yourself, for our parents."

His haughty tone made her cry harder. The tears felt like they were being squeezed right out of her heart.

"Why do you say that?"

"Sister, I know no pain, no hunger, no cold. I'm impervious to anguish."

"You are dead, then. Rizos, you are truly, truly dead. You will never come back, no?"

"Dead and happy." He smiled. He had no teeth; his mouth was a gaping black hole.

Cuca howled as loud as her developing lungs allowed. Rizos slapped her.

"Stop it!" he hissed. "Stop it!"

She shrieked louder. Pepe, her other brother, grabbed her shoulders. "What is it, Cuca? What are you shrieking at? Why are you sitting here alone?"

"He was here, Pepe! He was here in the house!"

"Who?"

"Rizos. I knew he would return, so I waited for him."

"Cuca, Cuca. He is dead."

"I'm telling Mamá, Papá." And she ran off to their room.

They did not believe her. Who would? An eleven-year-old child, maybe twelve or thirteen, with crazy ideas in her head, and an imagination that obliterated reason, and a willful, obstinate manner, sometimes sly, often sassy, hardly ever obedient.

"He slapped me, Mamá. Look, touch my cheek."

Her mother refused. Her heart could hold no more anguish.

Cuca grabbed her mother's hand and put it to the heat of her slapped cheek. Her mother drew it away quickly.

"Why did you do that to yourself? As if there is not enough tragedy in this family, now we will have to send you to Mazorra with all the crazy people."

"I am not crazy. Mamá, Papá. Please. I am not lying. I saw him. With my own eyes. I talked to him. He was wearing his white suit. His red rose, like if he was planning to go to a Saturday-night dance."

"Oh, it has come to this. A son dead, a daughter insane," her father lamented.

"Mamá, Papá, let me show you where I saw him. Get up! Get up!"

Cuca began to jump on the bed. She was in such a state and had created such a commotion that they knew they would not sleep unless they agreed. They followed her to the entrance, the father holding tight to the oil lamp, the mother stepping groggily, for she had, at her husband's behest, drunk too many rum-and-brown-sugar drinks. Cuca pointed to the chair where she had slept, and they saw Pepe standing by the window, staring at the full moon, entranced.

Cuca recounted what Rizos had said, what she had replied. "Then he slapped me."

Her father pulled her by the neck, close to the oil lamp, to get a second look at the imprint on her cheek.

"By the door," said Pepe, "what is that?"

The four of them drew close to the soft shimmering on the floor.

"A rose," said Cuca, who had the sharpest eyes in the family, and who, like a cat, could see for meters in the dark. "Rizos's rose."

Her mother reached out to touch it with her index finger.

"Oooh! It is hot."

"Leave it alone!" commanded Cuca. "Rizos forgot it. We should not touch it."

"What foolishness does this daughter speak?" her father said.

"Let's go back to bed. He will come back for it when we fall asleep, when no one is watching." Cuca was as sure about this as anything in her entire short life.

For a reason no one could explain, the family did as Cuca insisted. They returned to bed. Cuca vowed to remain awake, to spy on her brother when he slipped into the house to retrieve his rose, but as soon as she lay down beside her sister, who had slept soundly through the entire noisy scene, she fell asleep. In the morning, the rose was still there.

"Well?" her father asked her when the family converged at the entrance of the house, sleepy-eyed and disheveled and bitterly longing for the rest they had missed.

"I guess he is not coming back," replied Cuca.

"The rose still glows," Pepe observed. "Look at it."

"He left it for me," whispered her mother. "For my broken heart."

The man who made Rizos's coffin of the best caoba on the island also created a special glass case for Rizos's rose. The rose was buried along with their mother eighteen years later, still glowing, still as red and fresh as the menstrual blood Cuca found in her underpants that afternoon.

Ay, *Dios*. She remembered too much of the past and not enough of the present.

Remembering Rizos made Cuca very tired. Her right arm shook with the strain of her daily one hundred brush strokes. Why had she thought of this now? It had been years since she had thought of Rizos's rose, decades since she had stared into the glass case and wondered what it would be like to know no *dolor*? Dead and happy.

She lay down, without bothering to fold her Print of Paradise comforter at the foot of the bed, and looked up into the darkness. The keenness of her vision had dimmed with age, and the deaths of her brothers, her sister, her parents, her own babies, had closed her heart into a furious, hard ball. So she said a prayer: "God, God, send me a rose."

Then it struck her. She sat up so quickly her head spun: what if He already had and she didn't know it?

8

His heart, there was something wrong with his heart. It was too big, and even with its generous size, it could not hold everything. It could not contain all the love and pain of the world, this huge heart, so big and so full that it had arrived already broken.

"Two holes," said the cardiologist, a woman with mustard-colored curls and a German name.

She drew a picture that did not look like a heart but an oval with ribbons attached. A present. Her baby's gift to the world, with a couple of pieces missing.

Big heart. Brave heart. Victor Eduardo.

Maribel could not concentrate on the cardiologist's conversation, though the woman spoke slowly, enunciating each word as if Maribel were a child.

". . . congenital defects . . ."

The doctor's words flew into the air like birds. They did not hover, though, looking for a nest. They fled instead when they saw Maribel's face.

Big heart. Brave heart. Victor Eduardo.

". . . coarctation of the aorta . . ."

Where was Eduardo? She wanted him. She wanted to hit him, throw her shoe at him, spit in his face. This was his fault. His absence had broken their baby's heart.

"Every baby needs a father," she told the doctor.

The curly-haired woman stared at her, then smiled. "Yes," she replied simply. "Every child, but especially a baby, needs two parents."

Then the cardiologist continued her explanation. Maribel noted that she had blue eyes, as did Dr. Rothstein and Dr. Burton. Did angels have blue eyes? Or did their eyes come in brown and green? In purple and yellow and red, too? Maybe they had no eyes. Didn't need them because they were all-seeing.

"He's a little angel," Maribel said aloud.

"Yes, he is," the doctor assured her, and nodded. Curls bobbed.

Big heart. Brave heart. Victor Eduardo. Where are your wings?

". . . operation that would . . ."

Maribel jumped up. "You're going to operate, too? Another operation? Cut him up again?"

"No, no." The doctor patted her shoulder. "We're going to watch him for now. Continue him on medication, as needed. He's much too little for such serious surgery. He has to weigh ten pounds before we can even consider that."

A good sack of unrefined sugar from the mill near Lake Okeechobee weighed ten pounds. The neighbor's cat weighed ten pounds. Her mother bought ten pounds of red potatoes for $2.98. Her second cousin in Cuba, María Elena the Cross-Eyed, had birthed a ten-pound baby girl last year. Oh, Victor!

Maribel paced the room. The doctor watched her.

"Do you have family to help you?"

"Yes, my mother and grandmother," Maribel replied without missing a step. She walked from the bed to the sink to the window and back, left-right-left-right-left, passing a blur of mauve and violet on either side. She was sick of those colors, so pretentious.

"My husband should be here," she added, "but he isn't."

"We have a very good social worker," the doctor said.

Maribel did not reply. Something was choking her throat. An

invisible hand pressed her Adam's apple in, in, *in*. She couldn't breathe.

"I . . . I . . ." she stammered, and then began to weep.

The doctor matched Maribel's stride as she crossed from the sink to the window, and hugged her. She was a short woman, the cardiologist, and slight. "This is very hard, I know. Very, very difficult."

Maribel shook off the doctor's arms. "How would you know?" she sniffled, stopping short. "It's not your baby. You're just the doctor. You poke and pinch and look and then come deliver the bad news. It's not your baby."

"I can sympathize just the same, Mrs. Garcia." The doctor sighed.

"Sympathy is not the same as suffering."

"No, of course not. But I do understand how you feel."

"You understand nothing, doctor."

"Sweetheart . . ."

"It's not your baby! It's not your baby! It's not your baby!"

The words chased the cardiologist out the door and down the hall.

Maribel sat in the chair and buried her face in her hands. The hiccups managed to escape through her fingers anyway. It was her baby, her baby *and* Eduardo's, but he wasn't around. Eduardo was gone, perhaps far away, oblivious to her pain. He was probably sunning himself on some Caribbean beach. Eating a shrimp cocktail. Sipping piña coladas. Laughing with bikini-clad women. The bastard!

You just wait! she vowed. You just wait until I see you again. You are going to be so sorry.

Rage sapped the little energy she had. She sat in the chair, leaned back, and closed her eyes. She saw her baby, her baby and Eduardo's: his protruding eyes and sparse brows, his beak nose, his almost lipless mouth, his low-set ears, the hard forehead. And his enormous heart. Brave heart.

When the nephrologist visited Maribel in her room, about a half hour after Dr. Bauer, the cardiologist, had abandoned her to her screams, he was ill prepared for what he encountered. He was a tall man, bald, with a bulbous nose and exquisite taste in clothes. Had

Adela seen him, she immediately would have known he was a physician—Italian suit and dry-clean-only shirt.

"Who are you?" Maribel asked as soon as he walked in.

"Dr. Cox, your child's nephrologist."

Silence captured the room for several seconds before either spoke up again, and then both did at the same time. Dr. Cox smiled, apologized, but Maribel did not back off.

"Get out," she said.

"Excuse me?"

"I said, 'Get out.'"

Dr. Cox turned to look behind him. Surely she wasn't speaking to him. "I have some news about your baby."

"I don't care. Get out. You heard me. Get out."

"Mrs. Garcia, your baby's condition is very serious, a Grade 5 reflex problem."

"Get out."

"The urine is not flowing to the bladder . . ."

"Get out."

". . . dilated ureters . . ."

"Get out! Get out!"

"The renal sonogram . . ."

Maribel threw her slipper at Dr. Cox. It barely missed him, whizzing past his shoulder and smacking the wall behind him. Frustrated by her bad aim, she lunged toward the doctor, the lone slipper she still wore flap-flapping against the floor.

"Get out! Get out!!! *Get out!*" she screamed.

Dr. Cox had already left by the time she reached the door, but she banged it with her fists again and again until a nurse came and, meeting no resistance, put her to bed.

Just as she was applying the Poppy Red nail polish to the index finger of her left hand, Adela was struck by genius. And she was pleased the idea had bubbled forth at a time when she was, once again, feeling like a dead cuticle ready to be trimmed.

She dialed Eduardo's parents' house and did not worry about how her daughter would react to her meddling. They should know about their grandson, after all, and if anybody had a pipeline to Eduardo, they certainly did.

Sonia Garcia answered the phone. She was a short, stubby woman, a badly peroxided blonde who had worked most of her life at a garment factory in Hialeah.

Adela got right to the matter: "Maribel has had her baby. A boy."

Sonia Garcia howled into the phone, then called for her husband, Eduardo Sr., a forklift operator. Eduardo Sr. was as short and stubby as his wife but not nearly as gregarious. Adela had always wondered where Eduardo Jr. had gotten his looks.

Eduardo Sr. picked up an extension. Adela imagined him scratching his balls. That's just the type of man he was, crude. And Sonia . . . well, you could dress a monkey in silk but it remained an ape, didn't it?

"How is he?" Sonia asked.

"Not well. He has some problems."

A long silence followed. Adela finished the last three nails and blew softly to dry them while waiting for the Garcias to react. Come on, say something.

Finally, she talked into the vacuum: "I think Eduardo should know."

"Well, we have no idea where he is," replied Eduardo Sr.

"We haven't heard from him at all," Sonia added.

"Qué mierda," Adela mumbled under her breath. She did not believe a word. The federal agent who had visited several weeks ago had told her that both Sonia and Eduardo Sr. had quit their jobs last year. How could they live? he had asked her. She had shrugged and offered him Cuban coffee. But of course she knew very well how they lived—off their son's drug-running money. Which, by the way, her daughter refused to accept.

"Eduardo should know about his baby. He would want to know."

"I don't know how to get word to him," Eduardo Sr. insisted.

"Besides," piped in Sonia, "we heard he was out of the country."

"Eduardo would want to know about his baby," Adela repeated, and then hung up without saying goodbye.

She stared at her left hand for as long as her attention span allowed, thirty seconds, a minute. She thought of her grandson, that teeny infant alone in the hospital, and of her daughter, a bereft woman who was a stranger to consolation, and shuddered. *¡Qué vida!* She decided Poppy Red was too bright, too overpowering. She was getting a little old for the assault of such colors. Chica, now she was a grandmother. So she removed the Poppy Red with a cotton ball and polish remover and began once again on her left thumb, this time with something more modest, Seashell Pink.

I love you, Victor Eduardo. You are the crown jewel of my treasure, the love of my life, the sun in my galaxy, the reason for my existence, the cream in my coffee, the syrup on my pancake, the color in my rainbow, the center of my universe, the sand of my ocean, the rhythm in my music, the sweet scent from my gardenia bush.

Big heart, brave heart, bird-boy. Victor Eduardo.

Maribel returned home without the baby Monday morning. She returned to arid country, a dark, vast expanse of numbness that was filled with nothings. Adela tried to engage her in a conversation: What would she like for lunch? Did she need help putting away her clothes? Had the obstetrician told her how to care for herself? When did she plan to see the baby again?

Maribel ignored all questions, averted her gaze. She could not speak for the pain choking her. Her uterus cramped often, shooting bloody gobs of her insides onto the enormous sanitary napkin the hospital had provided. Her breasts throbbed. In the cavity of her chest, her heart lay as heavy and still as a domed boulder. She recognized neither language or sound. Her vocabulary was limited to one word, and that had no beginning or end or reason: Why?

Noise bothered her. Adela's laughter rang too loud, a cacophony, like a pile of dishes crashing. Odors made her nauseous. Had she found her voice, she would have begged her grandmother to wash off her violet cologne. Color insulted her. The impatiens in the garden appeared too bright, the ixoras too defiant, the early spring grass too thick. How could they be so alive, so brilliant?

She fled to the nursery. There she felt both a painful estrange-

ment from all the things she had collected for the baby and a yearning to use them. So many, many things—the framed Disney prints,
the matching lamp and crib and comforter and sheets and wallpaper
border and mobile and diaper pail and rug. So many, many useless
things.

She had grown so familiar with them in the past three months,
knew intimately the down softness of the comforter, the rough texture of the lampshade, the clean cotton of the sheets, and the tufted
feel of the Mickey Mouse–face rug. Shopping for them had brought
her such delight. Every Sunday morning she had settled at the round
kitchen table to look through the advertising circulars in the newspaper. Week by week, dollar by dollar, she had put the layette together—alone, because she had resisted her mother's insistence on
a baby shower. She touched each of the items now to make sure
they were real, to wish them into use, but the agony of her situation
clutched at her insides, a fist refusing to open up.

Maribel opened the top drawer of the white Formica dresser with
the red-and-blue handles. White pull-on T-shirts were stacked
neatly in the middle, between the pastel-colored Onesies and the
footed pajamas. She took one of the pajamas and held it before her:
enormous. And this was the newborn size! She would have to buy
Victor doll clothes, she supposed.

If he lived.

Doll clothes. Cabbage Patch diapers, Cabbage Patch shirts and
socks. Cabbage Patch bird-boy.

In the second drawer, she counted each of the flannel blankets
and each of the brushed-cotton ones, twelve in all, striped blue and
green and yellow. She never bought pink, not once had she considered it. No matter what Adela said, she had not, absolutely not,
been influenced by her mother's unwavering belief that the baby
would be a boy. Her decisions always were based on practical rea-
sons: a girl could wear blue but a boy in pink looked . . . well, effeminate.

The bird's-eye cotton diapers next to the blankets were as white
as whipped meringue. She had signed up for a service, but took her
mother's advice about buying a dozen at Kmart, cutting those in
half and using them as multi-purpose rags. Now she realized she had
not changed Victor's diaper once in the hospital. Not once. What

kind of mother was she? How would she know what to do? Didn't baby boys present special problems? Their penises, veteran mothers had told her, doubled as surprise fountains. She hoped his would. She hoped to bathe in his pee, delight in its hard stream. Oh, how she wanted this!

Maribel moved on to the last dresser door, where she had so patiently stacked most everything else that could not be hung in the closet: socks, hats, bibs, hooded towels, washcloths, crib sheets and pillowcases, infant-seat covers. The towels smelled like . . . like what? Like Downy, just as the television commercial promised they would—but something else, too. She pressed the towel with an embroidered yellow duck to her face and sniffed. It was the smell of baby's talcum powder, though Victor's real scent at the hospital had been of something else, of milk and newness and dry saliva and blood, a strange, living smell. Living smell. Living smell.

She slammed the drawer shut. She wished she could cry. Last time she had, she had emerged strangely uplifted, scrubbed clean. Since then, though, her tears kept wounding round her stomach like a string of black yarn, tight, tighter, unable to be released.

She threw open the closet doors to torture herself with the bright scraps of fabrics made into baseball suits and sailor suits and sun-suits with wide-brimmed cloth hats, suits of every kind and color except . . . except ones that would fit Victor. What she had bought was for giants. Giants! What had she been thinking of? Zero to three months, Newborn, Up to 11 pounds—God, God, God, what a sham, a heartbreaking sham!

She tapped the closet door with her forehead. She had done something to bring this on. Yes, she had—but what? Somebody please, please tell. If she knew, if she had an inkling, the slightest, she could at the very least repair, rework, redo.

Maybe it was the beer. The beer. She had a couple with Eduardo in the first month, before she knew she was pregnant.

Maybe it was the cough syrup she drank in her sixth month, when she got that terrible cold. Or the paint, the eggshell white she had used in this very nursery. Or the self-adhesive glue on the Mickey Mouse wall border. Or the dust and newsprint microbes floating over from the other side of the duplex. Or the air-conditioning in the office or the electromagnetic fields of the computers or the secondhand smoke she had not managed to avoid during those long focus meetings. So many potential hazards: the world was full of them.

And it could be any one of them. Anything. But it was something. Something, somebody was responsible for this.

A knock on the door. Her grandmother. She heard the jangle of her bracelets.

"Maribel, *hija*, I have made some red-raspberry tea for you."

"I am not hungry, Abuela."

"This is good for you. For your uterus."

Cuca was tempted to open the door, to barge right into the room, plant herself in front of her granddaughter and say: Shout! Scream! Howl! Break glass! Punch walls! Slam doors! But she wouldn't, of course. Couldn't. Everyone traveled through pain at their own pace. To interfere would only serve to prolong the arduous trip. To console prematurely was akin to offering a lifesaving device to a man before he jumped into the ocean. All she could do, Cuca knew, was to be here: a presence, a light, a rose.

"I will be out in a minute, Abuela."

Cuca shuffled to the kitchen, satisfied.

"Well?" Adela asked her.

"I could not hear a thing. Absolute silence."

"Oh, Mamá, I have not seen her cry once. Not once! That is not normal." Adela's hands pounded the air for answers.

"She may be crying alone."

Adela sighed. "Alone, to go through this alone . . ."

"She has us."

"How can we let Eduardo know? We should, you know. He is the father."

"Under other circumstances, Adela, I would encourage her to do that but now . . ."

"Mamá!" Adela faced her mother, arms akimbo, one hip jutting. Cuca's excuses for men were as varied as they were legendary. "He is as responsible as she is. He should carry some of the burden, too. We women are always excusing the men. No wonder they turn out the way they do."

"I am not excusing him. I just do not care for having all those detectives and agents hanging around the house again. Maribel does not need that now."

Adela laughed. She laughed because she wanted to hear the sound of her magic, listen to its comforting familiarity, but also because she had caught a fleeting vision of a stuttering Eduardo being questioned by the mustachioed federal agent. And she laughed remembering the short conversation with her daughter's in-laws that nobody knew about, and because she was desperate.

"It is good you have found laughter at a moment like this," Cuca said ruefully.

"Chica, we cannot bring that baby home to a tomb of silence. He needs sound, color, odors." She flapped her hands in excitement, in hope. "Besides, I remember what you taught me."

"Will we *ever* bring him home?" The question slipped from Cuca's mouth, a rebellious adolescent sneaking out past midnight. It had nagged her, this doubt, beat against the walls of her brain so violently it finally had found a doorway. She had never meant to give it voice, though.

"We will," Adela replied, hands clasped before her in supplication. "We must."

At lunch, Maribel did not speak. Her mother put a fork in her hand and her grandmother cut the *croquetas* into small pieces, baby-size pieces, next to the saltines. They sat her down, put the plate in front of her, a gray mug of red-raspberry tea, and a sweating glass of ice water. The older women's noises—the click-click of Adela's heels, the jingle-jangle of Cuca's bracelets, their rapid chatter— choked the air.

"Eat something, *hija*."

"Maribel, you need to be strong, now more than ever."

"Eat the *croquetas* first. They are more nutritious than the crackers."

"The milk, don't forget the milk."

"Adela, buy the whole milk, not this white water. This thing here has no *alimento*."

"Chew like you mean it, Maribel."

"Then finish with a fruit."

"Carlos brought them for you."

"Maribel, don't push your dish away."

"You cannot live off the air, Maribel."

Who says? Who the goddamnn fuck says?

"Greetings, brave heart." She brushed her lips against his forehead.

The baby slept, seemingly unaware of the tubes and machines around him.

"I know you can hear me. I know that somewhere in that deep, deep sleep you hear me."

Victor Eduardo moved his head. She thought it a reaction to the sound of her voice.

"Want to play?"

He twitched.

"The Chin Kiss Game."

He stirred.

"Fingers first."

Maribel pressed her tips to his.

"Let's get the hands to kiss."

She opened his hand. The palm was hot and moist.

"The knuckles now, *mi rey*."

Victor's were knobby and hard, like tiny garden pebbles.

"The wrists. Yes, those teeny-teeny wrists can kiss, too."

His were the circumference of a nickel.

"And we can't forget the elbows."

They touched elbows, hard bone to pliable one.

"And knees."

She grabbed the bassinet for balance, lifted her right leg, and pressed her knee to the plastic. Carefully, gingerly, she bent his leg.

"Oooh! You liked that, didn't you? Well, my love, my heart, my sky, my king, it gets better. Shoulder kisses now."

She bent over and met him halfway.

"Now back to the legs. Ankle kisses and toe kisses."

She rubbed his ankle, fingered each of his ten toes. Soon, she reminded herself, they also would be playing "This Little Piggy."

"And the hair kiss."

She brushed her raven's hair against his crow feathers.

"Ears. Ears, ears, ears. Yours are so low and so small they remind me of seashells."

Victor moaned, a soft purr deep in his throat.

"Let's not forget the nose, the Eskimo kiss."

Once, twice, she brushed her nose against his beak.

"And cheeks, just like if we were dancing. I wonder what kind of music you'll like."

His cheeks were bony. Her neck ached from stretching.

"Now, drumroll, please. The chin kiss. Tatatum."

As she leaned toward him for a last time, Victor opened his eyes and looked into his mother's face. In his pupils she recognized the infinite black of untamed space.

God, I hate you. God, I'll never forgive you for this. Never. God, you don't deserve a prayer. Doing this to a little kid. Bully. God.

9

The only good thing that could be stated with certainty about Miguel was that he had been well liked. By those who hadn't known him as well as Adela had, of course. He did not argue vociferously (as her own father had), nor did he interrupt or contradict. He was relatively even-tempered, eager to please, and never one to shy away from a favor—especially favors for strangers and acquaintances. Even when he was drunk, a state he had mastered in the last stages of their moribund marriage, he was neither morose nor violent, just a little more talkative than usual.

Otherwise, Miguel had been, as Adela's father liked to point out, *un cero a la izquierda*. A zero to the left, a loser. And yet . . . yet, she had fallen in love with him. And—God, could she admit this?—still loved him in that twisted way we love the people who are not good for us, the inexplicable way we yearn for things that we cannot have.

Why? *Why?* Adela asked herself as she leaned toward the stove, into the rising heat of a boiling pot of water. She could feel the steam opening her pores, cleaning them out, wiping away imperfections. Hmmm. Wet heat of all kinds was so much part of our lives, of the pleasures in our lives, that is. Think about it.

But back to the question: Why, chica? Why would she have taken him back had he ever demonstrated an inkling, a mere spasm, of an attempt to mend his ways? Why would she take him back if he walked in through the door right now, dressed as dapperly as ever, black wavy hair slicked back, slanted green eyes smiling, muscled arms reaching toward her?

She would take him back, that good-for-nothing, because— she leaned closer to the pot of boiling water, close enough to where the steam almost singed her brows, burned her nose—because deep down, deep-deep-deep-deep down, he had a good heart. And she was reminded of that generosity of spirit when she watched, through the hospital nursery window, Maribel playing the game with the baby, that silly exchange of kisses Miguel had taught their daughter. She had forgotten all about the game until she saw Maribel pressing her nose to the baby's, her fingers to his fingers, her ears to his ears, her chin to his chin, and in observing them play, Adela felt the breathlessness that comes with the rush of bittersweet memories.

She had met Miguel at a party. He was barbecuing chicken for their mutual friend, a man who had been in the Bay of Pigs invasion, and Miguel had looked at her through the heat and the smoke and smiled that expansive, welcoming smile that began with his lips but spread upward through his cheeks and eyes.

"Who's *that?*" she asked her host after she walked away with her chicken.

"Stay away," he replied.

And that was, of course, the wrong thing to tell her, a woman who liked to stand dangerously close to the heat, as she was doing right now, her face too-too close to the steam of boiling water. *Clean, heat, clean, clean.*

Their paths crossed, Miguel's and Adela's, several times after that. He always came or left with the prettiest girl at a party. He always laughed loud, attracted a crowd, brought the most beer or the finest wine. Yet nobody knew where he worked or how he got the money to buy his fancy clothes at a time when every other Cuban exile was shopping at thrift and army-surplus stores. The rumor in those days, those heady anxious days of the early 1960s, was that the CIA had every able-bodied Cuban man on its payroll, including Miguel. *La CIA* was the excuse and the reason for everything.

Miguel never told her if the CIA rumor was true. In fact, he did not tell her much of his comings and goings, of his whereabouts even after they rushed into marriage. When she asked, with uncharacteristic temerity, he skirted the question and made her feel as though she was prying. But she learned about him through observation, through the friction of daily living: sharing a bathroom, watching him dress, sleeping next to him, cooking for him, washing his clothes. And with time she realized that the expansive smile, the loud laugh, the easygoing nature were glossy varnish. Such a veneer.

He could not keep a job. He misspent his money, when he did have it. He was resentful and angry, with a seething, subterranean anger that expressed itself in unusual ways: he was hours late to pick her up from work, he would not call when he was away, he exalted the beauty and intelligence of other women in front of her, he drank too much and always at inappropriate times and places, he never apologized.

And yet . . . yet . . . how he loved Maribel. He fawned over her with a tenderness that melted the coldness in Adela's heart. Maribel, in turn, adored him. Worshipped him still, though surely her memory of him must be oh, so faint. Proof was that silly kissing game she still remembered.

Ay, chica, sighed Adela as she turned off the stove and patted her face dry with a clean hand towel. Why remember what could not be helped? It only served to make her feel so helpless and alone.

There is a not a mother who doesn't wish to rescue her child from the vicissitudes of life, to save him from the push and pull of dailiness, harbor him in the nest of her arms until vileness and temptation have eased, which is, of course, never. Any mother worth the label, Cuca quickly added, because she had read, with a horror that even jangling bracelets could not dispel, about mothers who abandoned their children, who beat them to death, who poisoned them or allowed them to be abused by men. Chilling memories of those news stories made her shudder. How could this be? How? How could it be allowed to be? Ah, those unanswerable questions.

Cuca had been watching Maribel carefully for signs of a rescue operation. She spied with a trained eye, searching for the telling detail, the giveaway gesture, the tears and questions and rage. So much of surveillance had to do with waiting, all of it practically. Waiting without being obtrusive, slinking through the shadows, melting into the wall. Patrolling. Guarding. This did little to ease her insomnia or curb her appetite because she seemed perpetually on hold. Already she had detected in Maribel symptoms of the first stages of denial: withdrawing silences, poor appetite, lack of tears. Denial and rejection, however, were the essential first steps before the salvaging and deliverance. They were necessary evils, and nothing one could do about them except pray and hope that they would blow away like a temporary bad wind, like the swath of devastation a hurricane cuts through once but never again.

Cuca sat out in the porch waiting for Adela to return from the pharmacy and for Maribel to wake from her nap. Afternoon was easing into evening, with all its accompanying noises of rush-hour screeches and honks, doors slamming, mothers calling out to children. She could smell barbecue, and her stomach gurgled in response. (The cantina today—*potaje de chícharo*, meatballs and noodles with a side order of wilted salad—proved no match for the inviting scent wafting from across the street.) She would have to settle for the delicious smell, so she sniffed hungrily and sighed. Maribel had no appetite, none whatsoever, and now more than ever she needed to eat, to fill her stomach and strengthen her muscles (along with her soul) for the task ahead. She needed to eat, eat, eat.

Oh, Maribel! Oh, *vida*! How desperately Cuca wanted to point the way, to the barbecue, through the pain, out into the world of light. Opportunity for this would arrive eventually, but Cuca knew she would have to be careful and guide gently, so gently. Maribel was a skittish child. Cuca could not afford to scare a seeking, stumbling girl away, yet she also had to be present whenever needed, available without being requested. This would require considerable finesse, but she was up to it, yes, she was ready for this most trying trial, her most difficult contest (perhaps her last, too). *Lista. A la orden.*

"Fernando! Fernando!" a voice screamed down the block. "Where are you?"

"One more minute, Mamá."

"*Ni un minuto más.* You march right into that bathroom."

"*Por favor, Mamá.* Pleeeze!"

Cuca giggled at the shouted exchange, so typical in its search and plea, surely a harbinger of what Fernando and his mother could expect in the future: push and pull, demand and bargain. Life had taught her much about the tension in the tug, so, so much, surely more than eight lessons. Those actually were just the start, an introduction, a summary to live by, to ease the pressure. And even with those (or because of those) she had made her mistakes, some more than once, a few that could not be corrected, but just the same she had mustered the courage to stand by them. In the end, life hadn't been so bad, still wasn't so bad at all, though she wished she could have made some changes.

For one, she would have raised Adela on a longer leash, allowed her a few more heartaches, more stumbles. Maybe she would have required more discipline and responsibility from her daughter, the same she demanded from herself. That might have had a settling effect on Adela, perhaps spawned, if not a more cautious woman, certainly one less averse to conventions.

When Adela announced to her parents her impending wedding (resulting of course from the surprise pregnancy, which she readily admitted), both Tony and Cuca had felt betrayed, destroyed.

"She's doing it to get out of the house," Tony whispered one night while both lay in bed, side by side, holding hands and staring at the ceiling. It was odd to hear him whisper, for he had met his daughter's announcement with apoplectic rage.

"*¿De veras?*" she whispered back.

"*Sí.* Why else would she do something like this? Ruin her future."

Cuca did not answer. Her thoughts were muddled at that time, and for several days later. Slowly, however, reason eased its way into her. Adela hadn't done this to spite her parents; she adored them and wanted to live right next door. ("Why would I want to move to an apartment far away, Mamá?" she had asked. "I still want to have breakfast and dinner with you. And who's going to make those *teas* I need for cramps?") Adela simply had been caught doing something she enjoyed; the baby was an occupational hazard, the bill due, for steamy backseat trysts. And let's not pretend they hadn't happened before, probably numerous times before.

"We shouldn't have been so strict with her," Cuca confided to her husband another night.

"What are you saying, *mujer*? We should have kept her under lock and key, that's what."

"Well, we shouldn't have. Being strict isn't the same as discipline. We were overprotective. We should have given her responsibilities little by little. Had her test the waters."

"Well, she sure tested them. Tested them real good."

So long ago, that conversation. Barely a memory, and now that baby was caring for a baby of her own, one link connecting to another, clasp to lock, a chain of joy and sorrow. Ready for the rescue.

Not that she hadn't been surprised at Maribel's pregnancy. Surprise? *Dios mío*, she had been shocked, flabbergasted, *espantada*, perhaps more so than when Adela had announced her own pregnancy. With all those creams and widgets to prevent pregnancies, the last thing she had expected was for Maribel to get herself in the family way. Oh, she was happy: how could Cuca not be? ("As long as you are adding to the family, all is well," Mamá Cleofe liked to say. "It's when you're subtracting settings from the table that you must worry.") But it was so unexpected, so uncharacteristic. And she had *chosen* to get pregnant, Maribel had, Maribel who liked things just so. Ignored the IUD, the diaphragm, the pill, the condom, the spermicidal cream, and certainly the unreliable rhythm method. She told her grandmother so.

"I want a baby," Maribel had declared defiantly while nibbling at saltines. (Morning sickness ran in the family.) "I planned it this way."

Well.

"Fernando! Who gave you permission to go outside after your bath? Get in here, *atrevido*."

"Ouch! I'm coming, I'm coming. You don't have to pinch me so hard."

Next door, Enrique, in plaid Bermuda shorts, sleeveless T-shirt, and black nylon calf socks in brown slippers, trudged to the side of his house and turned on the garden hose. He sprayed his rose garden and waved at Cuca, rolls of fat jiggling in unison. He grew larger every year. The Michelin man, Adela called him—and laughed uproariously. Cuca always missed the joke. Michelin who?

Maribel and her baby. Maribel with a son. There had been stranger couplings certainly, but this was about as close as Cuca had ever gotten to an odd match. Maribel, who could not abide a doily out of place, who always clipped her coupons with scissors and filed them in alphabetical order as well as by expiration date, who organized her closets by color, who planned her day like a military strike. How in the world . . .

Oye.

¡Mamá Cleofe!

Hija.

Oh, Mamá Cleofe. It has been so long, so long. Ay, Dios.

Listen. You are worrying too much.

I'm not worrying. I'm waiting.

You are worrying. And you are eating too much. Remember: the body is the temple of the soul.

I have to worry.

Why?

Maribel . . . the baby . . . this problem in his blood.

Can you do anything about it?

What do you mean?

Can you change what is in his blood?

Those chromo things? No. Adela says no one can.

There you go.

But . . .

But nothing. Focus on something else.

I want to help her. She needs a little guidance.

Perfect.

No, Mamá Cleofe. Not perfect. Haven't you seen? She's very stubborn.

A family trait.

She has no concept of the demands of an infant.

She will learn.

She is so fastidious.

People change, Cuca.

There are complications. No father, for one.

She won't be the last without a man.

You know, maybe that is why she wanted this baby. That's it, that's it.

What do you mean?

She wanted this baby, Mamá Cleofe, because the child cannot abandon her, not like her father or husband.

I beg to differ. A child leaves the house, marries, forms a separate family.

Not this type of child. No.

Ay, Cuca, I do not like to see that frown on your face. It worsens the lines on your forehead and around your mouth.

I'll try to remember that. But don't you think the baby is her security blanket?

And yours?

Mine?

Your tilos, Cuca.

You taught me.

Well, very well. Too well.

Yes, gracias.

On to the rescue, Cuca.

Wait! Don't leave just yet.

The visit has been much too long already. I do not like returning.

Too infrequent, your visits.

I want nothing more to do with these struggles. I had more than my share. Goodbye.

Adiós.

On to the rescue. To the rescue.

"Mamá?"

"What? What? Why are you shaking me?"

"You were talking to yourself again."

"Hrrmph."

"I hate it when you do that. It gives me the creeps."

"I'm glad something does, Adela."

"Who was it this time?"

"Mamá Cleofe."

"No! You're kidding, right?"

"Yes, Mamá Cleofe. After so many years."

"What did she have to say?"

"Not to worry."

"Not to worry? That's it?" Adela laughed. Around the corner, Fernando the mischievous boy heard a marching band. Enrique, surprised by the rockets in his ear, soaked his socks.

"*Más o menos.*"

"Why did she even bother?"

"She must think it important, Adela. Who am I to question? She doesn't visit because she's bored, I can tell you that."

"How do you know? I would think bliss might be boring."

"You would."

"Let's not argue, Mamá."

"I never argue with you."

"Okay, you disagree with me."

"What did you buy?"

"Kotex for Maribel. She only got a few from the hospital."

"And?"

"What do you mean 'and'?"

"And?"

"Okay, and a Cash 3 ticket."

"Aha!"

"Aha yourself."

"Aha back."

Before leading her mother back into the house, Adela turned to Enrique, now watering his lawn, and waved at him. A special kind of wave, flirty and noncommittal, the type a carnival queen uses while floating past a crowd, in a throne of cardboard and crepe paper.

10

On Tuesday, Maribel did not go to the hospital. She refused to get up from bed, a solid cherry French provincial four-poster with a white eyelet comforter and matching pillows.

"*Hija,*" said her mother, "take a nice warm shower, comb out your hair, and put on some makeup. You'll feel like a new woman."

Maribel did not follow the well-intentioned instructions. She snubbed the lunch of *tamal en cazuela* and then, later, the cantina dinner of breaded steak and black beans and rice. She asked only for *café con leche*.

"*Mi cielo,*" Cuca said, "staying in bed is the worst thing you can do."

"The worst thing in the world already has been done, Abuela," replied Maribel in a monotone.

Adela and Cuca went to the hospital by themselves. When Joanne the nurse asked after Maribel, Adela answered that her daughter was feeling ill but did not detail if it was a sickness of the heart or of the body. Joanne nodded, understanding too much. Then she allowed the two women to see the baby.

"The baby," Joanne said in broken Spanish, "needs *amor*."

Cuca had never seen an infant so small, and certainly not one sleeping face-up. Wouldn't he choke? Her children had all been big and strong, or at least seemed to have been, until they succumbed to some strange malady or other, and all had slept face-down. Maybe that had been the problem: those poor babies had thought of the world only as the immediacy of their blankets. No wonder they had preferred the other life. Only Adela, who had been lusty and demanding and a perpetual crybaby, had sought the world beyond the crib slats.

Cuca reached over the bassinet, but her hand froze in midair. She was afraid to touch him, to cross the boundary into that light that poured onto his tiny body like a viscous wine. And there were so many tubes and machines everywhere! One IV seemed to lead straight to his heart. In fact, just following the tubes to their destinations made Cuca dizzy with imagined pain. Ay. How could someone so new have so many things wrong?

"Go ahead. You can touch him," Joanne urged, reading her thoughts.

Cuca touched his tiny feet, then each of his hands. She felt the silkiness of his black hair.

"We love you," she whispered. "Oh, how we love you."

Adela asked Joanne for Scotch tape. She had brought a snapshot from last Christmas which pictured her in a green velvet and lace dress (vavavoom!), flanked by Maribel in a red sweater and Cuca in blue. She taped the photo to the inside of the bassinet, on the side the baby turned his head.

"Even if we're not here, Victor, you can always look at us," Adela said.

Then she sang him a song. Cuca joined in. The women had enticingly soft voices, like cool jersey rubbed against the cheek:

> *When you truly love,*
> *as I love you,*
> *it is impossible, my sky,*
> *to be separated from you.*

The baby continued to sleep, without acknowledging the attention, but both Cuca and Adela returned home pleased.

On Wednesday, Maribel again remained in bed. Again she refused to visit the baby at the hospital. Dust gathered on her cherry-wood dresser. The framed mirror looked streaked.

"What for?" she told her grandmother when Cuca urged her to get up.

Cuca and Adela visited instead. This time they explored Victor's little body more carefully. They discovered hair on his ears and above his lip. They noticed a tiny mole on the back of his left elbow. They traced the prominent bridge of his nose and took a detour to his eyes and cheeks. They peeked in his diaper and exclaimed with glee.

Cuca had brought an old black-and-white portrait of her family in Cuba, the bunch of them posing near the thatched roof of a *bohío*. She taped it next to Adela's Christmas photo.

"You come from good stock," she told him. "This here is your great-grandfather Tony and this one here . . ."

She stopped: she didn't need to introduce them. Victor already knew who they were, knew them better perhaps than she remembered them. When the nurse wasn't looking, she rubbed a little aloe around the IV needles that violated his soft skin.

On Thursday, Cuca and Adela dragged a listless, smelly Maribel to the shower. Adela stripped her and bathed her, raising her limp arms to soap her armpits, stretching her legs to dab at the back of her knees. Adela also shampooed Maribel's matted hair, then dried and dressed her indifferent daughter, while Cuca changed the sheets. Maribel stumbled back to bed and lay face-down. She did not notice the new pink-and-red-rose print. Grief throbbed through her veins, a pulsating heartbeat yearning for the child she thought she had carried in her womb for eight months, the child who never was.

Adela then swept and mopped her daughter's room. She sprayed air freshener—pinecones and evergreen—and sniffed.

"Do I need to dust, too?" she asked Maribel, hoping to strike up a conversation. She wanted reaction, any reaction, but really had no interest in straightening out the dresser or wiping down the matching night table or spraying the mirror. And she certainly wasn't planning on dusting the framed posters of the Coconut Grove Arts Festival and the Miami Book Fair.

Maribel remained face-down and did not respond.

"Open the windows at least," Adela said. "It still smells like mildew in here."

Still no reply.

In the hospital later that day, Adela pinned the black *azabache* stone to her grandson's bed. Maribel may have scorned it before, but surely Victor would not. Cuca recited a prayer. It contained no words, only hope.

On Friday, Maribel locked the door to her bedroom. She refused to take phone calls from her boss, Caleb, her in-laws, a co-worker or two. Cuca placed her ear against the door and listened. Adela waved her hands in inquiry, but after a few minutes Cuca shrugged and desisted.

"*Nada,*" she whispered, and fled to the kitchen in search of her chicken-bone lunch. How she needed the marrow! How she needed a lift!

In the hospital, Adela and Cuca met Dr. Rothstein as he left the nursery.

"He's a fighter," the doctor told them, pushing his rimless glasses up the bridge of his Greek-coin nose. "He's really hanging in there."

Cuca understood only one word—this *inglés* was such a barbarian tongue—and the image of the baby dangling from IV tubes prompted her to rush through the nursery door to the light. She hadn't run so fast since the last time she had forgotten to start dinner in her pueblo.

"Flesh of my flesh, blood of my blood," she gasped when she saw him, relieved he was not hanging from anything.

Suddenly Victor began to bawl, a howling so lustful that it filled the nursery with a cacophonous music, panicked the nurses who heard it, inspired the other infants to join in the chorus, and stopped the conversation between grandmother and doctor.

"See what I mean?" Dr. Rothstein asked.

Adela began to cry. She knew her mascara was running down her cheeks, making a mess of her freshly powdered face, but she didn't care. It was beautiful, that screeching, irritating bawling.

"We'll have the results of the karyotyping by tomorrow. Please tell your daughter," Dr. Rothstein said.

Adela watched him walk away. He was so tall, so handsome.

Patrician. And young. She sighed. She was glad he wore blue jeans to work.

Victor cried until, soothed by Adela's song and Cuca's stroking, he succumbed to an exhausted sleep.

When they returned home, Adela pounded on Maribel's door, shouting for her to open up. No movement or sound came from the other side. Cuca sent her daughter to the kitchen for a butter knife.

"Watch this," whispered Cuca, bracelets jangling. "Your father taught me."

She picked the door open. Maribel was lying face-up on top of the white eyelet covers, dressed in a pink-and-purple-flowered housedress, staring at the ceiling.

"He's a fighter," Adela said. "That's what the doctor told me. A fighter. Like me. Like Mamá. Are you?"

Maribel did not acknowledge the statement. Though she smelled of talcum powder and her hair was combed and clean, she appeared pale, sickly. She continued to stare at the ceiling.

"*Hija,*" said Cuca, sitting on the edge of the bed and taking Maribel's hand. "Your son needs you."

Actually, what Cuca meant was the opposite: You need your son. You need his dependency and his frailties and his trust. Only love will redeem your sorrow. The women in your family, women alone, women on their own, have learned this one way or another. And always through horrifying agony—some, in fact, would call it martyrdom. You, unfortunately, must, too.

"He cried today," Adela said. "You should have heard him. It was so loud, the wailing, that it could have raised the dead."

Maribel sat up quickly, as if pulled by a thread. She stared at Adela. She saw her for the first time as another woman, a woman aging but still attractive, with a punk haircut and dancing eyes, a woman other than the mother she always needed to save.

"Mami, when will the pain go away?" Maribel asked.

"What?" Adela replied in a vexed voice.

"Will it ever stop, the pain?"

These were Maribel's first words in almost two days, and their tone reminded Adela of the grating sound a plastic comb makes when its teeth are run against a hard surface. She wondered if such brokenness could ever be made whole again.

"I don't know, *hija*." Adela wrung her hands. "I don't know. I don't know."

Minutes later, Caleb arrived with a handful of daisies. Maribel ushered him in without paying attention to the bouquet, but Adela took it from his hands and exclaimed loudly. A man must be encouraged. Too bad, thought Adela, too bad this man was so ugly. Because he was a good man, a fabulous dresser (today, a striped Polo pullover matched to freshly pressed Edwin jeans), and with a respectable business, too. Chica, not many of those around.

"I'm worried about you," he told Maribel, and sat on Maribel's living-room sofa, a teal Italian leather that matched an easy chair Maribel favored and also played to the bright colors of a framed Guatemalan weaving.

"Don't be," she replied curtly, and flopped into the chair opposite her visitor. She was hardly ready for company.

Adela offered Caleb a glass of iced Coca-Cola, which he drank quickly to fill the silence. Once it was emptied, he placed the perspiring glass on the coffee table. Maribel watched a ring form beneath the glass but did not move to soak it up. Adela observed her daughter's nonchalance in horror. Should she wipe the ring or should she leave it as a reminder? What to do, what to do.

"I brought you another card," Caleb said.

"Thank you," Maribel replied listlessly and placed it beside the glass.

"Let me read it to you." He pulled the card out of the white envelope. It was a watercolor rendition of a basket of plump strawberries.

Caleb had a fine voice, as full-bodied and smooth as brown rum:

> *No silence can bloom into sound.*
> *No black can be filled with light.*
> *No scent can diminish the emptiness.*
> *No touch can pull the weight.*
> *Nothing.*
>
> *Brood not.*
> *Yonder, past the mist, beyond the hills, just over clouds,*
> *Awaits hope.*

"*¡Dios mío!*" exclaimed Adela. "I've never heard anything so lovely."

Caleb smiled. "Maribel?"

Maribel looked at him, tears brimming over her bottom lashes. "Oh, Caleb."

Caleb mistook the plea, confusing his emotions with hers after so many months of yearning desperately for an opening. As he reached for her hand, in his eager and willful blindness he bent too close to the empty glass and sent it shattering to the tile floor. Splinters shot out everywhere, and a two-inch shard impaled itself on Maribel's right shin. A rivulet of blood trickled down her ankle, dripdropped to the floor.

"Señora! Señora!" Caleb cried out. "Bring some napkins and water!"

Adela ran, amazingly quick on high heels. When she returned with a roll of paper towels, a plastic cup of water, broom and dustpan, she found Caleb kneeling on the broken glass, pulling the shard from Maribel's leg. Maribel did not wince. In fact, she simply let the blood trickle while Caleb cleaned her leg. Caleb was in a state, murmuring apologies, blushing in shame. After he had finished extracting the tiny sword, he brushed the glass from his pants legs and insisted on sweeping up the mess.

"At least it was empty," Adela said to ease the situation. She really liked Caleb.

Maribel narrowed her eyes at her mother, and Adela smiled so very pleased that, finally, fi-nal-ly, something had elicited a response.

"Caleb," Maribel whispered.

"Yes?" He leaned over, perched cautiously on the edge of the sofa.

"It hurts. It hurts so very much."

"Oh, God! Maybe a piece went into a vein in your leg." His brows knitted like beetles mating. Maribel laughed aloud.

Caleb wasn't sure what to make of it. "It hurts so much you are laughing? Crying?"

"No," she said. "Caleb, it hurts here." She crossed her hands over her heart. "Why does it hurt so much?" The plaintive cry of a bird in the night.

"Maribel, Maribel, Maribel." He pulled at his fingers so hard his knuckles cracked.

"It hurts, Caleb, it hurts. I can't breathe. There's this pressure on my chest."

Caleb sat on the coffee table in front of her and took her face in his hands. "Listen to me, Maribel. When Olivia first asked me for the divorce, I thought my heart had stopped. I couldn't feel anything, think about anything. Nothing, nothing, nothing. Then came the pain. And that was worse. It was like somebody was scraping my heart raw every minute."

"What did you do?"

"I got drunk a couple of times. Egged the house one night."

"No!"

"Yes. Oh, you wouldn't believe."

"I would."

"I even hired a detective to follow her around. I thought it was another guy."

"But you're okay now."

"Better than okay."

"How? I mean, all that pain doesn't just disappear, does it?"

"No. I wish I could tell you it does, but no. I just learned to look at it in a different light. I figured only so much sorrow could be packed into one day."

"I don't understand."

"Think of it as a purely mathematical equation. There are only three hundred sixty-five days in a twelve-month year, only twenty-four hours in each day, only sixty minutes in each hour. You can't add one more second of sorrow if you wanted. See? Pain is finite."

Maribel stared at Caleb's grin, his beetle-mating brows, his half-cocked eye—and she wanted to cry out. Because no, it could not be explained in a mathematical equation, not now, not ever. It defied language, numbers, symbols. To label this feeling . . . this oppression . . . this agony . . . with a simple word—"pain"—was to minimize it, simplify it. And no, she wouldn't allow it. She needed to *feel* the constriction killing her heart, give it free rein, in order to confirm she was still alive, still awake.

• • •

She knew how to pray, Cuca did. Always had, and yet, looking up at the iridescent green eyes of her black velvet Sacred Heart of Jesus in her living room, she remained wordless—and frightened. Mamá Cleofe had told her not to worry, but she wasn't the one suffering, was she?

Mujer, her husband called her.

Not again. She had tried to ignore him all day, but he was persistent. Always had been, and now even in death. No wonder he had been such a good lover.

Mujer.

I do not want to talk to you, Tony. You lied to me.

How?

You did not tell me the truth.

No?

No.

Cuca shuffled into the kitchen, turned on the light, and opened the kitchen cabinet. She needed some of her powders for insomnia. *Dios mío, Dios mío,* where could the valerian be? Aha! Hiding.

Mujer.

Her granddaughter had suggested several times that she alphabetize her personal pharmacy, and she had tried twice but lost interest somewhere along the way. Well, no, not lost interest. She simply had found something better to do. One time . . .

Mujer.

One time! One time she discovered an old recipe for *frituras de seso* and it had made her very hungry. She had walked to Fefa and Carlos's for fresh brains, then whipped up a batter and fried the delicacies—all before lunch. This had angered Adela immensely, though it had not stopped her from gorging herself with leftovers. Adela, you see, was scared that one day she would leave the stove on and burn the house down. What did Adela take her for, eh? And if the house burned down, so what.

The second time, she had found a condom among the herbs. Yes, a condom. She hadn't known it was a condom because it came in this fancy red foil wrapper, very nice, very discreet, and she assumed it was some kind of Alka-Seltzer.

¡Mujer!

There you go again. Forget it.

After a struggle with her arthritic fingers, she had managed to rip the foil wrapper and there it was, this thin, flat balloon. But no dick to wear it. To that, her life had come. Anyway, she filled it up with water and placed it carefully on Maribel's pillow. That was when she and Eduardo had just married and you could hear the bedsprings through the wall that separated the two sides of the duplex. The creaking reverberated always as the 9 p.m. *novela* was coming to a suspenseful close.

¡Mujer!

Maribel was not amused to return from work to find the water-filled condom resting on her bed. No sense of humor, that child.

¡Mujer!

Fresco. Do not touch me there. Cuca giggled because . . . well, because it still felt good.

I have your attention now. Besides, I am your husband.

And?

Listen carefully. The child's star . . .

I can't hear you.

The child's star.

What about the child's star?

See how small it is.

Cuca squinted to concentrate on the tiny, blinking light. Yes, it was small, very, very small—but how bright!

It will always remain small.

Why?

I miss you.

You haven't answered my question.

Rizos sends his regards. Your mother and Señor Pepe, too. The babies.

I haven't felt Papá around in a long time.

He is busy.

I need all of them now. I need them near me.

They are near you, Cuca.

I cannot see them. I have closed my eyes a million times this week and I have not seen Papá or the babies.

You cannot see everything that exists, dear.

Good point. You still have not answered my question. Why?

Why not?
Very funny. Still a comedian, hombre.
Look at the star, my Cuca. Do not lose the star.
Of course not.

Then he was gone. Cuca smiled at the faint streak his own large, overwrought star left. Always so exaggerated, this man. *Ay, Dios.* She would not lose the baby's star, of course. No reminders needed. She was not forgetful, only more enamored of what had happened and not necessarily what was to come. That didn't make someone absentminded now, did it? She jangled her bracelets for confirmation.

The star, she repeated as she readied herself for bed, scrubbing her teeth with baking soda and a moist washcloth, removing the bracelets, unbuttoning her housedress, untying her Reeboks, unwinding her braid. The star. How come the baby, now born and earthbound, still had a star?

One brush stroke, two, three, four. The star. A star. She stared into the dark universe of her closed eyes. Star light. Star bright. Why do you shine? She cut her brushing short this time, at fifty strokes. Too tired. Too confused. Too anxious.

The geneticist delivered the news. He was tall and thin, gawky, his face as smooth and unlined as a machete's blade. He did not walk: he loped like a giraffe headed toward a clump of trees, then sat hunched over the wooden conference table, struggling to meet her eyes.

Maribel stared at her reflection in his tinted glasses and knew she had aged a lifetime since she last walked this hospital's corridors. Her shoulders drooped. She had trouble lifting her feet, and she was tired just strolling from the nursery to this meeting room.

"Our suspicions, unfortunately, have been confirmed," said Dr. Burton. He had a very deep voice for someone so thin. "Do you have somebody else here with you?"

"My mother and grandmother, they went down to the cafeteria."

"Would you like to have them here with you?"

She shook her head no. These doctors were so nice, weren't

they? Maybe there was an equation for that: bad news = niceness × youth.

"Would you?" he repeated.

"No, I'm fine."

"As I was saying. Our suspicions have been confirmed. As you can see here"—he pointed to a photograph of connected tadpoles—"your baby has an extra chromosome. We humans have twenty-three pairs, or forty-six altogether. He has twenty-three pairs plus an extra single 18."

Dr. Burton paused. When Maribel did not say anything, he continued: "Actually, his is not a complete trisomy 18, only about three-quarters, which is, in this case, good news."

He paused again. She stared at his mouth, the way it worked so carefully, the smooth jaw a finely synchronized steel door. A trap.

"However, we believe your son's trisomy has a phenotype similar to that of the complete 18 trisomy. Some of his internal malformations—his heart, dilated ureters, incomplete esophagus—are very similar to the full trisomy."

"What does that mean?"

"Mrs. Garcia, we are talking about a severely retarded, medically involved baby here."

She shot up from the small conference table. "God almighty!" she shouted. "How many times do you guys have to tell me that?"

"I'm sorry."

Then more calmly: "Translate for me. Put it in plain English."

"I'm trying to." He motioned for her to sit down and folded his hands on the table. They were small, the nails manicured. A privileged man's hands. "I can tell you only from case studies in medical literature."

"What? What do the case studies show?"

"Most don't live past infancy, but in the case of a partial trisomy, the longevity stretches a bit. We know of at least a couple of partial trisomy 18s who are still alive at four years and another at three years."

"My baby?"

He shrugged. "He may not survive the operation next week. Then again, he might."

"Will he smile? Will he walk? Will he talk? Will he know I'm his mother?"

"I don't know, Mrs. Garcia." He shrugged his narrow shoulders. "I truly don't know."

"Then who does? I want to talk to whoever does."

"So do I."

There was not much to say after that. She remained seated at the conference table alone after Dr. Burton had loped away. Paralyzed in her chair, she recognized the ever-expanding sensation of emptiness inside. She saw its color, a gray sometimes but a dense black mostly, and felt its texture, a rough sackcloth, and heard its sound, oscillating, vibrating, with a life all its own.

¡Dios! ¡Dios mío! That anxiety was her life. It filled her like nothing else ever had. Frightened, she fled to the nursery, where Victor slept peacefully. His bassinet, awash with light, now was also filled with crosses, holy medals, prayer cards, and photographs brought by Adela and Cuca.

"Hey." Maribel rubbed his legs in greeting. "Miss me?"

The machines murmured unknown lullabies.

"We're moving tomorrow. Packing all your stuff and taking a trip across town. ¿Qué te parece?"

Maribel wondered what it would be like to pack and move across town—or what it would feel like to flee without a stitch of clothing or identification, destination unknown. Exciting, frightening, liberating. She lived in the same house she had been born in, knew the intimacy of no other kitchen or bathroom, took the same route to work day in and day out—an anomaly in transient Miami.

"I love you, Victor Eduardo."

Joanne the nurse sneaked behind her and patted her on the shoulder. "Feeling better?"

"So-so. The baby?"

"I reckon I'm going to miss him when y'all move. He's a tough cookie. Tough as they come."

"Yeah?" Maribel's heart fluttered with hope. Oh, oh, oh.

"He's going to give it all he's got. I can tell you that."

"You're not just saying that?"

"No, no. I think he's fixin' to give it a fight."

Careful, Maribel told herself as the emptiness filled with hope. Careful. Don't set yourself up for a fall. Heights are for the gods.

The house was a mess. Why hadn't she noticed it before? The week's newspapers had accumulated in a corner of the living room and her mother's magazines had made their way to her coffee table. Seashell Pink guarded the top of the television set, as prim and proper as its curved glass container. A water ring stained her prized coffee table. In the kitchen, breakfast dishes were stacked in the sink. A fading red stained the counters. Trash had not been taken out.

"Mami," she asked, "what is going on here?"

"You've noticed, eh?" Adela replied.

"You could at least have kept up appearances."

"I did, as best I could."

"It smells."

"Well, you know where the air freshener is, don't you?"

Maribel began to work. Tired as she was, confused as she appeared, the dusting and straightening, sweeping and mopping provided a comfort she had not known in the past six days. She rested at dinner. The cantina that night was tripe and garbanzos, one of her favorite dishes. She popped the last of the hot olives straight from the container into her mouth before returning to her side of the duplex.

Inspired, she began to look through the kitchen cabinets, organizing, sorting, rearranging. She kept only the essentials, throwing out bent forks, chipped glasses, saucers without cups, rusted ladles and spatulas. She then continued to the kitchen drawers, pushed by an energy to conquer, to methodize and regulate. By midnight she had moved from the hall closet, where she kept the few winter outerwear items needed for Miami's mild weather, to her night table and dresser drawers. She worked without stopping; she stacked, packed, divided without a second glance, a frenzy of thoughtless motion and feverish intent. At 3 a.m., her drawers and closets in order, her life in disarray, she fell asleep while filing her stockings by shade.

She dreamed. In the land of no time, love drew no blood and

every child was birthed beneath a star. In the land of no time, pain dissolved like sugar in one of her grandmother's hot *tilos*. In the land of no time, Fear renamed itself the Sun and wedded his sister, the Moon of Doubt. Their sons were called Courage and Fortitude, their daughters Patience, Grace, and Faith. In the land of no time.

Big heart, brave heart, broken heart. Victor Eduardo, which one will you choose?

11

Big heart, brave heart, will your heart be strong enough?

Stone Age man, Caleb was saying, probably performed the first operations with a piece of flint. Skeletons of that time show trephining, or a hole cut in the head of the patient to relieve pressure from a fracture. To demonstrate the technique, Caleb pounded the armrest of the sofa with exaggerated gestures and pretended to saw a hole.

"Pretty primitive," he observed, shuddering in horror.

Ancient Egyptians also performed certain operations such as castration and amputations. Caleb winced, crossing his legs tight. The Hindus of India originated plastic surgery and also perfected the removal of bladder stones. In Rome priests practiced sacerdotal medicine, and the Greeks were known for their operations on the battlefield.

"Kind of like M*A*S*H," Caleb said, chuckling.

Maribel nodded absentmindedly. She was counting the seconds between her breaths.

In France during the Middle Ages, continued Caleb, undaunted by Maribel's lack of interest, the surgeons were divided into two groups, surgeons of the long robe and surgeons of the short robe. Surgeons of the short robe were barbers who also had the right to perform surgery, usually bloodletting.

"Hey, Mac," Caleb intoned, "crop close on the sides and take it easy with the blood, okay?"

He laughed at the joke. Maribel continued to count seconds between her breaths.

Some French guy was the first to employ a risky method ligating arteries to control a hemorrhage. This eventually eliminated cau- terizing the bleeding with a red-hot iron.

"How do you know all this?" asked Maribel suddenly, between breaths. So, she had been listening all along.

"Read it somewhere. Actually, something I boned up on— excuse the pun—while trying to get on *Jeopardy*."

By the time Caleb had finished his explanation, Maribel's atten- tion already had flitted to something else. This did not discourage Caleb. He was willing to climb the Himalayas, swim the Arctic Ocean, cross the Sinai desert—anything—to ease her obvious an- guish.

He continued with his act, placing his handkerchief over his face and pretending it had ether. His eyes rolled upward, he slumped: the discovery of anesthesia back in the 1840s proved to be a real boost for surgery.

"Can you imagine, Maribel," he asked, straightening up, "getting cut up without it?"

Maribel nodded emphatically. "Oh, yes! That's exactly how I feel now."

They had been sitting side by side on a gray aniline leather sofa in a surgical waiting room at Miami Children's Hospital since seven- thirty that morning, when the baby had been wheeled out of the critical-care unit for the two-and-a-half-hour operation. The institutional-size, white-faced clock on the wall had just now ticked to eleven, and Maribel had lost count of her breaths nine different times, though once she had managed to reach up to seven thousand four hundred and eighty-two. Not bad. Her hands were folded neatly on her lap, and she had not moved all morning except to stand up twice to shake her legs and get the blood flowing. Both times she had felt dizzy, as if there were not enough oxygen to fill her lungs. Tottering, disoriented, she had looked at the swaying papers on a cork bulletin board across the room (announcements of support groups, advertisements for day-care centers, letters and photos of former patients), then at the two other families also awaiting news. She recognized the familiar fear in their faces. It didn't matter whether they sat calmly or paced anxiously, whether they held hands to comfort each other or sat on opposite sides of the room to avoid contact. Didn't matter. Despair marked indelibly.

Waiting proved a treacherous trial. She had not brought anything to read and the magazines on the gray Formica tables did not interest her. She was not hungry, either. And when Caleb brought some warm doughnuts from the cafeteria downstairs, she turned her head in disgust. Adela forced her to apologize. Caleb forgave her instantly, if he had ever blamed her at all. He was trying desperately to draw her attention outward, away from the sorrow that was quietly mauling her soul.

She did not want to talk. Her mother's tinkling laughter reminded her too much of a child's toy and Maribel banished her to the farthest corner of the room. Adela obliged because she understood: everyone's nerves were overly sensitive, like fair skin that had been sunburned. And Cuca? Cuca had exiled herself to the largest easy chair and proceeded to lay out her picnic of a thermos, two mugs, a bakery box of *croquetas* and other goodies, and a deck of cards for solitaire.

By midmorning, to pass the time, Maribel tried to make lists of anything she could think of. First, a list of all the things she needed to do when she returned home. Her mind went blank after three items. Then she listed shoes she owned, types of necklines on dresses, movies she liked, studies she had helped Caleb with, colors that suited her, books she would like to read, even the different ways she and Eduardo had made love. Nothing appeared remotely pleasant. And still, the minute hand on the wall clock moved more slowly than a child forced to eat his peas.

In the middle of her list compilation, as she enumerated types of fabric (cotton, rayon, organza, silk, velvet, taffeta, linen, satin), she remembered the sound of her grandmother's sewing machine. It brought her a momentary sense of peace, that wonderful whirrrrrrr-whirrrrrr of the motor. Stitching over gingham or brocade or polyester, the needle had sung her to sleep most every afternoon of her childhood, a tat-tat-tat lullaby of needle leading thread piercing cloth. Oh, Abuela! That's what I would like now, to nap the day away after a cold glass of milk and a peek at the dress you're making out of the dotted-swiss chambray.

A priest stopped by around ten. He was dressed in street clothes, navy-blue polyester pants, white shirt, and striped red tie. The hospital's social worker had filled him in on Victor's case.

"You must have hope," he told Maribel. His breath smelled like coffee, no cream.

Spare me, she thought.

"Do you know Father Peace? From St. Michael's?" Adela asked.

Cuca: "Are you assigned to a parish?"

"Put your faith in God, my daughter, for only He can guide you."

"How come you're not wearing a collar?"

"Nuns don't wear a habit anymore either, Mamá. The heat."

"Not the heat, Adela. It was the Pope."

"The Vatican Council, Mamá. That's what changed it all. Remember? Right about the time I married, I think."

Maribel glanced at the clock on the wall. Ten-oh-two. Two hours ago it had been ten o'clock.

"Let us pray together."

They joined hands, Adela, Maribel, and Cuca, even Caleb, who'd been raised Southern Baptist.

"Our Father," the priest began.

Maribel snickered. Fathers. Yeah, right. Fathers. She'd just as well seek solace elsewhere. But after the priest left, Maribel recited the prayer again in her head. Thy kingdom come. Thy will be done. In the land of no time.

Well, God, tell you what. Got a deal for you. My baby's life for whatever you want. Just tell me. Give me a sign. Work a miracle. Part the Red Sea. Multiply the fish and loaves. One goddamn sign, that's all.

Say something.

I'm waiting.

Please.

A family of redheads entered the waiting room, the mom pushing a baby in an umbrella stroller. They settled in near Cuca, who was wrapping up another game of solitaire.

God?

"Want some coffee?" Caleb asked. "I'm going down the hall to the machine."

Maribel nodded no.

"If there's espresso . . ." Adela said.

God? Okay, I'll start going to church every Sunday morning. Every single Sunday. What do you say?

No? What else, then? Money. Aha, money for the poor. Money for the church. Money for the priests and the nuns and the missionaries and the refugees and the homeless and the orphans and the crippled and all the damn people who . . . who . . . who . . . well, anyone who needs it. Okay?

I'm not asking for a lot. I'm not a bad person. No Mother Teresa but no Ted Bundy either. Just me, Maribel, trying to keep her duplex clean and her mother straight and her grandmother alive. Now I want one more thing. One very small thing. You know.

Why not, God?

Ten-oh-eight. A doctor entered the waiting room and everyone jumped from their seats, anxiety serving as springs. He spoke to a young black couple who had been weeping quietly since early morning. After the short conversation, the couple stumbled out of the room, sobbing. But, as if by design, another family, dragging an older boy by the hand, took their place. The father dropped a large white paper bag on one of the end tables. When he opened it minutes later, the mouthwatering yeasty scent of freshly baked rolls filled the room.

You have everything, God. You have bread and wine, the smells of a kitchen, the colors of all flowers, the sky, the sun, the moon, the planets and the galaxies and everything beyond. Why do you want my baby, too?

Maribel watched her mother as she struck up a conversation with the new couple. Did they know each other? No, but her mother exclaimed over the woman's hair color. Very becoming, she said, gorgeous color. The woman confessed: L'Oréal Burgundy Brown. Gorgeous, her mother repeated.

When Maribel was young, Adela used to rub a raw egg into her hair. Sometimes homemade mayonnaise. Very messy, but the red highlights in her black hair shone like a hundred candles. They caught the light, twirled it, reflected it—and blinded. When she was a little older, her mother rinsed Maribel's hair with beer, to add body and bounce. Never lemon juice, as Adela did with her own. No, never lemon. Her mother was fearful that it would lighten the black, dilute its power.

God, letting one teeny, weeny baby live is no big deal for you. For me, it's everything. I don't want a better car, a bigger house, a nicer job. *Nada.* Just my baby.

God?

Her grandfather used to tell her the story of an old man from the pueblo who had lost a leg during the War of Independence at the turn of the century. She hadn't thought about this story in a very long time. In fact, she hadn't remembered it at all until now, though the tale had been retold so many times that the images— the bloody stump of a leg, a grizzled old man, a hawk-nosed general—had burrowed into her unconscious:

Though the old man had learned to walk on crutches, had learned to brandish his stump at the town bullies who flung rocks at his dogs, he always told anyone who would listen that his missing leg, from the knee down, had been immediately placed on ice after the battle by the opposing Spanish general, then shipped in a zinc-lined icebox to the other side of the Atlantic, where eventually the son of this Spanish general stored it in one of the first refrigerators to hit the market. There was nothing the old man wanted more than to travel to Spain to see his frozen leg. And maybe, with some of the fancy surgeries doctors were experimenting with, have it sewn right back on.

Many years later, his granddaughter obliged. She had left for Havana at seventeen and returned sometime later, mysteriously but fabulously wealthy. She booked him a fancy berth north. Most of the pueblo's residents went to see him off. They waved white handkerchiefs, as was customary then, when the ship tooted and chugged away. On the fourth day of his voyage, as the old man was leaning over the railing to catch a glimpse of an enormous sea turtle other passengers had spotted, a gust of wind slapped him across the back, sent his crutches flying, spun him around, smacked him against the railing, lifted him off his lone foot, and toppled him overboard.

Maribel couldn't understand why she remembered this story at the hospital, of all places, but she smiled thinking of the improbability of a human leg preserved on ice and at the thought of her grandfather as one of the pueblo people who had waved a white handkerchief at the dock. Then she remembered something else: the granddaughter of the cripple was a madam. "And you better not know what that means," Abuelo had told her with a wry smile years ago, and kissed her good night.

God? That baby's like a limb. Amputated from my heart. I want him more than that old man could ever have wanted back his leg. Need him more, too. God?

Maribel went back to counting between breaths until ten thirty-seven, when Caleb's soothing voice, with its self-imposed rhythm and inarguable authority, began to massage her senses with tales of ancient scalpels and primitive clamps.

"Stone Age man . . ." Caleb said.

How about it, God? Do we have a deal?

Now Adela understood what was meant by hospital gray. Or was that battleship gray? Well, no matter. Either way dull, dull, dull. But maybe it would make an interesting nail color. Why not? Women wore black, which she thought tastelessly horrid. It was in style, it sold, customers asked for it. Gray couldn't be so bad, then. Gray nails for a courtroom appearance, say. Gray for a wedding you disapproved of, or for a meeting with a bank loan officer. Gray, so even, so muted, could be a statement of intent. But for a surgical waiting room? Absolutely not. A hospital deserved—needed—something more cheery: yellow. Paint the sun on your walls. Sketch a rainbow, a playground, a picnic at the beach. This room didn't even have a framed poster to brighten the place. Might be stolen, she supposed.

Oh, why was she thinking of nail polish now? To calm her heart, to steady her nerves. And because she could not read her book. The letters danced on the page; the words flew away. Concentration—what was that? She could think of only one thing.

Victor.
Victor.
Victor.

When you come home, my grandson, we will throw a big party. We'll roast a whole pork in the pit in the back yard. I'll make black beans from scratch, soak them the night before in water and love. I'll rise early that morning to bake the flan, slow-cook the sugar for the best *caramelo* in the world. Sweeten your tongue and your life.

Together we'll have so much fun. We'll go to the beach, the park, the grocery store. I'll buy you a bike, a horse, a car with a horn that goes toot-toot. Won't you like that? Please hurry up and live.

Adela sighed. The soles of her feet ached from anxiously clenching her toes in the prison of her gold-and-plastic, square-heeled sandals every time a doctor walked by. She needed to relax. Read and relax.

To the hospital she had brought her favorite book, *Unlock the Power of Your Mind*, and was now rereading the chapter on dream interpretation. She needed a review. The past few days she had been having very weird dreams. Worse, she couldn't remember them, only how strange and depressed they made her feel when she woke. Whatever their plot or purpose, they spoiled her mood, for she now did the most simple of household chores off-kilter, with neither rhythm nor desire. Chica, three days ago she had forgotten to buy a Lotto ticket! Hard to imagine, eh? But true. It had slipped her mind like water passing through a sieve. That was her memory now, *un colador*, and the clumps of matter that remained were unidentifiable. What was wrong with her?

Carlos had called Sunday, concerned by her absence. He had grown accustomed to her visits, her chatter, her laugh. She was flattered. She patted the wisps of her short hair into place now, remembering the echo of his voice, a baritone caress.

"Carlos," she had replied primly, "I have a lot of things on my mind."

Which was the absolute truth and not a teasing come-on in any way.

Her mind was clouded with this unrecognizable matter. She had never before forgotten to play the Lotto. Never, not once, since the state of Florida had initiated the lottery with much fanfare. Of course that wasn't counting the time she had been in the hospital recovering from an emergency hysterectomy. She had remembered and asked Maribel to buy her five tickets. Even given her the numbers written on a white napkin that came with her hospital food tray. But, chica, do you think her daughter would have done her a favor?

"You're thinking of that now?" Maribel had shrieked.

And, of course, Adela would have won had Maribel played the numbers, won with three numbers on her third card. Made a couple of dollars and change. But you don't win unless you play. Missed opportunity: that's what her life had become. One missed opportunity after another. Never remarried. Never had more children. Never owned her own salon. Never been to Niagara Falls.

Too depressing, this. Blame it on the color gray.

She closed the book for the umpteenth time that morning and opened her purse, a square black number with gold chain. She had bought it at Marshall's on clearance for less than thirty bucks. The thought of the bargain lifted her spirits, but only slightly: from the floor to just above the ants. She looked through the two compartments for the plastic Baggie with the nail polish. Aha! Seashell Pink. She had brought it along, hoping to do her toenails, but then realized that the waiting room, this horrid gray room of doom, was public and other families came in and out constantly, sat, ate, cried, prayed. Never would she paint her nails in public, of course. Muy *picúo, chica.* Like applying lipstick at a restaurant without bothering to go to the ladies' room. She twirled the polish open, turned to face the wall, and painted two dots and a curve. There! A Smiley face. Quick as a man without control. Oh, she was good.

Victor, I'm going to teach you to paint. We'll do murals on giant walls. You'll love color, I just know. Color and sound and smell, everything beautiful, everything in profusion.

What do you dream of? I bet they're violently beautiful, your dreams. You'll tell me all about them one day. And we'll figure how to play them. Fish bet eighteen. Mouse the twenty-nine. Dog . . . ? Dog—oh, she had forgotten, the number had slipped through her *colador* brain. Anyway, Victor, together we'll grow rich and move to the beach, to a condo on the top floor, where we can throw open the balcony door and smell the ocean and the fish and the clean air and the free sky and the hope of sailors and the gassy fumes from boats and the beckoning countries over the horizon and the visions of the Vikings and the courage of the conquistadores and the muted desire of all those who have died at sea. That, Victor, is the smell of the ocean, and you and I will enjoy it together.

Adela opened her book again, tried reading the dancing words, then shut it with a thump. She watched Caleb and Maribel whispering. Nice man, but almost old enough to be her father. So what. Because she deserved better. Who cares. He was a good man. Here he was on a Tuesday morning, a workday—and Eduardo? His parents? They didn't know about the surgery, but they could have found out. A little initiative, you know. Just a little initiative and curiosity. Now Caleb, in his fancy suit and wingtip shoes, his hair combed, his neck cologned, his tie perfectly knotted, his eye at half-mast—he was there. That counted for something. For a lot.

Oh, God. Meddling in her daughter's love life again. Hadn't she learned? Oh, God. I know you're up there. Don't hide. Okay, okay, so you don't recognize my voice. Didn't think the Smiley face was a contribution to the aesthetics of the room. Okay, okay. But oh God. Show some compassion, eh? If not for me—heaven knows I'm a sinner—think of that tiny baby. Don't let him hurt. Spare him the pain.

God. I know you hear me. Don't shut me out. I've been shut out from so many places so many times I can recognize the quality of wood by the slam of a door. God. *Por favor.*

God. My Virgencita de la Caridad del Cobre. My Sacred Heart of Jesus. San Lázaro. San Martín de Porres. Santa Teresita and San Antonio and Santa Ana.

God! A favor.

Cuca came prepared with a thermos of hot mint tea, a dozen *croquetas*, two bananas, one apple, a guava pastry (all of which she ate by midmorning), and assorted accessories for entertainment in her straw tote. Ready. For what, she wasn't sure. But for something. Actually, she did know what she had anticipated: the pain. It marked the lines around Maribel's mouth like parentheses. It furrowed her forehead, dimmed her eyes, blocked out sound. Ay, *dolor, tanto dolor.* If there was only something she could do about it, some herb to boil, some ointment to spread. Something.

"Listen, Cuca," her mother-in-law had once told her, "pain is part of life. You cannot *not* expect it."

This was after her third baby had died from diarrhea. She had cried a river. Then she had accepted the pain—clasped it to her heart like a rare jewel, worn it like a prized brooch. Anyone who had watched her knew. Noticed the agony that kept her heart beating. Noticed that every pain, every slap, punch, kick from life, was folded into that ever-present agony, like eggs into batter.

As it will be for Maribel. Sorrow such as this burrowed deep, a scalding, under-the-skin geyser of hope-cum-helplessness. And nothing you can do about it. Nothing. *Nada.* Ay, ay, ay.

The family buried her sons, all her live babies, in the family plot, down past the outhouse, under a ceiba tree. Three little marble markers all in a row, one two three, like children in line for recess. She had survived, lived on. A fourth, a miscarriage, more blood, hemorrhaging love, but she had persevered. Like a determined pit bull, toothless, limping, and blind in one eye, she had clamped onto the miserly bone life had thrown her. Cooked and cleaned and laughed and screamed and made love. Grown old. Grown wise. Still, her mind's image of the carved rock that marked those babies' short lives weighed down her soul, anchored it to the ground.

Now it was Maribel's turn. Now it was her granddaughter's turn to be taught. Oh, flesh of her flesh, blood of her blood, to be educated in the ways of love and hope invariably became an excruciating task! Sorrow, Cuca knew, considered neither youth nor old age, poverty nor riches. But in the end something good was produced, not less pain, not immunity, and not always acceptance. No. At the end of the lesson, like a pearl from sand, emerged truth. Yes, a steep price was exacted, but the best of those truths, the most lasting, was the one that nailed you to a cross. If she could explain this to Maribel, whisper it in her ear, translate it into her heart.

Let me be your guide, Cuca longed to shout across the room. *Tu maestra.* I know what it is like to see the flesh of your flesh, blood of your blood, slipping between paralyzed fingers.

But no, she could not speak or scream. No words. No chamomile, no mint, no anise. Plain pain, simple truth. That's all there was.

. . .

The fog lifted when the surgeon, still in OR greens, smiled at Maribel from the doorway of the surgical waiting room and gave her a thumbs up. Maribel gasped and hugged herself.

"Turned out a lot better than I thought," he said. He reminded her of Humpty Dumpty, egg-shaped and very fair.

"¡Gracias a Dios!" shouted Cuca, who understood the word "better" in almost any language.

"We went in through the side and attached the esophagus with very little problem. I'm pleased."

Adela took the surgeon's hands and kissed them. Blessed hands!

"When can I see him?" Maribel asked.

"In a bit. One of the nurses will come get you."

"Thank you, doctor."

"Now get something to eat downstairs. You're going to need your energy. As I explained before, and I'm sure Drs. Rothstein and Burton have, too, this is the beginning of a long haul."

Suddenly Maribel was famished. Her stomach gurgled. Her mouth watered in anticipation. More than anything, she wanted to freeze this moment, suspend it in the land of no time. More than anything, she wanted a cold, cherry-red Popsicle, just like the ones her father used to buy her from the ice-cream trucks that played merry-go-round music.

Eagerly, Caleb went off in search of one.

12

Through the shadows of the night, those holes of darkness where crickets seek to rub their legs and sing their songs and mate their mates, Eduardo found his way. It was nearing midnight, and except for a few mothers, almost every visitor had left the hospital. Eduardo spotted Maribel in the second-floor waiting room. And just as he recognized the blackness of her hair, so pure, so absolute, Maribel felt his eyes, the warmth of his hands, before he had crossed the threshold to her side. She lay curled on the sofa, her back to the door, under a white flannel blanket the hospital provided for parents who slept in the waiting rooms. She had folded the hospital pillow in two and turned to the backrest for company in her immense solitude. But like the chicken fleeing the farmwife, sleep eluded her. It was impossible to rest at the hospital anyway: the halls were lighted like a cloudless noon sky and strange noises—a beep here, an alarm there, screeching, moans, whispers, farts—filled the air.

Eduardo knelt beside her. "M-m-maribel," he whispered in her ear.

Without getting up, she turned to face him. She was happy to see him. Oh, she couldn't deny it. She was ecstatic. She wanted to run her fingers through his hair, bite his lips, bury her face in his chest. But she was angry, and exhaustion did not allow her to forgive.

"What brings you here?" she asked sarcastically.

"Our son."

She snickered, then sat up. She wanted to scream at him, but she knew she couldn't. There were two other mothers under blankets in the room.

"H-h-how is he?"

"What do you think? He's doing cartwheels."

"Maribel!"

He never stuttered when he was angry. She remembered that. He stuttered most other times, even in lovemaking, but never ever when he was angry.

"He's very sick, Eduardo. Very, very sick. The doctors say he might die."

A sob caught in her throat. One of the mothers stirred.

Eduardo took his wife's hands and led her out of the room, down the hall by the elevators.

"H-h-how sick?"

"He was born with an extra chromosome."

"So?"

"There are all these things wrong with his organs and he's got two holes in his heart."

"C-c-can't they fix that?"

She shrugged.

"The d-d-doctors, what are they f-f-for?"

"He's mentally retarded, Eduardo. They don't know if he'll ever walk or talk or even recognize me."

Eduardo stared at her. In his eyes, it seemed, she appeared as a ghost. She was a liar. She was at fault. Oh, how she recognized that look, would have known it anywhere. It was the stare he gave her when her mother or grandmother got in the way, when they meddled and she defended them.

"Eduardo?"

He did not answer; his stare drilled into her face.

"Eduardo, you need to be here with me. I wanted you here today during the operation. He's your baby, too."

"What the fuck did you do?" He grabbed her shoulders.

She shook off his hands and glared at him. "What do you mean?"

"How did the b-b-baby come out like that?"

"I don't know!" she shouted. She didn't care anymore who was sleeping. Why should the world rest when she was in misery?

"You m-m-must have done s-s-something."

"I didn't do anything. Maybe it was you. Maybe it was you doing drugs and all that stuff. How do we know it wasn't your sperm?"

"I-I-I don't do any d-d-drugs."

"Yeah, right." She turned and walked away. He tried to stop her, but she batted away his hand. She didn't want to leave. Truly she did not want to return to the dark waiting room to face her thoughts alone, but she had a little pride, you know. Being blamed for her baby. Being blamed for something she could not control. Incredible.

"P-p-puff," he called out her pet name. "P-p-puff, I'm sorry."

She faced him, his lopsided grin. "Do you want to see him or not?"

Eduardo nodded.

The baby slept face-up, under the heat lamp, entwined with tubes. He was one of five babies in the unit. During the day, each infant had a nurse who sat at the foot of the bassinet, watching the machines, adjusting tubes, jotting notes. At night, there was one nurse for every two patients. Maribel thought the young, cheery nurses in Teddy-bear-print uniforms were darling. She wondered if Victor noticed, if he saw, if he would remember.

"He's t-t-tiny," Eduardo whispered in awe.

Maribel nodded. She thought the baby looked better now than this afternoon. His cheeks glowed pink, and he seemed plumper somehow. She bent over to whisper silly endearments.

"W—w-what's this?" Eduardo asked, touching a rubber tube that protruded from the baby's stomach.

"They put that in during the operation. It's called a G-tube. In a couple of days the nurses are going to teach me how to feed him through there until the surgery is healed."

"Oh, G-g-god."

"Told you."

Eduardo put his arm around her shoulder. It felt so good, so reassuring, his arm, the heat of his body, his musky smell, the way his presence filled her space and her heart.

From the corner of her eye, Maribel saw the nurses in the room watching them.

"Did you n-n-name him?"

"Yes, Victor Eduardo."

Eduardo smiled. "He d-d-doesn't look like a b-b-baby."

"His features are kind of funny, but that's because of the extra chromosome. I think he looks like a bird."

Eduardo chuckled. "G-g-gonna fly off."

They watched their son for a few minutes, how his small chest rose and settled, rose and settled with the help of a respirator. Maribel wondered if the sight of someone so small and defenseless would anchor Eduardo closer to home. She dared not hope.

"H-h-how long does he s-stay?"

"About a month, the doctors say. If all goes well, three weeks."

They stood in silence a while longer, until Eduardo said he had to leave. Maribel grabbed his hand.

"Don't. Not yet." She hated to beg, but she did not want to tiptoe into the night alone. She did not want to entertain any thoughts, pursue any of those paths that darkness and silence pushed you through.

"I c-c-can't take the chance. It's t-t-too risky."

"The cops have been at the house several times. Some federal agent, too."

"I k-k-know. Don't t-t-tell anyone you've seen me."

"Eduardo," she said, and her voice broke.

"Yes?"

"Eduardo, why don't you come home? Just come home and be with us and whatever happens happens. It's better like that."

"N-n-no it isn't."

"You should be with the baby and me now."

"C-c-can't."

"Yes you can. You don't want to."

Eduardo dropped her hand and walked out of the critical-care waiting room. That was the thing about Eduardo. You couldn't pressure him. You couldn't push him or corner him or force him into a decision. He was slippery that way. Maybe he thought that gave him control.

Maribel did not follow him out immediately. She caressed Victor's face and kissed the tip of his nose.

"Don't fly away, bird-boy," she whispered. "See you again in a few hours."

Maribel found Eduardo around the corner of the hall, waiting for her. He was leaning against the wall, head tilted back, staring impassively at the ceiling. She noticed for the first time that he was wearing a white turtleneck and black jeans, an outfit she did not recognize. He looked good. No, he looked wonderful. And she probably looked a mess, in the same clothes for the past twenty hours.

"D-d-do you n-n-need money?"

"I don't need money, Eduardo. I need you."

He reached out to hug her. She leaned against him, pelvis to pelvis, in the familiar heat, and stared into his face.

"Yeah?" he asked, and grinned slyly.

"Yeah." She wanted to put her tongue between that wonderfully familiar gap in his front teeth.

"How about that g-g-guy who's been hanging around the house? Your b-b-boss."

"Caleb." She laughed. The jealousy delighted her. "Caleb's a friend."

"F-f-friend."

"He's good to me, Eduardo. He was here all morning with me. He visits me at the house."

"He w-w-wants something." Eduardo ground his pelvis against hers. She could feel his hardness through the jeans. She leaned over and kissed him, mouth open.

Then she said: "He's a kind person. Caleb's been through a lot with his divorce."

"He wants p-p-pussy."

"And you?"

Eduardo smiled.

"W-w-why don't you come with me, Maribel?"

"What?"

"C-c-come with me."

"Where?"

"To another c-c-country."

The image that had tortured her days earlier—a Caribbean beach, ice-cold piña coladas, half-dressed women—flashed in her mind. For a second, one fleeting moment of indecision, she considered it. To flee, to let go, to disappear, to forge ahead with no past—that was true freedom, wasn't it? To forget the raucousness of her neighborhood, the cramped duplex, the traffic from the dog track, all those neighbors with their rusted cars and noisy mufflers. Oh, yes! Then the picture of swaying palms and blue ocean was replaced with Victor's beaked face, his tiny body, the blinding light over his bassinet.

"The baby, Eduardo."

"He's g-g-going to die, isn't he?"

She disentangled herself from his grasp and took a step back. So that's how he thought about all this. Maybe that's how everyone else considered it, too. *He's going to die anyway.* Why hope? Why love? Why sing or caress or whisper or play with him?

"He's not, Eduardo. You'll see. The doctors have told me he's a fighter."

"C-c-come with me," he insisted, and tried to draw her to him again.

She held back. "I can't, Eduardo, I can't." And she realized that motherhood had indentured her to an inexorable servitude she had not yet understood.

Adela saved the best for last. After a late dinner, she showered and washed her hair, applied an orange-and-wheat-germ facial masque, soaked her feet, painted her toenails, plucked her eyebrows, and removed her masque—not once thinking about the sinkful of dirty dishes and pots waiting to be scrubbed. She would leave those for tomorrow, or for Cuca, who had gone to bed earlier, too tired to watch her nightly soap on Channel 23. Now, with her hair still damp—so much humidity, even in the winter in this Miami—Adela slid closer to the lamplight and began to read the weekly promotional letters that promised her riches. Perhaps in this batch she would find the winning one. Perhaps, perhaps. The tide was turning. Victor had emerged spectacularly from the operation only hours ago, so why not, chica, why not?

She put on her reading glasses.

"Dear Adela C. Menendez,

"Congratulations."

She smiled and adjusted the glasses. They all began with the same hype. Like men. Lot of fire at first but no lasting heat.

"You are on the brink of winning a Ten Million Dollar fortune to be given away just weeks from now. The name Adela C. Menendez has been paired with SuperPrize Number 83 4494 1942 16. Final processing may prove that number wins Adela C. Menendez ten million dollars in our 1992 Sweepstakes.

"However—"

She knew it. She could spot the "but" and "however" a mile away. Her life was full of them. She tossed the letter on the glass-and-wrought-iron coffee table, and ripped open another one.

"Attention Adela C. Menendez:

"This official notification is to inform you that as a resident of Florida having satisfied stringent selection criteria, you now have the opportunity to be a Final Stage entrant in the $12,250,000.00 Sweepstakes presented by . . ."

She scanned the next paragraph until she got to the instructions. She read them over carefully and followed them precisely. First, she removed the label in the left-hand corner of the letter and stuck it on the Entry Claim Voucher. She signed her name and slipped the voucher in the envelope provided.

"Your Voucher must be received no later than April 1, 1992, to secure its full entry value. Receipt of voucher by that date will secure the position of the Menendez name in the Final Stage of the $12,250,000.00 prize selection procedure, where winners are selected.

"THIS NOTICE WILL NOT BE REPEATED."

She reached for the book of stamps on the armrest, licked one, stuck it on the envelope, sealed it, and kissed it for luck. Normally she would have placed it, along with her lottery tickets, at the foot of her Virgencita, but she didn't want to be too pushy. She didn't want to ask for too much. She was counting on this

Sweet Mother to intercede on Victor's behalf: enough was enough.

She moved on to a third letter: "TO THE URGENT ATTENTION OF ADELA C. MENENDEZ," it began. How Adela enjoyed salutations with capital letters! She imagined typists crying out the words as they pressed the keys.

"Over recent months your name has caused quite a stir here. That's because it keeps coming up as that of a music lover in Miami."

Hmmm. Music lover. Well, she could still dance a pretty good merengue, that's for sure.

"Very recently in fact, the Menendez name has received a great deal of attention as we carefully put a group of people together to receive our latest offer and to win any of the 50,814 prizes worth . . ."

A loud knock on the door. Strange. It was so late. She called out, and Carlos replied. Panicked, she ripped the reading glasses from her face, ran to the bathroom, flung them in the medicine cabinet, finger-combed her short hair, pinched her cheeks, bit her lips, and squirted Emeraude behind each ear before returning to open the door.

"*Hola*," he said.

"Hello yourself," she replied, but did not open the door completely.

"Are you going to ask me in?" He held up a large package wrapped in a brown paper bag and taped on both ends.

"What's that?"

"A *paleta*, fresh. I seasoned it for you and everything."

She didn't reach out immediately for the package. She would have preferred flowers, really, or a box of chocolates, but then again . . .

"Let me in, *mi cielo*."

"My mother is sleeping."

"I won't make too much noise."

"Well . . . for a minute only."

Carlos walked to the kitchen, opened the refrigerator, and began to rearrange jars and plastic containers to find a spot for his pork. His white guayabera strained against his chest.

"Thank you," Adela said finally, and caught a glimpse of herself in the dark kitchen window. Presentable. Quite presentable, considering that mad dash to the bathroom.

Carlos walked to the living room and sat down on the upholstered chair. "Missed you," he said softly. His green eyes glowed in
the dim light.

Adela remained standing. "My mother's in the next room. Don't
make yourself comfortable."

"I brought you a Lotto ticket. With your regular numbers."

Adela didn't say anything, just looked at him, filled her eyes
with him: Yummy. But . . .

"Your daughter told me the operation turned out okay."

"Yes, it did. When did you talk to Maribel?"

"I called the waiting room at the hospital. She answered."

Adela sat down on the sofa, opposite Carlos's chair. She looked
down at her freshly polished toes, then at his smiling face. He reminded her of an overeager schoolboy, open face, smiling mouth,
green eyes like stone. She wondered why Fefa had let herself grow
fat and flabby, why she didn't color her roots more regularly or get
her nails done every Tuesday, when the bodega was slow. Why
didn't her friend care more? Why didn't she recognize and grab on
to what she had, what she could so easily lose?

"I want to console you," Carlos said.

"Oh, Carlos."

"Really, *querida*, I do. There's not one minute I don't think of
what you must be going through."

"Oh, Carlos."

He got up, moved the stack of letters onto the glass table, and
sat beside her. He took her hand, traced the outline of each finger.

"They're shaking, your hands."

"What do you expect?"

He kissed her cheek, her earlobe, her neck. Ay, *chica*. She closed
her eyes, and he kissed her lids. He turned her face and pressed his
lips to hers, gently teasing her mouth open with his tongue. His
mouth tasted like rum. Such intoxicating sweetness!

He rubbed her knee, the inside of her leg. Oh, oh.

"*Querida*," he whispered, before kissing her deeply again.

A loud noise outside made her jump back. "What's that?"

"Probably a cat, *mi cielo*. Don't worry about it, eh?" He reached
for her breasts. She was braless under her robe, and her nipples stood
at attention immediately through the fabric.

"My mother's in the other room, Carlos," she whispered, but the warning was halfhearted.

He unzipped the robe and cupped her breasts in his hands. "My precious beauties," he called to them. "My darlings."

He had a funny way of making love, Adela remembered. Every part of her body was given an identity, a name. Their purpose united in one: ecstasy. But suddenly she wondered if he acted the same with Fefa. Did he whisper, did he lick, did he grunt without differentiation? The thought was sobering, and she pulled away.

"What's . . . the . . . matter?" He was licking her neck now, between the whispered words. Undaunted, he pressed her against the armrest.

She couldn't do this to Fefa, could she? Fefa, friend and ally. Who trusted her. Who laughed with her. Who saved her the season's first mangoes. Actually, she couldn't do this to herself, could she? Could she?

He lowered his head to her breast. She could see his neck hairs standing on end, like tiny erections. He kissed, he suckled. Oh. Oh. Ay.

Chica, life was such shit anyway.

Maribel was nervous. She wished her mother or her grandmother could accompany her during this lesson.

"Relax," the nurse assured her. "It'll be okay."

The nurse snapped the lid off Victor's G-tube. Maribel held her breath.

"Now," said the nurse, holding a huge syringe in her right hand, "slowly you begin to push the formula into the stomach. Slo-o-wly. Like this."

The nurse began to inject the thick white liquid gradually. It was a special baby formula, chock full of nutrients and calories. About a half hour earlier, Maribel had watched the nurse feed him the same milk in a bottle. Victor had sucked hard at first, sweating profusely with the effort. He rested, then drank again. Rested, then sucked some more. Then passed out like a drunk. The nurse couldn't get him to suck anymore and he had consumed less than an ounce.

Maribel couldn't believe it: so much effort and struggle for so little. But the remaining liquid, about another half ounce, would be fed through the G-tube.

"Take your time when you do it. Real slowly. You don't want to rush it all in."

An alarm clanged somewhere, startling Maribel.

"Guess I'm a little nervous." She giggled.

The nurse smiled. Her name was Ellen and she wore a bear pin with a red bulb nose that lit up when you pulled a string. She had two children, including a six-month-old baby. Both were healthy. Did it upset her to work around so much sickness? Maribel had asked her. Oh no, never. It simply made her appreciate her children more. It made her appreciate everything more.

"Want to try?" the nurse asked her, and handed her the syringe without waiting for an answer.

Hands shaking, Maribel pushed the plunger. Slowly, slowly.

"Good, very good."

"I think he likes this formula."

"Looks like it. You'll see how big and strong he'll get."

Maribel clutched this hope to her heart. Victor was doing better. Big heart brave heart strong heart. Off the respirator, breathing on his own, he slept deeply and his sunken cheeks remained pink. But this small victory had exacted a price: her breasts, the breasts she had coddled in anticipation of nursing, throbbed with milk turned bitterly expendable. She didn't mind: her aching breasts were her sacrifice, and the throbbing somehow eased the pain inside.

That night, Victor had diarrhea. It was a lemon-green liquid and smelled like nothing she could name. The next day, the third day after the operation, the doctors switched formulas. The diarrhea did not abate. But Maribel and the nurse on duty, Ellen or Carmen or Mary Jo or Cynthia, continued the painstaking procedure of feeding him every three hours, first by bottle, then by syringe. By the time he left the hospital almost three weeks later, after countless turds of varying colors and textures, Victor had tried every formula on the market. Doctors finally settled, with some reservations, on a soy-based version.

13

Victor's formula was so rich and thick that Cuca could taste it for hours afterward. It filled her insides like a balloon, and she was constantly rushing to the bathroom.

"What's wrong, Mamá?" Adela asked her.

Cuca burped. "Oh, excuse me, but that milk . . ."

"What milk?"

"Victor's, the one they're feeding him in the hospital. It has such a strange aftertaste."

"How would you know?"

Cuca shrugged. "I can taste it in the back of my throat. Who knows why?"

Adela gave her a warning look, but quickly forgot the exchange. Her mind could not hold too many passions at one time, and currently it was brimming with Victor and Carlos.

The second formula the hospital tried made Cuca sluggish. It carried a faint mineral flavor; it was like eating a piece of chocolate with foil. She liked the third experimental milk the best. It was sweet, like mother's milk (Cuca had tasted her own), and creamy without being too dense, but it made her melancholic. And she knew how melancholy turned her skin sallow and made her breasts sag and her belly bloat and her hair kink.

It settled her into long periods of brooding. Today she had not done anything but brood. She had rested in bed until midmorning, when Adela, worried and annoyed, entered her room and demanded: "Are you sick?" With barely enough energy to toss the Print of Paradise comforter aside, she sat up in bed and nodded no, though she did feel heavy and slow-witted. After Adela left, Cuca studied the bright colors of her comforter, the green and purple and pink and indigo, for a very long time, long enough for her feet to fall asleep. She shook them and studied the comforter again because the colors were so bright and the print so appealing, and as she did, she began to remember the pain that had swallowed her heart for so many years after the deaths of her babies. "Remember" wasn't a precise enough word actually because she had never forgotten. Instead, she had learned to place the pain in a room in her heart, a room with an altar, like a flower-bedecked temple that she could visit when she needed or wanted to. Like now.

To lose a child was to lose one's sanity. To lose two was to desire death. And to lose three was to boomerang to a desperate hope, clawing through the anger, past disbelief and denial. When the miscarriages came, so bloody, demanding bed rest and concern from the family, she was stubbornly ready. But she wasn't ready for the surprises, the pinpricks and piercing thrusts to the heart of daily reminders. Any baby, spotted in his pram taking the air at the plaza, rendered her speechless. A mother bending down to pat a daughter's head paralyzed her. The smell of baby powder choked her. Everywhere, there were children, a bumper crop of babies. She seemed to be the only young woman in the pueblo who remained childless, and when Leticia, a friend since childhood, delivered healthy twin boys, she refused to visit. Entombed in her darkened bedroom, she locked her husband out and began her siege, welcoming, in a cotton nightgown and with black hair matted to her skull, welcoming an end to her sorrow, any way it came. By the third day, though, she was too hungry, too smelly—and her husband had macheted his way back in.

He bathed her. He spoon-fed her. In the night, he touched her limp body as the faithful venerate a statue. Eventually, something tripped in her heart. An insight, an epiphany, a realization that she wasn't going to die. Or worse: that uncertainty was the only certainty.

Still the pain did not disappear, no. It took new forms.

The L-shape of a knit baby bootie.

The sogginess of a neighboring child's diaper.

The pungent odor of sardines (which she always craved during pregnancy).

The melody of a lullaby.

The sight of a tall-backed rocking chair.

The smell of baby cologne.

The cry of a wailing baby.

The terry-cloth texture of a round bib.

The embroidery of ducks and bears on a towel.

The sun because it was the same sun her babies no longer saw.

The stump of the tree that had given wood for the crib.

Any lace trimming.

Bronzed baby shoes in a friend's living room.

A high chair, a stroller, a potty.

Every sentence that began or ended with the word "Mamá."

¡Ay! ¡Ay! Even now she could bear it no longer. The old sorrow sucked her breath away. She fell back and slept.

Mamá.

"Mamá! Mamá! It is three o'clock in the afternoon. Are you feeling all right? Mamá!"

"Adela, Adela, Adela."

"What's wrong?"

"Adela! You are real!"

"You're pinching me, Mamá. What's wrong? You haven't gotten dressed and your breath stinks."

"Adela!"

14

In the week that followed Victor's surgery, Maribel grew inured to
the night noises and the bright lights of the hospital. She slept well,
though nobody believed her when she told them. She slept straight
through the night, running past the darkness in one swift snooze.
The second-floor waiting room became her home, and with the
energy and righteousness of an avenging angel she tidied up after
other parents who left empty bags, scribbled papers, strewn blankets.
She settled into a routine between feedings, a routine that oriented
her to a familiarity that bordered on complacency. A tight schedule
allowed little time for her mind to wander. Mornings between 7:30
and 7:50, after Victor's feeding and before breakfast in the first-floor
cafeteria, she showered in a bathroom down the hall and around
the corner, a bathroom that only the nurses, ever sympathetic, knew
about. After breakfast, again between feedings, she read (9:30 to
10), she balanced her checkbook and analyzed her expenses several
times, always with the same numbers (10:45 to 11:30), she paced
the corridors for exercise (11:30 to noon), and she made lists of
things for her mother to do (12:45 to 1). After lunch, she clipped

interesting stories from the newspaper (1:45 to 3 p.m.) and in the afternoons (3:30 onward), she accepted visits—from Caleb, neighbors, Father Peace from St. Michael's, a co-worker or two. She expected, with hopeless desperation, that Eduardo would show up again. He didn't.

Adela and Cuca came every afternoon, laden with food for Maribel and songs for Victor. They serenaded the baby with classics: *Cielito Lindo, Naranja Dulce, Los Elefantes, De Colores, Los Pollitos,* and *Duérmete, Mi Niño.* They developed a following, and the admiring morning nurses waited for the singing women to arrive, even when their shifts had ended.

For Maribel, mother and grandmother alternated gifts: they brought her guava pastries one day, *café cubano* and oven-baked merengues the other, *pan de gloria* the next, chocolate eclairs and *señoritas* the fourth day. Maribel discovered, to her amazement, that she had a sweet tooth.

"No," said Cuca emphatically. "The sugar is what keeps your heart beating. I couldn't live without it."

Maribel did not laugh at the ludicrousness of her grandmother's statement; she simply held the illogical concept up like a ceramic bowl she might consider purchasing if the price was right. The accepting silence surprised Cuca.

One afternoon, Caleb brought Maribel a giant box wrapped in dinosaur-print paper with blue ribbon. Inside were twelve sets of preemie-sized clothes: pajamas, pullovers, pants, even a one-piece black-velvet vest outfit with a red bow. She kissed him in delight on both pockmarked cheeks. He apologized for not having had time to write her a poem.

The priest who had led them in prayer during the operation stopped by whenever he could. He still wore his navy polyester pants and white shirt and insisted on holding hands during the *Our Father.* In deference, she bent her head and closed her eyes when he prayed, even clasped hands with other parents, but she refused to cloud her thoughts with the possibility of God, the probability of true hope. Occasionally, though, between the eating, the bathing, the reading, the clipping, the balancing, and especially during the communal hand-holding, she entertained this fleeting yet indelible idea that horrified her: What if . . . what if . . . what if she was right? What if all this faith in a life after, in this cleansing of souls and redeeming of hardships, was a hoax? A cruel joke? Then what? *What?* She clipped faster, paced harder, read longer, and recited louder.

On the seventh day after the operation, with the blessing of the thoracic surgeon, the neonatologist, the geneticist, the cardiologist, and the nephrologist, she held Victor Eduardo in her arms for the first time. He fluttered like a captured bird before settling in close to her heart.

"Oh, my little man. My little king," she said, and tears rolled down her cheeks. Ellen the nurse patted them dry.

She felt a little awkward carrying him, though he was so light it was like carrying a down pillow. She adjusted his head this way and that, then his thin arms, and finally his feet. Oh, he was small!

"Does he look like he's all crumpled up?" Maribel asked her audience.

"No, he's perfect," Ellen replied.

"Chica," said her mother, "like every man, he's just the right size."

His skin was soft and pliant and pink; his hair stood on end, as straight and stiff as uncooked spaghetti. Teasingly, whispering *mi-cielo-mi-tesoro-mi-querubín*, Cuca dabbed the stray hairs with the violet cologne she had brought from home in her straw tote, then combed it to the side. Her bracelets jangled noisily, but Victor continued to sleep in his mother's arms. Adela took pictures with her pocket camera.

"I'm not pressing too close to his tube, am I?" Maribel asked.

Ellen laughed. "Relax. Look at you. You're an old pro at this."

Maribel sat in a rocking chair and rocked her big heart brave heart little boy. She could get used to this, all right. She could grow accustomed to aligning her body just so, like a curved nest, and rocking to and fro, to and fro, listening only to the inner music of this tiny soul. To and fro, to and fro. Ah, this helped the pain, it did.

"Mami," she asked Adela, "remember when Papi and I used to play the Chin Kiss Game?"

"Oh that."

"I'm going to teach Victor."

"*Mi cielo*, don't you think—"

"He likes it, Mami. He does." Maribel rubbed her nose against his beak.

"It might be better—"

"An Eskimo kiss. But we've done the finger kisses, the knuckle kisses, the elbows and shoulders and toes, too. The works." She pecked his ears.

"Oh dear."

Father Peace arrived with his mane of curly white hair, a stole, and a plastic bottle of holy water. At Cuca's request, he baptized the child. The ceremony lasted but a few minutes, and Victor did not stir when the holy water was sprinkled on his forehead. Adela took more pictures. To finish the roll, Ellen the nurse snapped a couple more photos of the three women with the baby: Maribel in the rocking chair, smiling as regally as a queen, Adela and Cuca at either side, preening.

Before his next feeding, to awaken his hunger and soothe his pain, Cuca sang him a folk song known for its magical healing power:

> *Sana, sana*
> *colita de rana,*
> *si no sanas hoy*
> *sanarás mañana.*

> Heal, heal
> frog tail,
> If you don't heal today,
> you'll heal tomorrow.

The song, suffused with memories of long ago, flung Cuca back to her youth when she had sung about frog tails and roosters riding on horses and elephants balancing on spiderwebs and bridges that collapsed over railroad tracks. Ay, such silliness! Such simplicity!

Remember, my dearest Tony? Remember?

Remember, hombre, when you bought me that rocking chair from that Polish Jew whose hands could create the heavens and the earth from a plain piece of wood? Remember how I sang our sons those songs, rocking-rocking-rocking in that chair?

Un elefante se balanceaba
sobre la tela de una araña.
Como veía que resistía
fue a llamar a otro elefante.

One elephant balanced
atop a cobweb.
When he noticed it supported him,
he called another elephant.

And:

Naranja dulce
limón partido
dame un abrazo
que yo te pido.

Sweet orange
cut lemon
give me the hug
I ask for.

And:

Duérmete, mi niño,
duérmete, mi sol,
duérmete, pedazo
de mi corazón.

Go to sleep, my little boy,
go to sleep, my sun,
go to sleep, piece
of my heart.

And:

Pipisigallo
montando a caballo,
Pasó la mula,
Pasó Miguel,
Mira a ver quien fue,

*Quita la mano
que te pica . . . el gallo.*

Pipisigallo
was riding a horse,
The mule passed by,
Miguel passed by,
Look to see who it was.
Take your hand away
or you will be pecked—by the cock.

Such nonsense words. Those melodies still make me tingle all over. Refreshing, like the cold baths you and I used to take in that old claw-foot bathtub during the long summers.

Remember when we rode in the backseat of Javier's sky-blue Buick Roadmaster, windows down, spirits up, hair whipping in our faces? How you shouted. How you sang. You were drunk, hombre, drunk on that hot rum and drunk with life and love and power. You wanted a car, too, an American automobile with no top and white wheels and long nose and an engine that roared. You didn't want your mule no more, no more. What would we have done with a car, eh? Riding with the dust in our eyes and bugs up our noses, at speeds only for God, over ruts and puddles in the unpaved roads. A car, ay!

Remember when your father rode his white horse into the bay in a storm? Oh, yes, remember! We weren't married yet. You were flitting around my house then, making eyes at me, a child of fourteen with a woman's body, full-breasted, full-hipped.

Wait, my father told me. Make him wait.

I did, reluctantly. Then your father rode his white horse into the pounding surf to rescue a boat that never existed, that only he saw.

Crazy family, my father said. I have been hearing about them. Crazy family. Miracle the horse didn't drown. Good horse, too.

He was a fine one to talk, my father. But he wouldn't let you in the parlor. Thought craziness might be catching. Almost two years passed before he forgot. Two years before emphysema and cirrhosis dissolved his memory. All the while, you still made eyes at me.

Remember those Sundays before the children, long before Adela came, when you walked with me to the plaza, then watched me enter the dim coolness of the church alone? Because you didn't want to follow. Because you preferred the company of men, their pretentious swagger and their loud boasts, men who exaggerated and smoked their cigars under the banyan trees, never losing sight of the church spires that jabbed the blue sky and swallowed their women. You should have come with me, you should have come along if only for the peace, the quiet.

And after church, remember? We went to your brother's for *arroz con pollo* and dominoes, and the men, they left the women at the table *again*, pretending they were off for a smoke, but we all knew you were marching over to El Viejo Felix's for the weekly cockfights. ¡Ay, que tonterías!

Remember the red hummingbirds in the spring and the song of the frogs when we crossed la Curva de Cantarana and the buttery taste of freshly baked *Panqués de Jamaica* and the colorful costumes I sewed for *carnaval* in Havana and your nephew Pedro's blow-out wedding to that snob from Oriente and making love on a blanket on the beach surrounded by sea oats and sand crabs (ay!) and the coal-black woman who beat the conga drums on the eve of Santa Barbara's feast and the snap of the sheets hanging under the hot sun in our back yard and the sickness that yellowed all the palms for five years and the moss that hung all weepy-like from the Witch's roof outside the pueblo and the *alcalde* who ran off with his partner's fourteen-year-old daughter, and the smell of night jasmine on summer evenings?

Remember?

I sing to Victor, that bright little star, and I remember. Tony, *mi hombre*, I remember so much. Too much.

Home that night for the first time in a week, Maribel was surprised by the dust, the dirt, the mess, the clutter. She thought she had left the house tidy just before Victor's surgery. Now this.

"Mami!" She knocked on the wall that separated the duplex.

Adela pranced over in her heels. She was feeling a mile tall tonight. Her gorgeous grandson was prospering—slowly, ever so slowly—and it was obvious to anyone who cared to notice his pink skin and his plump cheeks! Thank God. And then guess-who had left her a note in the mailbox:

Can't live without you. That's all it said. *No puedo vivir sin ti*. If Maribel were more of a confidante, Adela would have swooned right into the kitchen. *No puedo vivir sin ti.*

"Mami, look at this mess. The dishes, the newspaper, all that nail stuff. And the floor hasn't been mopped. Who was here while I was gone?"

Adela smiled sheepishly. "Me."

After Carlos's first visit, Adela had moved some of her stuff to her daughter's. It made his nightly sojourns into her life a bit more private and certainly safer. Cuca had a tendency to walk around the house in the middle of the night, talking to the air. And she had the ears of a bat.

"Whatever for?"

"Okay, okay," replied Adela, hands held up as shields against her daughter's onslaught. "It's a little messy, but it's not dirty. I mopped the floor this morning. And I dusted a couple of days ago."

"A couple of days ago!" Maribel rolled her eyes.

She marched into her room and slammed the door. Adela giggled. She felt like a derelict daughter, chastised for having left her chores undone—and this wasn't the first time. How had she ever allowed this role reversal to develop?

Adela surveyed the room. Yes, the newspapers were out of place. She had read her horoscope this afternoon, before leaving for the hospital, and forgotten to drop the papers back in the rack. Okay, Maribel was right about that. The dishes—well! One glass. One small, singular glass stood in the sink, filmy with dried milk. And the nail stuff, the nail stuff. There was the bottle of Seashell Pink she had used last night to touch up her fingernails, and a couple of cotton swabs. That's it. Nothing more, nothing less. No dirt, no dust, no sticky floors.

Adela sighed. She wanted to barge into her daughter's room and give her a piece of her mind: How dare you talk to me, the one who gave you life, the creator of your days? But what for? Adela knew Maribel had had an attack of nerves. Who wouldn't, after all that had happened. Ah, Maribel. She needed a little distraction, a pleasure to ameliorate the pain. Joy sprinkled among the sorrows, that's all that life amounted to, anyway.

She dialed Carlos to cancel their nightly rendezvous. He picked up on the first ring.

"Maribel's home," she explained.

He was disappointed. Good. Adela danced a little jig. He pressed her for another time, another place. She resisted. She didn't know Maribel's plans for the rest of the week, and she surely wasn't up to clandestine meetings at a sleazy hotel down on Southwest Eighth Street. She had a little pride, chica. She wasn't just a side dish, along with the plantains.

"I want to console you, *mi cielo*."

Consolation would have to wait a few days in this case. Not a bad thing. Time would make the consoling and the sympathizing and the kissing and hugging more effective when they met, that's all. And she wouldn't even daydream about their next meeting, no. She promised herself that. She'd let it percolate deep inside her for a few days, make herself hungry from deprivation, eager with anticipation.

Adela hung up and pressed her forehead to the receiver: he hadn't asked about the baby. Carlos hadn't asked how much Victor ate or how often, whether she finally had held him or simply sang him a song. Not a word, not a question. Yet, that was what she had desperately wanted to share with him. All the ride home, she had thought out how she would tell him about Victor, had even picked out the words and images she'd whisper over the receiver. And all of it had gotten lost in the discussion of time and place, of sex delayed. Details, details. He hadn't asked, and she had forgotten. She went outside and looked at the stars and listened to the crickets and sniffed the incoming rain. Winter nights were beautiful in Miami, clear and cool and tranquil, but now this one was spoiled somehow. Somehow, all she could smell was the rain.

Cuca was waiting for her in their kitchen, brewing chamomile tea.

"Have some," her mother insisted. "You need it."

Cuca had already let her hair down, and it hung like a white shawl over her pink flannel nightgown. It was strange to see her that way, stranger still not to hear the jangling of her bracelets as she moved around in the kitchen. Adela sat down with a sigh. She was more tired than she should have been: her bones weighed, her feet throbbed, her jaw, she was sure, sagged too.

Cuca joined her at the table with two steaming cups. "Adela," she said, staring steadily into her daughter's eyes, "isn't it about time you started acting your age?"

"What do you mean?" Adela put her finger to her lips, as if in deep concentration.

"I do not need to explain." Cuca sipped daintily from the cup. The tea scalded the roof of her mouth, her tongue. She blew on it, her eyes still on her daughter.

"Oh, Mamá!" Adela gestured wildly to underscore her words. "My age, my age. What *is* my age—the one told by the calendar or the one singing in my heart?"

Cuca did not reply. She simply kept staring at her daughter, steadily, steadily.

"And you of all people to tell me that, Mamá."

Much later, on the other side of the duplex, a deep, abiding sadness jolted Maribel awake. She was surprised to find herself in her bedroom, in her cherrywood bed, under the white eyelet comforter. The mattress felt too soft, too smooth, too ample.

Victor.

She sat up and turned on the night-table lamp.

Victor was alone in the hospital.

A cool breeze whispered in through the window. She shivered and pulled the covers up to her chin.

Victor was alone in the hospital without her.

She looked at the time on the clock radio: 2:37. Twenty-three minutes before his next feeding. Cynthia was on duty tonight.

Victor was crying. She could hear him all the way here, in her house. Would Cynthia hold him? That's probably what he wanted. Now he was used to being held. All it took was one hug, one melding of skin and soul, to accustom a child to his mother's arms.

She turned the light off and settled into bed. She needed to get some sleep. She needed her rest and her strength and her humor and her smile and her voice. She needed everything.

Sleep. Rest. Death. With the lights out, she thought of death. She thought of it as an eternal blanket of nothing, an inviolate space. But how would she know? Maybe it was a nice nap, a long rest. Maybe it was another dimension, a universe of sound and smells and sights we could not experience though it existed just the same. Death.

Waa-waa. She could still hear his cry. He was hungry early tonight. Oh, big heart brave heart, working up an appetite.

He would not die. He could not die. She wouldn't let him. She turned on the light. She could not get rid of the constriction in her throat. Maybe she needed some refreshment, yes. In the kitchen, she poured herself a glass of water and a mug of orange juice.

Waa. Waa. She could still hear Victor bawling. In the kitchen, with the lights on, the refrigerator humming, the crickets singing, the wind blowing, she still heard his cry.

He needed her.

Quickly she dressed. Quickly she closed the front door, got into the car, and zoomed west on Flagler, south on Red Road, and west again. She parked in the visitors' lot, under a bright light. Waa. Waa. She heard him so clearly now. He was just on the other side.

The elevator took forever, though there was nobody riding it at night. She sprinted down the hall, turned the corner, slammed the metal button on the wall to open the sliding doors to the unit. Waa. Waa. Waa. Waa. Waa. It was him, all right. Victor crying, Cynthia trying to soothe him.

"Victor!"

Cynthia was startled to see her.

Maribel's words rushed out of her mouth: "Why is he crying? Is he hungry? Does he hurt? What are you doing to him?"

"It's the G-tube," Cynthia replied.

"What?" But Maribel wasn't paying attention. She was stroking her son's face, cooing, humming. He had started to hiccup.

"G-tube's leaking," Cynthia repeated.

"What do you mean?" Maribel half expected an alarm to clang, a troop of doctors to march in for the rescue. But just one nurse? What was wrong with this hospital?

Cynthia lifted Victor's T-shirt. Bloody gauze circled the rubber tubing. Pain lacerated Maribel's heart.

"Oh, my God!"

"It'll be okay, Mom, it'll be okay." Cynthia rubbed her back. "We're taking care of it."

"But he's crying!"

"Of course. He's hungry and it hurts. There's a lot to cry about."

"Can I hold him?"

Cynthia hesitated.

"I'll be very careful," Maribel insisted. "I won't shake him. I already held him this afternoon."

Still wailing and hiccuping, Victor settled into her arm. He was sweating and his face was red with anger. His hair was matted down over his forehead.

"Oh, sweetie," Maribel cooed. "*Tesoro mío*. What have they done to you? Tell your mamá now. Tell your mamá."

She caressed his sparse eyelashes, rubbed his hot cheeks, cooed, cooed, a mother sparrow comforting her chick. Slowly, with sound and touch, she led him away from the pain and the anger and the noise and the dark and the tears. Slowly, slowly, no rush. She had all the time in the world, her whole life.

Eventually, he fell asleep. In her arms. Next to her heart.

Back home, Cuca waited for Maribel in a lawn chair on the porch, a blanket thrown on her shoulders. The rain had blown over, but the night had turned chilly, surprising for this time of the year, mid-April. Cuca's white hair glowed in the moonlight, and her voice was as soft as the fog and light rising in the east.

"I was worried about you, *hija*."

Normally Maribel would have chided her grandmother, but she had no energy left. Just a warmth inside, phosphorescent, radiating.

"Victor needed me, Abuela."

"I heard him crying, too."

Maribel narrowed her eyes, then smiled. She sat on her doorstep, next to the lawn chair, and was quiet for a while. She listened to the crickets, then to a plane rumbling overhead and the neighbor's cat prowling in the bushes. Adela's impatiens winked in the fading darkness: pink, red, purple, white.

"Abuela?"

"Yes?"

"How come it turned out like this? How come?"

"Ay, *hija*." Cuca sighed. It had been a long night, a long dark night, and without the entertainment of Adela and Carlos's gropes and grunts to shove the hours along, either. "This is how it is."

Then, after she had pronounced those words, Cuca wasn't sure if she really knew how it was. Maybe life had taught her nothing. Maybe eight lessons were not enough. Maybe seventy-seven years added to zero.

"Like how?" prodded Maribel.

"There are questions you don't ask, questions that have no answers. They are nonsense, *hija*. *Sin sentido*. We can't possibly understand everything, you know. Too much, there's too much for our little brain to comprehend."

Cuca paused. The crickets sang. The cat meowed. The flowers blinked, blinked, blinked. Above, the sky was empty, silent, dissolving into light.

"What does yellow taste like, Maribel?"

"Yellow?"

"What color is anger? Can you measure hope with a ruler? Does fear smell like dying flowers or baking bread? What shape does love take?"

"Abuela?"

"Yes?"

"It is round. Love is round, like a circle."

In the fading darkness, Cuca smiled. In the fading darkness, her bones creaking, her bad back whining, her husband calling-calling, she rose from the lawn chair and opened the door, holding back the bubbles of incorrigible mirth.

"I have to get some sleep, *hija*. This is the day I wash my hair."

15

Easter was a fistful of calendar days away. In Cuca's pueblo years ago, everyone would have been preparing for the visit of Casimiro, the midget magician with copper-red curls and eye-catching tattoos who always began his performances on the afternoon of Easter Sunday, in the empty lot beside Claudia the Witch's home. ¡¡¡CASIMIRO EL MAGO!!! his banner screamed. He tied the ends around two trees and let the banner flap in the spring breeze, though the letters had faded over the years and no advertisement was needed to announce his expected return. All the pueblo's children knew him, and they trudged en masse first down the cobblestone roads, then along the dirt paths to the outskirts of town where the Witch lived. Though their parents warned them not to, the younger children skipped out whenever they could, usually right after the big Easter meal or during siesta when the adults were too busy to notice. Even the older children, the teenagers, met their *enamorados* under the banyan trees, exchanging furtive kisses while the midget magician pulled white doves and brown rabbits from his frayed top hat.

One year, when Cuca was about ten years old, her friend Carmen volunteered to be Casimiro's assistant. He put her in a box the size of a child's coffin, muttered words over the closed lid, and made her disappear. Then he couldn't bring her back.

At first, everyone thought it was a joke. The younger children clapped and hooted. The teenagers continued to kiss under the cool shade. Casimiro seemed to believe it, too, for he chortled loudly and moved his small, hairy hands like wands over the closed lid again. Nothing. Casimiro tried, and tried, and tried. Still nothing. By now the younger children had stopped clapping; they fidgeted nervously on the flour sacks used as seats. The teenagers' smooching had given way to morbid curiosity.

Night fell and still no Carmen. The children returned to their homes, whispering along the way, not daring to make any noise that would awaken the malevolent spirits roaming the province. Casimiro, confounded and concerned, took the box apart, plank by plank. He searched the nearby woods with the help of the Witch and an oil lamp. No Carmen.

He was looking through a black leather manual when the men of the pueblo found him and chased him down a dirt road that led east to Matanzas. The men's torches threw angry heat and light at the incredibly fleet-footed magician, who managed to escape unharmed but without his magic book or his banner. Carmen's mother, who had not seen her husband for at least three years, wept bitterly into the night, assisted by other women who gathered in a corner of the plaza, their wails curling into the black sky like the exhaust from a sugar-mill smokestack. At supper that night, Rizos said Carmen could not find her way home. Cuca and her brothers were eating beans and yuca leftovers from the day's earlier festivities because their mother had joined the crying women in the plaza and their father was chasing the midget.

"There is no magic," Rizos said to Pepe and Cuca. "Only temporary blindness."

At dawn the next morning, a search party found Carmen sleeping on a mat of dry grass at the edge of the woods. Beside her lay the stray yellow dog Benjamin *el boticario* fed behind his pharmacy every night. Carmen could not remember being lost and expressed bewilderment at the town's concern for her safety.

"I guess I fell asleep," she mumbled.

Her mother slapped her, right there in front of all the nosy people who had gathered for the free show before going to the fields or opening their shops. For Cuca, the slap only confirmed the mother's ignorance and pettiness. Rizos agreed. Nobody forgot the incident with Carmen, but Casimiro returned the next year and every year thereafter, until he died of rabies. Carmen moved to Havana. By then Cuca had married and lost two babies.

Cuca remembered Casimiro the Midget Magician as soon as she smelled the honeysuckle seeping through the crack under the door again. This time she translated the scented mist like a spy deciphering a memorized code: he was coming home. A week earlier than expected, yes, but she knew in her bones and in her soul, as Rizos had known about magic and temporary blindness, that her great-grandson, flesh of her flesh, blood of her blood, two generations removed, was taking his place among the living.

And she was ready. Her kitchen/medicine cabinets were, at least for now, full.

After a cloudy beginning with threatening thunder, the morning turned glorious. It erupted in an April light that was pure and clean and sweet. Maribel could smell the outside air in the hospital; it overcame the usual stench of alcohol and shit.

"Hot date today, Mom?" Ellen asked Maribel.

"Hot as they come," Maribel joked. "I'm robbing the cradle."

Carefully, the two women slipped Victor's arms into the sleeves of a green cotton pajama, trying not to wake him. Maribel had preferred the black-velvet-vest outfit—it suited this special homecoming occasion—but it had no opening in the front to accommodate the G-tube. She reminded herself to check the rest of his clothes for the same problem as soon as she got home. Oh, so many details to remember—feeding times, medicine dosages, cleaning schedules, doctor's appointments. On and on and on.

"Look this way, Maribel," called out Adela.

Part of Adela's face was hidden behind the camcorder she had borrowed from Carlos and Fefa. She had never operated one before and the instructions Carlos had given her were flimsy, many of the details having been lost between gropes and kisses. Ah, well. Victor was coming home. Victor was coming home. That's all that mattered today.

"Mami, you're filming the floor."

"No, I'm not. I just turned it off. See? Here. Oh, I guess I am. The red light is still on." Adela laughed, and the trembling of cymbals and the ringing of xylophones filled the hospital room. She pushed the pause button, placed the camcorder on a chair, and started snapping photos with her own trusty pocket camera. The sleeping Victor posed with all the nurses, even an orderly who was captured for posterity with his eyes closed, a sheepish grin carved from a fat blob of face.

"Hope we never see you again," Maribel told each of the nurses, after thanking them.

"Yep," retorted a moist-eyed Ellen. "That's what I tell my mechanic, too."

Maribel waltzed out of the hospital, her feet barely touching the floor. She looked up at the lapis-lazuli sky; she sniffed the clean air; she felt the cleansing heat of the sun.

"Big heart, brave heart Victor, isn't it a beautiful day?" she proclaimed.

The baby responded with even breaths. He slept quietly, a speck of a child in the infant seat his mother had bought him for an imagined life that would never come true.

"Finally," said Maribel, as they packed the belongings in Adela's Ford Escort. "Finally."

"I feel," Adela added, "like I've won the Publishers Clearing House Sweepstakes."

The car started on the first try—surprise!—a healthy revved-up engine ready to race anywhere. Oh yes, it was a good day when the old clunker turned over just like that, a blessed hour. On the way home, as she sat in the backseat with her son, everything appeared new to Maribel. She stared out the window at other cars, other drivers, pedestrians, cyclists, joggers, little dogs and big ones, a calico cat darting after a squirrel, two shirtless boys playing catch in their front yard, a woman sweeping her front porch, another weeding her garden, and she wondered why she had never noticed the brightness of the colors that flashed before her or the graceful rhythm that defined all movement. Where had she been?

North on Thirty-seventh Avenue, nearing home, they got stuck in traffic for the dog track's weekend flea market. Maribel listened to the car horns, the shouts of the street vendors, the whistle of the policeman just ahead, the Spanish words that floated up in the air before descending with a plip-plop on the other side of the street. They were like a Gershwin symphony, these cacophonous sounds, simultaneously melodious and grating.

"Want a Sno-Kone, Mami?" she asked when she spotted Chucho in the corner.

"Why not?"

They ordered two reds. When Chucho realized the women were bringing the baby home, he refused to charge them. Maribel insisted. The drivers behind them leaned on their horns as the two argued. Finally, Adela drove off, leaving Maribel to pocket the two dollars.

"Let Chucho feel good, too," Adela said. "Let him feel like a man." Her fingers drummed the steering wheel, keeping the beat of an imaginary song.

Maribel suggested a stop at the bodega before turning homeward. She needed milk and orange juice. Adela readily agreed, insisted on getting the stuff herself.

"Hey, stranger," called Fefa as soon as Adela stepped in.

"Hey!" Adela answered, and then she noticed. Fefa wasn't looking too good. Chica, she was looking horrendous. Her roots showed badly now, telling white in the fading black, and she had gained weight overnight, it seemed, at least twenty pounds. Some pounds sat heavily in her jowls, and though Adela couldn't see because of the counter, she suspected the rest had settled in her already ample hips. Fefa looked old and spent and . . . yes, long-suffering.

Adela grabbed the jugs of milk and juice and took them to the checkout counter for a closer look. Oh, her friend looked past horrendous! She was positively gross—dark rings under her eyes, two-toned kinky hair, pasty complexion, dull stare, chipped nails, a rubber band choking her fat wrist.

"We're bringing the baby home," Adela announced, trying to keep from staring. How could anyone change so in three weeks? A slow, steady decline due to age was one thing, but this? No, this was something altogether different.

"That's good." Fefa's voice was flat.

"What's the matter?"

Fefa shrugged.

"Are you sick? Any of the children sick?"

"No, no, no." Fefa shook her head emphatically.

"What is it?"

"Oh, nothing." The way she said it gave Adela the chills.

Fefa rang up the purchase. Adela handed her a five-dollar bill and wondered where Carlos was. Fefa's appearance had side-tracked her intentions, and now she couldn't very well pretend to be looking for a can of peas or a bag of sugar, especially with Maribel and Victor in the car. Maybe if she dallied a bit, struck up a conversation, acted like she had forgotten something—bread, rice, ham. Distracted by her thoughts, she dropped the change Fefa had returned to her. Bending, she heard his footsteps, a sound she would recognize anywhere, and his voice booming as he approached from another aisle:

"Is that Adela?"

"Yes, Carlos, it is," replied Fefa.

"Hey, stranger," he greeted. Funny he should use the very same words his wife had. "You dropped your change."

He bent down and picked up the coins. On the way up, he caressed her ankle, her shin, her knee. It was a swift touch, but tingling all the same. Adela couldn't believe his boldness. Had Fefa noticed? She searched her friend's face for a sign, but Fefa had already moved on to another customer and her pound of green plantains.

"The children are in the car waiting," Adela mumbled, and rushed out with her bag.

Her heart seemed to beat right out of her chest, and her hands shook so much she couldn't grip the steering wheel. She must have blanched, too, for Maribel asked, "What's the matter, Mami? You look like you've seen a ghost."

In the Mickey Mouse–decorated nursery, the women gathered to welcome Victor home. Early-morning preparations of this very room had been both fickle and intense, with neither Cuca nor Adela able to make any decisions without heated discussion, and Maribel drifting through her shower, her grooming, her breakfast, in a fog. Adela had changed the crib sheets four times before settling on a cotton

that seemed soft enough. Cuca had rearranged the tiny plush toys—
a white lamb, a gray elephant, a brown monkey—this way and that,
here and over there, finally moving them to the dresser and propping
them against the wall. They had argued about the windows (open or
closed?), discussed the window shade (up or down?), and debated the
guests' placement (keep them in the living room or give them access
to the nursery?). They wanted the homecoming perfect.

Now, windows open, shade up, and room empty of visitors, they
watched Victor as he slept in this unlikely throne. They counted
his breaths, the twitching of his eyes, the times he sucked at the air
with his lipless mouth. Maribel believed the steady rise and fall of
his chest was as entertaining as the advent of television.

"A miracle," Cuca agreed. She did not want to leave the room,
fearful that whatever had cursed her baby sons would find its way
to the next male in her line.

Adela remembered the surprise and delight of Maribel's newness,
and Miguel the Scoundrel's rapt interest in his firstborn. His only
born—well, that Adela knew of. Chinita, he had called her. Chinita, and his words had stilled her cries during those interminable
evening bouts of colic. Chinita. Miguel. And Victor. Endless the
chain, endless immortality.

So they watched, the women, an immortal chain, and they giggled, and they told stories of each other's childhoods, memories that
were really fantasies twisted into reality. Finally, a few minutes before his feeding time, he cried—oh, glorious sound!—and Maribel
ran to the kitchen to warm up the formula and sprinkle in the rice
cereal as the nurse had taught her at the hospital. Proudly, she demonstrated how Victor clung to the nipple, sweating in his efforts to
drink, and she demonstrated, too, how the remaining portion of the
formula was injected slowly into the G-tube. Cuca and Adela were
mesmerized.

"¡Qué hombre!" Cuca exclaimed. She had never seen anything
quite like this. It was better than Casimiro el Mago's white doves
and brown rabbits. This truly was magic.

Later, they gaped as he reddened and strained to move his bow-
els.

"¡Mira! ¡Mira!" They shouted in unison and with glee.

Red, red he would get, and he held his breath and pushed and pushed, strained and strained, his eyes staring blankly back at them, his concentration so intense that the women cheered his efforts.

"It's the rice cereal," Adela complained, wiping tears from her eyes. "It constipates babies. It always does."

"I have a little something for constipation," offered Cuca. "My grandmother used to . . ."

"Abuela, I'm not sure he's ready for that."

"Pffft! First you must give him more water. Distilled water. Then . . ."

"Abuela . . ."

"Listen to me, *hija*. My grandmother would take onions and cook them in sweet beer and drink a portion of that for three days."

"Beer, Abuela? Beer?" Maribel laughed. It was a sweet sound, Adela thought, a sweet, sweet sound because it was so rare.

Victor continued to strain. At one point, he wailed loudly but briefly. The women gasped.

"I'll have to call the doctor," Maribel said softly.

"I'll have to get some psyllium seed," Cuca vowed to herself. "Doctors don't know everything."

When the straining and the pushing and reddening had passed, the women joined forces to clean him. Cuca got the tiny diaper— a doll diaper, an angel's cloth wing, she thought. Adela went for the moist Wipe-ees—oh, these Americans thought of everything, didn't they? And Maribel moved him to the changing table, pulled away the soiled diaper, and began dabbing his groin. It was not messy shit, not like the diarrhea of those first days in the hospital. Now the stool was hard as a baseball, and the color of fresh mud.

"*¡Bolitas de china!*" exclaimed Adela in wonder. "Look how tiny!" Indeed, they looked like pellets, only smaller.

"That's the only thing that is small. *Dios mío*, look at the size of his balls!" Cuca giggled. "Who does he take after? His father?"

"The nurses," replied Maribel, suddenly prim and huffy, "said all baby boys are born with swollen balls."

"Chica, and some men keep them the rest of their lives," Adela retorted, and laughed loudly.

Music filled the room. Church bells rang. A band played a *dan-zón*. A trumpet blared. The sounds were so clear, so real, so very near, that Victor's penis stood at full attention and sprouted a warm geyser of pee. This surprise did little to dampen the women's enthusiasm for the baby's bodily functions. They simply clapped appreciatively, and Maribel sighed with gratitude, for now she knew she had been baptized. Finally, finally, she had been welcomed into that mysterious sisterhood.

Over the next few days, Victor's face began to fill out. His eyelashes and brows thickened, his mouth developed thin lips, pink like a little girl's bow, and the prominent bridge of his nose, though still beakish, widened and appeared to fit in better with the rest of his face. His interest in the formula increased daily, and it was a pleasure for the women, a break in their routine, to watch him sweat as he sucksucksucksucked on the nipple, howling loud if one of them pulled it away, mistaking rest for sleep.

The windows were always kept open for fresh air and the shades stayed up for the spring sun. Cuca worked her magic, her temporary blindness, with an infinitesimal fraction of psyllium seed she bought from the Cambodian man who ran the Asian import store in the strip shopping mall on Flagler Street. Victor's stool turned soft and brown, the texture of clay used for sculpture. It was discussed at length by the three women every evening for size, shape, and weight. The Caca Committee, Adela teasingly called the meetings.

The milestones of development were small, perhaps unrecognizable to the world which measured progress with the popular child-rearing manuals. There were no first smiles, no turning over in bed, no raising of the head. And yet . . . yet . . . Maribel was sure Victor recognized her voice, for his hungry fretting stopped, at least briefly, when she talked to him. Several times he held her gaze, especially while they played the Chin Kiss Game, and the blackness she saw in those pupils was unblemished by knowledge or intent.

Every night Maribel slept in the twin bed she had moved into the nursery, and every night she left the hall light on. She adapted well to a life compressed between feedings. She enjoyed the meticulousness required for her baby's well-being, thrived on the methodical medical care that allowed little deviation. Though her day was predictable, there was a frenetic quality to it, a sense of having to pack in more than twenty-four hours' worth. But Victor was accommodating. He was such a good baby, Victor big heart brave heart was. He rarely cried and then only in hunger, a timid wail unable to disturb someone's sleep or hurt someone's feelings, or when the skin around the G-tube, which seemed perpetually irritated and red, oozed with stomach acid and spilled milk. But he never protested the medicine he took for his heart or renal troubles. He did not complain about soiled diapers, either, as other babies tend to do. Because his delicate skin blistered easily, Maribel was constantly checking him to make sure he was dry. She had discovered the consequences of a dirty diaper left against skin too long, when an angry rash spread over Victor's buttocks and scrotum after she had forgotten to change him between meals. She wept bitterly at her neglect, teardrops falling on her baby's face like soft rain. But he had simply stared at her, yawning once, twice, forgiving her inexperience. Ever ready with her apothecary, Cuca had tended to the diaper rash with compresses of Maalox and chamomile.

No visitors came. Caleb was in Montreal for a conference and to drum up corporate sponsors for a study on Latin American consumers' brand preferences. He sent postcards almost daily, short greeting verses on the back of the Botanical Gardens at Maisonneuve Park, St. Joseph's Oratory, Château de Ramezay, Basilica of Mary. The dwindling Canadian winter made him cryptic, turned him inward.

> Angels caught in the snow
> Wings trapped in cold
> Looking for your face.

Another time he scribbled in his shy, condensed script:

> A ship sails past its dock
> A gull flies southward, beyond its nest
> A sailor, the captain complains, has forgotten to pull in his net
> Only I have not forgotten your eyes, your smile, the way you
>   hold your head.

Maribel received a note on lined paper from Eduardo, too. Unsigned, postmarked Naples, a town on the other side of the state, the three-sentence letter carried his imprint, if not his name. There was no doubt in her mind that he had written it, and she treasured it as a young widow cherishes the only photograph of her soldier husband. "Come sale away with me," he printed in block letters, apparently unaware of his misspelling. I ♡ U. How is the baby?"

Time seemed to have met land, the Sun wedded the Moon, and the stars winked in the dark, if anyone cared to look.

16

Who's the woman in the mirror? The woman with the black hair and slanted eyes and broad cheekbones? *China. Mi muñequita china.* She applied the blush carefully over those bones everybody so admired and powdered her mouth the way her mother had taught her, to prepare her lips for color. Pat pat pat. She traced the outline of her lips with her pencil, then crayoned in the color over the powder. She took a tissue, folded it, pressed her mouth against it. Smooch. A perfect kiss, the shape of her son's heart. She applied the lipstick again, a ruby red that infused her face with a glow, but this time did not blot the color on the tissue. Lips, ruby lips, solid and long-lasting. Color of a rose, a heart, a cherry, an apple. She stared at her reflection: Maribel, I do not know you.

She considered dabbing on some perfume, just a teensy-weensy bit behind the ears, but decided against it. Perfume would make this seem like a date, an official meeting, and she wanted nothing to hint in that direction. She couldn't bear it, and it would be unfair to him, too, wouldn't it? Still, here she stood in black pumps and a linen coatdress, lips red and moist as a plum, ready for her foray into the world she had forsaken. It wasn't going to be pleasant, this outing. It was going to be just like a visit to the dentist, something you did without wanting to, for a greater, imagined good and not momentary pleasure. At her mother's insistence and Caleb's persistence, she had agreed to leave the house for a couple of hours. To walk in a room she had never visited, share a dish she had never eaten, converse about something other than diapers and feeding schedules.

"*El mundo te espera*," her mother had said. "The world awaits you. You are young."

Well, the world could wait, if it was up to her, which apparently nothing was anymore. She had carved, with the scalpel of her fear and the hammer of her pain, a contented complacency from her cloistered surroundings. It was the only way to stay the course. Except for rushed visits to doctors' offices, she had not left the duplex, not even walked to the corner, since she arrived with Victor from the hospital, and the mere opening of the front door—wind rushing, birds trilling, traffic honking—pushed her adrift in a turbulent sea she could neither control nor name. She had no need for this confusion. Secluded, monastic, ever vigilant of her big heart, brave heart bird-boy, she clung to the anchor of the familiar and predictable. This did not prevent her, as Adela suspected, from drawing small satisfactions from the mundane. She still reveled in the spring's growing warmth and the longer days of approaching May and the crickets' song at night, but it was a celebration behind closed doors. Until this. Why had she agreed? Foolish fool. She could have pleased Caleb with a simple thank you. She could have repaid the caring, the concern, the poems, all of it with a smile, a touch to his hand. That's the way Caleb was, low maintenance. But no-o-o, she had weakened in a moment of indecision, because her mother and grandmother thought they knew it all when they rarely conceived of anything that was not backward, barbarian. Oh, foolish fool. Foolish Chinese doll.

She tottered to her kitchen, where her mother was rinsing dishes. Adela was always dressed for a party, short hair fluffed and clean, eyeliner smooth and black, clothes stylish and fitted. Maribel realized that if not for her mother's influence she would have tended to the slattern, despite her maniacal sense of order.

"You look stunning as always," Adela observed approvingly. Chica, her daughter could be a real beauty, if she tried, if she smiled. She had good genes, good bone structure.

Caleb arrived shortly, dressed in a dark gray double-breasted suit and baby-blue shirt, thin red-striped tie knotted hard against his neck. Adela thought he appeared dashing, if not handsome, and if you didn't look too closely at his thick, uneven brows, the blue eye that remained at half-mast, or the scarred cheeks, he looked a little like Mel Gibson. A little.

"Where you off to?" Adela asked to fill her daughter's silence. Really! She had taught the girl better.

"Sushi." Caleb smiled and his perfect teeth flashed white.

"I have to be back by nine," Maribel said curtly, and thought: Raw fish, yuk! I'm going to eat raw fish!

"*Buenas noches, mi rey,*" Adela singsonged to her sleeping grandson. "It's you and me tonight. You and me against the world—if your other grandmother doesn't decide to intrude."

She put her manicure box on the dresser and opened the TV tray table she had dragged into the nursery.

"Don't worry. She probably won't come in jangling her bracelets or mumbling any *brujería* over her herbs. She's organizing her cabinets. That should keep her busy into the next century."

She brought the portable radio from the kitchen and put it beside the manicure set. She looked around for an outlet and plugged the radio in.

"I wish you could listen to music round the clock. It is good for the heart. And the mind, too, I guess, but I don't know as much about that. Anyway, my sky, my sun, my king, you and I will listen to this music as soon as I get this old thing working. Maybe we can dance a little merengue, cheek to cheek. Would you like that, eh?"

Adela stretched the antenna as far as it would go, and then moved the radio around until sound blurted from its speaker:

Miénteme una eternidad
que me hace tu maldad feliz

> *Y qué más da la vida*
> *que es una mentira.*

Summoned by the music, Adela began to dance beside the crib of her sleeping grandson, heels clicking against the tile like high-pitched maracas. She wiggled her hips, shimmied and sidled and sashayed until the song came to a close. Then she sat on the edge of the bed to catch her breath.

"It's ... kind ... of ... like sex ... you know, *mi . . . cielo.*" She fanned her face with her hands for several minutes. "Yes, it is, dancing is. Both put a little oxygen in your blood and springs in your feet. Oh, yes, yes, yes."

She stood to look at the baby. Victor was sleeping quietly, head turned right.

"Good music," she thought aloud, "calls for a celebration, don't you think? I'll have to go into my hidden stash."

Adela found four Coronas in the utility room. She stuck two in the freezer for a quick chill and returned to the room for another look at Victor.

"I'm back, *tesoro.* Missed me? Need me? Love me?"

She caressed his cheeks. He felt unusually warm, but maybe that was because her hands were cold from the freezer. She sat on the bed and started painting her left pinkie with Poppy Red. Olga Guil-lot's soulful voice returned to the radio with another song, *La Noche de Anoche.*

"Listen, *mi rey*, I want to plan a little. Give you something to look forward to. I don't want you to think that this life is like what you see here, full of silence and routine. Life is so much more. It is color and music and flowers and men's cologne and a kiss on the lips. It's a lot of things. You know?"

She looked through the crib slats at Victor. He was twitching. He appeared restless. Hmmm.

God, it feels good to laugh! thought Maribel. I like the way it rumbles up my belly like a burp, then explodes out my mouth. Hahahahaha. The joke wasn't even that funny. I just wanted to laugh.

The sushi wasn't bad, the ambiance passable, the company superior. Caleb was a good storyteller. Still, her mind flitted to Victor again and again. Was he sleeping? Would her mother remember to change his diaper? Was he still fussing?

"First," Adela said, "I would like to take you to the beach, to see the sun rise over the ocean and watch the gulls tiptoe to the water's edge and all the people march to the shore with their umbrellas and chairs and balls and tanning lotion. You would love that."

She blew on her nails, then sprayed them with a drying agent. The color was . . . shocking? No, it was eye-catching. It drew the eye to her hands. She had a young woman's hands, soft and sleek. She had made sure of that. No man wanted to be touched by hard hands.

"Then I would like to take you to a park with lots of swings and monkey bars and a fancy store with marble floors and soft music. Give you a taste of the good life, no?"

She stood over the crib to look at her grandson. He was still sleeping, but his face was pink and his hair was matted with sweat.

"Hot, *mi rey*? Maybe I'll bring the fan. It is getting a little warm here."

She brought the fan from the living room and turned it on. That meant she would have to raise the volume of the radio to be able to listen to the music, but she was afraid of waking the baby. Well, she could listen to music any old time. She turned off the music. Now then, her right hand, pinkie first.

"Back to the fun, *tesoro*. We could also go see a mountain, visit an Indian reservation, make a snowman—though, you know, I don't care much for snow. The people up north, they live with the heaters on all the time. Horrible what it does to your skin. You can always tell the women who have lived up north. So wrinkled!"

She blew on her right hand and headed for the kitchen. She moved one beer down to the refrigerator and opened the other. Aaah! Aaah! She danced back to the nursery.

Adela thought she heard a soft whine. She looked down at Victor, but he continued to sleep. His hair was dry now, but his skin was still flushed.

"Yes, we would go somewhere cool. And, chico, for sure, I would take you back to Cuba. Not to live, no. For a visit. Now, that is a real country. The sand in the beaches is sugar, *tesoro*, pure sugar. Imagine building sugar castles with your pail and shovel, eh? Sugar castles. And we could ride our horses into the mist of the green hills and drink the coconut milk for breakfast. Would you like that?"

She took a long swig of beer. It was good, refreshing, but nothing like the coconut milk of her childhood. There was nothing quite like that, really.

Eight-twelve, and they were waiting for dessert. Maribel had wanted to skip it, come right home and rush into Victor's nursery. But Caleb had assured her there was plenty of time. They were fifteen minutes away, and that was in traffic; he could probably make it to her house in ten.

"Relax," he insisted, but she had already drifted away. He had lost her during the story of how the Iroquois had attacked Montreal.

Victor, she thought. My big heart brave heart bird-boy.

The waiter brought the ice-cream sundae, but suddenly it turned insufferably hot in the restaurant. Sweltering. Beads of perspiration formed on her upper lip; sweat dripped under her breasts and armpits.

"You okay?" asked Caleb. "Your face is flushed."

"I feel feverish," she replied.

He leaned over and felt her forehead. "Lord God!" he exclaimed.

They skipped coffee.

"I don't know what your mother has told you about me. She can be harsh in her judgment, but I'm sure you'll be able to figure things out on your own. I may not raise you well—well, by some imagined standard, I mean—but, *mi rey*, I will raise you with love and laughter. That's for sure."

She set the empty beer bottle down on the TV tray table and stood. The beer made her feel light-headed. She had never been able to drink well, maybe because she was small and slight.

"Oof! I think we have celebrated a bit too much. One beer and I'm ready to dance on the tabletop. Hey! That's an idea!"

She touched his sweet face, that face she loved beyond reason and logic and imagination, and jumped back, startled. He was burning. A spasm of terror shook her. Victor was burning with fever. What should she do? She ran next door, hollering for her mother. Cuca stopped her halfhearted cabinet organizing and followed Adela next door.

"¡Ay, *Dios mío!*" Cuca exclaimed, hand on forehead. "He is burning."

"What are we going to do, Mamá? I don't know what medicine to give him."

"Quick, let's get some cool compresses on him."

Adela rushed to the linen closet, grabbed washcloths. In the kitchen, she poured water into a dishpan and brought everything to the nursery. Then she searched for the thermometer while Cuca applied the damp, cold washcloths to the baby's forehead, neck, and chest.

"Oh, dear, the milk is leaking out of that tubing," Cuca called out.

Adela hurried back to the room. "It is something else, too. Not milk, something else."

Victor began to cry. It was a weak wail at first, but then it grew louder, louder, loudest. His face turned crimson. The thermometer showed 42 degrees Centigrade.

"Oh, he's going to die!" blurted Adela.

"We have to continue to sponge him off."

The two women worked frantically. Both broke a sweat. Adela cried. How could this be? How? How?

Cuca began to sing to him:

> *Y si vas al Cobre*
> *Quiero que me traigas*
> *una Virgencita*
> *de la Caridad.*

> And if you go to Cobre
> I want you to bring me
> a little Virgin
> of Charity.

In accompaniment, Adela clucked her tongue to make a light maraca sound.

> Yo no quiero flores
> Yo no quiero estampas
> Lo que quiero, Virgen,
> es la libertad.

> I don't want flowers.
> I don't want prayer cards.
> What I want, Virgin,
> is liberty.

Cluck, cluck, went Adela's maracas. Dance, dance, went her hands, her fabulous hands.

> Y si vas al Cobre
> Quiero que me traigas . . .

The baby quieted. Adela went for more tap water. They sponged him again. It was just past 8:30 p.m.

Adela fled to her bedroom on the other side of the duplex. She attacked her night table. Pushed aside old newspapers and unopened letters, dress patterns, *Vanidades* magazines. Tossed her books across the room. Threw the spool of green velvet ribbon and the stack of Lottery tickets and sweepstake entries against the wall. Found a black lace push-up bra she thought Carlos had taken. And then—aaah! There she was. Her Virgen de la Caridad. Black heavenly hair and black toes over blue sea and tiny dark hands folded in prayer.

"*Por favor, mi Virgencita,*" Adela pleaded. "*Por favor.*"

Maribel did not wait for Caleb's car to come to a complete halt before she jumped out and bounded through the open door of her duplex.

"Victor! Victor! Victor!" she cried. Oh, she knew she shouldn't have left him.

It was so noisy in the emergency room. Too bright, too smelly, too full, too everything. Noise, noise, noise. Lights, lights, lights. Everyone shuffling, moaning, asking questions. Hell. This was hell. The other side.

Victor, the emergency-room physician told her, had an infection.

Infection.

The fect goes in or on. The ions of infect. The ins and outs of fection. How does that work? How do little organisms creep under your skin and enter your bloodstream and attack?

Caleb's voice. Oh, he was in command. He asked questions. Yes, no, maybe, it was like this but if you tried that and we will talk to the surgeon, of course. Words ran together. Good Caleb. Constant Caleb.

"Maribel." Caleb shook her gently. "What medications is Victor on?"

She was surprised she remembered them.

Caleb and the physician conferred again. The phone rang. Victor's surgeon was on the line. Yes, yes, they had checked the G-tube. Yes, it was working fine.

"It leaks too much," Maribel said softly.

Yes, the skin around it was very tender, inflamed. Yes, the patient's mother was putting gauze around it.

"It leaks too much!" Maribel shouted.

The patient's mother insists the tube leaks too much, the doctor passed on. Make an appointment? Yes, okay. Say hello to the wife.

Next the nephrologist called. Long conversation in a mysterious language. So many fancy words. Maribel wanted to hold Victor, comfort him. He seemed so tiny in that big white stretcher. A fly on snow, a cinnamon crumb on rice pudding. Her bird-boy. Big heart, brave heart. But at least he was not crying. The fever had abated. They had won. They had won.

They waited. Admissions. Overnight. Observation. Precautions.

No, no, no. Not the hospital again. Victor, Victor, Victor. Victor Eduardo. When will this suffering be over? The white-clad doctor slipped out through an opening in the curtain, on to another patient, another tragedy. Maribel was allowed to hold the sleeping baby while the nurse started an IV with a stronger antibiotic.

"*Mi cielo*," Maribel cooed, and then began to weep. She could cry now, Maribel could, without making a sound. The silence of her pain was deafening.

Later, in the hospital room, she looked out the window through the black latticework of treetops at the starless night sky. A full moon, as white and round as a scoop of vanilla ice cream, hung over the city. Maribel noticed it was not wearing a wedding dress. The clock across the hall in the nurses' station ticked noisily: tocktock-tocktocktock.

Over in her daughter's side of the duplex, Adela finished the last beer from her stash and fell asleep on the couch, heels and all. She sank into a restless sleep, fraught with misplaced dance steps and forgotten sweepstake entries.

In the kitchen on the other side, Cuca drank whiskey straight from the bottle. Oooooh! how it burned her insides. The hot liquid gurgled around in her stomach, along with all the food she had devoured in an attack of nerves after Maribel and *el americano* had rushed the baby to the hospital. Sighing, she twirled the blue feather she had just found in the baby's crib. It was soft and small and very blue. Bluer still than the one she kept in the kitchen cabinet.

17

Doctors' offices, with their muted conversations and long waits, intimate questions and hopeless answers, elicited odd musings from Maribel. She and Victor visited so many—the cardiologist, the geneticist, the nephrologist, the neonatologist, the pediatrician, and now the surgeon—that the offices were becoming interchangeable in her head, a parade of pastel-colored rooms with vinyl-and-chrome furniture. In her case, frequency had engendered neither interest nor pleasure. She hated waiting in the foyers, hated how the rest of the patients stared at her son, whispered among themselves, accused, doubted, misspoke. Some were bold in their ignorance.

"What's wrong with him?" one mother asked at the pediatrician's the other day.

"There's nothing *wrong* with him," Maribel retorted, venom in her voice. "He has a special condition."

The woman recoiled in fear. She took her little girl's hand and moved to other seats. Maribel got so angry that just to keep from marching across the room and slapping the stupid woman's face she had to bite her lower lip until it bled. But she also was relieved that Victor was sleeping and hadn't noticed. He sensed those snubs.

She resented the fathers who accompanied their wives, too. She turned her face away when they cooed at their babies or rough-housed with their preschoolers. Their doting, their pride, their obvious pleasure in the flesh of their flesh, blood of their blood, made Eduardo's absence more conspicuous. She cursed him under her breath, cursed the twists of life that had led her to be alone. Alone like her mother. Alone like her grandmother.

Doctors' offices also made her wonder why the medical profession preferred to wear white. White shoes, white slacks, white lab coats. White simply reminded patients of butchers, plus it contrasted so sharply with the vermilion of blood. Why not black? Now, there was a thought: the absence of light, the negation of possibilities—and black hid imperfections so well.

Hearing someone call her son's name at the surgeon's office, she shook off morbid thoughts and followed a nurse inside, leaving Adela in the foyer with her purse and blue baby bag. The nurse closed the door of the examining room. On the pale pink walls hung two framed certificates with the surgeon's name, one from the University of Miami/Jackson Memorial Hospital, the other from Shands in Gainesville. A mobile of papier-mâché planes twirled gently under an air-conditioning vent. A small metal tray with various scissors, tweezers, and other tools lay near a sink toward the back of the small room.

"Mrs. Garcia?"

The surgeon—Mr. Humpty-Dumpty, she called him—had entered her room now. He smiled, fiddled with his stethoscope.

"So the tube is leaking a lot?" he asked, reading from the chart. His deep voice rumbled like the bass on the stereo of a souped-up car. He had deep-set brown eyes, like small buttons sewn on a plush toy, and a flat, wide nose.

"Yes, the skin around it is always raw."

"Hmmm." He warmed the stethoscope against his white lab coat and then listened to Victor's chest. He examined the wound on the side, where two months ago he had spliced, sliced, and stretched to perform a miracle. His hands were gentle, slow.

"Healing well," he commented, which was true. "Now let me see the tube."

The surgeon touched the opening, felt the skin around the baby's stomach. He looked and touched for a long time, long enough for Victor to blink awake. The surgeon shook his head. He took a syringe and inserted it in a small side opening in the G-tube and sucked the air out.

"Now we've deflated the balloon at the tip," he explained.

With a yank so swift that Victor didn't even have time to cry, he pulled the tube out. Maribel felt her insides rip. She didn't dare look at the gaping hole in Victor's belly.

The surgeon examined the tube and the small balloon at the end.

"The tube's okay," he observed. "It seems to be performing as it should. How much is he eating now?"

"About two ounces." Her voice sounded so mousy. She cleared her throat.

"Whoa! Two ounces every time?"

"No, not every feeding, but he's doing it maybe half the time."

"Good." He called for a nurse on the intercom, then turned back to Maribel. "I'm going to help the healing along a little."

The nurse entered, a young, solemn-faced woman in white slacks and pea-green top. The doctor mumbled something to her and she slipped out, returning shortly with a brown bottle, gauze, cotton swabs, and other materials Maribel could not identify.

"We're going to cauterize the wound, Mrs. Garcia."

"What exactly does that mean?"

"Well, we get rid of the dead tissue around here"—he outlined the opening—"and hopefully prevent the spread of infection."

Maribel felt her intestines twisting into knots. She did not think of pressing the doctor for details. Carefully he inserted the G-tube into Victor's stomach and turned back to the nurse.

"Would you like to hold him or should I ask my . . ."

"No!" she answered quickly. "I'll hold him."

She took him in her arms and stretched him flat on her lap. The doctor sat on a low stool and rolled over to her. His gloved hand reached for the brown bottle, the gauze.

"Silver nitrate," he said.

Maribel did not know what the compound was, but somehow she remembered an old black-and-white photograph she had once seen of her grandmother in a petticoat, with laced-up boots and a big bow in her hair. Wasn't silver nitrate what photographers used?

The surgeon moistened the swabs. Slowly he dabbed the edges of the wound. Victor screamed. He screamed so loud Maribel could not tear her eyes away from his terrified stare of surprise. She smelled the burning skin. He screamed so shrilly that miles away Cuca dropped a plate she was soaping in the kitchen sink, and in the doctor's waiting room Adela peed on the doctor's furniture (much to her chagrin).

The surgeon swabbed the wound twice. The screams pierced Maribel's heart both times. She felt her belly button engulfed in flame. The invisible blaze seared her clear through to the back.

"I think this should take care of it," the surgeon said.

"It better," she retorted heatedly. "That hurt him."

The surgeon did not reply. Victor's crying was eventually replaced by hiccups. Maribel's hands shook as she placed him back in his infant seat. She dried his wet cheeks, then her own. She kissed his nose, cooed. So much suffering, she thought, so much pain. For what!

Maribel felt the hole in her stomach, just above her navel, growing, expanding, becoming the size of a golf ball. Look, she wanted to yell at the world, can't you see my intestines? Look how my stomach acid bubbles and oozes like Victor's? She was fascinated.

When Caleb visited, she tried to show him. She had lost all shyness with him, if she had had any before.

"It's there, Caleb, it's there." She lifted her yellow-striped pullover and showed the hole burned into her belly. "See the opening?"

She traced its outline, so vividly red in her eyes that it glowed. Could he not see it?

"Sympathetic pains," Caleb said, and grinned.

But she knew he did not believe, that he did not see. How could that be? It was so . . . so visible!

"You don't see it, do you? Tell me the truth, Caleb."

Caleb stood up from the chair and went to the kitchen.

Just before he had arrived, Maribel had tossed a piece of lemon down the disposal and the fresh citrus smell filled the air. He poured himself another glass of Coke. Today he was dressed in blue jeans and a Tommy Hilfiger collared pullover. He was going shopping for Mother's Day presents and had invited Maribel along. He wanted to make a day of it, strolling the outlet mall, eating at the food court. Why, he had planned it to the minute, just as Maribel liked her day to be. But now, after last week's rush to the emergency room, she did not even sit out in the porch. Her boundaries, instead of receding, had moved even closer to corner her.

"Caleb?"

"No, I do not see it, but you know, Maribel, it does not matter if I don't see it. You feel it, don't you? You see it, don't you?"

She nodded emphatically.

"Then that's all that matters."

They were silent for a few moments, Caleb sipping his soda, Maribel staring down at her stomach, not understanding her friend's inability to see. Jangling bracelets announced Cuca's entry. She walked in holding a steaming cup of catnip tea. It was not as good as garlic for a sore throat, or as good as chicken soup for that matter, but what could she do if her granddaughter refused those other time-tested remedies? If only she could show this child that ignorance was simply the turning away from the obvious.

"*Buenos días, señora*," greeted Caleb.

"*Señor*," Cuca replied. His Spanish was getting better, Cuca thought, and he could charm the straw hat off a *guajiro*, but heavens, that man's face needed a little rearranging.

Cuca set the cup on the coffee table. "Drink it all at once and try not to take a breath in between."

"I'll choke."

"No, you won't. I have seen toddlers drink this in one swig and nothing ever happened to them. It's the only way to loosen the phlegm."

"Abuela?"

"Yes?"

"Do you see the hole in my stomach?" Maribel stood close to her grandmother.

"Ay, *Dios mío*, look at that!" Cuca reached out and marked the exact configurations of her granddaughter's hole.

"See?" Maribel told Caleb triumphantly.

"The skin is so red, *hija*. I think you need to put . . ."

"It doesn't hurt anymore, not since yesterday at the doctor's."

"Still, *hija*, that is so raw."

"When I move around, I think my intestines are going to fall out, but they haven't."

Caleb stood again and refilled his glass in the kitchen. Maribel knew the conversation was making him nervous.

"Caleb," she called after him, "you think I'm going crazy, don't you?"

"No, no," he said quickly. "I just don't want you to hurt."

"It doesn't anymore. Really. I wouldn't even have noticed if I hadn't changed into pajamas last night."

"In my pueblo," Cuca volunteered, "such wounds are called stigmata."

"Oh, Abuela." Maribel laughed dismissively. "Those are for religious fanatics."

"Not always."

"Really?"

The fleeting doubt pleased Cuca. She walked out to the porch and performed a cha-cha-cha step.

After Caleb left, Maribel washed the glass and dry-mopped where he had paced. She didn't like the shadow mark shoes left on the white tile. Then she prepared for Victor's sponge bath. This was her favorite time of the day. She enjoyed playing with him, cooing and giggling and singing, watching him watch her. And when he watched her, she felt she knew more than the doctors' learned knowledge, more than their passel of theories. Unlike theirs, lifted from between the covers of a book, replicated and regurgitated, her knowledge was original and without peer, stored in her heart, not her brain.

"How's my big heart brave heart boy?" she asked Victor as she placed him on a hooded towel on the changing table.

She removed his shirt, his socks, his diaper. She inspected the skin around the G-tube. It was dry, yes, with a lining of new scabs. Hers was just plain red.

"*Mi rey*, I have a hole just like you. Except mine is brand-new."

He stared into her eyes. She loved it when he held her gaze. She felt they were communicating on a level beyond words, one that was pure emotion, unadulterated by labels.

"Want to play the kiss game, *mi rey*? You like that so much."

She began mopping his brow with the moist wash towel, then his face, his ears, his neck. She was very good at giving him baths because she was methodical, just as in her house cleaning, always working from the top down, left to right. A couple of weeks ago, Adela had insisted on trying to help, and by the third time she had dipped the washcloth in the warm water, she had forgotten the last limb she had cleaned. Maribel was furious at first, then forgiving. Her mother would never change, and it was unreasonable to expect she could. It was like demanding that Victor sing or walk.

"Press your fingers to mine, *mi cielo*, *mi rey*, *mi tesoro*."

She cleaned each of his tiny fingers. They were shaped like his father's, thick at the bottom and tapered near the nails.

"Now the knuckles. Yes, very good. Then the wrists. Hey, you're getting the hang of this."

She sponged his upper chest, bony still, but now filling out. At least it didn't look like it was caving in between his ribs anymore.

"Let's have the shoulders kiss. Yes, yes. And the elbows. Oooh! What a smooch."

She dabbed carefully around the G-tube, stroked his balls, up around his butt, round and round his thighs, before moving to his knees and ankles. She cleaned each toe carefully, one by one.

"We'll skip the ankle and toe kisses because I can't get my feet up."

Victor let out a little cry of complaint. He sounded just like a hungry bird.

"Oh, sweetie. Look, I'll make it up to you."

She leaned over to kiss his knees, then each of his toes: one-two-three-four-five, one-two-three-four-five. She dabbed him dry. He gurgled with pleasure. Victor liked to be rubbed and stroked, she once told her grandmother. Like every man, Cuca had replied.

She wrapped him in his diaper, fitted him into his T-shirt, and slipped on his socks. He began to whine softly.

"No, no, I haven't forgotten, *mi cielo*. I just want to make sure you're not cold. We'll finish the game. I promise."

She dabbed some violet cologne on his stiff hair, combed it to the side. He looked just like a little man. A bird-man.

"Okay, okay, the hair kiss. Good. Now the ear kiss and eyelash kiss."

Victor groaned with pleasure.

"And of course the Eskimo kiss. Nose to nose."

Rub-rub-rub, mother to son, nose to beak.

"The cheeks. Right, *mi rey*. Always right first. Now left."

He could not smile of course, and he could not talk. He could not communicate in the language of this world. He never would. But he purred and moaned and groaned, and they were beautiful sounds, a timeless song.

"We're finishing up, *mi rey*. Tatatatum: the chin kiss."

In the kitchen, the wall clock stopped.

The cuckoo clock had come with instructions in English and in French, no Spanish whatsoever, and no one seemed to be able to make the damn thing work. Miguel sat at the kitchen table in his undershirt, fiddling with the key and the levers. He had bought the clock for Maribel from an old Cuban man peddling wares downtown on Flagler Street. Adela was angry, angry at the money he had spent for a stupid clock that did not work, angry that he had quit his latest job earlier that morning, angry, too, that Maribel stood so patiently and so eagerly by his side while he tried to figure out how to get the clock to tick.

"Incredible," Adela muttered from the living room, where she sat soaking her feet in a warm bath of Epsom salts. She had weathered a frenetic day at the beauty shop, teased and curled and combed and dyed more than a dozen clients' hair, until past eight o'clock. Tomorrow, Saturday, her first client, who wanted both her nails and her hair done, was scheduled for 7 a.m.

"Incredible," she repeated, this time louder, to make sure Miguel and Maribel heard her.

Neither acknowledged her presence. She sighed. The clock, Swiss-made and too large for any wall in their tiny duplex, had been a bargain for twenty dollars, Miguel said. She scoffed at the suggestion but had to admit the clock was a pretty, if ostentatious, ornament—for another house, another family, another time.

"Incredible!" she shouted. "I can't believe you spent twenty dollars, a week's worth of groceries, for a stupid clock. Do you have sawdust for a brain?"

Miguel stopped his fiddling long enough to look up at her benignly, as one glances at a misbehaving child who will be reprimanded at a later time, in private. He curled the tips of his mustache.

"And what about the job?" she asked, hands flailing as her anger grew. "What was it this time? An overbearing boss? A bigoted *americano*? Too much work for too little pay? Substandard conditions? What? What?"

Her words echoed in the silence of the room. Miguel did not even deign to look at her. He whispered instead to Maribel, their heads bowed conspiratorially over the clock.

Then Maribel began to jump and clap. "Mami! Mami!" she shrieked.

Tick-tock, went the clock. Cuckoo! went the blue wooden bird. Cuckoo!

Maribel threw her arms around Miguel's neck. Square chin on his daughter's shoulder, green eyes smug with knowing satisfaction, Miguel stared across the room at Adela and smiled his expansive smile, the smile that began at his lips but spread upward to his eyes and cheeks.

Late one night, Adela was bidding goodbye to Carlos through the back door when she heard it: a keening so baleful that it stopped her cold.

"What is that?" she asked.

He shrugged. He wanted one last kiss, and she had pulled back from him to listen to that woeful sound.

"Is that a cat?" she insisted. She glanced over at the bushes and at the neighbor's yard, then at the sky, so dark, so ominous. There were few stars and only a sliver of moon. Evenings were turning muggy now, in preparation for summer. From somewhere far away, she could smell the night-blooming jasmine, sweet and cloying, a scent of her childhood.

"Don't you hear it?"

"Yes, of course."

"I can't make out what it is."

"*Cielo*," said Carlos, exasperated, "it's a woman's lament. Don't you recognize it?"

She shooed him away and let herself into her daughter's house with her spare key. She followed the keening past the foyer, through the living room, down the hall, to its source. There, over the crib, stood her crying daughter, barefoot, bundled in her peach robe, and as wilted as a collar waiting to be starched. The weeping was, yes, a woman's lament but also more, a mother's dirge. In the shadows of the nursery doorway, Adela watched as the tears ran down her daughter's cheek, so many, many tears that they formed a puddle at her feet. Endless those tears, endless. She watched as Maribel leaned over to stroke the baby's face, hiccuping now with the rhythm of her grief. She heard nonsense words, soft cooing, a language she did not understand, a voiceless prayer. And tears, still more tears, always tears. A flood with no end. Still Victor did not stir.

Then Maribel looked up, straight into the penumbral hall. Her eyes glowed with moistness, two beacons of sorrow.

"Who's there?" she called.

Adela stepped into the dim light of the nursery. "I came to see what was wrong."

Maribel did not reply, and Adela did not dare break the silence again, not so much for fear of waking up the baby as in sudden realization that, at 3 a.m., she was still dressed in gold high-heeled sandals, black pullover, and jeans. How would she explain? But Maribel did not notice her mother's attire. For a long time, both watched Victor sleep. Minutes elapsed, perhaps hours, maybe days. Neither knew. Neither cared. Victor slept, Victor breathed, Victor lived. That's all that mattered. And somewhere during that period of time, hour or day, decade or century, daughter's hand met mother's across a great divide.

"I'm just tired of hurting, Mami." These words were spoken so softly they did not break the silence, only continued it in another octave.

For a moment Adela glimpsed the image of her daughter as a pigtailed child coloring within the lines in her first coloring book. Adela began to cry, a weeping chorus of low notes.

"I'm scared something is going to happen to him when I'm not watching, Mami. No, worse. I'm scared of what will happen to *me* after it happens to him."

"*Sabes, mi cielo*, it takes enormous courage to love. To connect with someone is the biggest leap in the dark you will ever take."

Adela wanted to add that many, herself included, leapt, only to miss the other side altogether, but Maribel was sniffling and there was no need to add reality to misery. And anyway, the fall didn't stop people from trying, did it? Did it? Chica, here it was three o'clock in the morning and she was dressed to go to a party. What did that say about leaping?

Maribel shut her eyes hard against the light of the Mickey Mouse lamp.

"Yes, Mari," Adela whispered, using a nickname she had not spoken in two decades, "just close your eyes and step ahead. Step ahead."

18

The impatiens wilted in the late-spring heat. Their petals drooped, their leaves crinkled, their stems leaned against each other, a shriveled, multihued assemblage. Adela began to dig them out, the pink ones first, for their soft coloring seemed to make them more susceptible to Miami's sweltering weather, but of course she eventually would pull all of them out, the reds and whites and fuchsias too, and leave the flower bed that bordered the duplex with nothing but black soil until autumn, when she could replant and enjoy the parade of color once again. Her neighbors often told her that this was a lot of work, spring planting, fall planting, unplanting, digging, spraying, fertilizing, weeding. They sat in lawn chairs on their porches, sipping soda or *guarapo*, probably a rum drink or two, watching her on her knees and in her straw hat until something more entertaining passed by, like a couple of men in drag or a shoplifter running from the flea market's security guards. The women never had time to sit around for too long, though. Always too damn much to do around the house, and the heat discouraged even the best intentions. But the men, they were thick-skinned and slow and knew everything about anything. (Dicks apparently gave them that knowledge, a special power of sorts, even if the men had stopped using them for anything but waste disposal.) The men in her neighborhood, most retired or nearly so, most with paunches that confined them to a straight-ahead view, came over sometimes to offer their opinions and their advice. They pointed their cigars at a caterpillar or a mealybug, expounded with exaggerated waves of their arms. She listened and smiled, smiled and listened. Then she did what she damned pleased. Chica, it was the only way to deal with men.

Just last fall, Luis from down the block had stopped at her yard while walking his German shepherd. He twirled his thick gold chain as she dug. He did not move when she began slipping each impatiens and its dirt-bound roots into the moist holes.

"You need to plant them closer," he called out.

The dog barked in agreement.

She wiped the sweat collecting on her upper lip with the back of her gloved hand, turned to look at him, and smiled. She was digging six inches apart, just as she had always done, just as the instructions called for. And damn if she was going to change that.

"They're too far apart now, the holes," Luis called out again. "They'll take too long to grow together."

She nodded again. Idiot. Five years ago, defeated by chinch bugs, Luis had poured concrete over his entire front yard. In the summer, if one looked east from Adela's porch, heat waves rose from his paved yard. Still, here he was giving free—and unwanted—advice.

More and more she was beginning to feel men behaved in ways she wasn't sure she wanted to accept. The Americans had a way of putting it, no? Couldn't tell their ass from a hole in the ground, men couldn't. Didn't know the difference between their two heads, men didn't. Take Carlos as a for instance.

Carlos. The mere mention of his name did something to her insides. It watered down her anger, weakened her resolve. Oh, those strong arms. That muscled chest. The slow hands. His tongue, his mouth, his kisses, his sucks. Oh. Oh. Oh. But—she stabbed the ground hard with her spade—consider Carlos. Already he was getting a little demanding. Like she owed him. Like he owned her. He just expected things. Expected her to be available and willing and eager. And then acted like he was doing her a favor. Chica! All because she had said she was concerned about Fefa's health.

"Fefa doesn't look too good," she had told him one night. They were lying in each other's arms after lovemaking. (Great session, by the way, the kind that lasted an eternity and eventually made you beg-beg-beg.)

"Yeah, well," he replied. He nuzzled her neck.

"She does. I'm worried about her."

"She's okay. Just getting old."

"It's more than that. Has she gone to see a doctor?"

He shrugged, then kissed her nipples.

"You should get her to a doctor. She looks like she's got cancer."

He stopped kissing her breasts and leaned on his elbow, stared at her in the dim light of the night-table lamp. His green eyes twinkled.

"I mean it," Adela repeated. "She looks like a cancer is eating her up from the inside."

"Don't tell me what to do."

"I'm suggesting." She pulled him back and kissed him deeply. Ay, could this man kiss! But even with his tongue down her throat, she couldn't get Fefa's haggard countenance out of her mind.

"*Mi cielo,*" she whispered, nipping at his lips playfully, "you should take her. Make an appointment, put her in the car, and drive her there."

"Mind your own business."

"It is my business. She's my friend."

"And I'm your lover."

"Still."

He got up from bed and began to dress. She loved the swirl of curly black hair on his lower back and wanted to reach up to stroke it. She didn't.

"Don't leave mad."

He didn't reply.

"Look, I was only trying to help. I do care for her."

"You're not my mother, okay?"

After he had left through the back door, Adela could hear her mother's occasional snore.

Now she thrust the spade into the soft ground with all the festering anger of the past week, for all the nights she had waited for him to call since their discussion about Fefa. That's what she liked about gardening: the pure physicality of it. It was dirty, yes, and she was always careful to wear gloves and wash her hands carefully and apply lots of moisturizer afterward, but nothing matched the feel of yielding soil or its wet, mineral smell or even the grainy taste of earth. (She always spit dirt out as soon as it touched her lips or tongue, but she had heard of women who craved its taste and texture.) Only sex and dancing came close, she thought. Sex, dancing, and gardening—her physical entertainment, her relaxation and excitement. So much alike, but each so different. All three could be done slowly or quickly, and were considered actions of leisure, though it was quite difficult not to sweat or feel spent if one performed any of the three masterfully. But her gardening remained a solitary affair: the digging and covering, the pruning and clipping were fun only when done alone. Alone with one's thoughts.

¡Ay, chica! She hoisted the bucket full of wilted pink impatiens to the side of the house and dumped its contents in the large metal trash can. She supposed she could save them somehow, but she liked starting anew, preferred fresh, perky plants every season. Maybe that was one of her problems, a character fault: always wanting something fresh and unused. She returned to the front of the house and knelt beside the red impatiens. She mopped her brow with the back of her hand.

Cuca occasionally lamented the fact that Maribel was alone. She hinted that Maribel's ways, her maniacal sense of order, her oppressive loyalty to routine, had driven Eduardo away. Not so. Slowly Adela was beginning to understand that women were not the ones who drove men away, as if men were oxen to be led by rings in their noses or stallions that startled easily when surprised. No, no, no. Men *chose* to go away. As she pulled the first of the withered red blooms, it struck her how the three generations of women in her family were variations on a theme: her mother widowed, she divorced, her daughter abandoned. They had not pushed their men away. They had not tossed them out, or ignored them, or turned their backs on them. Yet here they were: alone. Neither by choice nor intent, mind you, but alone all the same.

She pulled at the drooping blooms angrily, one after another, quickly, until her bucket brimmed full again, and the space where the red impatiens had blinked and winked turned bare and black. Good. She walked over to the side of the house and dumped her dying plants in the metal trash can on top of the pink corpses. Overhead, the sun crawled up, up, up, a gradual ascent. She knew she had to finish before 11 a.m., before all her energy was sucked out of her, before the outdoors became an open-air sauna.

She knelt and jabbed the earth once to the right, then twice to the left. She repeated those motions again and again, digging up the fuchsia blooms like a mechanical hoe. The very same hands that had cut, combed, teased, curled, straightened, and tinted the hair of thousands of women could also excavate with expertise. They were hands of many talents and many uses, no? Just last week they had run the length of a man's body, from shoulder to private parts and back, in one swift, irresistible caress. Last night, they had rubbed Victor's congested chest until he breathed more peacefully. And now, now they were one with the earth.

There was a unique smell to these withered flowers, a vegetable faintness that was simultaneously attractive and disgusting. Unwillingly she thought of Carlos's sweat after lovemaking, the muskiness she longed to bottle one minute, then sought to turn away from the next. There she was again, thinking of him. Imagining, wanting, wishing. Tonight. Not now. Tonight. Nights were when she needed a man. Nights were when she forgot her resolve.

Days? Days were easy and populated. Days stretched out like cats in the winter sun. She had gone so long without men during the day that it was only in the closing hours, when the demons had to be put to rest, that the insatiable yearning rose from her loins. Chica, nights were so long!

Cuca did not like the baby's cough. No, not one bit. She lay in her bed, covered by the Print of Paradise comforter, staring at the bumps and ridges of her low ceiling, thinking of the dry, hacking cough that made the milk come up through his G-tube. How could she be expected to sleep worrying like this? Ay, Dios. The pediatrician had sent him a mild expectorant, but it had done nothing. Doctors knew nothing, anyway. They were in it for the money.

Dinero, dinero, dinero. Life, it seemed sometimes, had been reduced to that.

Bad cough, said Rizos.

Oh, Rizos! Cuca exclaimed. *Long time no talk.*

That's like a cough from our youth, sister.

Not TB, no?

No. A bad cough, though, a very, very bad cough.

I prepared a little boneset for the baby and—

Some Eupatorium perfoliatum, eh?

Show-off. Cuca giggled. *Forget the Latin. I started putting a little of the watered-down boneset tea in his formula four days ago, three times a day, and nothing.*

Hmmm.

Yes, and Maribel, I'm afraid, is becoming suspicious of me.

Well, yes, you were always the sort to be suspicious of.

Rizos?

Yes?

He's going to get real sick, isn't he?

You're always trying to get me to help you with the future.

Come on.

No, sister. That's why I stopped visiting.

Rizos? Rizos? Rizos!

Damn her brother. She pulled at her loose hair, trying to sit up quickly in bed to get a better look at his streaking star as it disappeared from her room. Ouch! She had wanted to ask about the ephedra (*Ephedra sinica?* he would have teased) but hadn't been given the chance. She was hesitant to use it on a child so small. It was a powerful herb, so powerful it stimulated the heart and increased blood pressure. A risk she dare not take. Damn Rizos. Damn-damndamn!

It crept into his lungs stealthily, a bandit on stocking feet. It clogged, it filled, it took control—bacteria known as pneumococcus.

Victor cried now with every little movement. He wheezed. He choked. He was comfortable only when propped up by pillows, happy only when the women sang. They had taken turns all day in their serenade, and now, as night closed in, Maribel crashed into the inevitable. She refused to wait for further instructions over the phone.

"I'm taking him to the emergency room."

"What does his pediatrician say?" Adela asked.

"I've done everything he's told me to since this morning, and the fever hasn't gone down."

"Go! Go!" Cuca insisted. "You must go!" Rizos's visit had pestered her for the past three nights. The issue needed to be settled, she knew.

Within minutes, they had packed the baby's bag and were zooming south, then west, then south again and west. Sometimes it seemed to Adela that she did not need to steer her car, so familiar was it with this trek—south on Thirty-seventh Avenue, west on Flagler, and south again on Red Road. Nearing the hospital, Victor began to cough. He hacked hacked hacked. He turned red. He gasped for breath.

"Mami!" screamed Maribel. "He can't breathe! He can't breathe!"

Adela swerved like a drunk woman from the left lane, nearly missing a white van passing on the right, then stopped hard on the grassy swale across from a pink house with white shutters. Cars honked. Someone shouted a curse.

Victor's feverish flush was giving way to a pallid blue. He was shivering and only the bloodshot whites of his eyes showed.

"Do that thing to his mouth!" Adela shouted.

"W-w-what t-t-thing? W-w-what t-t-thing?" Maribel shuddered to Victor's shivering beat.

Adela opened the door, hopped out, and jumped into the back. "Like this! Like this!" She put her mouth over Victor's and inhaled, exhaled. Victor coughed harder, gagged, then coughed again, letting a green wad of mucus fly right into his grandmother's gasping mouth. Adela shot back, surprised, than spit on the car's carpeted floor. Victor began to breathe again raggedly; the uneven breaths seemed to take all the energy he could muster.

"He was choking on the phlegm," Adela cried, trying to catch her own breath.

She staggered back to the front seat, and though her hands shook and her knees wobbled, she managed to get the car started after only three tries. She eased herself into the westbound traffic without using indicator light or mirror, only a strong sense of conviction. She turned where she needed to, without taking note of the street, and headed steadily to the night lights of the hospital. She could not hear Maribel sobbing. She didn't see the cars darting out of her way. The remnants of Victor's phlegm tasted sweet and hot in her mouth, like room-temperature vermouth before dinner.

In the emergency room, with its familiar sounds and smells, the physician listened to Victor's heaving chest. The diagnosis was prompt. The X-rays, he said, would certainly confirm it: pneumonia. Victor was put on oxygen to help his breathing, and penicillin dripped into his veins through an IV. He was admitted to a different unit, where Maribel had to learn the nurses' names all over again. Though the workers' faces changed, the ambience did not. The linoleum remained nondescript, as did the walls and crib and chair. Austere, an old vocabulary word from high school, was what came to Maribel's mind when she settled in.

She tried to sleep in the room's gray recliner, wrapped in the hospital-issue white blanket, but the noise of the clock outside kept her awake. Its hands made a staccato sound—ping-ping—for every second-change and clapped plunk-plunk when they moved up to the next minute. So distinct was this sound in her head that it drowned out all the other alarms and bells of the hospital. She tried for a long time to ignore the ping-ping and plunk-plunk, but it echoed in her head, underscoring the pain in her chest. She lifted her shirt and looked at the hole the surgeon had burned into her. Still there. It glowed now like a Christmas light, and its edges remained red and slightly tender, though she couldn't truthfully say it hurt. No, her pain had nothing to do with her physical being, not a bruised muscle or a torn tendon or stretched ligament. Her pain was something else entirely; she could describe its jagged thrusts in detail as it changed patterns and movements. Sometimes the pain ran straight like the infinite lines she had once studied in geometry. Sometimes it was circular, without beginning or end, self-contained. Other times it displayed a herringbone pattern or houndstooth check or paisley print. Many times it looked like Egyptian hieroglyphics, defying translation. Always it made her think, as she thought now: If *I* feel this, how much must Victor, big heart brave heart Victor, suffer? She winced.

The clock continued to ping-ping and plunk-plunk outside. Exasperated, she turned on the TV set. She flipped through the channels until she found something pleasant: Annette Funicello at the beach. She wished she were at the beach. She wished she were a child at the beach with her Abuela and her Abuelo and her father and mother, chomping on cold watermelon from the cooler. She wished she was four years old again, with little knowledge of the world and even less of English, and the sun beating on her shoulders and the fishies nipping at her heels and the endless ocean extending past a horizon she could barely make out in the brightness. She wished for summer and for Sunday and for simplicity. The intense wanting of the past, the pure yearning, seemed to soothe the thrusts of her pain. Memory was an ointment, a salve.

She remembered how summer Sundays dawned with the glorious explosion of lights and chirps. She remembered the inviting scent of simmering onions and garlic wafting into her bedroom from her grandmother's kitchen, jolting her awake when everybody was asleep, everybody except Cuca, who was frying plantain omelets and potato omelets, lots and lots of them. Barefoot, Maribel would walk to the other side of the duplex, following the garlic and onion scent that knew no walls, to watch her Abuela place the plantain and potato tortillas, one by one, on pieces of wax paper inside a large pot. Cuca did it always in the same way, tortilla–wax paper–tortilla–wax paper, predictable as the tide.

Abuelo Tony awoke with first light, too. Before breakfast, he lit his cigar and puffed large clouds of choking smoke. Cuca cursed at him, tossing her long braid back. He laughed and pinched her butt, fled into the yard. As the gray mist of morning turned to brightness, Maribel watched him from the window, pacing in front of the house until he had almost finished his cigar; then he came back into the house to drink the *café* Abuela had put out for him.

Spotting her in the corner, he'd shriek: "¡*Dormilona!* Sleepyhead! Hurry, if you want to come along."

Maribel peeled off her pajamas, struggled into her swimsuit and thongs, and followed her grandfather to the bathroom, where they both brushed their teeth with loud gurgling noises. Off they went, hand in hand, to the bakery on Thirtieth Avenue to pick two box-fuls of pastries.

Maribel's mouth now watered at the thought, at the memory of the smell and the taste and the sight of the neat rows of pastries in the refrigerated window of the bakery. She longed for a baked me-rengue she could devour in two bites or a sugar-topped *pan de gloria* to dunk in *café con leche*. (Oh, Victor, if you could only taste such delicacies! When we get out of this prison, you will. You and I, we'll go to the bakery and eat whatever you want, however much you want.)

By the time Abuelo Tony and Maribel returned home with the pastries and two fresh loaves of Cuban bread, her mother and father were puttering about. Miguel was dressed in blue swim trunks but shirtless. Adela was applying her makeup.

"Bring anything for me, *mi muñequita china?*" Her father called out.

"Now, Miguel," her grandfather would answer sternly, "you know the pastries are for the beach."

But as soon as Abuelo Tony disappeared into his side of the duplex, Maribel slipped her father a chocolate eclair. Pleased, he tousled her hair and wolfed down the sweet. She climbed onto his lap and listened to her mother singing in the bedroom: *"Coge tu sombrero y póntelo. Vamos a la playa, calienta el sol. Chiribiribi para-papá, chiribiribi parapapá."* Get your hat and put it on. We're going to the beach, the sun is warming up. Chiribiribi parapapa . . .

Until now, it had never occurred to her that her grandfather might have willingly left the pastry boxes behind so she could do what she enjoyed most: be her father's little China doll. The reali-zation filled the empty spaces of the hospital room. It stilled her heart. She wiped the tears from her cheeks and stood to look at Victor. He was whimpering in his sleep, pink with fever. She knew the television bothered him, so she turned it off. But he still fussed. His eyes seemed to have sunken in on either side of his beak. His tiny mouth twitched. The ping-ping and plunk-plunk of the clock outside was making him restless. Anger bubbled in her like yeast in dough, anger at her helplessness to maintain routine, to stabilize her life or his. Of having no say.

She marched out of the room, into the hall, and five or six yards down to the nurses' station. A young black woman with cornrows looked up from a medical chart and smiled.

"Will you turn off that goddamn wall clock!" Maribel shouted.

"We—"

"Shut the damn thing off before I break it. My baby can't sleep with its noise."

Maribel marched back into the room, leaving the startled nurse mumbling in her wake. The clock was moved to a utility room and kept under sheets. A red stick-on circle was placed on Victor's chart, a warning to staff. The pediatrician and neonatologist offered advice, and the social worker left a pamphlet for a parents' support group. Maribel laughed in their faces and behind their backs. What did they know of the spasms and twists of the spirit? What did they know of heaven or hell? Had they ever stared into the depthless dark of the beyond? When had they ever danced with an angel?

Victor's fever succumbed to modern medicine on the fourth day. His breathing turned smooth, his skin cooled. He choked less and less on his phlegm.

"Out of the woods," said Dr. Rothstein.

"Beat it again," said Dr. Herrera.

Maribel nodded. She knew there would be an again again, but she also knew that eventually, in the land of no time, she and Victor would go to the beach, Crandon Park or Hobie Beach or South Beach, with a red pail and shovel, blue thongs, and striped swim trunks, singing: *Chiribiribi parapapá, chiribiribi parapapá.*

Every night of the week Victor remained in the hospital, Adela downed a shot of vermouth before dinner. Alcohol, Cuca told her, would kill the sly bacteria that had invaded the baby's lungs. And the old woman was right: it did. Adela didn't develop so much as a cough, and the taste of vermouth never left her mouth. Never.

19

Random thoughts from the Beyond:

So much thrashing about! So much fight and struggle and resistance. Let it go, my darling wife, my Cuca. That's what I want to scream at her. To her and to our daughter and to my precious grandchild who is now a woman with a child of her own. All these women, tantas, tantas mujeres, in an endless struggle.

If they could see me. Oh, but Cuca does, doesn't she? My essence she sees. That fire we called soul because on earth we must label everything; we must tag it and sort it, put it through some point of reference. But yes, she can see my fire, that which has existed forever, before my time on earth, and will live forever afterward. Forever. Let that word caress her tongue, roll out her mouth, out into the open. Forever. Forever. A concept so difficult to explain. Nothing to compare it to because everything we have known is finite. Birth and death, that is all our finite little minds can understand: beginning, end. Our grasp is so pitiful, our intellect so minuscule. Forever.

I see them, my child and my child's child, the product of my loins, that which came from many nights of something so beautiful, and I suffer with them in the body that once cloaked me, with the feelings that once assaulted me, but something beyond that, my soul, that kernel within all of us, comprehends that the suffering is temporary, a blip in the time line. Blink and you will forget it. But how do you tell this to somebody racked by life's events?

I remember, even now in the fire-essence of my being, separated from the struggle, having ceased the thrashing forever, and comfortable about it, I remember waking in the middle of the night and finding Cuca at our bedroom window, staring out at the fields, past the outhouse, toward the ceiba tree, where the three little stone markers gleamed in moonlight. The pain, you could stroke it with your hand.

With all its anguish and convoluted turns, there is a certain majesty to life. Watch for it.

A little about myself: I was never old. I died thinking myself young. Died? Ah, such a useless word. An earth-word. A life-word. A word that must serve its purpose: to frame a concept, to make tangible what is intangible. I can explain it better. I passed to another world, another life, still thinking I was young. I crossed the boundary in my sleep, from one state to another, that easily. A massive heart attack. I faintly remember a sharp pain in my chest and then a sudden easing, floating away, a rush to light, music, angels, light light light so much light only light light light. And peace. That peace is indescribable.

The peace. After the blinding, glorious light, that is what you notice. You are still seeing, but your sight is all-encompassing. You are still feeling, but your touch is not reluctant. You notice the peace before anything else, I believe, because it is so different. There is a starkness to it that mesmerizes, but a soft simplicity, too. You want it. It calls to you and more than anything else you desire it. The yearning drives you to move toward it, but of course you have no control. You cannot move as you once learned to move, with your legs, willing your muscles to do your bidding. No, you do not move, because it carries you like an ocean current. That peace, and you say, ah, ah, ah, that is what I have always been seeking, tranquilidad, this is what I have wanted, something that feels like silk but is warm like wool, and comforting, and serene, and all-knowing. Finally. Finally.

I knew to live at only one speed. Intensity was both my grace and my undoing. I died because of it. I crossed the boundary because I wanted so much to hold on to what I had. How pitiful! What I had compared to what I have now—I will not bother to explain. It is inexplicable, the bounty of now.

And still, it is not as though you do not miss those you love and those things that brought you measured joy. I reach to touch the velvet of my Cuca's skin, for the pleasure of the connection, but she is untouchable, another dimension entirely. How many times have I shouted at her only to realize that my voice, this fire-voice that is part of this essence of my being, is but a whisper. She hears, it seems, only when she wants to, and then pleads for what I cannot give her. She must continue her life without my guidance. She can only draw comfort from me, a sense of security from memory.

I had a great deal of education, for my time and place in the world. Eight years. It was enough to learn that wisdom is not knowledge, though sometimes, if you are a good listener, the former rides the coattails of the latter. The school I attended was built by the district, not too far from the clump of trees people later began to call the Witch's Woods. It was a one-room building with wide windows that we opened for a breeze and a heavy wooden door that creaked; about thirty of us, give or take a few, went there to be taught by Señorita Patricia.

My father, an old man who could not read, nor did he care to, left me in school, an able-bodied boy, imagine, for so long because of my mother, who had great ambitions for me and my five brothers. She knew my three sisters' lives already were circumscribed. He was not crazy, my father, as some would have you believe, but he did have a talent, as Cuca does, and, with variations, Adela and the child as well. (Oh, yes, yes! Give it time.) He heard and saw what others could not. I know much was said about my father on his white horse rescuing the ship in the storm. Much laughter was wasted, and we his children were the butt of jokes for days. As a result, I was exiled from Cuca's presence for two years by her father, a drunk and womanizer and hypocrite. My brother Juicio, a year older than I and as far from judiciousness as anyone in the family, was knifed in a barroom brawl defending our father's honor. He survived, a scar running like a huge centipede the length of his right arm. And so did I, marrying Cuca soon *after the exile, my scar invisible to the eye, but it also ran the full length of my hard body, only where no one can see: the pained solitude of someone forced away from love. She was barely seventeen, and I just on the other side of twenty-four when we wed.*

The house I grew up in was, by today's standards, nothing more than a three-room shanty. My father added to it, in the afternoons he did not work in the bakery, as the family grew, a slipshod room here, another there. It withstood two or three hard winds from Africa-way and various downpours, so it probably wasn't as badly constructed as we thought. Many times my mother cooked outside, and if there is one thing I remember clearly of my childhood, in this vast place of all memories and no time, it is the scent of roasting pork between the trees, a woodsy smell of crackling pig fat. The home Cuca and I had when we were first married was an immediate improvement. Not just in physical surroundings, but also in the emotional splendor of coming home to a bed with cool sheets and a warm woman.

About Cuca. There was a silent fierceness about her that blinded me, made my heart quiver like a young girl's. I looked at her and knew. A man knows. We are strong and weak, both at the same time, and that is why we always flee so frightened. Knowing makes us skittish.

But yes, there was an untamed quality about her, an impetuosity well guarded by the strictures of her day. She was heat and cold, light and dark, summer and winter: passion. A man knows. He knows how to kindle it, though few, I must admit, know how to tend it. In our case, it burned effusively, and then slowly the color of brightness evolved, eased into a comfort that was gentle on our bodies despite our arguments (loud) and our lovemaking (spectacular). Such is a love that outlasts death.

The woman who buried me was not the girl I married. I would not have expected different, yet her changes seemed more profound as we moved into maturity. As a girl of fifteen, she was kinetic energy. Watch Adela's movements and coquettishness and you can trace the fluidity— and defiance—from mother to daughter. But the death of the babies slowed her down; she turned inward, reflective. I did not stop loving her— how could I?—but I wondered what had happened to the girl with the flare for the dramatic. She solidified, that's what. She learned magic and herbs, though she told me she had always known about them and rarely used them. Then there were a few years of peace and a modicum of prosperity. Adela grew into a woman, uncontrollable and playful and with strong ideas her mother had put in her head and then regretted. I should have taken a more active role in raising her: one of my regrets. I, too, spoiled her. She was our only.

Then exile. I no longer understand the meaning of diaspora. I am home now, in such peace and comfort that being ripped from everything known seems otherworldly, impossible. And it is. You carry home within your heart. Nomads understand.

I remember the taste of fear in the night, when the only sounds you hear are the creaking of the house and the call of a wild animal in the distance. (If you are fortunate, you might also hear the soft snoring of a woman in your bed.) Do you know the taste of fear? Have you savored it, bitter as a coffee bean?

Men are not supposed to know fear, but courage, I learned along the way, is ill-defined. Rarely is it grandiose. Or impetuous. Or reserved for important events. It was the bravery of daily life that fascinated me as I moved closer to the end, fascinates me still: the courage to face the morning, to not fear sleep or darkness, to take a step when movement is frightening. Cuca is the bravest person I know. Maribel will learn from her. To stare back at pain, that is bravery: the dissolving of bitterness in the back of your mouth.

I was not a saint. There were infidelities of the body and the mind. With age the body dared less, but the mind always. I am not proud of this.

Cuca knew of only one time. I don't think she suspected otherwise. I was more careful perhaps. Or perhaps I was so desperate to get her attention that one time that I did not bother to hide my nighttime excursions. I am not proud of this, I want to repeat. Even now, the pain of the knowledge of my own weakness shames me, but shame is not something we practice here. It is a belittling sensation, and it smothers our fires.

Why would I seek what I so easily found at home? I am sure every man—man of conscience, I mean—has asked himself that question. I did not look elsewhere because Cuca was not available, or willing. In fact, sometimes I wondered at her stamina. I worried about it, so much of it sometimes, overwhelming. And though her interest ebbed and waned with the babies, I knew, from experience and with growing anticipation, that it would eventually flare with unbridled passion. So why, why risk? I was an angry man. I was angry that our babies died while others thrived. I was angry at myself. (How strong can I be if my own offspring wilt into death?) I was angry at death, for being so effective. I was angry at the world. I was angry at her, for letting it happen.

And convenience, let's not forget the matter of convenience and happenstance. I was at the botica buying some headache powders for Cuca, talking to Benjamin, that old goat who had so much money but lived like a pauper. (Do you recall the old pharmacies of small towns? Sometimes they doubled as medical office, mail-delivery service, and news-dissemination center.) Claudia arrived. La bruja, the witch. I had never seen her out in daylight, and was stunned to find her at the botica. Stunned, too, that she did not appear as old as I had thought, maybe ten or twelve years older than I, and not ugly, not beautiful either, but certainly no wrinkled, long-nosed, curved-back witch. She had long black hair, rippled like a washboard, dark, brooding eyes that darted from shelf to shelf, and soft, full lips that I'm sure—it struck me right away—had known the taste of many men.

Claudia limped toward me: she had a clubfoot. She spoke. I heard but did not listen. Her voice . . . her voice. An angel's voice. A siren's call. Label it as you please. Bewitching. I could not resist.

Her house was one room with many purposes, made of cement block and topped with a tin roof. She had no bed. We made love on the sofa. I later found out she was my mother's age.

I was not a risk taker by nature, but there was a period or two in my life when I was daring. In my youth, before I married, Fernando and I would get drunk every Saturday after work and, naked and blindfolded, ride our horses over the misty hills and into the fast-moving river that came down from the mountain. We wanted to hear the voices our father heard. But in our ears only the ringing exhilaration of death sounded. I am surprised we never drowned. Oh, they weren't horses, either. They were mules, and they tended toward stubbornness.

When I worked at the sugar mill, I also liked to push my hand as close to the blades of the cutting machine as gravity allowed. It was fool-hardy, but knowing it was foolish did not stop me. I did it, anyway: tempting, enticing. More than a few men left their fingers there. I died with all ten. Foolishness is never rewarded.

And so, in some fashion, I am at the threshold of my granddaughter's life. I left when she was a child, almost an adolescent, shy as a newborn panda bear but with a zealousness that always surprised us. I don't re-member any of her friends, certainly none who came over or invited her to an outing. She stayed to herself, occasionally played with cousins who visited. She seemed fond of a younger boy with a cleft palate. He lived down the block, Marianito. His family moved away, shortly after Miguel suddenly stopped showing up to visit her. Though there was no connection between the two, I'm sure she made one. She was a child, and is a woman, who seeks effect from the cause. Did this change her, the father leaving? You tell me. Alterations are often invisible, and she continued to keep her own counsel. I admire that in a person.

She always liked to sit on the front stoop of the duplex and, after Miguel left, did this more than ever. Fewer cars traveled the roads then, and the traffic from the dog track was seasonal, with the white-legged, blue-haired americanos throwing away their money only during the balmy cloudless winters. There were no paved driveways on our block back then, or sidewalks, just tightly tufted grass that ended at the edge of the blacktop. Later, when exile lengthened, bush and flower planting began in earnest, along with the paving. It was quiet, our neighborhood, with none of the frantic and frenetic rushing and noise that later invaded.

Maribel was not a loquacious child, as I said, but she was responsive. Inviting her along to the bakery on Sundays made me feel magnanimous. She took to the outings like an enlisted seaman invited to the captain's table, and grew to expect them. You could not change something once you had started with her. If you were gone longer than estimated, she panicked. She assumed you were not returning, and she was right most of the time. To sense abandonment before it happens is a terrible gift, the curse of foresight.

She senses it now. Watch her. One minute, she clings to that baby; the next, she recedes. She blames, as I did. She draws inward, as her *grandmother tried. She touches, then cringes. The very passion of her love repulses her. You doubt me? Watch her. Watch her. She already knows what is going to happen, has been told what is to happen, but believes she can change it. Can she? you ask. Oh, what a question! Like all of us, she is both free and destined.*

20

Upon returning home from the hospital, Maribel took to the habit of the siesta during the long, languid afternoons of late spring. She napped with her eyes open, staring at the ceiling, inventing names and lives for the stucco animals and plaster faces she saw above her. (She did not like to close her eyes because she was always surprised by a shock of blinding, violent light that greeted her inner darkness, like a star out of control, a galaxy's sun.) Her favorite stucco animal was a dancing horse she nicknamed Mambo. Mambo had one beautiful wing, feathered and round and whole, and a crippled one that hung limply by his right foreleg. Maribel figured the winged horse had moved into the ceiling when she brought Victor home; she did not know where he had come from or where, eventually, he would go. Not far from Mambo was a rooster without feet, a hound dog without ears, a lamb without its curly tail, and a very fat pig without its corresponding fat snout. Along with the animals, two children populated her ceiling. One was a little boy—or possibly a girl with short hair—who wore billowing pants. His left leg was much longer than his right, and when Maribel squinted, pretending to sleep if her mother or her grandmother walked in, the little boy seemed to hobble from Mambo to the pig, then to the hound dog and back. She named him El Cojo, the Lame One. The little girl wore a long hoopskirt and was missing half her face: a stucco ridge flattened into a plateau just where her right features should have been. Some days Maribel saw other images she had never seen and wondered who had given them life—a vindictive stucco god? her own wicked imagination?—and why had she not noticed them before. Her ceiling became a haven for the crippled and deformed, the impaired, maimed, or otherwise mangled, and though she would never have told her mother—and certainly not admitted it to her grandmother, either—she was happy Victor, her big heart brave heart bird-boy, had company of some sort, even if only in the reality of coarse white plaster.

Sometimes, to rest her eyes and steady her nerves, she also napped watching the intriguing movement of the red worms that were her intestines. Her hole was small, but its edges were well defined. The view? Spectacular, if a little filmy and occasionally bloody. The worms gurgled, stretched, frothed, contracted. (As Victor's probably did, too). They were at peak performance after meals, frantically squeezing, mauling, breaking, chomping, pounding, pinching, tearing the bits of food her stomach had passed on. For all their hard work, the intestines were not nearly so entertaining as her stucco farm, but either way she rose from siesta time feeling relieved, her eyes never having closed, but the wrinkles in her brains smoothed, the knots in her muscles unknotted, the welts in her heart leveled, the doubts in her soul assuaged.

Before and after, but especially during such naps, time collapsed. It followed a rhythm she could not understand—and how could she, this woman of timetables and schedules. It folded back onto itself, time did, stretched new legs, grew tangents, developed new entryways, a starfish regenerating itself. Victor's meals were at the same hour, every three hours, and his medication—for the heart, for the ureter, for the infection, for whatever else the doctors thought he lacked, which sometimes seemed like everything—was delivered in a pattern that was consistent with the one taught by the nurses. Still, she could not grasp the passing of day into night and then the gradual easing back into light. It made no sense. Her inner clock seemed to remain stuck on an hour she could not at first define and only later realized was Now, the present separated distinctly from the past and future, precious and inviolate because Victor was alive, breathing easily and ostensibly unhurt. A Now without intrusions.

Lying atop the twin bed in Victor's nursery, fully dressed but not wholly conscious, she contemplated the parallel road that ran alongside the one she had taken, a path invisible but beckoning: an alternate life. She began at the beginning, the only logical place, for nothing can be built without a foundation, and she imagined what her childhood might have been like with different parents. Surely she could have had a father who left for an office in a white button-down oxford shirt and striped tie, and returned home at dusk, hair disheveled, and bellowing for his slippers. She could have had a father who asked, because it was his business and also because he was interested, what she had done in school *every day*, not just on Saturdays or never. The luck of a different draw also might have assigned her to a normal mother, a reflection of the ones she had studied on TV, with their hair pinned back and always in an apron. No need to worry about that kind of mother, what she wore or said or dared to do. They remained in the background, spatula in one hand, cookbook in the other, and as allergic to the spotlight as Maribel was to mosquito bites. They wore sensible shoes.

Maribel chuckled at the thought of her mother in flat loafers and long, formless skirts. And with spatula and cookbook? Now, that would be a sight. Amusement aside, however, she cornered the fantasy of that other life and riddled it with the doubts of reality. Surely, with a sensible mother and a hands-on father, she might have turned out to be someone quite different, but she couldn't possibly imagine who. She disliked the flirty, flighty girls she had known in high school, felt humbled by the brainy students and spastic beside the athletes. Yet, the quirks of her family—gambling mother, herb-cooking grandmother, disappearing father, and doting, raging grandfather—had provided a solace that welcomed her as openly and patiently as the shore receives the pounding of the surf, time after time, endlessly. Their vagaries gave her a sense of responsibility; their peculiarities centered her. Without knowing it, they had taught her acceptance, and only now did she truly know the value of that lesson.

Aloud she said into the silent room: "We become what they are, though neither of us might recognize it."

She thought she heard an echo, or possibly the murmur of an answer, but knew it was only her imagination trying hard to soothe the revelation. And that was comforting, because the rage balled in the pit of her stomach seemed to unclench, if only briefly, at her announcement.

After toying with what-might-have-been during her open-eyed siesta times, she begged her grandmother to recount the stories of women who had been anointed in some way by wounds of the spirit, tales that had not been retold in several years and which seemed simultaneously eerie to her innate logic but normal in a world where parents beat children, husbands abandoned wives, children left home. She listened to them with the eagerness of a child opening a birthday present. Her favorite was the one about the woman who suffered through the Crucifixion every Good Friday. Cuca described the woman's hairline oozing blood, bruises rising long and narrow down her back, and nail-wide holes bursting in her palms and feet.

"They came from miles around to see her, a pilgrimage of believers and nonbelievers," Cuca said.

Maribel imagined the stir such a scene would cause in another country—and the profit to be made in sleazy mementos: vials of oozed blood, photographs of the back lashed by an invisible whip, fragments of the woman's hem stapled to prayer cards.

"Did they get close to her, the people who went?" Maribel asked.

"Yes, of course. She lived in a little *bohío*, far from any main road, so people had to walk to her place. She kept the door open during those days. You came, you saw, you touched, you poured her a glass of water if she needed it, or held her hand. Whatever."

"Was she in physical pain?"

"Oh, great suffering."

Maribel thought about this for a moment. She tilted her head to the side and narrowed her eyes. In the late-afternoon light that poured through the window, her face was suffused with a sallow color, making her appear frail and frightened. She wasn't.

"Did she cry?" Maribel asked.

Now it was Cuca's turn to pause. Had anyone ever mentioned tears? And if there had been none, if the suffering had been as parched as a summer drought, would it have mattered?

"I don't remember."

Maribel stood abruptly and walked to the nursery. She looked down on Victor, sleeping, twitching in his dreams, silent. He rarely cried. When she returned to the living room, where Cuca had remained with her eyes closed and her hands clasped in prayer, a soft wetness shimmered under Maribel's eyes like a spray of glitter makeup. She plopped down beside her grandmother.

"When did she start showing the signs? I mean, how did they know what it was?"

"According to the story, Maribel, it began on the first Easter after she married, and her husband thought she was going crazy."

"From the sex?"

Cuca laughed, the full-throated laughter of a woman who has lived a lot of life but can still be pleasantly surprised. "What would sex have to do with it, *hija?*"

Maribel shrugged.

"No," Cuca continued, "not from the sex of newlyweds. He thought she had gone crazy because she had suffered a miscarriage and nearly died from it."

"How many years did she go through it?"

"Every year of her life."

"I can't imagine."

"Oh, I do not think it was so bad. I am told she led a very happy life otherwise. Her husband prospered. They bought a house in town. She had many children, smart, beautiful children. In fact, I think she was quite fortunate."

"How do you mean?"

"Her suffering had a prescribed time and place. What more can you ask for?"

Yes, her grandmother's stories were interesting, and not nearly so unnerving as the voices. Voices. Where did they come from? Voices like fleece or sandpaper, cold sheets and warm blankets. Voices. She heard them calling. Mami, do you hear them, too? Maribel wanted to ask. Abuela, do you? Listen, listen. They are soft and loud at the same time, beckoning and rejecting, blessing and accusatory. They follow her. At first she wanted to get away, but now she strains to listen. Quiet! Quiet! They may speak at any time, voices without sounds, pleas without words:

Mami, says one voice, *I call you, your son. I am not the way you see me. In another world, I have no holes, no pains, no need of anything. My heart is solid, a bloody muscle that beats regularly to match your own: Bupbupbupbup. A wonderful sound. If only you could hear it. Hold a seashell to your ear. Listen to the murmur of the faraway sea and you will know that my heart endures like those waters. It is big and brave, yes, yes! It is not broken. I breathe air and water and nothing. I am whole, as complete as a circle, bright as the eastern sun, permanent as the firmament. Mami, I call you. I ask for your acceptance. What you see is transitory, a flight of fancy. I'm here, I'm gone.*

Whispers the other: *Hey, you. Yes, you. Don't turn away. Mírame. Confróntame. Do you see what you want? What you expected? I am the son you thought you would have. My face your face. My body's the body of my father. I smile. I turn my head this way and that. I nurse from your engorged breast. Soon I will reach out for the noisy rattle. Already I am mesmerized by the Mickey Mouse mobile. I am perfect. Yet I do not exist, never did except in your imagination—but oh, how you cleave to me! I am your precious and your lost one, your now and your forever. I can never be.*

Oh, the voices, they were as familiar as the curve of Victor's cheek.

For about two weeks, Maribel received strange missives. They arrived unsigned, undated, unstamped, without a return address or postmark, and once she learned to recognize them, she ripped open the envelopes or note cards, even a small, taped package once (containing a small ballerina music box), with damp hands and dry mouth and a constriction in her throat that did not allow her to breathe. Though the letters were pocked with misspellings and grammatical errors and not one contained a shred of poetry, she initially mistook the messenger and thought Caleb had sent them to her. But when he denied authorship, she concluded with a fierce desperation that they were Eduardo's, though the handwriting var-

ied from letter to letter, and two were typed on Hilton Hotel let-
terhead. He did not know how to type, so she imagined him in his
white uniform, sleeves rolled up, matching cap on desk, pecking his
way through a sentence, smiling sideways in concentration. Some
days she received two or three short notes, though most of the time
only one letter was left in the mailbox—by whom, she didn't even
try to guess. She did not show them to her mother or grandmother,
but kept them, as Cuca kept her list of eight life lessons, in her
underwear drawer, between the plain white cotton-crotch panties
and functional eighteen-hour bras, under the nylon slips and not far
from a potpourri sachet she had received from her mother a few
Christmases ago. She brought them out every night, after Victor's
nine o'clock feeding, before she went to bed. This is what she read:

Dear Maribel,

In the woods hear, sometimes I see a rabbit or deer jumping from
behind a tree. I had never seen one. They are smaller than I imagined them. We see lots of squirrels too, and raccoons. Possums come
right to the cabin and eat from the garbage. Anything they eat,
plain garbage. I didn't no there was so much wildlife around these
places. Once we saw a fox. It is cooler here than in Miami, but
around lunchtime it gets hot. I think of you. What are you thinking?
What are you wearing? What are you saying? I wish you would think
of me, of times together. I can't understand your [indecipherable]
and you can be so hardheaded about change. Why not? Not too
many of us ever get the chance to be someone else. We're always
stuck being the same peoples. Think it over. I think of you all the
time.

My dearest,

How do you like that? It has rained every day here. Mud all
around us. My friend is an idiot. He wants to go into town to buy
cigarettes. I tell him no and he does it anyway. I'm frustrated. Nobody seems to listen to me and I'm supposed to be the boss. You
listen to me okay. Get out of there okay. You belong with me okay.
I no this is not the life you want. I no you like things planned out
and to be told with lots of warning but hey baby you need to learn

to go with the flow. Surprise me. Send me a message. You know how.

Maribel,
 That guy visits you almost every day don't he? Why?

Sweetheart,
 How did we get ourselves into this mess anyways?

Puff,
 I miss you.

Dear Maribel,
 This new place is very hot. If you turn the oven up and open the door that is how this place feels. Miami is snow city compared to this hell. I have lost wait but that is good because I had gained some pounds around my belly and I wasn't like you liked me because the food wasn't good food we were eating and we had no place to exercise or walk or lift weight so not to make noise.
 I think of you every night before falling asleep. I imagine you naked on top of me and then me on top of you kissing you everywhere especially there where you like it and then you kissing me where I like it. It is lonely here and this other guys an asshole. I do anything to touch you and taste you. You know how.

Dear Maribel,
 When I was a kid I remember how popular The Beatles were and how I liked to listen to Creedence Clearwater Revival and my father who was a bastard sometimes would come into my room and give me a backhand across the face because he had had some problem at work and the music was too loud and he didn't like it. I no that never happened to you. I no I used to get mad at your mother and grandmother but they are good people and they always took care of you and liked me only because you loved me. That was all. I no you don't like my mother so much but she is better than my father but a wimp anyway who won't stand up to him. She is afraid of the bastard too.
 Have they called you?

Sweetie pie,

I past the time away thinking of your face sweet face. On the radio now Elvis sings Are You Lonesome Tonight and I guess I have to say yes. It seems to me that you have to lose something to really know what it means to you. Why is that I think? You no how we fought about my friends. I wish we hadn't fought and those friends aren't friends because if they where I wouldn't be in this mess running and not noing where I am going or how really you are doing. I no only because word gets back to me. I pay someone.

Dear Maribel,

Sometimes I just miss the safety of the house. Me in the bedroom knowing you're in the kitchen fixing some thing. I think alot about that in the dark. It seems that's when I do all my thinking, kind of like a voice speaking inside me and I can't see it so I have to listen to it.

One time your grandmother saw me with these sisors about to cut a knot on a plastic grocery bag. You know how the bag boys tye them up so the stuff doesn't come out kind of stupid you know. Anyway she came up to me and told me to untye the knot like this and that. She said you gotta undo a knot to figure how it's put together and if you keep cutting the shit you won't know how to untye it the next time around. I think about that in the dark.

Maribel,

Wanna fuck?

Hey,

Tell that guy to stop coming around so much. What does he want with you. I know he brought you pink roses the other night.

Dear Maribel,

The beach is okay but not the same without you. Nothing is the same without you and that is why I love you. Do you want money? I think at times that I have made lots of misteaks because I didn't think before doing but also because I didn't pay attention to you. Your grandmother used to tell me stories about your grandfather what a piece of work that man and how they had some years were they didn't have no money and times were hard but she knew God would do alright by her. I think of God sometimes now can you believe it? I wonder what does he look like. You know like that painting your grandmother has in her living room, the one were the eyes follow you everywhere. Or maybe he is like a gas, you can't see it but it's everywhere. I know there's got to be a God. How else did all these things get made, like the sand and the ocean and the fish inside the water and the sun upstairs and the white clouds and all that other stuff. I'm not religious you know that but I just can't see how there can't be a God. I just can't see where I fit in all this. I'm like a nobody.

Yeah I'm kind of low today. We've been eating tuna fish for three straight days. I want a good *bistec* with chopped onions on top and a slice of lemon over it and a big plate of steeming black beans and rice with plantains. You wouldn't believe the shit they eat hear.

Maribel,

Do you know what goes on in your house some nights. I laughed so hard when I was told. Who would have thought.

Maribel,

The ocean water here is bluer than blue but they've got something called sea lice and you no who got it when we went swimming. I'm chugging Benadryl and putting stuff on the bites. Where's your grandmother when you need her?

Dear dear,

My balls are on fire.

Honey,

It's night and it's dark and it's warm. So close to summer. I am afraid but who can I tell about that. I don't want to get laught in the face.

Every time Maribel reread the letters, she worried that he never mentioned the baby. Not once.

21

In her dream, Cuca wanted to scream out that she did not doubt, had never doubted, but dreams allow no lies, only imaginative embellishments. And oh yes, she had doubted. She had doubted the scent of honeysuckle, second-guessed the hints from Rizos and Tony, even Mamá Cleofe's teaching—but doubt, she knew, was essential to her passion; it was the too hot fire that forged eventual faith. Perhaps this is why Cuca, sleeping on her side, bottom lip hanging softly over a row of perfect teeth (all hers, still), left hand tucked under her face, mother-of-pearl hair unbraided and spread about the pillow, arms free of her forty-six bracelets, perhaps this is why Cuca's subconscious simultaneously accepted and rejected the scene it was creating with great flourishes. The dream was reality and reality a dream, an inexorable link between doubt and passion. *¿Entiendes?* the voice of her dream asked. Do you understand? The well-kept secrets of the human heart—*her* heart and everybody else's, too—unfolded before her, a white carpet rolled out toward a marble pedestal. In this dream, she settled for a glimpse of the altar, and a glimpse, too, of both the demons and the angels. Doubt was not the enemy, only an accessory.

Ah, this dream. Do not forget it.

In her dream, every dream, anything is possible, everything is probable. Animals talk, men fly, night disappears, the poor grow wealthy, heat is cold, courage is common, fear nonexistent: perfection.

There is a meadow in this dream. See it? See how far it stretches, past the horizon, to forever. The meadow has flowers, and the flowers have colors, colors we've seen and colors we cannot imagine. Vivid colors, so vivid: a blue so deep you have to touch it, a red so bright you cannot fathom it, a yellow too passionate, an orange that is blinding. Such are the colors of these flowers. Daisies. Poppies. Orchids, peonies, gladioli, morning-glories, lilies of the valley, dandelions, jonquils and daffodils, begonias, pansies and violets, asters and nasturtiums.

Oh, and the herbs! The herbs! Where to begin? How to gather them? Where did they all come from? Of course this is a dream, a dream of medicine and remedy, a dream of infusions, concoctions, and salves. Should they be listed, the herbs? Of course, of course, and in alphabetical order because this is a dream, and in it she is organized: alfalfa, aloe, anise, barberry, blackberry, black mustard, bladder wrack (though the meadow is far from the coast), boneset, chamomile, cloves, coltsfoot, comfrey, cranberry, echinacea, ephedra . . . Ay, so many! Sniff, sniff—a bountiful delight! (Who says we cannot see color or smell odor in dreams? Who?)

The music. Do you hear it? Listen, listen. Heavenly. In this dream, it is both toneless and full of sound, an ancient beat and a new rhythm. We've heard it before, in the message of snare drums from another continent, carried by the harps of David, haunted by the reed flutes from the Andes. Oh, turn up the volume a bit, just enough to fill the soul. And it does, the music, it enters the body and invades the soul, overpowers the mind. This is the sound of harmony, of bliss. Listen to it as it curls in wisps into the heavens.

The heavens. Cuca is struck by the heavens. In her sleep she stirs. What the flowers and the herbs and the music could not do, the sky does: bewitches her. In this dream, the heavens part like two slices of blue being separated by a pie knife. Light pours into the meadow, an amber wine, illuminating a path she had not seen until then, a path that in the reflection of the light appears paved with perfect intentions. Her closed eyes follow the light into the path, and though she wants to open them to see more, to grab greedily what is so obviously special, she cannot open her eyes. She can only see the light through her lids and know what she has known for years: the freedom of surrender.

Then she sees him. He is unmistakable. She is overjoyed, the rapture is like no other she has ever known. In this dream as in reality, he is small but perfect, smiling toothlessly, eyes opened wide in understanding. She calls to him. He answers, not in words but with arms outstretched, recognizing her: the movement is louder than any syllable or intonation.

He walks. He takes a step toward her, then another. Cuca can see Victor walking toward her, each of his movements well defined. She sees the muscles through the skin, the tendons and ligaments working oh so perfectly. Now he runs, little legs pumping hard, puffing, puffing. He is running toward her, all movement and motion, unstoppable and whole. He is running so fast that he takes flight, rising above the path paved with perfect intentions. She savors his flight for the eternity that is her dream, until sunlight forces itself furiously between windowsill and shade and the rudeness of day intrudes on what she knows she will never see.

Victor, oh Victor!

Through the side window of the kitchen, Cuca watches Maribel removing Victor's sun-dried laundry from a thick wire strung between two oak trees in the back yard. She possesses an easy fluidity, a sense of self that makes every movement a dance step, even if it's simply unpinning the tiny, stiff clothes and dropping them into the basket. Cuca remembers moving in the same way, with a quiet determination and unaware of the passage of time. Of course, washing laundry was different back then, fifty, sixty years ago. At least Maribel has a washing machine, a heavy-duty Sears Kenmore with four cycles. Cuca used her hands against a washboard in a tin tub filled with water carried from the well. Life was very rudimentary then, and though others speak longingly of those simple times, their retrievals of the past as ignorant as they are innocent, she knows progress has had its definite benefits, chief among them a woman's smooth, soft hands—regardless of her station in life. Cuca traces the knobby knuckles and old calluses on her hands, badges of past labor and triumph. She remembers, too, the stabbing pain of her lower back from carrying the buckets of water and boiling laundry and cooking soap. Ay, in her youth life was as tough as the sole of a shoe. It had been even more difficult for Mamá Cleofe; she can-not forget the tedious, backbreaking, sidesplitting, blister-forming housework of her grandmother's time. No wonder nobody made it past fifty then: they were all too tired and wanted to die, to find a final resting place where food never had to be cooked and laundry remained immaculate. Now, of course, there were fancy gadgets, the electricity that made night day and telephones that forced faraway voices into neighbors. The microwave, too. Sí. If she had had a microwave in her youth, she would have served dinner on time every night and her relationship with Tony might have been, if not per-fect, at least a lot smoother. Ay!

And yet . . . yet . . . she misses the slower pace that too much work sometimes imposes on the laborer. Paradoxical, no? But now she thinks that most everybody she knows misuses their time. What has freed them also enslaves them. Nobody wears a piece of clothing more than once before washing it. Floors are expected to sparkle. Everybody hurries so they can sit in front of the TV. Women have moved into the office, and men—well, men go to gymnasiums now to work out. That's what Eduardo used to do almost every day after work, meet his friends and pump iron. In her time, men walked everywhere: their leg muscles lengthened and strengthened. They had to carry heavy packages on their backs, saw large pieces of wood manually, machete through dense undergrowth. Lift weights? Who would have thought, eh? Who would have needed to? Ay.

Maribel finishes gathering the last of the small socks and stops to look around her. Except for the two oak trees, the back yard stretches uninterrupted as a flat plain of green lawn, though there are small patches of yellow in the far west corner. (Chinch bugs?) There isn't much to look at, no flower beds or lawn decorations, but Maribel stands very still, head tilted to her side, as if considering a deep thought. With all her senses, Cuca watches her. Maribel leaves the laundry basket and tiptoes slowly toward one of the trees. What could she possibly be doing? Cuca presses her nose against the window. She hears Maribel whistle in a high staccato pitch—tweet, tweet, tweet, tweettweettweet—and sees her granddaughter stretch her arm toward a branch above her head. Then suddenly: a flutter of leaves, a dash of blue. Maribel turns to catch the bird in flight, but the streaking proves too quick, and for several seconds thereafter, until Cuca wills movement, Maribel remains paralyzed, outstretched hand frozen in midair.

Tweet tweet, her granddaughter calls out.

Tweet tweet, Cuca whistles back, but knows her song is not loud enough.

Back in her living room, Maribel begins to fold the tiny clothes on the coffee table. The air-conditioning, which the women decided to turn on just last week, hums rhythmically in the background. It gives the enclosed air a pure, metallic scent, a stark contrast to the earthy spring warmth they have grown accustomed to.

"You look tired," Cuca tells her granddaughter when she joins her. "Want me to make you some *café?* Mint tea?"

"I'm fine."

"You're quiet today."

"Where's Mami?" Maribel asks, without acknowledging her grandmother's observation.

"Where else?"

"You would think that her devotion alone would have won her the Lotto by now."

"Persistence isn't always a guarantee of success, *hija.*"

"Well, it should be."

"Lots of things that aren't should be. Here, let me help you."

Cuca begins folding Victor's pajamas following Maribel's methodical lead, left arm first, then right arm across, both pants legs up, finally squared off. Working together, they finish the laundry in less than five minutes. Neither in the firmness of Maribel's chin nor in the erect line of her back, not even in her words or mannerisms, does Cuca detect any of her granddaughter's familiar arrogance. She feels that sitting together, shoulder to shoulder, folding pieces of clothing is an accomplishment. Cuca is encouraged.

"What kind of bird was it?" Cuca asks.

Maribel turns abruptly. "What?"

"The bird, the one in the tree in the back yard."

Maribel stares at her grandmother. A blush suffuses her face.

"*Hija*, it is all right. I was in the kitchen and your movement caught my eye."

"A bird, that's all it was."

"But you tiptoed to it. I saw you."

Maribel stands to dismiss the conversation. "I'm going to put away the clothes before the next feeding."

Cuca follows her to the nursery. "What kind of bird?" she insists.

"I don't know about birds. It was some bird."

"But it caught your attention because of something, Maribel."

"So what?"

"Oh, I'm curious."

"I know what you are thinking, Abuela. You are looking for signs for all that hocus-pocus of yours."

Cuca laughs. Maribel slams the dresser drawer shut, and joins in the laughter. The moment of humor is an unexpected victory for Cuca.

Together they walk to the crib and watch Victor sleep. Despite the slew of antibiotics and other medications, or maybe because of them, he appears to have gained weight and his face, that little bird-face with the beak nose and the lipless mouth, is slowly rounding out.

"I'll be going back to work soon," Maribel whispers, as she strokes her son's knee.

"How do you feel about that?"

She shrugs.

"Do you want to return, *hija*? Or would you prefer to stay home with Victor?"

"It depends what time of day you ask me," Maribel replies, smiling.

"What about right now?"

"Right now I wish time would stop and I wouldn't have to worry about Victor's next operation or the severe growth retardation the geneticist talks about or the holes in his heart."

In the land of no time, no time, no time.

"Maybe returning to work," Cuca offers softly, "will take your mind off those things."

"Oh, Abuela! It doesn't matter what I'm doing. I can be sleeping and my mind gravitates automatically to that."

"The tongue always finds the hurt tooth."

Victor whimpers as though in agreement. Maribel coos to her big heart, brave heart, mending-heart-boy.

"You know, Abuela," whispers Maribel, forcing Cuca to lean closer to catch each word. "All I ever wanted was an ordinary life. I mean, I don't really have much ambition. Just an ordinary life is what I aspired to, with a job, a house, a car, a husband, two or three kids, everything in its place, simple meals at their right times. Do you know what I mean?"

"*Sí, sí, sí.*" Cuca takes Maribel's hand. "And you already have it, *m'ija.* You do. All our lives are ordinary."

"Oh no, Abuela. Ordinary unlike yours or Mami's. Like other people's."

"And what makes us so different, so extraordinary?"

Maribel pauses.

"Don't be afraid to hurt my feelings, if that is what you are thinking."

"Well, Abuela, most people I know have different kinds of grandmothers and mothers."

"How so?"

Maribel giggles. "They don't talk to spirits, for one. They don't play every single game of chance ever made. They behave like . . . like, well, like adults."

"Ay, *hija,* you are still a child. You do not know what calamities of spirit and body befall others, and how very strange and like us they truly are."

"Maybe."

"No maybe. That is a certainty."

"Abuela, there are no certainties." Maribel stares at her grandmother, tears in her eyes. "None at all. How is it that you do everything you're supposed to do, follow the rules, stay within the lines, and something like . . . well, what you did not expect . . . happens anyway?"

Cuca takes Maribel's face in her hands. "Oh, my dear, dear child, that's just the way life is."

"No, Abuela, not for others. I watch how others live."

"And what do you see?"

"Ordinary normalcy."

Cuca snorts. She rubs her granddaughter's face as though she were still a little girl. "Give or take a few incidents, we're all the same. You're captivated by an illusion, *mi cielo*."

The doorbell rings. Maribel answers. She takes the dozen velvet-red roses from the deliveryman and arranges them in a cut-crystal vase.

"From Caleb," Maribel tells her grandmother.

"*¡Dios mío!*"

"Today is my seventh anniversary with the company."

Cuca wants to ask if *el americano* sends flowers to his other employees, too, but decides against it. Why spoil the gift?

"Did he write you a poem?"

"Of course," says Maribel, and laughs. "I'll read it to you."

And she does, though Cuca cannot understand a word her granddaughter recites:

> *One report, two reports, three reports, four*
> *We've done so many together to fill up an entire store.*
> *Five studies, six studies, seven studies, eight*
> *In case I haven't told you before, I think you're top-rate.*
> *Happy anniversary!*

The moment of communion is lost, but brief as it was, Cuca knows Maribel is on her way. Cuca has left out one thought, though, and she doesn't know when another opportunity will come up to share it. Moments of vulnerability and confession are rare with Maribel. Oh, flesh of my flesh, blood of my blood, Cuca muses silently, in the end you will have something much greater than normalcy or an ordinary life. Something much sweeter and satisfying.

22

Before Carlos and Fefa bought the bodega, a fat man nicknamed El Gordo owned it, first as a hole-in-the-wall that stocked the bare essentials and then, after yearly expansions, a neighborhood market that also sold top-quality meat. El Gordo was an excellent butcher and it was well known that he was tied to his wife's apron strings— choked, some said. El Gordo, he was immense. Everything about him was circles. He had a moon face, a round body that resembled a child's drawing of a snowman, and arms that hung like large hams from his shoulders. He wore a white apron that was never clean (blood spots formed different patterns, like Rorschach inkblots, in the front), and he greeted his customers with a flourish of his butcher knife.

"¡Viejo!" he shouted at old men. Or: "¡Hombre!"

At the women he singsonged a "Doña" or, if they were obviously young, "Doñita."

When he flirted or whispered innuendoes, nobody took them to heart. He was a fat, bored man, that's all. So, of course, it shocked his customers—and his wife, too—when he ran away with a widow who liked to buy the *boliche* on special. He disappeared with all the couple's savings, too, and the stunned wife was forced to put the bodega up for sale. "Cheap, real cheap," Carlos once told Adela about the purchase. "She was ready to give it away. A fire sale."

The possibility of Carlos repeating El Gordo's mad but lucrative escape was an idea Adela had entertained the past few days, though she would have denied it vehemently to anyone else, perhaps even to herself. She did not want Carlos to leave his wife; she simply wanted Carlos as a bedmate, a playmate. Didn't she? Chica, her head hurt if she tried to figure it out. Whenever she got involved with a man, *really* involved, she suffered disorienting headaches, and she was beginning to wonder if the nightly pleasures were worth the daily discomforts. The trade-off wasn't as appealing if you considered it that way, eh?

Anyway, she had come to the bodega to buy the weekly Lotto tickets and a smattering of cooking necessities, but, more important, to figure out if the other week's disagreement over Fefa's health had turned out to be a farewell conversation. Wouldn't that be ironic, chica? Her concern about his wife turned into his excuse to flee. Men were so childish—and so vastly complicated. Adela had learned to allow them to believe they were in control, that they ruled, that their word was law; she had learned to give them a sense of power, but sometimes it was difficult to keep herself in check. She was always wanting to fix the mistakes they made. Like her mother, she too often and too readily accepted excuses or made apologies for their behavior, anguished over their words and their actions. Men, on the other hand, were so much better defended that way. She could not imagine Carlos suffering wretchedly over their ten-day separation, let alone any conversation. If he had felt any twinge of remorse (which she doubted), it probably had been thrown out like so much trash. Waste of the heart examined endlessly by women was useless flotsam for men.

The bodega smelled of earth just tilled. It was a good smell, and it was strongest in the produce aisle, where the bins held the fundamentals of Cuban cuisine: *ñame* and *boniato*, *plátanos*, *yuca*, *malanga*, *calabaza*, and onions and garlic and peppers and all those wonderful earth things that made food taste like manna from heaven. Still thinking of Carlos, Adela began picking out her weekly selection of vegetables and roots and fruits. She took great pleasure in pinching and kneading the hard skins and fibrous coverings. She always did this before moving to the butcher counter, though it would have been more expedient to order the meat and, while waiting for Carlos to cut it, do the rest of the shopping. Expediency was not her forte. She liked, first, the anticipation of knowing she would see Carlos at work, the tingling that spread from her center to the very ends of her limbs, and then she also liked to watch him cut the meat with the sharp-sharp knives, the tension across his T-shirted back and the ripple of the muscles in his arms and how his green eyes locked with hers in an untouched embrace across the counter. Drawing from her experiences, she had arrived at the conclusion that there were essentially two types of men: those who looked good in clothes and those who looked better without any. Carlos definitely fell into both categories, a rarity.

You know what her problem was, chica! She had taken her mother's lessons too much to heart. She loved completely, turning herself inside out, becoming as raw and vulnerable as a shucked oyster. One had to keep something to oneself, an inviolate core, an inner sanctum, protected at all times, unreachable. She had never quite managed to do that.

And another thing—and this, too, she had learned from her mother, that enlightened tutor—she allowed herself to make mistakes. She never said never; she accepted possibly, maybe, perhaps, and that usually opened the door to complications.

She put three *boniatos* and a slice of *calabaza* in her cart, then considered the plantains. This week they appeared small, anemic, but the price was attractive—six for a dollar. She took six, selecting the plumpest, firmest ones, which wasn't saying much. Ah well, she did what she could with what she had. From the produce aisle, she moved on to the bread aisle for Cuban crackers and cornmeal, then to the canned and packaged goods for guava shells and *membrillo*. She bought a can of Spanish olive oil, then in the next row Cuban coffee, Materva, Ironbeer, and Malta Hatuey. She could hear Fefa ringing up the purchases of the other customers, some of whom had been coming to the bodega, as she had, from when El Gordo owned it and the Cubans played *bolita* instead of the state-sanctioned Lotto and the talk had always turned to celebrating New Year's in Havana instead of Medicare and the *novelas* on Spanish TV. Now Fefa's voice served as a counterpoint to the merry ringing of the cash register: her tired contralto matching the machine's metallic soprano. Poor Fefa! She still looked the worse for wear.

Adela continued to meander through the aisles, waiting for Carlos to finish with a sudden rush of customers. He was patient with them, and friendly, tossing in an extra pork chop for an old man or a big bone for the Great Dane of a woman wearing pink curlers. He offered advice on everything, from when to fertilize the mango tree to where to buy a car. As in the time of El Gordo, the meat counter proved to be the heart of a bodega, the place where intimacies were revealed, marriages planned, divorces discussed, the future contemplated. Carlos was a confidant to his customers. "The stories I could tell if I wanted to," he whispered in her ear when they were in bed together. He promised, he hinted, but never told. She liked that about him; if nothing else, he was trustworthy that way. She despised men with big mouths, braggarts who could lift themselves up only through the power of their empty presumptions.

A discerning customer could buy any type of meat at Carlos's and, better still, get it cut any way she wanted. Hanging above the freezer counter were hand-lettered signs in red Magic Marker: *Patas Saladas* (salted pigs' feet) or *Lacón* (ham hocks) or *Lomo de Res* (beef loin) or *Bacalao* (codfish) or *Carne Molida* (ground beef). If Carlos happened to have something very special, the sign would be taped on the white wall behind him, beside a calendar with color photographs of half-naked women. Sometimes that sign would say: *"Especial: Conejo"* (Special: Rabbit) or, around the Christmas holidays, when everyone was planning the roast-pork meal, for Nochebuena, the sign trumpeted: *"Ordene pronto. Paleta. Pierna. Entero."* Order soon. Shoulder. Leg. Whole.

When the other customers dispersed, Adela was ready to order her usual, a small *cañada*, which Carlos would hack into thin *palomilla* steaks, then chop into square pieces of *falda* before finally feeding the leftover meat into a spitoon-shaped metal contraption that ground the contents when you pushed its handle around.

"Well," he greeted her. That's all he had to say. It was more than enough. She felt the bolts electrifying her.

"The usual," she said primly, but her hands danced with glee in front of her.

Without another word, Carlos pulled one of the smaller sides of beef from the freezer and dropped it on the scale.

"Almost eighteen pounds."

"Fine."

He began stripping away at the surface fat first, then slicing long strips to make the *palomilla* steaks. He placed the steaks in pairs on pink paper. Adela couldn't stand the silence.

"So how has business been?"

He looked back at her and grinned. "Not very good."

Now, what was that supposed to mean? Adela wondered.

"Maybe people are saving up for vacation," she offered.

"They still have to eat. How about you?"

"I still eat, as you can see."

He turned completely toward her now, sharp knife glinting in midair, and laughed. "I mean, how have you been?"

"So-so."

"Oh?"

"Victor was in the hospital, you know." She couldn't avoid the tone of recrimination in her voice. Stupid to get herself into such a petty possessive state. Stupid, stupid, stupid, but she couldn't stop herself now. Chica, look at his arms! His green eyes!

He returned to the slicing. "I'm sorry to hear that. Is he doing better?"

"Yes, but the doctors warned he will always be very sickly."

Carlos didn't say anything else. He stacked the *palomillas* diagonally on a large strip of white paper, wrapped them in four fluid movements, tucking in the corners and taping the sides. He wrote the price on the package with a black wax pencil, then finished grinding the meat and chopping the *falda*. Adela, too, remained quiet.

When he finished, he asked, "A pound of ham?"

She nodded. "Sliced thin, please."

"You going to be home tonight?"

She wasn't sure she heard right. Her delayed reply prompted him to ask again.

"Depends," she answered, feeling more sure of herself. This was the thrust and parry, the give and take she was accustomed to. Silences confused her.

"On what?" he asked.

She laughed. Cymbals clashed. Bells clanged. The customer who had bought two whole snappers swore to Fefa that their tails were still snapping against the conveyor belt of the checkout.

"I love to hear you laugh, Adela."

"Really?"

"De veras."

"That comes as a surprise."

"It shouldn't."

"Well, your absence speaks otherwise." She paused. "Let me have a half pound of salami, please."

He sliced the salami effortlessly and wrapped it for her. "Anything else?" he asked.

"You tell me," she replied, looking as serious as she possibly could under the circumstances.

"See you tonight."

At the checkout, she paid Fefa quickly, unable to meet the woman's tired eyes, and then nearly ran home, rushing past the bumper-to-bumper traffic on Northwest Seventh Street, waving dismissively at Chucho the Sno-Kone man, barely greeting neighbors walking their dogs. She had lots to do to prepare herself for this sacred offering.

Then she remembered she had forgotten to play the Lotto.

Chica, that chest! Those arms!

"It took your mother long enough to fall asleep," he whispered between nibbles on her neck.

"Oh, she's probably not asleep yet. She suffers from insomnia."

He kissed her, prying her willing mouth open with his tongue.

"Mmmm!" He savored her. "You taste . . ."

"Sweet?"

"Sí, but with a little hot punch to it."

"Oh, that's because of Victor."

"What?"

"Well, I drank vermouth for a week to make sure I didn't get his pneumonia."

He laughed. "Haven't you heard of antibiotics?"

"This was better, and now I taste like vermouth all the time."

Carlos propped himself on his elbow. He lifted the covers from her naked body. "Vermouth and cream and chocolate and a touch of hot pepper."

"He was really sick, the baby. They had to try a couple of different antibiotics. Then they had to be careful that whatever they gave him did not counteract the other medications he takes for . . ."

He kissed her in midsentence. She struggled to finish her thought.

". . . the other medicine he takes for his heart and some urine problem he has. Did I tell you he's going to have at least one more operation in the next month or so?"

"Let's not talk, *mi cielo.*"

"No, let's talk. We never get to talk."

He kissed her hard; she swallowed her words. Such pleasure!

Later, he dressed quietly in the dark. She wrapped her throbbing body in a blue velour robe and watched him, wanting to ask about the next time but knowing she couldn't. There existed no swifter method of scaring away a man than pushing him against a wall of commitment. She wanted, too, for him to linger in conversation, but he was in an awful hurry to get home.

"You missed a loop with your belt."

He laughed nervously.

"You're in a big hurry, aren't you?"

He didn't answer. She felt reprimanded in some way.

"I forgot to buy the Lotto tickets when I went by today."

"You mean yesterday."

"Well, yes, yesterday. In any case, I'll have to drop by again. It's up to seventeen million."

He nodded and finished slipping on his shoes. They tiptoed down the narrow hall arm in arm, through the living room, and to the door. He turned and bent to kiss her. The smell of his Paco Rabanne cologne stirred her again.

"Let's not be strangers," he said as his lips met hers.

They were out the door, nuzzling each other, copping one last feel, when Adela felt the unmistakable presence. Was it her daughter's shock she sensed first? The unspoken recriminations? The bewildered pain? Or the quick, unforgiving judgment?

"Maribel!"

"Mami, Carlos." Maribel's voice was as cold and dry as ice.

Carlos stumbled down the steps without saying another word. His car tires screeched as he fled the scene. The two women watched him wordlessly.

"Maribel . . ."

"I don't want to hear it, Mami."

Maribel turned and went into her house. Adela tightened the sash around her robe and followed her in.

"Listen, *hija*, I know what this looks like. Let me explain."

"I don't want to hear any explanations."

Maribel stepped into the nursery, Adela at her heels. Victor was sleeping quietly, his mouth open. Gently Maribel nudged it closed.

"He has to learn to breathe through his nose," she said softly.

"I know what you're thinking, Maribel."

"Does it matter?"

"Of course it does."

"Too late now."

"I want you to understand."

Maribel climbed into the twin bed and pulled the baby-blue chenille bedspread up to her chin. Adela sat beside her. She remembered doing this almost every night many, many years ago. Remembered how shiny her child's hair looked in the lamplight. Remembered how her black-black eyes glowed. Remembered the copper sheen of her skin and the dazzle of her smile and the trust in her look. Especially that, yes, especially that trust.

"Anything you say will make no sense, Mami." Maribel sounded as though all the air had been sucked out of her lungs.

"I guess not," Adela admitted sheepishly.

"Please leave."

"I can't."

"Don't tell me your conscience is bothering you."

"As a matter of fact, it is."

"Jesus!"

Adela refused to move. She placed her perfectly manicured index finger on the side of her face and tried to concentrate on some plausible explanation for what Maribel had stumbled on. Of course she could find none. She didn't have to dwell too long on that. Besides, the hum of the air-conditioning made it hard for Adela to stay the course of her thoughts.

"How could you, Mami!" It was an accusation, not a question.

"The flesh is weak." Adela covered her mouth to obliterate the rising giggles. The phrase was so inane, even to her ears.

"He's married."

"Yes," she agreed stupidly, "to Fefa."

"How could you!" Maribel blubbered. "I mean, do you even love him? Does he love you?"

"I haven't thought of that." Which was not true. She had contemplated the possibility on either side, from both ends.

"And you brought him into this house." Maribel sat up. Tears of reproach welled in her eyes. "This house. Our house."

Adela leaned to touch her daughter's face, but Maribel shook her off. "I don't know how you can live with yourself." The words carried a spiteful ring but an honest confusion, too.

"Maribel, Maribel, Maribel." Adela's voice cracked.

"Don't."

"Do you know how lonely it is without a man to hold you at night?"

As soon as the words were out, Adela knew she had made a mistake. Of course Maribel knew.

"I'm sorry," Adela said quickly.

"You should act like a mother, for heaven's sake." There was no mistaking the inflection in Maribel's voice.

"I'm also a woman, Maribel." Then, clinging to the last remnants of her dignity, Adela left her daughter and grandson's room. She was barefoot, and Maribel realized she couldn't remember the last time she had heard the soft patter of her mother's feet against the tile. It was always the sharp tic-tac of her heels.

The next morning, with the rising sun shining off the toaster, Maribel faced a day without illusions. She burned the bread and angrily threw out the two hard black slices. She sniffed the air and smelled the faint odor of mildew and waste, of something not quite right. She noticed spots on the polished chrome of her sink, an opaqueness filming the windows, dust in the corners of the rooms. Everything, the very existence of her environment, upset her.

Suddenly Cuca was at her elbow. Maribel was surprised: she had been too discomfited to smell the violet cologne or hear the jangle of bracelets.

"I was already told about last night's surprise," acknowledged her grandmother.

Maribel snorted.

"Judge only as you yourself would like to be judged, *hija*."

"Save it, Abuela."

"I made some chamomile tea. Like some?"

"I want to be left alone."

And for the rest of the day, that's precisely how Maribel found herself: isolated in her righteous anger. The sun rushed through the morning and peaked in the afternoon. Night fell, cooling the air only slightly, and the full moon rose, stripped of dress and charm. As the digital clock flipped to midnight, Victor developed a fever that his mother reluctantly recognized.

23

Big heart, brave heart, Victor Eduardo, do you want to play?

"Yes?" Maribel whispered between the metal slats of the hospital crib. "Do you? The Chin Kiss Game?"

Victor slept, wheezing noisily. Maribel imagined the pneumonia bacteria fighting against the antibiotics: soldiers ready, shields up, guns loaded, cannons aimed. The war had started fifteen hours ago, when two nurses had shaved a swath of hair on his right forehead and pricked his scalp with an IV. Now she wasn't sure who was losing or whether there would be any winners in this battle at all. Victor looked like a war casualty, pale as a tourist and so, so frail. She wondered if he understood what she said. Did he make out the words? Or was it something more elemental, an understanding of her tone, a reception of her intent? Surely he comprehended *something*. He responded to her touch, the caress of her cooing. She knew that. And could he see her? How? In color or in black and white? As an enormous form looming in the distance or a loving face pressed close to his? Would he be able to pick her out in a roomful of mothers? Recognize the blackness of her hair, the slant of her eyes, the full mouth gloating over his triumphs?

Oh, Victor, big heart, brave heart, bird-boy.

Dr. Rothstein appeared at the door. She greeted him effusively. He was such a kind, patient man. Every time they met—in his office crowded with diplomas and photographs of his patients, or during these tense visits in the hospital, when her nerves were on edge and her despair in clear view—the echo of their conversation from months ago nudged her into a weary acceptance: *It's the quaking of the soul, my dear.* Oh, yes, he had been so right. How her soul quaked at times! A solid ten on the Richter scale, shaken by the fear of loss, the fear of pain. But the quaking softened when the doctor was around; it eased into a tremble, a quiver, a tic. The neonatologist's quiet demeanor, the gentle way he touched Victor, the soft cadence of his voice, everything about him soothed her. She knew it was momentary, fleeting, but valued it just the same. Let the inevitable wait.

"How is he?" she asked as he examined the baby.

"Better than last night, Mrs. Garcia."

"Overall?"

He turned to face her. She read his expression clearly but wished she hadn't, wished desperately to cling to hope. She covered her face with her hands, and before the first sob passed her lips, Dr. Rothstein took her hands in his large ones.

"He hasn't gained much weight since I last saw him," he murmured.

"I know, but he *feels* heavier. Lots heavier."

Dr. Rothstein smiled.

"And his face looks fuller. Doesn't it?"

"You are a wonderful mother, Mrs. Garcia."

"Lot of good that does," she said sarcastically.

"You're wrong. It does do him a lot of good. More than any medicine can."

"Then why isn't he cured?"

"There is no cure, and that's not what we're looking for. Please understand that. It may be the most important lesson in all of this."

"Then what *are* we looking for?"

He took back his hands and looked down at them for several seconds. In the background, Maribel could hear the voices of two women rising and falling outside the door. She repeated her question.

"I've asked myself that for as long as I've been a medical doctor. No, before that, in medical school."

"And?"

"I think," he began, adjusting his rimless glasses, "I think we are looking for a place for each life, a reason for our existence, so to speak. On the other hand, I also think we can never truly find what we are looking for . . ."

"Why?" she asked angrily. "Why look for it, then?"

"Because it is part of our nature to search, though the answer may be beyond our comprehension."

There was a familiar message in the doctor's words, one that Maribel recognized, a thread that pulled at her heart the way her grandmother's words did—with a prodding yet calming confidence. Maribel sighed loudly.

"My specialty, Mrs. Garcia, is not metaphysics. The hospital has an excellent chaplain."

"I've met him." She immediately conjured a faceless figure in navy-blue polyester pants, white shirt, and striped red tie.

"Or your own clergyman."

Despite herself, she tittered, trying to imagine a visit to Father Peace, in a dark confessional booth, whispering her secrets through the grate. Bless me, Father, for I have sinned. It has been aeons, a lifetime, since my last confession.

"If it is any consolation, the surgery seems to be healing quite well."

Yes, that was a consolation, but only like an honorable mention in a contest.

Shortly after Dr. Rothstein left, Caleb arrived with a box of Godiva chocolates, dressed dapperly in a gray double-breasted suit with a blue flowered tie. Maribel opened the card on the chocolates and read to herself:

The gentleness in your face
is a beacon of hope and faith and grace.

She carefully untied the red bow and opened the box, offering him first choice. He took a deliciously molded seashell.

"He's doing better," she said before he asked.

"Out of danger?"

"Not quite, but he's a fighter, Caleb. He fights and fights and fights."

"I saw one of his doctors at the nurses' station. The big guy. What did he have to say?"

Maribel put the box of chocolates on the tray table and walked to the crib. Looking down at Victor, she replied, "He didn't have to say anything to me. I read the message as plain as day on his face."

"Oh, come on, Maribel, I know you're not into face-reading."

She turned and lifted her Hard Rock Cafe T-shirt. Pointing at her gurgling hole: "You don't see that, Caleb, do you?"

Caleb nodded no, sheepishly. He looked hurt.

"I'm sorry, Caleb. I'm upset about the baby and about my mother and about being at the hospital again. About a lot of things. You shouldn't pay for my moods."

"I'd pay for everything or anything if I could."

His smile was such that she had to turn back to Victor because she could not stand the silent pleading in his look or her inability (or was it unwillingness?) to respond.

He spoke again before leaving: "I don't want you to feel you have to hurry back to work. Take whatever time you need."

And how long, she asked herself, would that be? A week? Two months? A year? Ten?

Updown, up-down, ar-r-round. Up-down, up-down, ar-r-round. Cuca scrubbed her teeth with a washcloth and baking soda. Once, then twice for good measure. Aah. Fresh breath, clean teeth. What a lucky woman she was. Seventy-seven and all of her own teeth. Every single one of them. Amazing, if she said so herself. A country woman with little access to dentists, and a mouthful of teeth.

She breathed at the mirror; a foggy circle formed, obstructing the view of her face.

She smiled. Life was like that, no? Breathe out, savor the moment, pat yourself on the back, and then watch out for the fog that obstructs your view.

In the bathroom she could hear Adela on the phone. She could not make out the words, only the hard rapid consonants, the flirtatious intonation. Incorrigible, her daughter.

She dabbed the Agustín Reyes violet cologne on her head and behind her ears. Today on the crinkly skin between her breasts, too. Tony had loved to bury his face there and in his memory this morning she would honor him in this way. We never forget the dead, eh? They may forget us, become citizens of the otherworld and renounce their nationality in this one, refusing to visit, refusing to answer our pleas, but we the living continue with the memories: flowers at the grave site, framed photographs on night tables, tears at anniversaries. Today: fifteen years since his death. *Ay Dios, una década y media.*

She divided her hair, that mother-of-pearl mantilla, into three even sections and began to braid: over and under and through. Again. Again. Again. Her hands worked without direction, in an automatic rhythm imprinted by the years. Hair, beautiful hair. A promise kept.

Adela's laughter rang through the walls. The power of bringing joy from your insides, from the very pit of your belly, was a force like no other. That laughter had carried Adela through some difficult times, long periods of loneliness and doubt, yet she had not made use of that anguish as Cuca would have hoped. If only Adela would have, if only she could. A life turned inside out can be straightened so much more easily than a mediocre one that has never lost its form. Cuca knew well that it was the forced solitude of pain that drove people to discovery. It led one to the core, through fire and storms and disasters, all manner of obstacles; once that core was spotted, tracked, and mapped, anything and everything was child's play: exercise strengthening. Adela hadn't been willing to put in the hard work: she kept running in circles. In this, Cuca had failed; she yanked at her braid angrily. She blamed herself for not guiding Adela correctly, for not setting up the kilometer markers along the way. It would not happen again with Maribel. No, no, no.

You have not failed, mujer.

Ay, mi cielo. You.

Not happy to hear from me?

I'm always happy to hear from you. But today is not a good day. Or have you forgotten?

You call it death, mujer, but it is a rebirth, a passage into another dimension.

I believe that, but it doesn't lessen the pain. Fifteen years. Fifteen long years.

You are still counting.

Shouldn't I?

If you must. But remember that what truly matters cannot be quantified.

Easy for you to say.

Yes, because I know that the grief in your heart now is pasajero, a blink into nothing, a blip in the time line, and I know, too, that you fully understand what I have to say, though you can't always assimilate it.

It's the worries, Tony. The worries over the baby, over Maribel. And Adela . . . ay, Adela!

Not what we expected, eh?

Yes and no. She is like a geyser that you try to control.

Let it go, mujer. Let it go.

But Maribel, she is hurt by this discovery of her mother's nocturnal life—you know, with Carlos the carnicero—and that child does not need anything else to complicate her life. She has more than enough with Victor.

Cuca, dear, you are only skimming the surface.

What do you mean?

Precisely that. You are skimming the surface. A surface pain. A paper cut. A scrape. Don't confuse the different depths of Maribel's suffering.

Oh, but I don't. Still, one suffering at a time, por Dios.

Who says? Did you make up that rule? How many people are afflicted all at once, curse after curse, plague upon plague.

A few, I suppose.

This small matter with Adela is a diversion. She may not see it that way, my darling Maribel, but it is. Afflictions come in many guises.

You've learned to speak in riddles.

I've never spoken clearer, mujer. Now, just listen carefully to what I must tell you. Close your eyes and tell me what you see.

A star. Victor's star.

How do you know?

It's tiny and bright. A lone candle in the immense dark.

Yes, yes, yes. Maribel sees it too, when she closes her eyes to sleep. She just doesn't know it.

Ay, I must tell her.

With care. She may have questions that you cannot answer.

She's more perceptive than I once gave her credit for.

Like her grandmother.

My darling man, I miss you in my bed.

Oh, such passions of life.

Sí, a passion I miss sorely and regret we did not partake of more. Every night, and every morning, the touch of your hands, the weight of your body, the softness of your lips.

Time does not affect you, my Cuca.

But Maribel . . .

Sí, Maribel. She knows what awaits her. She sees it clearly but feels that she can change it.

And she can't?

The outcome is . . . well, it is best I do not get into that. But, mujer, change is inevitable. She must simply understand the type of transformation.

I'm not sure I understand what you mean.

You shouldn't. But remember what you told me about Victor's star, how it flickers in the dark much the same as a candle does. I like that. A candle transforms its wax into flame and disappears in the sacrifice.

Ay, Tony, do not go. Stay. Stay. Come back. Tell me more about the candle. Tony!

Cuca reached into the mirror. She wanted to touch his hair, his chest, his face. She wanted to feel his lips, the pressure of his body on hers, taste his mouth, his tongue, his sweat. But she stared at her reflection and saw only her face. Ay, so many wrinkles. Time had worked its troubles, hadn't it? She rubbed her face, caressed her hard-earned wrinkles. What to do, what to do? All that information from Tony: a candle, a transformation, change in the air. *¿Qué significa?* She didn't know what to think anymore. With a sigh that left its foggy mark on the mirror, she shuffled back to her bedroom to make her bed. Cautiously, for her back was creaking like a rusty hinge, she bent over to extend her Print of Paradise comforter. Such pretty bright colors, and a bargain, too. Small pleasures. She sat on the bed, removed her slippers, and slipped into her size-six Reebok sneakers. Her marching shoes, her pathfinders. Cuca knew she had first agreed to wear these rubber implements with the sky-high price and aerodynamic styling because of Maribel. ("Abuela, you have to wear flats. Comfortable flats." Or, "Abuela, once you wear these shoes, you will never want to wear anything else." Or, "Look at Mami and all the crimping she goes through to look good. You have more sense, Abuela.") But now she wore these funny-looking modern inventions because they fit so well, and they were light, and as with the damage to her skin, time had marked her feet with an increased heaviness.

She moved to her dresser and began the process of putting on her forty-six gold bracelets, one by one, twenty-three on each arm, and remembering the occasions on which they had been presented. Not every one was a pleasant memory. Tony had left the eighth gold band (or was it the ninth?) on her dresser one morning with a love note. That night, as he had so many other nights for two months, he disappeared into the darkness and returned with a smell she refused to remember now. Another bracelet reminded her of Adela's hurried wedding and the loud dissatisfaction—directed at her, the questioning of her mothering skills—from the man who should have shouldered as much of the blame as she had. And there was one wedding anniversary, into the second decade, when they were fighting spectacularly (the walls shook when they clashed) because Tony wanted to invest their meager savings to buy the town bakery with one of his brothers. Ay, remember that? Her dear husband—so stubborn sometimes. Only sometimes? Ha!—thought there was a fortune to be made in this endeavor, and perhaps he was right, but never with that brother, a cheating scoundrel who had stolen money from his own mother. If only they had had enough money to buy it on their own. How sweet life would have been, full of syrup and confectioner's sugar, eh?

Most bracelets, however, represented joyful times, passionate moments of ecstasy the body knew, as well as the soul. Ay, the mere thought made her quiver. People thought age whittled away at desire, as though time deadened the nerve endings or something. What did they know? Had it happened to her? Hardly. Her only problem was that the object of her affections (though it was much more accurate to label it a fiery craving) had been removed from her life, and she was forced to use the heated dreams of the night to replace what had been a guiding light of her days. ¡Ay, ay, ay!

Jingle-jangle, she shook her arms. Magic music.

She waited until Adela had left the house to phone Maribel at the hospital. It took several rings for her to answer. She had fallen asleep in the recliner, Maribel admitted. Yes, Victor was still running a high fever, but it was controlled. The doctors were optimistic. He battled, this tiny baby, with the strength of a grown man. Brave warrior. Cuca was encouraged by Maribel's cheery optimism.

"*Hija*," she began, and wished she could press this point in person, "you know that bright light you see when you close your eyes?"

Silence.

"Like a star or a very powerful candle?" Cuca insisted.

"Abuela."

"Do not fear what I have to say to you, my child. I see it, too, that is why I need to speak to you about it."

"What is it?"

"Victor's soul."

Maribel laughed.

"I'm serious."

"Oh, Abuela!"

Cuca imagined Maribel's expression at that very minute: an annoyed grimace, disbelieving one second, desperately hopeful the next.

"I can see that hole of yours, Maribel, as well as I can see that star."

More silence. Cuca jingled her bracelets to interrupt its deafening depression.

"Okay, Abuela, I do see the blinking light. It's so . . . so violently bright sometimes."

"A north star."

"So what?"

"It's there for a reason."

"What reason?"

Now Cuca was stumped. She shifted her weight on the living-room sofa and looked up, for inspiration, at the iridescent eyes of the Sacred Heart. She wasn't sure she herself had understood her husband's message. What was it again? Something about transfor-mation, a particular kind of transformation. And the candle, *sí*, something about the candle losing itself in the sacrifice. *What did it all mean?*

"I'm not sure what it means, *hija*, but your grandfather . . ."

"Oh, no, Abuela, don't start on that."

"You must remember that faith . . ."

"Is all we have when there is nothing else. I know."

"Just be open to what you see and feel, Maribel. Don't build walls. And remember that illusion is part of disillusionment."

"What's that supposed to mean?"

"Just what it says. You can't be disillusioned if you don't have some illusion in the first place."

After she hung up, Cuca wondered if she had garbled the mes-sage in the retelling, or maybe she had never understood what Tony had tried to tell her in the first place. Was it a warning, the starlight in the darkness? A prophecy? Or just her too vivid imagination?

Ay, Dios. Cuca realized she was growing increasingly confused. Time for the morning tea. She needed a cleansing of the poisons confusing her body: dandelion.

Dandelion leaves, Mamá Cleofe used to tell her, must be gath-ered when they are young. Left to age in the fields, they grow much too bitter. ("Like some folks around these ways," Mamá Cleofe whis-pered.) The flowers with the top leaves are especially good for bil-iousness due to stomach problems or heartbreaks and deceptions. A handful of those thrown into boiling water, steeped for about ten minutes and strained carefully, make a good hot tea. Honey sweetens the herb. Mmmmm! She didn't feel so confused anymore, only a little light-headed.

Adela sprinkled cinnamon over the warm *arroz con leche* she had just finished making. It was a peace offering she intended to take to her daughter at the hospital.

"I can't understand her reaction," she was telling Cuca.

"You're not that stupid, Adela. You should understand, and you do. You just do not want to accept it."

"Whatever."

"Shame is a most uncomfortable feeling."

"Is that a new cologne you have on, Mamá?"

"No, the same *agua de violeta*. Do you know what day it is today?"

Adela looked up at the calendar and gasped. "Papá's anniversary! Do you want me to take you to the cemetery?"

"Yes, of course, so don't dawdle."

"I'm not. It just bothers me, her holier-than-thou attitude. Who does she . . ." Her hands grabbed at the air for words.

"She's your daughter, Adela, and she has every right. *Un hijo es el peor crítico.*"

"Well, I'm not your worst critic."

"Really?" Cuca arched an eyebrow.

"She shouldn't judge, that's all."

"She will."

"Well, then, not so harshly."

Cuca took the plastic container with the rice pudding from her daughter and pressed a lid on it. Then, like a queen bearing a royal present, she paraded out of the house in her flower-print shirtdress and Reebok sneakers, bracelets jangling, violet cologne scenting the air in her wake. Adela, primped up in a narrow black skirt and form-fitting white mock turtleneck, followed her to the car, heels tap-tapping to a silent music.

24

So what was she supposed to do with the *arroz con leche*? Accept it as it was intended, an olive branch? Or could she do with it as she really wanted—throw it against the hospital room wall and watch it splatter and stain, a visible sign of her anger and disappointment? Taste it, taste it, her mother was saying. I even left the lemon rinds in, just the way you like it. I brought a plastic spoon. You need to eat. Blah blah blah. Why so much talk? Why the overtures? Words meant nothing to Maribel now, though she suspected that an open apology, an admission of guilt, would have gone much further than food. What did she want from her mother? What did she need from her? What could she expect? Oh, she wasn't so sure most times, but this once she knew she wanted the traditional "I'm sorry," and also something else: heartfelt remorse, a promise. But Adela couldn't say "I won't do it again"; it was beyond her. Her mother was rarely sorry about anything, and she had such little self-control that one minute she promised to abstain but the next . . . she couldn't resist. So immature, really.

Maribel sighed.

"Eat something!" Adela and Cuca chanted in unison.

Theirs was an unusual relationship, Maribel thought, a complicated, erratic pas de deux with no end. Growing up, she liked to think of it as a complementary partnership that benefited both of them, mother and daughter, but later, as Maribel gained maturity and experience and knowledge of the world beyond her house, their alliance shifted, lost its footing. In the dance now, they were no longer touching hands, and sometimes they had their backs to each other, moving to the rhythm of individual songs. After Victor, Maribel thought that the music had blended together once again, like a piano duet. But now . . . now . . .

"Taste it, why don't you?" her mother insisted.

The words echoed in Maribel's head: Taste it, why don't you-you-you. Maybe she was coming down with a cold, her brain was so clouded. Maybe she had caught Victor's pneumonia. Her big heart brave heart bird-boy. Victor Eduardo.

"Aren't you hungry, *hija?*"

Aargh!

Maribel traced the dissonance in their relationship to her conception, that sudden, surprising result of a coupling that had no basis in love or shared interest, only mutual lust. Yet she blamed it not on Adela (though she was tempted to, and Adela probably did need to share some of the blame) but on the man they shared in common: her father. Without ever truly knowing him, Maribel had created a character for Miguel, imbuing him with the qualities she thought would have served to balance her own rigidity (yes, she admitted it) with her mother's impulsiveness. Her father was fulcrum, but more than that, too. He was catalyst and circuit breaker, judge and jury, diplomat and doer. He possessed what the two of them were missing. Or he would have, had he not died.

His death, even before that, his departure, had formed an annoying but ever-growing secret pebble of resentment toward her mother in her heart. She dared not exhume it now, when Victor was in the hospital demanding an emotional energy and support only she could give. The resentment simmered, though, a stewed secrecy ready to boil over into anger. She felt its heat sometimes, flushing her neck and face, suffusing the rest of her body with an electricity that agitated her. Resentment, even if safely secreted, gathered a life of its own.

Yes, it had a long history, this exasperation. It began in the womb. Others did not believe in pre-birth memory, but Maribel did. She remembered. Or perhaps it was not memory at all but whispers overheard, muddled stories deciphered, blanks filled in between the lines: a slow but cumulative process. Over the years, she had accumulated these nuggets of information, and they formed the framework of her identity.

Begin at the beginning: Abuelo Tony had forced her mother to marry. In essence, she owed her life, her very being, to an old-fashioned, machista edict. Her mother, young, pert, and hopeful, had consented, but treated the pregnancy—by all accounts, in stories she had heard both intentionally and unintentionally—with equal measures of jubilance and disdain. She knew, too, about the time her mother, fully into the second trimester, had gone roller-skating. (Yes!) And from a slipped word here, a telling phrase there, Maribel had also managed to pick up on how Adela had drunk beer and wine, sometimes smoked, behind her husband's back—while pregnant. (And to think how she, Maribel, had suffered stoically the caution of her own pregnancy, how she had read aloud to Victor in the womb, sang to him, talked to him, eaten her vegetables, her fruits, her carbohydrates, never forgotten to take her vitamins!)

And that was just beginning at the beginning.

"Well, if you're not going to have any pudding, I'll try some," Cuca said.

"Go ahead, Abuela."

Should she go on with her story of betrayal and confusion? Details or general description? Either choice was fine. Maribel had plenty of examples.

Her earliest memories were of Adela's beauty, a jealously guarded, often flaunted beauty. Adela was not like other mothers, and had no intentions of being. She was not fat. She danced to music on the radio. She flirted. She was up on the latest fashions: white go-go boots, miniskirts, fringed vests, platform shoes, bell-bottoms, halter tops. Get the picture? Maribel's childhood was governed by a mother who danced with the pink hula hoop better than her daughter ever did.

Adela taught her many things, sometimes unwittingly. At times the lessons were formal. How to walk. How to get in a car. What to say to someone you have just met. Which fork to use. How to cross your legs. When to smile and when to bat your eyelashes. When to touch a man. In other words, manners with flair. These were the small formal lessons that took a few minutes of any given day, and were often mentioned in passing. "Mari, *hija*, do not slouch. Do not walk like you don't want to get there. Now stand up straight. See? See my back, a perfect line? Go on, straighter. Your head. Up. Look ahead. Point your chin, *hija*. More. Okay. *Bien, muy bien.* Now you look like a princess. Walk over to the door and back. Slowly. No, no, no! *¡Dios mío!* Listen to the rhythm inside you. Do you hear it? Why that face? Don't you hear it? Everyone has a rhythm. Listen closely. Concentrate. Now walk. No, no, no. Come back over here. Walking is not throwing out your legs or strutting like a peacock. Walking is the movement to your inner rhythm. Watch me. Watch my hips. See? A smooth glide and a little hip action. Not too much. Just a little. Try it, Mari. Okay, okay. Better. Now you have to practice in front of the mirror. Do it slowly first, then work into it, until you find your own rhythm. Listen to it. Do you hear it?"

Then there were the Lessons, with a capital L, ones that should have been serious, thoughtful, insightful, but instead were simplistic, irreverent, sometimes funny. They made Maribel nervous. Like when they talked about menstruation. And sex. And men.

About sex: "It's a little giving and a lot of taking. *Una taza de arena y otra de cal.*" A cup of sand, another of quicklime, that was Adela's favorite saying. Maribel never understood what she meant, and was too embarrassed to ask.

About men: "They're all after the same thing." Adela pretended an obliqueness, but the dance of her hands, the emphasis on *all* and *thing* left Maribel with a strange doubt, almost a hope.

About menstruation: "Men worry about impotence. All we have to worry about is our monthly flow. I think we got the better end of the deal, eh?"

Much of what Maribel had learned, though, was passed down

not by words but by actions. Maribel observed: the way her mother applied her makeup, the smile with which she anointed her men, the aura she exuded, and of course, always always, the stares she received from the opposite sex. Maribel noticed, because Adela stared *back*. She was unflinchingly consistent about this, her mother.

"I'm hungry. I think I'll have some of that pudding," Adela said.

"Go right ahead, Mami."

"Let me go and ask the nurse for an extra spoon."

Adela sashayed out of the room, the black skirt outlining the tight roundness of her buttocks, her shoes click-clicking daintily.

"How can she walk in those heels?" Maribel asked her grandmother. Maribel, in one of Eduardo's University of Miami Hurricanes T-shirts and jeans (freshly pressed, of course), always felt underdressed around her mother.

"Well, she can't imagine how you can be so fastidious about so many things," Cuca replied. She licked her lips with delight. Adela had oversweetened the pudding, but that's exactly the way Cuca liked it.

"Maribel . . ."

"Abuela . . ."

They laughed. Maribel motioned for her grandmother to continue.

"You know, *hija*, your mother is beside herself with that incident of the other night."

Maribel rolled her eyes.

"Now listen to me. She is. She wants to make amends."

Maribel snorted so loud that Victor blinked his eyes open. She cooed him back to sleep. Cuca carefully placed the plastic container with the rice pudding on the tray table and shuffled to the crib to stroke Maribel's hands.

"One of the most comforting things for me these past few trying weeks has been seeing how you react to what many would think of as a tragedy. If nothing else, Victor has brought us all closer together."

Whether it was the way her grandmother held her hand or the mention of her son's name, one or the other brought tears to Maribel's eyes. Or maybe it was just listening to truth spoken so plainly.

"*Hija*," continued Cuca, "help your mother with the apologies. Don't close her out of your life."

"It is inconceivable to me . . ."

"In a few months or maybe a few days, nothing will be inconceivable."

"I'm not closing her out. She is doing it to herself."

"Rejection is shutting somebody out of your life. So are disdain and arrogance."

"Why did she get involved with Carlos, of all people? And at this time, of all times?"

"Security."

"Security?"

"Ah, a strange concept, no? Listen, *hija*, there's a memory of pain in all of us. Touch a bone somewhere and we may wince though there is absolutely nothing wrong with us now. But the imprint is there. Your mother carries that imprint."

"She should know better by now."

Cuca laughed. "So should you about her. You've known her for almost three decades."

Adela sashayed back into the room, humming, smiling. "I've got two more spoons," she said cheerily, waving them about like trophies. "One for you, Maribel, and one for me."

Maribel and Cuca exchanged glances. Maribel thought she heard harpsichord music, a harmonious duet. Where was it coming from? It was so distinct, each note resounding with a depth and tone that surpassed any other music she had ever heard on Muzak. She joined her mother at the tray table. They reached for the *arroz con leche* at the same time, and their hands—Adela's flighty, dancing one, Maribel's steady, searching one—met on the rim of the plastic container.

"I just want a little bit," Maribel said softly.

"Well, I want more than that."

Mamá Cleofe was waiting by Adela's Ford Escort, a muted star that could barely be seen in the constellation of parking-lot lights. She commented on the fading red plastic carnation Adela had rubber-banded to her antenna. This made Cuca laugh aloud.

262 • Ana Veciana-Suarez

"What are you laughing at?" Adela asked.

Cuca did not answer. She was busy listening to Mamá Cleofe.

That dear child thinks there are antidotes to life's pains.

What do you mean, Mamá Cleofe?

Maribel expects age—youth—to serve as shield.

Well, so would I.

There are no antidotes, Cuca. Not experience. Not beauty or brains or money. Not even faith. You cannot inoculate against tribulations.

"Mamá," Adela whined, "who are you talking to now?"

Do you know, my Cuca, that the life you lead, that we all once led, is like exile.

How so, Mamá Cleofe?

It is a separation from our true home, geographically, emotionally, spiritually. A journey.

And home, you are telling me, is where you are. That other life. The life after this life.

I will not define home for you. I will leave that to your imagination. I will define exile for you, though, and perhaps you will recognize displacement. You are living it, exile.

"Mamá, will you get into the car before somebody arrests us for loitering or talking to the air?"

Cuca, my little one, exile is more than separation and absence. It is memory erased and reconstructed.

I don't understand why you are telling me this.

Doubt is the worm in the apple.

What?

Because you cannot remember or you cannot imagine, you doubt. But be careful: the worm is dangerous.

You make me feel ignorant, Mamá Cleofe.

Intelligent, caring people can be blind. Do you want more proof than the child.

"Mamá? Mamá? Who the hell are you talking to?"

Ay, Mamá Cleofe, you have given me much to think about, but there are always things I do not understand.

Good. To understand often means to simplify. Simplification is not always possible, should not be possible. You cannot reduce what is bigger than yourself.

Mamá Cleofe! Wait, there is something I want to ask. Mamá Cleofe!

"Insanity has reached new heights. Get in the car, Mamá. I think there's a security guard headed our way."

"Oh, Adela, you would not believe . . ."

"Hmmm. I like the way he struts. Nice ass."

Chica, he looked so good. Watching Carlos sitting in the dim light of the living-room lamp, legs crossed, head tilted just so, Adela wanted to rub up against him like a cat just let in from the cold by its benevolent master. His eyes were so green, the smile so winsome! Oh, and the breadth of his shoulders. *¡Chica, chica, chica!* This was proving to be a lot more difficult than she thought.

"I can't understand why, all of a sudden . . ." Carlos sounded perplexed.

"It's not all of a sudden, and I don't expect you to understand."

"Then I want you to think about it. We are so good together."

"In bed, Carlos, in bed. We are not together in any other aspect of our lives."

"You look nice, very nice in that black skirt."

She laughed. He heard a flute, then the trombone. "Stick to the topic at hand."

"You make breaking up sound like a business transaction, Adela."

"It isn't?"

He reached across the coffee table to touch her knee. His fingers seared through her hose, her skin. She remembered the taste of his kiss, the stroke of his tongue against her nipples, the pressure of his hands when he searched, the thrusting and nibbling and panting and nuzzling and rubbing. All those things, she remembered and wanted—and knew she must give up.

"Think about it," he insisted.

"I have."

"Not enough, *mi cielo*."

"Yes, enough."

He knelt beside her, held her face in his hands, caressed it. "I know what you want."

Adela smiled. She knew what he was thinking by his silly grin, and he was so off the mark. "Do you really?"

He leaned to kiss her. She dodged his lips. Maybe it wouldn't be so difficult after all. He recovered, the Cheshire grin now replaced by a befuddled look.

"Well, you know where to find me," he told her as he left.

She did not reply. She did not nod her head. She did not even dare to stare at the door closing behind him. But she did hug herself. Then she closed her eyes and hummed a strange piano-like melody that echoed in her head and rocked to and fro and thought that it wasn't so bad being alone at night and congratulated herself for acting responsibly and tried to remember how Cuca prepared that mint tea that made her insides sparkle.

"Put a half-dozen fresh sprigs into a teacup," Cuca said.

"Mamá!" Adela sat up, startled. "How long have you been there?"

"Do you want to know about the mint tea or not? Fill the cup with boiling water and set the saucer on top. Keep it that way for five minutes. Add a pinch of bicarbonate of soda and stir."

Peeking in on this scene, someone else may have nodded in recognition of two women stripped of pretensions, alone, in the dark. But Cuca observed something else entirely: one woman who had finally donned the gold-threaded garment of responsibility, another helping with the tiny matching buttons. Adela would have agreed.

25

This time the mist arrived bearing a scent Cuca readily recognized. It seeped in through her closed bedroom door in the middle of the night, when she could still taste the freshness of the mint tea on her tongue, and in the middle of a vivid dream that she would never confide to anyone because it was so pleasurable that the roots of her hair tingled and her fingertips went numb and her toes twitched. (¡Ay, cielo, qué rico!) She did not want to leave this dream; in fact, she wanted to delve deeper into it, savor its sensations, envelop herself in the color and the music and the taste of this sensual past she could never get back.

But that scent: sweet, cloying, penetrating. It nudged her awake, beckoned. She refused to sit up. Instead, she pulled the Print of Paradise comforter over her head and willed herself back to sleep, back to that dream, where touch became electrifying and her skin was stretched taut and her eyes grew clear and her hair turned the black of the coal used in the stove. The dream, the dream.

She was home, in the massive marriage bed carved from good Cuban caoba. She was naked. The sheets were cool; they smelled of Caribbean sun. He was warm. And he was patient. There was none of the rushed lust that marked their lovemaking at night. Kisses deepened, touch lingered. In the distance, birds harmonized with the lights of early morning.

The fog, however, was much too strong, the scent too over-powering. It soaked the comforter, settled over the sheets made hot by this old body, hers, with wrinkled skin and myopic eyes and white hair. It spoke to her, the scented fog.

Fiel. Ser fiel.

Faithful? She had always been faithful. And Tony, he had tried. Give him credit for trying.

Fidelidad.

Faithful to what? To her husband? To her daughter, granddaugh-ter? To her life? She sank lower into the bed, pulled the comforter higher, over her head.

Fiel. Fidelidad. Fidelity to your vision.

What vision? *Dios mío*, what was all this about?

Slowly, steadily, in the same way night lifts itself into day, letting in warmth and light and hope, the scent of honeysuckle receded, but Cuca, confused, cowering still under the Print of Paradise comforter, did not leave her bed until she was convinced she could no longer reenter that dream, that wonderful, sensual dream, again. *¡Coño!*

In the fifteen days that followed Victor's release from the hospital, a quiet ache settled into Maribel's soul, yet she managed to cling, with a ferocity that would have surprised even her grandmother, to a daily schedule of Chin Kiss Games. They played whenever he opened his eyes, whenever he was strong enough to remain awake (a few seconds sometimes, minutes rarely), and she thought of her father then, how tall and handsome he had appeared to her, how very manly, and she thought, too, of the calliope music of the ice-cream man and the brain-freezing coldness of red Popsicles licked carefully on a porch stoop. Sometimes she wondered if she should prefer a variation of the game—perhaps add thighs in the middle, or remove references to toes or knees—but she decided that pre-dictability was something to be treasured.

"Big heart brave heart Victor Eduardo."

The baby blinked awake. She thought he smiled, but his small, round eyes, sparrow eyes, wren eyes, hummingbird eyes, drooped closed.

"*Mi cielo, mi tesoro, corazón de melón.*"

"Oh, let him fall asleep," Adela snapped.

"Why, Mami?" Maribel asked crossly. "He likes playing this way, and it's good for him. Stimulation."

"*Ay, pobrecito.*"

"Victor."

Victor's eyes opened. The depth of their blackness was frightening.

"Chin kiss time. Let's start with the fingers."

Maribel reached for his fingers, white worms curled toward the warmth of his palm.

"Kissie, kissie, kissie." Her index finger, with its nail recently painted a Blossom Sweet shade by Adela, met his.

She pressed knuckles to knuckles, wrists to wrists. He seemed to smile, to move.

"Hey!" she greeted his efforts. "Hey!"

She rubbed elbows.

"Victor," she chirped, "a nose kiss. An Eskimo kiss."

Nose to beak. Then she moved right into the cheek kiss, left, right. She sensed Adela waiting for her to finish, waiting warily, and was annoyed at her mother's perseverance. But it was a fleeting exasperation, like a muscle twitch that settles smoothly under the skin after its first warning.

"Okay, now, Victor. Stick that chin out. Out, out, out. Ta-dah—the chin kiss."

In addition to the game, Maribel also wrote letters to Eduardo, letters she never mailed but that served as outlets for her rage and disappointment. The crumpled remnants of her attempts sat in her bedroom wastebasket. Even the salutations, something as simple as that, had proven to be irksome: Eddy or Eduardo or My Dear Husband or My Sweetheart or *Mi Cielo* or Dearest or, as she scribbled in her last feeble try, You Bastard.

She had a vague notion of what she wanted to say—When are you coming home?—but during different drafts, her feelings ebbed.

By the fifth draft, she was wondering about, or perhaps longing for, the freedom of being a fugitive. Running away appeared more liberating than acceptance, running away with Eduardo but also escaping alone.

"I have been thinking of your offer of going away. Remember?" she wrote. (She had a very neat, schoolteacher-like hand, circumspect, without the flourishes of her grandmother's or the fickleness of her mother's.) "I have thought of what it would be like for us to live alone, without a past, on some island in the Caribbean." She had paused here in the writing to consider if her mother and grandmother would be able to handle Victor alone. "Then I think that after a while we wouldn't like it, living without a past, I mean, no matter how much we enjoyed being together. Besides, where would we work? What money would we have? What names would we use? Would we ever see our families again?"

None of the other attempted letters carried that tone of measured wistfulness nor did they broach the subject of escape in any way. On the contrary.

"Your son is the sunshine of my life," she began in one. "I can't understand how you would choose to live in darkness."

In another: "When we're all together watching Victor open his eyes or turn his head to look at us, I feel your absence more than ever. Where are you? Where are you?"

In another still: "You got a lot of balls leaving me. Abandoning me. And your parents? Haven't heard boo from them."

"You don't know what you're missing," she wrote, too. "Might as well return home and see what happens. Take a chance."

Of course she never took the chance of putting any of these letters in a white envelope, sealing it, printing his name on it in simple block letters, and leaving it in the mailbox for the unknown messenger who had once left a flurry of Eduardo's notes in the very same black metal box. Too much time had elapsed since their separation, and it was he, she believed, who needed to come to her, not the other way around.

So much time had passed, yes, so much time. Already the weather had stumbled into the steaminess of June. (Summer in Miami does not move in overnight; it creeps up before it can be officially welcomed, its hot, humid breath like a vaporizer on one's neck, sweat drip-dripping from armpits, under breasts, between thighs, where silky skin tends to chafe.) That she had noticed the weather—and the depth of their separation—pleased her. She wanted to believe that recognition of detail, amid pain, was a sign of healing, or of promise. Cuca would have told her otherwise, but the temperature, for all its torridness, never came up as a topic of conversation that summer, until deep into August, and no one ever spoke Eduardo's name to her face.

During those first sweltering days of summer, Maribel found herself cleaving to her mother's company, her grandmother's wisdom. Many years later, when she looked back at this particular period, she would remember not the mounting tension that accompanies all fatal illnesses but the gentleness of the hours as these drifted and bumped into each other. They became halcyon days, paradoxically so, for they were pregnant with impending anxiety, like the bruised clouds of a summer thunderstorm, while also being blessed with the peace of acceptance, the satisfaction of knowing she was managing to stay the course.

As she spent more and more time with her mother and her grandmother, she began enjoying their stories, their idiosyncrasies, the very fact that their brains, illogical, circuitous, never worked the way she expected them to, certainly not the way hers did. For instance, Adela had a surprisingly agile head for numbers, a fact her daughter had failed to notice before. But that extraordinary ability translated itself into something Maribel considered totally useless: Adela could figure out the odds of winning almost anything with the speed and accuracy of a calculator. How does she do that? Maribel would ask herself, watching her mother from afar, as she ripped through piece after piece of junk mail, looking for entries into sweepstakes, possible announcements of finalist status, declarations that yes, you are our lucky winner.

Maribel, who always had tossed out every piece of junk mail, now read the letters avidly, scanning the sections in red or blue or bold print for important information. She did not fill out forms, no. That would have been going a step too far, but occasionally she did read them aloud to her mother and giggled over various passages, primarily those that tempted with schlocky gifts or gifts she knew she would never receive:

"I knew that *Homemakers* would want nothing but the best for their friends," Maribel read from one letter, chortling. She paused and looked up at her mother, who was heating up a can of Campbell's Golden Mushroom soup. "Shouldn't it read 'the best for *its* friends'? Isn't a magazine an it and not a they?"

"Who cares? What are they giving away and what do you have to do, that's what I want to know," said Adela, anxious for the information.

Not only did they read mail to each other, together they also played with Victor, dressed him, changed his diapers. They washed clothes, folded them in tandem. Maribel picked up the habit of watching the *novelas*, the Spanish-language soaps on television, and was surprised at how she, too, found herself spellbound by the ridiculously contorted story lines. Every night at ten o'clock, she and Adela splurged on a plate of cream cheese with guava marmalade, a sticky sweetness she somehow had forgotten from her childhood.

These were not days without squabbles, of course. Closed surroundings, forced familiarity, tentative discoveries of each other made for misunderstandings. Adela remained sloppy, Maribel tidy as a mortuary. Adela continued to visit the bodega to play the Cash 3 daily, and Maribel warily watched her mother leave every afternoon and wondered if "the affair," as she called it, was being rekindled.

One day, as Adela pranced out of the house, rosy and perfumed for her daily stroll, Maribel confronted her on the porch. "You're running over to meet him again, aren't you?" Maribel demanded.

Adela's hands danced nervously in front of her. "Don't be ridiculous. I'm going to play the Lotto."

"Play it at the gas station."

"I've always played it at the bodega."

"Change."

"Don't be ridiculous."

When Adela tried to pass on Maribel's left side, Maribel grabbed her by the arm. "Are you, Mami? Are you seeing Carlos again?"

"What do you think?" Adela looked straight into her daughter's slanted black eyes.

Maribel let go of her mother's arm. "I . . . I . . . ."

"I am a lot stronger than you give me credit for, Mari. Much of my life has been spent conquering my tendencies."

Maribel stepped to one side and watched Adela sashay down the street, tall heels tap-tapping the very same road her husband had used to walk away from their lives, the same street that, in Maribel's mind, had led away from her childhood. For a fleeting moment, she was assaulted by one vision: her father's back moving steadily away, leaving, defecting, his back so tall, so proud, so erect, so much part of the Papi she had adored. Then aloud but softly, to herself but also to the hot, humid air surrounding her, Maribel repeated her mother's words: *conquering my tendencies.* Funny her mother should say that. Strange that she should describe her life that way. Conquering, overcoming, mastering.

Mastering the mysteries of life was so much her grandmother's domain, the field where Cuca served and dealt, listened and opined. But Adela?

"She has learned my lessons better than I might have thought," Cuca answered Maribel when she asked for a translation of her mother's words.

Grandmother and granddaughter had talked often and at length the past two weeks about Cuca's eight lessons of life—which, by the way, Maribel had found endearing, the way her grandmother had written them on the legal-pad paper with her exaggerated, fancy writing, then folded the paper in threes horizontally, then vertically again, and placed it in her underwear drawer close to the smell of dried-flower potpourri. Maribel wondered what lesson her mother had found particularly difficult, impossible to truly master.

"Every lesson has varying levels of difficulty, *hija*," she replied, bracelets jangling. "Some of us find one more difficult than the other because of our personality or our—how would you say?—tendencies."

"Which has been the hardest lesson of all for you, Abuela?"

Cuca considered the question. The two women were sitting on Cuca's living-room sofa, Maribel in the middle, Cuca on the end, leaning lightly on the armrest, the TV set on low to Channel 23, the iridescent green eyes of the black velvet Sacred Heart of Jesus staring down on them. Quickly, Cuca ran through the lessons: To love. To care for one's own. To accept, to fight, to surrender. To build a home (not to be mistaken for keeping house). To allow one's children to take flight. To dance, to laugh, to cook a coconut flan. To never forget. To never say never.

"So?" Maribel insisted.

"I think it has been to allow one's children to take flight. Or maybe to never say never. One of those two. And you?"

"To accept, to fight, to surrender," Maribel replied without a second thought. "I can't always distinguish between them."

"Yes, tough lesson. *Difícil*. Anything else?"

"To laugh," said Maribel, and laughed hard, from the very center of her belly, with the eagerness of someone who has just learned to blow bubbles with her gum or ride her bike without training wheels. "Yes, to laugh."

And so the women, for those two weeks, immersed themselves in the quotidian, in the thrill and relief of texturing one's life with the ordinary. Later, much later in her years, Maribel realized that those fifteen days of ridiculous readings of sweepstake entries and childish kiss games and talks of life lessons had provided her with sanctuary, a journey into restoration and renewal. In her old age, the appreciation of this reprieve, and the vivid joyful memory of it, tempered the pain of having felt too much—and having lost it so quickly.

The surgeon greeted her with a smile as he closed the door behind him. Maribel and Victor were in the same waiting room as on the last visit, the room with the pale pink walls and the mobile of papier-mâché planes twirling under an air-conditioning vent. This time, though, Maribel was confident there would be a better outcome.

"How time flies, Mrs."—he glanced at her file—"Mrs. Garcia."

"Yes."

"Time to remove that tube. And it seems like yesterday we were performing the operation."

Like yesterday? Who was he kidding? It had been an eternity, an infinite stretch between then and now. But of course she said nothing. She returned his smile and continued to hold Victor tight to her breast.

"Now, why don't you put him on the examining table here, so we can take a good look at him." His deep voice rang hypnotically, with an authority no one dared question. But he still looked like Humpty Dumpty.

The surgeon beeped the nurse, who padded into the room and acknowledged Maribel with a nod. Reluctantly, she placed Victor on the table and stepped aside for the examination. What would they do? Would they hurt him again? Would he scream in agony as last time?

"Very good, very good," said the doctor, as much to himself as for her.

She felt the surgeon's fingers on her own skin, pressing the side of her chest, tracing the wound in her own belly, probing, prodding. Victor, awake now, eyes fixed on the ceiling above him, neither winced or whined. The doctor took the syringe his nurse handed him, inserted it in the smaller opening of the G-tube and sucked the air out. Swiftly he pulled the tube out: the hole remained the size of a dime.

"There we go," the surgeon singsonged. "That wasn't so bad."

He was right. Victor seemed not to have felt it; he continued to stare at the ceiling. But Maribel clutched her stomach. She felt as if someone had pulled a thick rope through her insides.

He quickly began giving her instructions about the care of the wound. She listened carefully, but they were so many details and all seemed so complicated. She couldn't stop thinking about her own wound, still open, still gurgling.

"You mean you're not going to sew it shut?" she asked when he finished his discourse.

The surgeon frowned. He tilted his head, the head with the glue-on button eyes and wide, flat nose.

"Won't he bleed from there? Won't his intestines fall out?"

The solemn-faced nurse giggled. The surgeon patted Maribel on the shoulder condescendingly.

"No, of course not, Mrs.—" He mumbled, continued: "The wound will close on its own. Slowly the edges will meet."

And he was right. Eventually Victor's G-tube hole crept in on itself, the skin inching across, regenerating, covering ground. Some days it seemed as if it would never close, and Maribel twice called the surgeon to complain. "Patience," he advised. "These things take time." Most days, though, it seemed as if Victor's skin, growing too quickly, was reaching out from one side to another in a desperate attempt to make him whole, to make him right.

Her wound never closed. It remained as red and as round, gurgling as fiercely as the first day she had discovered it, invisible to those who could not see, but a strange and wondrous miracle to those who could.

26

June sweated into July. Maribel, anxious as a college graduate heading for her first day on a new job, returned to work on a particularly muggy Monday that set records for humidity and heat. Once there, she couldn't concentrate. At first she blamed the distractions created by her co-workers, the effusive greetings that appeared disproportionate to her nervous reluctance.

"Welcome back," chirped Vivian the receptionist, a thin woman with bright red acrylic nails and long, lank hair that she liked to toss back when the phones rang off the hook.

"Promise you won't leave us anymore," said Carmen, another research assistant.

Letty in her high-pitched voice hissed: "Well, well, well. It's the new mommy. We sure missed you."

Tim: "About time."

Chantal: "Girl, this place just about collapsed without you."

From his glass office, Caleb smiled and waved several times.

Her thoughts invariably drifted to the air-conditioned nursery where Victor slept. Was he comfortable? Had her mother warmed the formula correctly, thickened it with just the right amount of rice cereal? Had she checked his diaper? Oh, big heart brave heart Victor.

Her cubicle was piled with unopened mail, reports waiting to be corrected, charts that needed to be proofed, a couple of thick, scholarly books, several small gift-wrapped boxes, and, in a clear glass vase, a fragrant bouquet of red roses and baby's breath Caleb had sent upon her return. Sitting at her desk (an oak credenza with matching keyboard drawer), leaning back on her ergonomically approved chair, fingering the outline of her PC, she drew some satisfaction knowing that everything had remained as she remembered. But the mess, the mess! She stared at the clutter her working area had never known, unclear which stack of unfinished business she should attack first. She decided on the study completed while she was gone. Caleb had told her about it: several multinational corporations had sponsored a survey about Hispanics' use of coupons. Testing brand loyalty, he added. She opened the report and tried to read. After the second page, she looked up and sighed.

"Hey," said Tim, whose own desk was as exemplarily neat as hers had once been, "everything okay?"

She reassured him with a nod and turned her attention back to the report. But the pages moved, the letters danced. Sentences did not make any sense. The charts—they seemed overwhelmingly confusing. Focus, Maribel. Focus. Focus. She couldn't. Her mind was like a Mexican jumping bean, bouncing here, hopping there, unable to settle for very long on anything. And when it did, when her thoughts alighted on something constant, it was always the same image: Victor. Though literally separate from her, he was still figuratively attached by an invisible cord vibrating with love and devotion and doubt.

Oye, Mari.

Maribel glanced around her. That voice . . . it was so familiar. The cadences of its Spanish, melodic and baritone. The lilt at the end of the words: a singsong.

Mari, el juego. Mari, the game.

Who was talking? What game? Maribel scrambled up from her seat, hoping to surprise whoever or whatever was talking to her. Across the room? On the other side of the partition?

Cuando jugábamos eras feliz. When we played, you were happy.
Played what? Happy about what?

"You okay?" Tim asked.

She nodded much too quickly. Tim, a slightly built middle-aged man with a graying goatee, watched her with curiosity. Maribel smiled, hoping to dispel his concerns. Surreptitiously, she surveyed the room in search of the voice. The office—its fine credenzas and pleasing blue-gray carpeting, the espresso coffee machine they had all pitched in for last year, the thriving philodendron in the corner, the fax that made too much noise, the copier that reduced, enlarged, made colors, even the level of water in the water cooler—had changed little since that Leap Day in February. But she had. She had changed. The Maribel who thought life could be simplified into charts, where had she gone? With embarrassment she recalled that equation that she had so painstakingly put together, the explanation that reduced what was far too complex and certainly insoluble. Love = intensity + attachment squared by time − distraction. The thought of it, the mere suggestion that she had been so ignorant, made her shudder. Such equations, no matter how perfectly crafted, were theorems, that's all, ideas twisted into facts, based on assumptions and beliefs that could be proven in a limited universe. They were not truths.

Mari, cuando jugábamos eras feliz. Mari, when we played, you were happy.

Where was that voice coming from? So familiar, from somewhere deep in her past.

Bewildered, she sat down again, returned to the report, yellow highlighter in hand, which meant business, serious concentration. She read the first two pages again, the executive summary, and understood nothing. She blamed it on the din of the office, the normal noise of people working in close surroundings, a sound she had long forgotten in the solitary exclusiveness of her home. She tried hard to tolerate the conversations (Chantal laughed too much, Carmen talked too loud, Leticia gestured wildly), tolerate, too, the ringing of the phones, the hum of the air conditioner, the annoying underbeat of the Muzak, the insignificance of it all.

Suddenly she realized the sad duplicity in her life. It did not mean anything, this report. Brand X or brand Y? Fifty cents off or

free trial package? Spring or winter expiration date? She wondered
who really cared how many coupons were used by a family of four
with an annual income of $35,000. Well, not who cared exactly, for
someone obviously did, companies with money, because they had
funded the survey. The question really was: Did it matter? Could it
change fate? Save a life? Bind a family? Force a change? Make one
pray?

Te gustaba también el heladero. You also liked the ice-cream man.

What ice-cream man? Where are you? Oh, that voice, that voice.
She shook her head because the voice, that voice with the familiar
lilt, was inside her head, wasn't it? Exasperated, she tossed the cou-
pon survey aside and began looking through another stack for the
first draft of a report Carmen had completed recently. She couldn't
remember what it was about, though Caleb had told her. Everything
went through her, past her; her brain had become porous. Nothing
stayed in for very long except . . . except . . . It wasn't about coupons
of course, the new report, but something vaguely familiar, if only
she could pick through the flotsam of her brain. She did remember,
though (and she smiled gratefully at this recall), that Carmen had
completed it with Hiram, the statistician, before he had left for
another job in . . . where? New York. No, Los Angeles. Or was it
Boston? Newark? Oh, what was the use? Hiram had been replaced
by Paul, who was out of town for something else. A conference, a
workshop, something. Whatever it was, it had not stayed in her
brain.

No use, this.

Lo único que siento, hija, es no haber pasado más tiempo contigo.

*What regret? Spend more time with me? Who are you? What are you
talking about? Am I your daughter?*

She rushed to the bathroom, anxious to get away. Not much
had changed there, either. The same white standard-issue toilet that
choked when you flushed, the same blue-and-gray chevron-print
wallpaper, same plain sink with the rusty drain and round, fogged
mirror. Only the old soap dispenser—which had either dispensed
too much or too little, never the appropriate amount of creamy
liquid—had been replaced. But then, why should anything have
changed? What narcissistic idea had possessed her into believing

that because she had, everything that had once been important to her would be transformed, too?

Aquí más nunca se pone la luna su vestido de novia.

Maribel agreed. The moon would never wear its wedding dress here.

In the full-length wall mirror, Maribel checked the hole in her belly (still gurgling) and her makeup (blush, lipstick, mascara), fluffed up her hair, and rearranged her panty hose, white slip, and blue linen suit skirt.

Chiribiribi parapapá. ¿Te acuerdas?

"Remember what? Who are you?" Maribel demanded aloud.

The faucet drip-dropped in answer.

Coge tu sombrero y póntelo. Vamos . . .

"What hat? Go where?" She screamed. She smacked the paper-towel dispenser with her open hand. The clang of metal echoed in the small room. Frightened, Maribel scurried back to her desk.

She began to open the mail, dividing it into three piles: letters that needed to be answered, letters that required immediate attention, and everything else. She did this for half an hour, straining her muscles and her brain to stay on task, to focus, focus, focus, though her thoughts treacherously drifted home. Victor, my Victor. Big heart brave heart Victor.

Could her mother take care of Victor? She was so ditsy sometimes. She didn't exactly inspire confidence in her abilities outside the realms of betting odds and manhunts. Maribel shuddered at her vicious thoughts. Worry lured the demons into one's heart, didn't it?

Amé siempre a tu madre. Always I loved her.

"Hello, Mami," said Maribel, without any memory of having picked up the phone and dialing the numbers. "I'm coming home."

But Maribel did not return home. Not on the first day. Adela managed to convince her to stay, explaining that Victor was sleeping peacefully (*¡Chica, como un angel!*) and had not noticed her absence. Caleb, sensing the tenuous hold the office and its residents now had on Maribel, cajoled her into lunch at her favorite spot, a hole-in-the-wall eatery that specialized in *caldo gallego* (a hearty soup which she ate with great gusto despite temperatures that hovered around ninety-five by one o'clock). She worked diligently on Tuesday and Wednesday. On Thursday, a morning on which meetings with various clients pulled Caleb away from the office, Maribel sorted mail, answered letters, finished proofing a report, wrote the summary to another survey, typed three memos, including her resignation, and then went to lunch. She did not go back to the office, did not return for the velvet-red roses, now opening like hungry mouths, or the framed photograph of the entire staff—Maribel in the center, huge with child—posing under last year's Christmas tree. She wanted nothing to remind her of that chapter in her past. And she did not want to hear the man's voice singing: "*Coge tu sombrero y póntelo. Vamos a la playa, calienta el sol. Chiribiribi parapapá . . .*"

Ay, Dios mío, she had him all to herself this morning—Maribel running an errand, Adela at the bodega—and the promise of this communion, however hurried, however temporary, brought a smile to her lips. Cuca and Victor, a duo. Finally. They would go for an outing. Not far, just to the back yard, something she had meant to do for several days now but didn't dare. It took a good deal of sleuthing to find the white-and-blue Aprica stroller, fancy thing, an expensive import Maribel had bought the baby before he was ever born. It was stuck in the very back of her granddaughter's closet, behind some dresses, leaning against boxes, folded like a circus contortionist. Then, of course, she had to figure out how to open it, make it stand, so many metal parts and screws, plastic knobs and metal levers, with directions she could not understand (even the diagrams seemed drawn in a strange language), but Cuca managed somehow to get it working. It was these mechanical contraptions that underscored the painful absence of a man in the house. Or, as Maribel likely would have suggested, the contraptions simply pinpointed the type of important education women lacked—and needed—in certain fields of endeavor. Ay, but why bother thinking about that now? Why, why? She was going to take her own lessons to heart: she would laugh today, laugh a lot, laugh until her insides filled and rumbled with mirth.

Bracelets jangling, she lifted Victor from the crib and placed him in the stroller. He blinked awake and, she thought, he smiled, lipless mouth spreading, beak nose widening. Cautiously, she rolled him out of the room, down the hall, through the kitchen, bump-bump (carefully, carefully) down the back steps. She would have preferred to stroll to Douglas Park, where an old, majestic oak spread a wide shade over a green bench on the edge of a playground that offered an enticing view of dimpled knees and sneakered feet pumping hard on swings. She wasn't taking any chances, though. The heat, even this early in the morning, was brutal in July, and though Victor's health seemed to be flourishing, she did not dare parade him around, lest she attract . . . jealous spirits? The evil eye? She did not believe in those, such ignorant superstitions, but you never know, never know. Besides, how long would it take her to hobble down those blocks, dodging traffic, skirting barking dogs? A long time. She was an old woman with a young heart. Ay. Ay.

Years ago, in her pueblo, when the day unfolded into something as mellow and sweet as honey and smelled like sun-dried wash fetched in midafternoon, she used to take her babies out for strolls in an American-made carriage Tony had bought at El Encanto in Havana. So ostentatious, that carriage! How she had enjoyed showing it off, its big, wide wheels and solid navy-blue canvas, but she'd enjoyed most exhibiting her babies. Back then, one never took an infant out of the house before its first month. The threat of premature death blanketed the region and any hint of illness (cold, flu, malaria, pneumonia, dysentery, scarlet fever, rubella, mumps, chicken pox) sent Cuca rushing through the house, closing windows, drawing curtains, locking doors, and seeking the help of backyard herbs and the guidance of a fickle spirit, Mamá Cleofe's. Those were the times when mosquito netting was the only safeguard against the devastation of disease. Oh, but that stroller, how fine, how very fine! She would take her babies—Emilio, the only one who had survived the first month, a spunky infant until the dysentery killed him, and Adela, who had pouted and demanded in the womb, before she was ever born—on the cobblestone streets of her pueblo, to the beauty shop, maybe to the dressmaker's (though she could not afford any of her gowns, of course), to the butcher's, and to Benjamin *el boticario* for headache powders. Along the way, she always stopped to gossip, to listen, to pick up information that textured the lives of all the pueblo residents. No television then, some radio, but nothing else to divert the attention away from life and into fantasy. Many, many conversations, though, always plenty of that, and plenty of rich details that were savored along with the night's *potaje*. Cuca liked to talk and was often both the source and the disseminator of town news, occasionally perhaps its subject, too. Somehow these stories she shared gave another dimension to her life, a life she regarded, at times, as flat and monochromatic.

The stories she heard were fascinating. If only she could remember them all now. Sad stories, sexy stories, stories with happy endings, stories that were repeated from house to cabin to shack to restaurant to bakery shop. She remembered now the one about Pablo, who had left his wife, pregnant with their fifth child, for a cabaret dancer he had met in the capital, and Marta *la tortillera*, the town dyke who had taken up with another woman the next pueblo down and was committing despicable acts that both repulsed and intrigued Cuca—repulsed and intrigued her to such an extent that she whispered them to her husband that very night. (What possibly could women do to each other? It was difficult to imagine, though she had heard of homosexual men and had noticed an effeminate gesture or two. But women?) And there was Melba, the woman with three breasts, who had farmed herself out as a wet nurse to a wealthy family in Pinar del Río, and Martin's son, whatever-his-name, who had stolen his parents' savings (all thirty dollars) and stowed away on a ship to New York (good riddance! Cuca thought), and Humberto, who was experimenting with an engine that ran on sugar water, and Guillermo, who had left his perfectly good job as a teacher in Güines to write books (imagine! as if words could buy food), and Diana, who had walked to the field down the dirt road past her house and never returned (Cuca thought she had been abducted; everybody else said she ran away), and Mili, who finally—finally!—had left that no-good wife-beating son-of-a-bitch husband, moved to Havana, returned two years later pregnant with twins and no one to care for her, and the daughter of Francisco and Silvia, who had died in a diabetic coma on her wedding night (now, that was a tragedy). Oh, and also the very romantic tale of Margarita's niece, a slight Havana girl who gave in to vapors, and her torrid love affair with an American sailor she had met at a club dance, a handsome Texas-tall sailor with—oh—my—blue eyes, who also happened to be married, so Margarita's brother had threatened to send the law after him, but he returned north, divorced the wife, took the Key West ferry back to Havana, and began the long and silent courtship of this vaporous child, a courtship that seemed to proceed chiefly through long, meaningful looks and tempting smiles, for the sailor knew no Spanish and the girl only a few English words. Maybe that was better. Language tended to interfere with love. Ay, *tantos cuentos.*

Sometimes, after rambling through town, sipping some coffee at the stand or buying a *boniatillo or granizado* from the vendor, she settled into one of the black wrought-iron benches under the majagua trees in the plaza, breathing in the breeze, taking in the sun, preening, showing off. (With a good dress on, a fine dark cotton with a square sailor's collar, cinched tightly at the waist, flaring over the hips.) Other mothers congregated there, some young girls looking for husbands, too, and a few men loafing about. They discussed the war, first when it was Franco's, then when it was Hitler's, and sometime later, much later, the peace. Everyone talked about the wars and the government in the capital and whoever was in power at that time, but these were not favored subjects. The families of the pueblo were so infinitely more fascinating. And the babies in their carriages or in their new walking shoes so much more entertaining.

Before heading back home from the plaza, occasionally she stepped into the dim coolness of the stone church to cross herself and her baby, flesh of her flesh, blood of her blood, with holy water. The echoing silence of this old, old building filled her with a sense of peace, a satisfied need to belong. She wondered now how true those feelings had been or whether her reading of those emotions had been influenced by the strict conventions of the day. As she lived and suffered—was that redundant?—she discovered God in the most unusual places, sensed calm in the most tumultuous times. She had learned her way to and from, but especially through, the dark passages of pain and regret. She had discovered how to sit still through the urgency of life. Sitting, watching, waiting—ah, yes, that waiting, such patience and rigor in that waiting—had pushed her into another dimension of existence, and for that she was grateful.

Ay, what memories.

Now in the back yard of her Miami house, a home she had never expected, in a land she could not always understand, she glanced at what served as a substitute for the pueblo plaza: a long expanse of grass with patches of yellow, a laundry line strung taut between two anemic oak trees. These were not the majaguas of her youth, but they would do. The sky was the blue-black of a new bruise, and the air was redolent of rain. Not the weather she would have wanted, but she would make it do, had always settled for what she had been given, fighting it at first perhaps but then making do, making better. She pulled a lawn chair beside Victor's stroller, and she began to sing the songs she had sung in the hospital for the nurses and this beloved flesh of her flesh, blood of her blood, but primarily she sang to ward off the debilitating effects of fear and loss of hope: *Cielito Lindo* and *Naranja Dulce, Los Elefantes, De Colores, Los Pollitos.* And later, as she sang that timeless love song of fond memories—"*Quiéreme mucho, dulce amor mío, que amante . . .*"—a yellow dragonfly with transparent wings skimmed the stroller, then flitted to her. It was soon joined by a second dragonfly and a third; a fourth flew in, too, with sequined wings and a thorax like stretch lamé, and then dozens more arrived, until there were so many dragonflies, so many, so many, that they formed a dense cloud of whirring bodies and flapping wings, an assemblage of dizzying, streaking color, metallic gold and blood-crimson and the indigo of a jacaranda flower, wings of silver and hand-blown glass, wings of satin and velvet and chiffon, so many, so many of these astounding dragonflies, a tribe, a colony, a world. Cuca, rendered speechless, without melody or beat, remained utterly still, perfectly quiet. In sacramental reverence, heart burning, she shaded her eyes against the brilliance of the sun that appeared suddenly between the dark clouds, a pure light dappled and diced by the fluttering dazzle of wings.

Such beauty, such grace! Cuca thought she, too, might take flight.

Caleb arrived unannounced, solemn-faced but dapper as usual. Adela let him into the house, holding the door for him almost reverently, and after the politest of exchanges, he strode past her, into the nursery, and closed the door. He was not there for more than ten minutes, only long enough for Adela to make a *colada* of coffee and wonder what Maribel and Caleb could possibly say to each other, whether they discussed the surface issue—the resignation—or the seed, root, and stem of the matter. Unrequited love, Adela knew, was the most painful emotion of all and perhaps the most lasting; the reality of daily living never tarnished it. She heard their voices—Maribel's even, firm tones, Caleb's softer ones—but could not make out the words. When he walked back into the living room, without Maribel, she quickly offered him a cup of the freshly brewed coffee. He nodded no, but hardly put off by his quick rejection, Adela walked him to his BMW.

Outside, under the lavender light of the full moon, Caleb reminded her of an animal who senses its coming slaughter and accepts it with eyes wide, possum-still and lamb-gentle.

"I am sorry," she said simply.

He smiled but did not answer. He looked up at the stars, the few that could be seen in the urban light.

"I wish I could do something about it," Adela added, and then felt like a fool for saying it. Chica, she wasn't very good at conversations of the heart, eh?

He put his hand on her shoulder; it felt surprisingly light but warm.

"You are a good man, Caleb," she went on, and wondered why she could not keep quiet. She should let him go, let him suffer in peace, but the recognition that he had come to terms with the truth propelled her into offering consolation. "You have been brave, kind, generous. You deserved something."

He shrugged halfheartedly.

"I mean it. No one deserves rejection, but certainly not you."

"There are no coincidences, señora," he whispered, and leaned over to kiss her on the mouth. She stepped back, stunned. Then in one fluid motion he opened the car door and climbed in. Bewildered, she watched him drive away. The vermouth tasted a bit sweeter in her mouth, and the crickets had changed their cacophonous tune to welcome the night.

In the nursery, Adela hugged her daughter.

"Mami," said Maribel, her eyes filled with tears. "I never meant it to turn out this way. I love him."

"I know," Adela said, stroking that black hair she had washed and combed and cut so many, many times. "I know."

But she didn't know, not really, because Adela wasn't sure whether Maribel's love referred to Eduardo or to Caleb, or to both, and the teary silence that enveloped mother and daughter brooked no inquiring interruptions. "I love him" could mean just about anybody, just about anything.

Unannounced, too, Eduardo showed up at her doorstep. It was the middle of the day, a Friday, wash day, grocery day. His curls had been shaved off, and he wore a baby-blue guayabera over jeans. Maribel noticed, after she got over the surprise of his presence and of his hairless head, that he had been working out: his biceps bulged against the short sleeves.

"Come inside," she managed to say. "It's cooler."

"I don't want your mother or grandmother to know I was here."

"They're at the bodega."

He hesitated. He was tanned to a walnut-brown. She, who never saw the sun except to hang laundry from the clothesline in the back yard, appeared pale next to him, an inhibited, sickly, pasty white.

In the living room he refused to sit down. "I can stay only a few minutes," he kept telling her.

She reached out to touch his hand. He drew her close. They kissed.

"Don't you want to see the baby?" she asked.

She led him to the nursery, where Victor slept. He stared down at the crib; Maribel could not read his thoughts.

"You can touch the baby, you know," she whispered, not quite managing to keep out the accusatory tone.

Eduardo did, gingerly, running his finger down the side of his son's face, across his son's chest, the length of his son's tiny leg.

"I came for you," he said then, without looking at her.

And for an instant, a moment that seemed both eternal and ephemeral, she felt herself consent. Yes! Yes! A thousand times yes! Take me away from this. But apparently she had said nothing, for Eduardo repeated his statement.

She walked away from the crib, to the window, and looked out.

The street and sidewalk were empty. It was too hot for anyone to even think about taking a walk. Diagonally across from where she stood, an old mango tree was heavy with ripening fruit. She opened the window and heard the hum of the air-conditioning unit, the call of a bird, the screech of brakes, the rustle of leaves, all familiar sounds, all bearing the comfort of daily life.

"What about the baby?" she asked Eduardo without turning around.

He was silent. She knew he could not answer, and she also knew what he wanted: for her to leave Victor behind.

"Don't be afraid, Maribel. I have everything figured out."

She turned away from the window and stared at Eduardo. She felt she was seeing him for the first time. She wondered, as she had never before, about the frivolity of their relationship. How much had been based on their intense animal attraction, that muskiness that bewitches and blinds, instead of some other, more reasonable foundation?

"What should I be afraid of, Eduardo?"

"You are afraid of change, but you shouldn't be of this change. It is for the better, for the two of us."

"Yes, you said it. For the two of us."

"Well?"

"I'm not going," she said softly. Then she thought such a phrase did not truly convey what she meant. She wanted to say it in a different way: "I'm staying."

She knew that, in this instance, staying put demanded courage, Herculean strength, and she had that. Oh yes, she did, and the realization gave her a lift, some hope.

27

Soon after Maribel quit her job, Victor grew restless. He developed a cough, then a mysterious rash, finally a low-grade fever that refused to recede. He cried, a low, whining plea as if the pain he felt needed noise, an annoying sound, to make it real or worthwhile. Even when he did not cry, Maribel heard the plaintiveness of his request. She heard it in her sleep, tangled with nightmares of ambulances and long-needle shots. She heard it above the dull roar of the shower, a sharp, cold, persistent drip-drip. It erased, this lamentation, all sweet memories of past halcyon days, at least temporarily, for Maribel took Victor's slow deterioration as a harbinger. Of what, she did not know, or refused to know. She tried to prepare for whatever awaited her by reminding herself of Victor's first days: the hopelessness of the doctors, their plain and unaffected honesty, the pain of her realization. It was coming, she knew, whatever it was, whatever was meant to be, *whatever she could do nothing about*, and she wasn't sure she could accept it. She wasn't ready, no. All her life she had thought actions had consequences, but now she was being forced to come to terms with a consequence that had no action to justify it, an effect divorced from a recognizable cause. The randomness that had chosen her had chosen wrong, and she chafed at its injustice. She had done nothing to deserve this, nothing.

She nagged the pediatrician. Daily phone calls led to daily visits to nighttime interruptions. She lost the feel for the boundaries of propriety; she threw off her natural recalcitrance, a yoke that had bounded her to a measure and a system. The pediatrician pretended patience. In his white lab coat, tall and stoop-shouldered, weathered face open to her fear, furrowed brow creased with consternation, Dr. Herrera listened to her rambling description of her son's varied symptoms. He patted her hand, much the same way he had patted her hand after Victor was born, with a certain condescension, yes, but also with a sense of Hippocratic obligation—and something more. Pity perhaps. Disbelief maybe. Outrage.

But no matter how much hand-patting the pediatrician did, no matter how many phone calls he answered, there was a certain emptiness to his explanations, a tone of futility in his voice as though nothing he could say or do would matter. She sensed it, Maribel did, as easily and vividly as she heard her son's cry in the shower and in her sleep. The pediatrician, exhausted or impatient with her relentlessness, referred her to the neonatologist and to the geneticist for the questions that dug too deep, and later, much later, at the hospital he would admit to Adela a feeling of guilt for having deflected Maribel's concerns that were not of a purely medical nature. When it was their turn, Drs. Rothstein and Burton, inured to the gradual deterioration of the majority of their patients, also preached patience and acceptance. But their words rang hollow. How could you accept surrender, Maribel wondered. How could you be patient when sucked into a maelstrom? How? How? Why?

Between visits to medical offices and the filling of new prescriptions for the variety of maladies that preyed on Victor, Maribel devised a shortened version of the Chin Kiss Game, skipping over the parts that required more effort and limb movement on his part. She kept all the face kisses—the eyelash, the nose, the ears, and, of course, the chin. It was a sacrifice, a shortcut, like reading the Cliff Notes instead of the novel, but she thought it was best to keep his interest and to savor the silence, for it was only during this seconds-long game that Victor's toneless, heart-wrenching wail subsided.

And even then, the game proved to be too much of a strain. He barely remained awake long enough to play.

Victor appeared to wilt, his body assaulted, weakened by time, the elements, fate itself. His skin grew ashen. The edges of his face, when lit by the pallid light of early morning or late afternoon, shone a dull green, the color of a long, useless convalescence. And no matter how frequently she fed him, or how much rice cereal she added to thicken the special formula, he did not gain weight. He looked like a shrunken little bird, the beak of his nose growing more prominent, his small eyes sinking into the hollows of his cheekbones. His arms were impossibly thin, his legs too skinny. So fragile he was, so very delicate. Maribel's heart ached at the sight of him, at her helplessness and his frailness, and it ached, too, in the middle of the night, when, awakening for a feeding or medicine, she glimpsed her own reflection in the bathroom mirror, under the fluorescent light, and noticed Victor's same pale green suffusing and bordering her features. She recognized the green as a slow fading of life.

One evening, as she fed him a dropperful of antibiotic, she was struck by a sudden frightening thought: *Every day we move closer to death, every single day a push toward the grand finale.* The realization paralyzed her. She wasn't sure how long she stood beside the crib, medicine dropper in hand, weeping fear, weeping denial. But she recovered. Somehow. She dried the tears on her face and on Victor's bed. She closed her eyes and imagined herself in a secret garden, overrun by color: allamanda yellow and ixora red, impatiens fuchsia and gardenia white and violet blue. A refuge, a heaven. And she walked among the flowers, and bowed to savor their varying scents, and traced the velvet petals, and from this image in the center of her heart she snatched a sliver of peace for herself, a soothing liniment to ease the anxiety.

Still, Victor's condition worsened. In the span of four days, he was rushed to the emergency room twice—once for a seizure and then for a high fever of unknown origin. Both times doctors kept him overnight for observation. Maribel did not leave his bedside, but she resented the false cheeriness of the hospital staff, the decorations, the bear-print hospital gown, the concern displayed by Caleb and others who visited. The smell of disinfectant and impending tragedy nauseated her. Dark circles formed under her eyes, giving her the appearance of a raccoon. And though the neonatologist insisted she return home to rest, she stubbornly refused. Instead, she asked questions. She demanded answers. All she received, though, were shrugs, sentences with no meaning, words she could not understand.

"The Shrug's Hospital, that's what this place is," she complained to Caleb when he visited, dutifully as ever. "They don't know anything."

Fear made her sarcastic, and it tinged her vision with a paranoia she had never experienced. When a nurse took too long to answer a call, her mind ran away with a furious thought of willful abandonment: her son was being left to die. Even the mellow entertainment of her siestas turned ominously dark when she returned home. She no longer saw stucco animals and faces in the ceiling of the nursery. Mambo the dancing horse's lone beautiful wing became crippled and featherless. The rooster without feet, the dog without ears, the lamb without its curly tail, and the fat pig without its snout disappeared from the stucco terrain. She narrowed her eyes, strained to see, called them, but they were gone. She missed most, not the animals, but the little boy who had hobbled from one side of the ceiling to the other in his billowing pants and the girl in her hoopskirt. She did not see anything in her ceiling now, just a white, seamless plateau that had closed its doors to her sanguine imagination. They, too, had abandoned Victor, perhaps moved on to another child's room, another stuccoland, where chances were palpable and the future more promising.

One night, under a full harvest moon, Maribel lay wide-awake in Victor's room, scanning the ceiling in the lamplight, hoping that the dimness would cast telling shadows and bring back her stucco friends. She saw nothing, of course, and the more she searched the corners, the crevices, the middle of the ceiling, working her way by squares in a grid fashion, then diagonally, trying to fit madness into pattern, the more desperate she became to find something. Her legs tensed. Her eyes twitched. Her shoulders knotted. Her heart beat madly. Her fingertips grew numb. Eventually she lost her ability to focus, and the faint light taunted her into action, because it is at this shadowy time of the night that we lose hope. Without knowing what she was doing, she lumbered into the living room and picked up a small Lladró figurine of a shepherd girl from the end table and threw it against the wall. She slammed the lamp next, then a heavy, cut-crystal ashtray that broke into glass tears, and a beautiful porcelain apple Caleb had given her as a paperweight one Christmas, and, still incoherent but shaking with rage, she tried to smash two brass candleholders against the floor but one bounced back and landed on her right toe. She shrieked in pain. Adela and Cuca, in their pajamas, ran from the other side of the duplex, threw open the door, and gaped at the mess.

Dry-eyed, Maribel stared back at them. She told them she felt she had been scraped raw by disappointment and pain.

"It's like I keep falling on the same knee over and over," she said. "It's a wound that never heals."

Adela and Cuca stared at her, surprised and speechless.

"I can't take it anymore," Maribel whispered, and looked, not at her mother, for she did not expect an answer from Adela, but at her grandmother, for if anybody could help her, if anyone knew of a miracle or a helpful herb, it would be Cuca.

"Yes, you can," Cuca told her emphatically, wishing she had on her jangling bracelets to ward off the dismal, pessimistic air that surrounded them. "You most certainly can take it."

Maribel accepted this. Silently she swept the shards and splinters, while Cuca brewed some chamomile tea. Cuca figured this was the last of the uncharacteristic eruptions, because her granddaughter was too even-keeled, too programmed, too much in control to lose it entirely.

Cuca was wrong. Another night, in a horrific moment of desperation, exhausted by lack of sleep, weakened by anxiety, Maribel began to scream at Victor when he fell asleep sucking. The yells were so shrill, so cutting, so absolutely delirious, that Adela and Cuca ran from the other side of the duplex once again, thinking the worst, the expected, had already happened, and then were amazed to find the red-faced Maribel holding the still-full baby bottle, Maribel as they had never seen her, spent and hoarse and lost. Again Maribel wept, and desperately, in forgiveness and in shame, she stroked and rubbed, whispered, giggled, cooed:

"*Mi rey, mi cielo, mi tesoro. Chinito. Caramelito. Corazoncito. Precioso mío. Corazón de melón. Sol de mi mañana. Querubín.*"

Victor slept.

Maribel thought she had exorcised the demon of her anger in that incident. "Primal-scream therapy," she called it, joking with Adela. "The Japanese use it all the time." But she had not weathered the storm within, had not yet faced the initial terror and final relief of surrender.

Chica, Adela never would have imagined the long days and insufferable nights, the anguish. Not in her wildest dreams, and she had some of those, plenty, too many, where she still strutted around in tall-tall heels and clingy pullovers and tight skirts, her derriere as firm and yielding as gelatin, leaving the men panting. Still, this was . . . was . . . How could she describe it? *Esto le puso la tapa al pomo.* This put the lid on the jar. What more? What next? How? Why? So many questions. Too much, all of this was too much. But maybe Adela was getting ahead of herself here. She was always operating at 78 rpm while everybody lolled about on 33.

This is how it all began. Or how it began so many days ago. Victor's health deteriorated rapidly after Maribel, in one of her odd decisions, surprised everyone by quitting work her first week back. Plain-out quitting. No, not taking a leave. Not asking for a break, a vacation, a longer whatever-you-call-it. No, none of that. She quit outright. This Adela knew because Caleb had told her. Anyway, the descent into the inevitable was surprising for Adela, because it came so suddenly, and because there had been those wonderful days before, that period of union and bliss. The calm before the storm, Caleb said. ¡Ay, chica! Then Victor started with the fever and the rash and the restlessness. And then came the mad, teary rushes to the hospital, the stays for observation, the lack of knowledge, the dimming of hope. That, all that, Adela thought, they could have withstood. Yes. But that third dash to the emergency room, that horrible horrible scare, watching the life ebb way from her grandson, screaming at the nurses that this was not how he always was . . . well, that was enough to shake the wind out of you, to knock you senseless. And it knocked all of them, knocked them cold.

This was how it happened. Adela remembered most of it, but not all. Details slipped away, blurred. Chica, her memory was never good. And now . . . well, now. But this was how it happened. Listen.

Victor was burning. Hot as cooking oil. They rushed him to the emergency room, she and Maribel. Same old story, same old car, through the same old streets, even the same parking space. Amazing.

"One hundred and three," the nurse read the thermometer. "Not good." They were sequestered in one of three tiny ER rooms that provided a little privacy from the commotion of the general area. The nurse was petite but wide-hipped and horse-faced. Adela noted her bleach job was cheap.

The nurse disappeared. Minutes elapsed. Neither of them spoke. Adela could not look at Maribel, but she thought she heard her daughter humming. What song? she kept trying to figure out. Such a lovely melody.

The nurse returned. She undid Victor's diaper and placed a plastic bag over his penis. She covered him with a white sheet.

"Urine culture," she pronounced, and disappeared again.

More humming from Maribel. On the other side of the door, alarms, bells, crying, a scream. The smell of blood and alcohol, smoke.

The nurse appeared in the doorway. "We're going to do a spinal tap now, so I have to ask you to leave."

No question: a command. But Maribel, apparently awakening from her humming stupor, did not move right away.

"Why?" Maribel asked.

"We're going to check for meningitis."

"What are you going to do to him?"

"We take some spinal fluid for a culture."

"How?"

"With a needle. Lower back, just below the waistline."

Maribel shuddered but managed to compose herself long enough to lead her mother by the hand to a waiting room. She already knew her way around this place, Maribel. ¡Qué triste! They sat in two straight-backed upholstered chairs and listened, stiff-lipped, to Victor's crying. It was easy to distinguish his from all the other misery around them. Adela looked down at her hands, her beautiful hands that had created so much and made love so often, and saw that they were shaking.

After about fifteen minutes, the nurse led them back to the room. Victor lay in a small stretcher, tiny arms tied to the railings, white as confectioner's sugar.

"He is so pale!" exclaimed Maribel.

The nurse stopped writing for a moment and nodded. "Well, yes," she said.

"Look at him," Maribel insisted. "He is so pale."

The nurse glanced at him, shrugged, returned to her writing.

"There's something wrong with him. It looks like the blood has been sucked right out."

The nurse put her pen and paper down on the counter. She took his pulse, then stumbled to the wall phone.

"He needs oxygen. I'm calling for help."

"What's wrong?" Maribel stroked Victor, whispered something to him.

"*¡Dios mío!*"

Another nurse, large, with short black hair and an air of authority, marched into the room without knocking.

"What is it?" she asked. "What is it?"

She did not wait for a reply. She grabbed Victor and ran out, Maribel and Adela jogging behind her. She shouted orders. The crowd parted for her. They ran and ran and ran and ran. They ran probably ten or fifteen yards, no more, across the emergency room, behind a curtained partition, where an oxygen tank stood. The big nurse flipped it on and slipped the mask over Victor's tiny head. Slowly, as if an invisible hand were dabbing color into his face with a child's paintbrush, a rosiness claimed his features, a rosiness Adela and Maribel had not seen for a long time.

"Jesus!" the big nurse exclaimed as she lay Victor in bed. "Jesus! Jesus!"

"*¡Dios mío!*" echoed Adela.

When Adela returned home, she could not feel her fingertips or her toes. She felt faceless, a mystery to herself. Carefully, with trepidation, she tapped her nose, traced her lips, touched her eyes, desperately wanting to assure herself she was still there, or at least part of her was there. Another part—the part of her that was invincible and coquettish, sly and steely and sassy—that part had been erased, obliterated. She sat on her teal living-room sofa, mere feet from the iridescent green eyes of the black velvet Sacred Heart, and buried her face in her hands. She sobbed. Her mascara ran into her palms, black hieroglyphics of sorrow and sadness. Oh, how stupid she was, how very stupid! Senseless, ridiculous, addle-brained! For so many years, so much useless, wasted time, she had believed so wholeheartedly that beauty and brains, and perhaps a little spunk, would protect her from pain. What a laugh, chica! There was no antidote. None whatsoever. You lived: you hurt. They were interchangeable, those two actions, synonyms that should have been listed side by side in a book somewhere. You could not have one without the other. Oh, and how she hurt now! To see that tiny child, that frail *inocente*, that creature of God, *her* grandson, suffering so. And that she could do nothing about it. Not a single thing. Now, that was pain. Pain pain pain painpainpainpain. Everything that had happened to her before this—Miguel's drinking and abandonment, the death of her father, the insensitivity of other men, the silent recriminations of her daughter—they were nothing. Her Victor. Her grandson. Agony.

Suddenly Adela jumped from the sofa and tottered to her room. She began to sort through the mess on her night table, tossing the magazines, then the books, the ribbons and crossword puzzles, the Lotto tickets, a past-due bill from Burdines, four unopened letters and a Hallmark card from Carlos. All this she scattered about the room, madly searching for the beautiful plaster figure of her Virgencita, and when she unearthed it and saw the beatific smile and the black toes over blue water, the hands clasped with much more reverence than she had ever mustered, her knees buckled and she fell to the floor, hiding her mascara-blackened face in her chenille bedcovers. She wanted to pray. She wanted to ask, to plea, to beg, but she wasn't sure she knew exactly what she wanted. Her heart and her mind, her very soul, were as blank, as empty, as the promises she had heard too often from others.

"I don't know what to pray for anymore," she gasped, and then suddenly knew this to be the best prayer of all.

• • •

Lo llamo a casa.

What home are you calling him to?

Cuca, no te metas en esto, mujer.

How can I not interfere, hombre? How can you expect me to accept this so quickly?

No tiene nada de pronto. Han pasado meses, un siglo, una vida entera.

You think a few months is a lifetime? Where did you learn to count? He is still an infant.

No limites tus pensamientos, mujer.

What limitations? I do not think wanting to keep him a little longer means my mind is limited in any way.

Egoísmo

Nor am I selfish.

Suéltalo, mujer. Enséñale a Maribel.

I cannot let go, Tony. Not yet, not yet. I have lost so many other babies. I cannot let him go.

Ya sabes.

No, that is not true and you know it. One pain does not soften the blow of another.

Suéltalo, mujer.

I can't let him go. I can't.

Relief comes in many guises. Some we never recognize, others kiss us wetly on the mouth. At Victor's five-month birthday, during a routine visit to the cardiologist, Maribel learned the two holes in her son's heart had closed. Surgery would not be necessary. He was taken off medication.

"I've never seen anything quite like this," mumbled the doctor with the German name. She rubbed the lapels of her white lab coat and shook her head. Her mustard-colored curls bobbed.

That afternoon, a glorious rain shower lowered the steaming temperature several degrees. It washed the heat away, temporarily refreshing the parched grass, the wilting bushes, the beleaguered trees. Maribel walked out of her house and stood in the middle of the front yard, arms extended at her sides, palms up, face turned to the sky, black hair streaming water. She thought she saw the moon trying on a new dress for the night.

"What are you doing?" Cuca called out from the porch.

"What does it look like, Abuela? I'm standing out in the rain."

Cuca remembered what Mamá Cleofe had once said about the miracle of water as source of life, as cleansing agent and miracle fluid. Rivers, oceans, streams, brooks, ponds, lakes, rainwater and running baths, showers, springs and geysers, all provided refuge from something. Oases.

In her purple paisley-print housedress, bracelets jangling, neck smelling of sweet violet cologne, braid wound tight about her head, Cuca shuffled over to join Maribel in the yard. She looked up at the purple sky, ferocious with dark clouds, and at the raindrops splattering her face, neck, shoulders, hands, knees, feet, and felt her nipples harden in the ecstasy of release.

Yes. She could let go, she could and she would.

28

Tu hijo, madre, te llama.

Do your hear, Mother, my mother, sweet Mother? Do you hear me calling? I knew you before you had a sense of your self, before you had discovered the cacophonous magic of a rattle, before you stared into your own mother's eyes, before you savored the texture of a mashed malanga, before you took your first step over there, in that corner where the pothos thrives in the morning's faint light, before you completed your first homework, swallowed your First Communion wafer, nursed your first crush and first menstrual cramp, cashed your first paycheck, made love for the first time. I knew you. I knew you would have me, and I you, in a love that would be both pure and selfish as only temporal love can be. I knew before the start of time, before your first first and my last last, that this love would ravage, dig a hole in your insides, splinter your heart. I knew all that. And I came anyway. For you.

I came to visit. To play your game. To light your way.

I fell in love with you, as only little boys can fall so madly in love with their mothers, when you were twelve and your grandmother had twined your black-black hair into two stiff braids and given you a shoe

box full of S&H green stamps and several books made of coarse newsprint
paper. How patiently you separated the stamps of ten into clumps of five.
How patiently you counted the smaller ones, one-two-three-four up to
fifty. Not missing once, not skipping, not hurrying. You licked them with
your small pink girl's tongue, tasting the spearmint of the glue, and pressed
each of the stamps in its place, sometimes in rows, sometimes one by
single one, with the same care a surgeon makes a first cut, scalloped edges
matching, the insignia right side up, perfect.

I knew you were the one.

Tu hijo, madre, bids you farewell. Adiós.

And still there were dark days, days of depthless despair when, unable to reconcile herself to the inevitable, Maribel had trouble getting out of bed, dressing herself, combing her hair, keeping Victor's schedule. What was the use? She felt she had developed Victor's own listlessness, and the lack of interest doused her sense of direction, of purpose. She lost her appetite. The cantina, delivered every afternoon, its garlicky, oniony, spicy scent filling the duplex, did little to awaken any hunger. Adela and Cuca tried to entice her with old favorites: *arroz con leche, merengue* and *pan de gloria* fresh from the bakery, *boniatillo, tamal en cazuela, ajiaco, flan* and *natilla.* Visiting faithfully every evening, dapper as ever, interests widening, Caleb arrived lured by these Caribbean kitchen scents, which he found simultaneously delectable and repulsive, and lured, too, by an abundance of emotions that he could not define except to recognize them for their exaggerated expression: Adela dancing about in her heels, perfumed, coaxing, enigmatic; Cuca fretting over Maribel and all those mysterious potions she concocted; Maribel sulking and sullen, barely able to meet his glance, not bothering to acknowledge his smile.

Maribel, oh Maribel. That is how everyone thought of her now. Their concern was not for Victor. But Maribel, oh Maribel. Led to the table in her mother's kitchen, she sat glumly in front of the plate set before her, face in her hands, not hearing orders or encouragement. Her head felt like a gourd, a pumpkin, a cabbage, porous and dense at the same time, useless. Her neck, she thought, had lost all muscle tone. She could not hold her head up. This inability was, like the gurgling hole in her stomach, a sympathetic symptom of

Victor's own growing debilitation, for his head had grown so heavy that it hung like a too large sunflower on the thin, weakened stem of his neck. Not that he had ever managed to hold his head up like other babies, or move it from side to side. Never that, but weeks earlier, in the blissful period of his life, that period of illusion and false hope, she had thought his muscles were strengthening and that if she hoped for it enough, fiercely and long enough, one day he would lift his head from the mattress and look right, then left, straight up, like a little turtle coming out of its shell.

Her turtle with a mended heart.

Also, when she was deep into her despair, unsigned missives from Eduardo began to appear again in her mailbox. She read them and then tossed them out, believing that nothing he had to tell her mattered. Only what they had not shared—Victor and his illness—was of significance now. Shared pain, anguish endured together, bonds a woman to a man in ways that neither love nor lust can. What could a handwritten note, hurriedly composed, telling of his longings and the weather, possibly mean to her? So irrelevant, so petty. They had told each other everything the Friday he had appeared at her door. Still, she read the letters carefully.

"Mi querida," he wrote, "the days are long and hot now again even when it rains and that is just how I feel about you. One of the guys was able to go back home to Colombia and I think about how I wish I could go home to you two."

Another time he penned: "Maribel, I believe you will change you're mind. You belong to me. Keep my uniform clean at all times." She thought this should give her hope, but it only made her sad because she knew, if and when he did return again, which she wasn't counting on, it would be to the same heart that had greeted him days before: an empty heart.

Her doubts increased further when in early August, after several days of not receiving any notes, and in the middle of an insufferable heat wave, she opened an envelope and read:

"Dear Maribel,

"I was listening to Elvis singing Are You Lonesome Tonight and thinking of you and that I think is what you need to keep in mind. Sometimes we do things because our bodys need to like when your hungry and you eat a candy bar instead of an apple or when you gotta go and you just do it in some bushes. You know? I hope you will forgive me for what I've done. I am missing you & I think I am sorry if I ever hurt you but you are stubborn when you could be with me enjoying each other. Why work at some dumb ass office."

The last note she received was postmarked San José, Costa Rica, August 6. It was written simply, in elegant handwriting as though Eduardo had practiced his loops and swirls several times on lined paper before penning the brief note: "What gets your motor running now?" She pondered the question for several minutes, worried that maybe she had no motor at all.

Then she became angry that he had not mentioned his son, not once had he acknowledged the life they had created together, their shared genes, the flesh of their flesh, blood of their blood. Reading the letters, she clenched her hands so tight that they left indentations shaped in half-moons on her palms, and she gritted her teeth so hard her jaw locked and her gums grew too sore to be stroked with a toothbrush. But the pain was not so much physical as soulful, intangible and irredeemable. Maribel felt she had squandered too much energy, too early on, on useless hope.

Cuca watched her granddaughter's inner turmoil with trepidation; she struggled for words to console, a gesture that would soothe and settle this adult child. So much wasted anger! She observed how the eddies of discomfort and rage widened instead of receding, and she felt she had been betrayed—or, at the very least, she, Cuca, had somehow let Maribel down. But what could she do? How could she help? Where would she lead? She could not perform miracles. The medicines of this world—those herbs and potions, the endless list of roots, powders, and oils—could do nothing now. To survive the ravaging and devastation, one had to have something else, and it was in this that she had failed: she possessed it, had earned it and crawled and clawed her way to it, but she could not offer it to Maribel. No. Maribel had to find her way to it herself.

Cuca called to Mamá Cleofe. The old woman did not answer. The star appeared so faint in the darkness of her closed eyes. Blinking, blinking, winking. Oh so far.

Mamá Cleofe! Mamá Cleofe! Help me.

No reply.
Tony!
Rizos!
Had they abandoned her, too?

His fourth and final bout with pneumonia was the worst. Victor dwindled for days, a slow descent that seemed, at first, imperceptible because of its gradualness. Maribel moved into the hospital room, wincing at how the green-grayness of its walls echoed with familiarity. Maribel thought she had been at the hospital forever, had lived her life in the sameness of this room even before Victor was born, and that she would remain here long after, a fixture.

She tried to keep to a schedule as she had in the past, after his operation, but time rushed past her. It was as though all the clocks everywhere had been put on fast forward. Time ran away from her, flung her into territory that was unknown and bleak and bereft of landmarks. She went from feeling nothing to feeling too much, from numbness to intensity: emotional whiplash.

Cuca and Adela visited every afternoon. They brought songs, pastries from the bakery, whatever color and music they could snatch from the day. Unlike Maribel, they did not feel the onslaught of time; without thinking about it, on a subconscious level they would recognize only much later, they strolled into destiny. Yes, Cuca still called for Mamá Cleofe, for her brother and for her husband, and Adela, marveling at how effortlessly she had eradicated the passion for Carlos from her life, still had trouble looking Fefa in the eye. But they walked anyway, forced themselves to walk the path, singing the silly songs that had worked in the past but that now they knew would not work again.

"So be it," Cuca often said to no one in particular, but sometimes to Maribel, who did not understand, who clung to her misunderstanding.

Adela, whose insights tended to be like fireworks, illuminating but brief, spoke rarely but wisely. Her words surprised even her mother. "So this is how we learn," she said one evening. Another afternoon: "Chica, you survive the devastation as you do everything else—one second at a time, one minute, one hour, one morning, one day, one week, one month." And to Maribel: "*Hija,* forgive yourself. It is the best gift."

It was only fitting, Maribel thought, that Dr. Rothstein, who had initially delivered the news about Victor's chromosomal abnormality, would also bring the final news. If it had to be any of the doctors, Maribel clearly preferred him to the others. She had always been taken by his warmth, by the way he looked her straight in the eye, by the feel of his large hands as they took hers. She remembered their first meeting, when he had explained Victor's incomplete esophagus by drawing it on a notepad, remembered, too, how carefully he had chosen between the truth and a merciful lie by giving her hope in a dismal situation, and remembered that phrase he had uttered so clearly and with so much conviction: "It's the quaking of the soul."

Her soul quaked now. Probably it had been quaking all along.

"There is very little we can do for him now," said Dr. Rothstein, thick black brows knitted in concern.

She looked out the window of Victor's hospital room, into the empty vastness of morning sky. She considered, fleetingly, the possibility of opening the window, leaning over the ledge and tumbling down, down, down. Or maybe she could hurl herself instead—and fly, fly, fly.

"I am so sorry, Mrs. Garcia." His hands lay like heavy blankets over her own.

"Is he hurting?"

"No."

She looked into his blue eyes for a long time. A tranquil blue, a blue forged in pain and redemption.

"I am sorry," he repeated, and patted her hands again.

She did not see him leave, but when she finally noticed his absence, she wished she had asked him if his experience could put a timetable on her anguish. How much longer, doctor? How much worse will it get?

Maribel stared at Victor in the hospital bassinet, frail and emaciated, bound to this earth with her hopes, tethered to this life by too many tubes. Medicine dripped steadily into his veins. His beginning and his ending, how alike they were! How painfully alike, surrounded by tubes and machines and a great desire. She patted the blanket that covered his body. She cooed. She wept.

And she said: "One last Chin Kiss Game, *mi rey*."

He blinked his eyes open—for a second, maybe in recognition of her voice, maybe by instinct, most likely by reflex.

She didn't choose the shortened version of the game, though the myriad tubes and beeping machines made it difficult to connect, to touch, to feel the bony limbs that were as light as bird-bones. She wanted the details that had textured their games together, the rubbing of cheeks, the fluttering of eyelashes, the stroking of knees. She wanted all that, wanted never to give it up.

As she bent over, chin thrust closer and closer to his face, a speck of blue caught her eye. She finished rubbing his chin, the blue streaking in the corner. She turned toward it, reached out, felt its fine tip, the hard stem: a blue feather lay flat against the whiteness of the sheets. Frowning, Maribel picked it up and twirled it close to her face, then tucked it in a pocket of her wallet. She clasped the wallet shut, pressed it to her heart, and patted it for a long time, strangely comforted.

As night fell and Victor's fever climbed, as the nurses whispered more conspiratorially and the drip of drugs into his tired veins rang in her ears, the comfort eased away, replaced by a simmering rancor that began in the center of her stomach, gurgling in her hole, then rippling to her ribs, her waist, her arms, her loins. A rancor that demanded justice. A rancor that expected miracles. A rancor that knew no bounds. Her heart beat fast, faster. Her hands shook. Her throat closed. She could not see what was in front of her, not the crib, or the checkered curtains on the window, not even the sliver of moon rising in the coal-dark night. She was blind.

"Mrs. Garcia?" a soft voice inquired at her ear.

She turned to a bespectacled nurse. Her face, except for the large, round glasses, was the face of every nurse she had ever encountered in this forsaken place, in this hellhole.

"Dr. Rothstein and Dr. Burton will be coming later. Perhaps you would like to call your family."

"My family?"

"Yes."

"It's the middle of the night, isn't it?"

The nurse nodded. "Close to three, yes."

The nurse walked around the crib to the phone on the night table, the swooshing of her thick-soled shoes breaking the dismal silence. "The number?"

Maribel recited it mechanically. The nurse spoke into the receiver briefly and then, before leaving Maribel in the darkness of the private room, whispered, "I'm right down the hall."

Adela and Cuca arrived within minutes. Adela's face was pale, without a hint of makeup. Cuca's white hair hung limp over her shoulders. She was without her bracelets. Though dressed in street clothes, both still wore their bedroom slippers and Maribel noticed that her mother's shirt was buttoned wrong, and the right corner of the stiff collar stuck out at an odd angle.

"*¡Dios mío!*" Cuca and Adela exclaimed together.

They gathered around the crib and held hands, closed eyes.

"We should pray," said Adela, and immediately both she and Cuca fell into a silence that gradually became a deep trance.

Maribel could not keep her eyes shut, though. They blinked open as her rancorous anxiety mounted. She squeezed her grandmother's hand to the right, her mother's to the left, but neither acknowledged the tension in her desperate grip. She stared at Victor, at the deathly paleness that glowed in the darkness: his beak nose, his closed, beady eyes, his lipless mouth, the cheeks and brows that were ridges and ledges of bone.

She threw her words into the silence: "I have to eat something."

And she grabbed her purse from the closet, ran down the dimly lit hall, banged the elevator button, barely waited for its doors to open, and zoomed to the lobby. But instead of turning right, in the direction of the cafeteria and the vending machines, she veered left to the sliding glass doors and entered the artificial lights of the urban night, walking quickly, feet barely touching the ground, down the pathway that led to the covered parking lot where her own blue Toyota was parked. Hands trembling, she unlocked the door, slipped into the seat, turned the ignition, flipped on the lights, reversed, turned, and headed out the narrow hospital road into a residential street and more lights but little traffic. Trembling still, the rancor shaking her to the bone (at the first red light east on Coral Way, she looked both ways and sped through it, shaking shaking shaking, shaking as if being thrown by huge hands, spinning like a roulette wheel, remembering what Dr. Rothstein had told her, so long, long ago, about the quaking of the soul)—she realized she did not know where she was headed and decided to follow wherever this . . . this torment was taking her, east and east and east, then north briefly, down streets darkened by despair and homes somnolent with sorrow, and east again, until she discovered herself in the vastness of the expressway, stopping at the tollbooth just east of Twenty-seventh Avenue, following the road ahead, following the stars, east and east and east, until, crossing the MacArthur Causeway, she noticed how the stars above and the lights from the port glinted and shimmered in the blue-blackness of the ocean and how the neon of Fifth Street on Miami Beach burned as intensely as that gnawing feeling inside her, and then turning right, away from the blue and green and pink of glimmering, desperate fashion, into a quieter street, curving past Joe's, where she had eaten a plateful of stone crabs once with Eduardo, the man who had given her pain and pleasure equally, then farther east and east and east until the car slipped perfectly into a parking space. She turned the motor off and opened the door into the darkness, leaving the keys in the ignition, not thinking of all the horror stories she'd heard whispered of this neighborhood, and walked and walked, walked aimlessly but knowing full well where she was going, to the packed white sands of the beach, to the susurration of the ocean that so resembled the rhythm of her heart.

She knelt at the shore. She inhaled the saltiness, the fishiness, the endless possibilities. In the distance, the lights of a ship flickered. The water spread vast and wide ahead of her, into the infinity of the horizon, but she knew it ended in land. Eventually. She knew that. It calmed her. It soothed her, the knowledge of a spit of earth decorated by a lone tree. She turned her face skyward, rubbed the wetness of her own salty ocean into her cheeks, and screamed: "What do You want from me?"

Her anguish echoed upward, and her despair spread east and west, then north and south and all points between, the rancor easing, settling in: What do You want from me?

29

On a Tuesday of the week in August that Cuca's great-grandson left this hard world, high-velocity winds blowing around a low-pressure center pushed northwesterly away from the doldrums, a narrow equatorial belt characterized, as Victor's life had been until then, by intermittent calm, light variable breeze and frequent squalls. But the three generations of women bound to this boy did not know, and would not have cared to know, about the hurricane off the coast of a continent halfway around the globe. Their own storm seemed so much more precious, their turbulence so much stronger and more vital. When they asked to take Victor home to die, standing side by side before a phalanx of white lab coats, creating a formidable, forceful wind, they appeared attached by an invisible but intricate, inextricable cord, a rope thickened by sorrow and faith. The physicians, after consulting each other and considering the possibility of lawsuits and dismissing that idea as out of character for any of the women, agreed to the plea. (Not an easy thing to grant in a litigious society.)

So Victor traveled home in a special ambulance, a mournful look spreading across his tiny bird-face as though he had been born to personify sadness. Maribel carried him to the nursery, whispering sweet, small lies, cooing nonsense, her voice like a soothing rub-down. (Big heart, brave heart, mended heart, Victor Eduardo.) This, she knew, would be his last night in his room, with his Mickey Mouse lamp and the white dresser with matching crib and bumper— all the possessions he owned but never noticed, all the things that bound him to a life he had never lived.

Though he slept soundly and she was exhausted, Maribel sang him a song, the last time. She made up the words as she went along, and forgot them as soon as they floated into the air. The melody was as familiar as her own skin, the beat the rhythm of her own heart. She kissed him good night, a last time. She cooed to him, a last time. She whispered endearments, and wished she could con-tinue forever, whatever forever was, whatever she had once imag-ined it to be. *Mi cielo, mi rey, mi corazoncito, sol de mi mañana.*

The next morning, as life ebbed and the day opened in light and noise, Maribel carried her son to the back yard, to the narrow but protective shade of the oak tree, in the shadow of the laundry clothesline, trailing blue feathers, a steady stream of such fine plum-age she could not imagine how her child's body had been complete without them until now, so perfectly did they match the blue quill she had found on his pillow at the hospital. She collapsed into one of the three lawn chairs her grandmother had so thoughtfully placed beside the stroller that had been used so rarely, and immediately kicked off her peach bedroom slippers so she could place her feet on the dew-dampened grass and the still-cool black earth. Ah. Aaah! She did not lay him down in the expensive blue-and-white Aprica, though; she held him in her arms, clasped to her heart, fiercely, mightily. She would never let go. He would leave, but she would never let go. Never. Never.

She turned her face toward the sun, the yellow-orange half ball peering over the Nicaraguan couple's red-tiled roof and the low-lying branches of a mango tree the next yard over, and toward the cloud-pocked infinity that surrounded so much fire, and she thought of how the dark ocean she had seen on an earlier night extended in a parallel boundlessness and yet also ended somewhere, anywhere, with a spit of land. Wouldn't the heavens end somewhere too, if not in a sliver of earth, at least with a pocket of pillow clouds to serve as both floor and roof, wall and window, haven and home? Wouldn't it?

Adela and Cuca sat in the lawn chairs, too, flanking Maribel, three women lined in a row, three generations of power and pain, flesh of his flesh, blood of his blood, settling in for his last breaths, a temporary goodbye. The August morning was developing into something glorious, unseasonably and surprisingly cool, spring-like. Cuca thought a morning such as this had been made for death, for a passage of time, a change of shape and form, for it was like a special creation: sunlight both dense and clear, warm and refreshing, the shade providing enough shadow for privacy but no chill, the blue jays and sparrows trilling at a respectful distance, clocks marking no seconds. Time stretched into distance, blending past and future. The morning smelled of strawberries and cream, of melting chocolate, of a gardenia's first bloom, of all those wonderful scents that inspire us, however momentarily, to think all is well, as it should be. She knew Mamá Cleofe was near. Cuca closed her eyes and saw her grand-mother's star blinking so bright that it blinded. And she saw, too, that Tony and Rizos hovered close, as did her sister and her middle brother, her father, her mother, and all her babies, all the babies she had loved and lost, their stars approaching, so very close, waiting for Victor, ready for him. And Cuca sighed in relief. And Cuca turned to look at Victor as he gasped for breath, uhha, uhha, life fading, uhha uhha, moving on, forward, his paleness running pure and white, stillness becoming stiller still, the beak of his nose grow-ing more prominent, and the feathers, so many feathers, forming wings, forming a tail, forming flight. And Cuca glanced at Maribel and recognized the sorrow in her granddaughter's wide-open eyes but saw the relief, too, the relief in the knowledge that what was destined would finally transpire and relief that for five months and a few days, Maribel had tasted a bit of everything, the bile of rage and the nectar of joy, too much to ask and too little to know. And Cuca saw, too, that Maribel knew all this was enough. And Cuca then examined Adela, whose hot tears formed rivulets of black mas-cara on either side of her chin. And Cuca thought: If only I could put into words what I feel, what I've come to know: that her soul, in spite of immense suffering, or perhaps because of it, has finally achieved the fullness of a late-spring bloom. Deprivation taught as much, maybe more, than bounty. But she could not find the words to state this so precisely, only the burning idea of them.

And Cuca wept, her bracelets as silent as they ever would be.

Adela, in the darkness provided by her closed eyes, listened to her mother weep, and touched the black tears on her own cheeks. She heard her grandson's breath grow shallow, shallower, distanced, less frequent, and she reached to touch his closest limb, that tiny bone-thin leg that had never withstood its own weight or taken a step or run a race or danced a silly jig. Never known its function, and perhaps never cared. She touched. She felt a feather, the fringe of fine plumage, a tuft so strong but so yielding that she opened her eyes and looked at the sun rising into the heavens and the cumulus clouds drifting in infinite blueness and the earth rotating. She heard her heart beat, expand, accept the immolation she had long expected.

Then Maribel said loudly, "I love you, Victor Eduardo," and these words were meant for the world, because surely he already knew.

Maribel sighed. She had neither questions nor answers. She had stopped asking herself, "How can this be?" because nobody knew how it could be, only that it simply was. She sighed again, longingly, languidly, and her sigh was Victor's last breath, one and the same.

He rose, floated, soared, feathered and beaked, free, unshackled, bodiless, no suffering, no pain, no medicine, no tubes, a gossamer spirit borne upward by a breeze, above the majestic shade spread over the three women, above the blue jays and sparrows, the red-tiled roofs and laundry lines, above the children playing box ball and the neighbor watering his lawn, above the blinding flash of faded metal from the old neighborhood cars, to the land of no time.

He flew, he flew.

"Free at last," Cuca said. *"Libertad."*

And they cried, the three women, into the afternoon.

Acknowledgments

I would like to thank the following: my children, for their patience; my parents and sisters, for taking care of those patient children while I wrote this book; John Barry, Tananarive Due, Ileana Oroza, Sonia Ramón, and Janet Mondshein, for their suggestions.